'A love letter to the classic country [
If Agatha Christie had written *The Big*
very much like [
J.M. Hall, author of A *Spoonful of Murder*

'Jensen has a wonderfully descriptive style, pin-point accurate
and loaded with atmosphere. If this is the start of Scandi-cosy,
I'm all for it'
Ian Moore, author of *Death and Croissants*

'Oskar Jensen is a sparkling new voice in crime fiction'
S.J. Bennett, author of *The Windsor Knot*

'A wonderful mix of Golden Age tributes, Scandi not-so-noir,
puzzling mystery and a study of the sort of friendships that linger
across the years, often against the odds. A belter of a book, and I'm
already anxiously awaiting the sequel'
Katy Watson, author of *The Three Dahlias*

'A glittering jewel in the crown of modern country house mysteries.
We must have more of Torben Helle!'
Marion Todd, author of *Old Bones Lie*

'Full of skulduggery and humour and with a denouement
that will take you by surprise. A fresh fix for lovers of
Golden Age crime'
Anita Frank, author of *The Good Liars*

'As cunning as Christie, as elegant as Sayers, with a dash of Donna
Tartt thrown in for good measure. Not only a fiendishly clever
mystery on par with the best the Golden Age has to offer, but a deft
character study in the complex entanglements of old friendships'
William Hussey, author of *Killing Jericho*

HELLE & DEATH

OSKAR JENSEN

 VIPER

First published in Great Britain in 2024 by
VIPER, part of Serpent's Tail,
an imprint of Profile Books Ltd
29 Cloth Fair
London
EC1A 7JQ
www.serpentstail.com

Text design by Crow Books

1 3 5 7 9 10 8 6 4 2

Printed and bound in Great Britain by
Clays Ltd, Elcograf S.p.A.

A CIP catalogue record for this book is available from the British Library.

Hardback ISBN 9781800811720
Trade paperback ISBN 9781800811737
eISBN 9781800811751

For my friends

HELLE
&
DEATH

DANISH GLOSSARY

Det blæser en halv pelikan	It's blowing half a pelican (cf. 'It's raining cats and dogs')
Det ved jeg sgu ikke	Roughly, Damned if I know
Dit svin	You swine ('you bastard')
Er du sindssyg?	Are you serious? (John McEnroe, 'You cannot be serious!')
For fanden!	For the devil! (expletive)
For helvede!	For hell! (expletive)
For Satan!	For the devil! (expletive. It's good to have options)
Frisk som en fisk	Fresh as a fish ('fit as a fiddle')
Fuck dig	Fuck you
Gå som katten om den varme grød	Walk like the cat around hot porridge ('pussyfooting around the subject')
Gerningsmand	Perpetrator
God nat	Good night
Hyggelig	Cosy (sort of. Oh come on, we all know this one by now)
Hold kæft!	Shut up! (Often used to express incredulity or awe, cf. 'Wow!')
Hold op	Hold up, wait up

Ingen ko på isen	The cow is not on the ice ('everything's OK')
Jeg elsker dig	I love you
Klap lige hesten	Pat the horse ('hold your horses')
Lort!	Damn, bugger, oh shit!
Morgen	Morning
Offer	Victim
På god fod	On good foot (on good terms)
Så er den ged barberet	So the goat is shaved (a difficult task completed)
Sluge en Kamel	To swallow a camel (to put up with something, cf. 'no use crying over spilt milk')

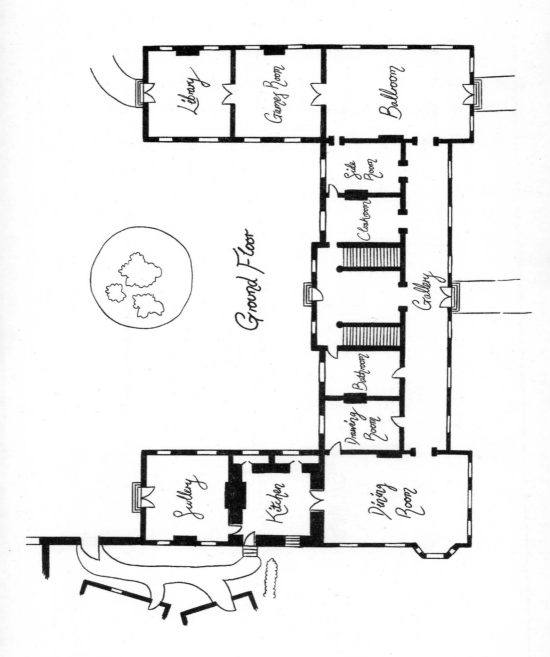

Ground Floor

Library

Games Room

Ballroom

Side Room

Cloakroom

Gallery

Bathroom

Dining Room

Gallery

Kitchen

Dining Room

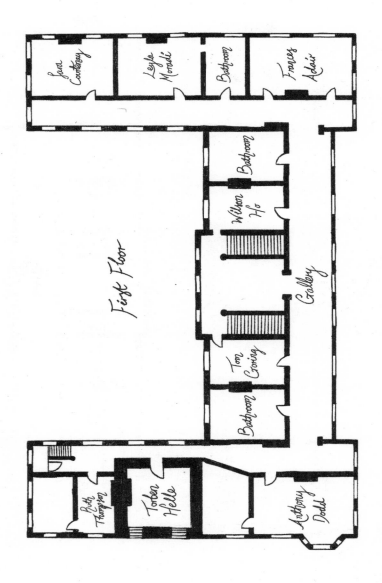

First Floor

Jан Courtenay

Leyla Moradi

Bathroom

Frances Adair

Wilson Ho

Bathroom

Gallery

Tom Goring

Bathroom

Betty Thompson

Torben Helle

Anthony Dodd

I

SATURDAY, NOON

It was easy to overlook the bullet wound. The dead man lay back on the narrow bed as if asleep, large left hand across his chest, his right arm dangling. The gun had fallen to the floor, just out of reach, looking for all the world as innocent as the cast-off slipper lying beneath a bare right foot. The corpse was dressed in a pristine white nightshirt. Were it not for the gaping entry wound in the right temple, itself almost lost in shadow, the rumpled bedclothes and sprawled limbs might suggest nothing more than a restless night.

Torben Helle's eyes roved quickly round the room, taking in the scene. The cheap chairs with their rush seats. A skull tucked away upon a shelf of books and jars, and the mundane explanation for its macabre presence – an artist's palette. A painter must study anatomy. The morning light from the single window was poor, revealing only that too-pure nightshirt and a rent in the mattress, its spilled stuffing somehow more violent than the fatal injury itself. So dark was the room, that Torben first took the scrap of white upon the floor for a nightcap, before realising what it really was: the suicide's final note. He straightened up, lifting his eyes from the page. What was Decamps saying in this image?

Torben had been asked to review the first English-language

7

monograph on Alexandre-Gabriel Decamps, a Parisian artist more famous for his oriental scenes, and the book's author was clearly struggling to make sense of this painting. Her argument was that it was a forgotten milestone in French depictions of suicide, halfway between the grand heroic scenes of David's *Death of Socrates* – the noble martyr surrounded by mourners – and the nihilism of Manet's *Le Suicidé*. The Decamps painting dated from the 1830s, and the author saw it as a move towards Manet's vision of the pointless death, in an image literally stripped of meaning by the removal of all the 'clues' that an artist would generally include for the viewer. To Torben, that spilled stuffing in the mattress was clue enough. And if this author was going to reference David, why had she not thought to bring in his *Death of Marat* – the famous body in the bathtub – and, though not a suicide, visually a far more obvious—

Torben looked up. A change in the train's motion had brought him to his senses just in time: they were pulling in to Newcastle, and passengers were stirring all around him. He took the handwritten invitation that he had been using as a bookmark, tucked it in at the page of Decamps' *Suicide*, and crammed the book back into his battered leather holdall.

As the train juddered to a halt he glanced at his watch. Nine minutes to twelve, two behind schedule. That gave him precisely four minutes to cross the double bridge to platform seven, where the eleven fifty-five would take him on to Bastlehaugh. He was encumbered by the holdall in his left hand, and the umbrella in his right. And by his hat, which might cause problems, given the strong wind. Oh, and there was the small matter of about three hundred other passengers, all bent upon the spot where stairs, bridge and barrier met. Maybe it was the malignant influence of the suicide paintings, but something about all those milling bodies unnerved Torben. Coupled with the grey and the grime they had something about them of an old war film, of going over the top. His umbrella was a solid stick, its handle of bark ash, and unconsciously he adjusted his grip, holding it like a sword. Time to go.

The wind was high upon the bridge, licking at the tails of his coat, tearing holes in the mist. Torben danced between the oncoming fools who were heedless of the signs to 'Keep Left', and slalomed down the ramp to the platform. He had a minute, maybe less. But there was the train ahead of him, its carriage doors still open. On the edge of his vision he glimpsed a man in uniform with a whistle between his lips. But Torben had almost made it, just behind a small, huddled figure who was struggling with something, blocking the way.

Lort! Without a thought, Torben stooped, taking up the old woman's surprisingly light luggage with what he hoped was a friendly smile. He was about to heave it on to the train when he became conscious of an unpleasant sensation, and looked down to see the woman battering him with her fists. 'Get off me bags! He's got me bags!' Her screams rose to mingle with the whistle and the screeching of unknown machinery. In the absence of any better plan, Torben threw their cases in, then, losing his head completely, he picked up his assailant and lifted her bodily aboard the train, jumping in after her an instant before the doors closed upon him. Grimacing, he wrenched his hand from their grip.

'Sorry,' he panted. 'Thought you— you needed help, or we might both have missed the train.'

The woman glared up at him, her face incredulous. 'Missed the train? *Missed it?* I've only just bleedin' well got *off* it!'

Torben blinked. 'Off it?'

'I was goin' into town for me shopping, wasn't I?'

'Oh. I thought—'

'You thought! I should have the law on you.' And she fetched him another blow with her handbag.

Eventually, the combination of a full carriage, the train's motion, and the realisation that the train carried on to the Gateshead Metrocentre, all served to pacify his abductee, who turned her back on him with a final '*gnarh*'.

Torben took stock. Had he literally just *picked up* an old woman? It appeared that he had. Apparently emergencies turned him into some sort of … molestatory stevedore? Still, he had caught his train. One finger was bleeding; his bag had a new scuff to add to its war record. And his umbrella, presumably, lay where he must have dropped it when he had embarked upon his act of unsolicited chivalry. '*For helvede*,' he swore.

The second carriage was a little emptier, and Torben threw himself into a seat in time to see the Tyne roll below him. The great river was battleship grey, mists curling across its surface. Normally he was comforted by large bodies of water. Today, this one looked like it was lying in wait. He felt the tug of melancholy, of the grey river beneath him. His mind went back to the painting. Had Decamps been right to suggest there was something heroic in the act of suicide? It was the way Torben would want to go, given the choice; there was something comforting about death at one's own hand. How much better that would be than to fall, trapped in metal, into the grey waters below. And again he felt that leaden tug.

Then someone snatched his hat.

'Torben!' He turned. 'I knew it was you! Didn't I say so, Frances?'

He began to get up, one hand instinctively ruffling his hair out of its hat-bound flatness. Two faces close to his: one pale, high cheek-boned, framed by long black hair; the other green-eyed and grinning, alive with inner light.

'Sara! Frances!' he beamed.

Next instant, he was enveloped in a whirl of copper-coloured hair as Frances caught him in a three-kiss hug. As he struggled free, Torben felt the envious eyes of two men across the aisle – before they switched back to appreciating Frances' slender form, wriggling in beside him. Naturally, he told himself, he deplored their objectifying gaze. But he couldn't pretend the seat next to him hadn't been significantly improved by the presence of its new occupant.

Across the little plastic table, Sara slipped in quietly, her knees skimming his. 'Let's have a look at you then,' she said. 'Frankly, Frances, I don't think he's changed a bit.'

Frances offloaded a bag on Torben's feet, leaving her gloved hands free to cup his face. The gloves were made of butter-soft leather, moss green, and supple as skin against his jaw. 'It's this beard,' Frances said. 'He's all braw and bonnie now.'

Torben caught Sara's eye, mid-roll. Frances had always played up to her Scottishness. He smiled. 'It's been a criminally long time, I'm sorry. And I must say, to see you both still looking so outrageously gorgeous is—'

'Surprising?' said Sara.

'Colossally unfair,' he finished. 'How was your journey?'

'Grand,' said Frances. 'Bit of an early start, but we've been self-medicating so it's all been rather … you know, like a holiday,' she finished up, with a belated attempt at schoolgirl innocence. Well, that explained the exaggerated accent. And the slight whiff of whisky.

'You came up together?'

Frances paused, looking, for once, at a loss for an answer. For perhaps the space of two seconds, no one spoke.

'We happened to have booked the same carriage,' said Sara, her voice smooth. 'First class, if you can believe that. It was practically cheaper once you factor breakfast in.'

'I wasn't sure who else was coming,' said Torben, 'except Ruth, who said she was travelling last night. And Wilson's been in touch.'

'Tom Goring will be there, I suppose,' said Sara. 'Anthony will have tried for the usual boy-girl matchy-matchy thing – you know how anal he always was about planning things – so if Leyla's made it too, that's more or less the whole set.' She grinned. 'Classic setup for a country house party. The tycoon, the lawyer, the actor, the – well, whatever you are, Torben. Not a professor yet, I trust? Of course, we women aren't keeping our end up as femmes fatales but we can boast me as impecunious literary scholar, Fran here as *enfant terrible* of the art world—'

'As the struggling sculptor of Shoreditch, more like,' said Frances.

'And Ruth and Leyla as more agents of law and order,' Sara finished up, ignoring Frances' interjection. 'I make that all eight of us, the original first-year line-up, the cream of Staircase Two!'

'I wonder,' said Torben, 'why we've all been brought back together.'

Frances beamed at the two of them. '*I* wonder,' she said, 'why we never thought of doing it before.'

The train ploughed on up the Tyne Valley. At every little station, damp ferns sagged over the brick banks, lurid in colour, somehow Jurassic. Beside the sulky band of river at their right, the town was giving way to sodden fields and clumps of marshland, stretched beneath a February sky. Rooks stalked the barren pastures; a few sheep hunkered down. With great deliberation, a heron lowered its head to murder a frog. To the left of the track, the hills rose high, and bare spindled trees thinned into pasture, itself soon replaced by a parapet of jagged fir trees. It was, thought Torben, an uninviting landscape, for all its brutal grandeur. He couldn't see why his fore-fathers had made the effort to conquer it, a thousand years ago.

But then, hadn't he felt something of the same pull himself? That was the reason he had given his family when, uncomprehending, they had challenged his decision to burden himself with the debt of a for-eign education, to estrange himself in an institution that was, in the words of his parents – school-teachers who had grown up in the heady days of '68 and, unlike so many, stuck to their principles – 'nothing more than an archaic bastion of establishment privilege'. Torben had entrenched, argued for its beauty – its exacting standards – even its convenient bus connection to Heathrow airport. If there had been a subtext, he had allowed it to be the appeal of a world-famous univer-sity set against his own upbringing: a small farmhouse outside a small town, a humble life in what, even for Denmark, was a backwater. But what had really won the day, he thought, was his parents' guilt. Both taught at the same *Gymnasium* where Torben had done his A levels, and after three years of that, they had to concede that he'd earnt the right to get as far away as he liked.

He remembered the excitement of getting into Oxford, an early Christmas present in a family where no one had ever been educated further afield than Århus. And when he finally made the move, he had welcomed the unknown. Eighteen years old and brimming with newness, revelling in a language, a culture, that had fascinated him from afar. But he had not accounted for the loneliness. It would have been better, surely, to make the adventure surrounded by fellow war-riors, than to leave as he had done, alone?

That was also why he had accepted Anthony Dodd's invitation to this little reunion. As a student, he had swiftly overcome that initial isolation. He had flourished, made himself anew – not without missteps, granted, but by the end of his first degree, he was happy with the person he had become. Now, nearly a decade on, living alone in Oxford and London … well, he was not so sure. But that was the beauty of seeing old friends: they assumed they knew who you were. To them, Torben was still a lovable fool, and the role suited him perfectly. That was who he wanted to be, for a weekend at least.

Ruth had noticed, though, the last time they had met. She had seen the hardness that was in him. What had she said? 'No man is an island.' Torben had laughed it off, as usual. 'Clearly John Donne never visited the Isle of Man.' He loved that about the English language, its capacity for playfulness. He had once discovered, delightedly, the irony that in English you could be described as both gauche and maladroit – an observation that had sent Anthony, no scholar of French, scurrying for his *Oxford Dictionary of Etymology*—

'Oo, this is us,' said Sara, scrambling up. 'Torben, could you manage—' she flapped a hand at their cases. Frances winked at him. The train shuddered to a halt, and 'Bastlehaugh!' was called.

'Funny,' said Sara, as they alighted. '*How* – like Aslan's How, I suppose. I assumed it was pronounced "whore". Ah well. Oh, and I never thought about taxis …'

'I've ordered one,' said Torben, from behind a stack of luggage.

'Excellent,' said Sara. 'Thanks, Torben, that'll save us a fare.' She always had been ruthless when it came to money.

Frances smiled, making the corners of her face do that crinkling thing he remembered so well. The part of Torben that was still emerging from his melancholy liked to think he was above being placated by a Glaswegian lass with auburn curls and a retroussé nose. But he had to admit he was not.

As she very well knew.

The window of a cab wound down. 'Taxi for a Doctor Hell?'

Torben sighed. *'Helle,'* he said, 'it has two syllables.' But he said it only in his head, as he stacked their cases in the boot of the cab before clambering in beside the driver. The girls – forty minutes of their company had transformed them ineluctably in his mind from women to girls – took the back.

'Bastle House, is it, sir?'

'That's right, thank you.' Shameful, of course, but he sort of enjoyed those rare occasions when people called him 'sir'. It seemed so ridiculously English.

The driver started his engine. 'And picking up on Tuesday morning?'

'Yes, it's sort of a long weekend.'

The driver shook his head. 'Well, I will try. But it is a bad road at any time, and snow is forecast.' He sighed, putting the car into gear. 'But I will do my best.'

Torben had encountered this before, the fuss the English made over a few flakes of snow. They had no conception of a real winter. Of the great drifts that remade the world, the long nights and the bone-cold, the thoughts that came unbidden through the cracks … He shook himself. This *was* England, where snow was picturesque. *A holiday*, he reminded himself. *A jolly holiday.*

Bastlehaugh was a tiny place, crooked in the elbow of the hills. A straggle of slab-stoned houses, a pub and a post office, all on the point of capitulation to assault by ivy and the damp, pervading mist. The little taxi growled as the road grew steep.

'So, is it far?' said Torben, conscious of his social duty. It was too loud for general conversation, and the other two already had their heads together.

'Not as the crow flies, no. But it takes time – with these roads, and the hills. The fee is fixed, sir.'

'Oh, sorry, I didn't mean …' Torben trailed off.

'Now, Doctor Hell,' said the driver, 'is it a party you are going to?'

'I suppose so,' said Torben. 'There's a group of us – we were something of a set at university, though all that was years ago. Then at Christmas I received – well, we each received, I imagine, a letter from Anthony, inviting us for this weekend. Anthony Dodd,' he added with emphasis, glancing at the driver.

'Yes?'

'Oh, I just thought you might have heard of him; big name, small place … in fact it's all rather mysterious. He made a fortune almost straight after leaving university through, well, an invention I suppose you'd call it; the papers were full of it at the time. Big business. Then only last year, just when he was all set to become a Captain of Industry' – Torben pronounced it so the capitals were audible – 'he chucked the whole thing in and retired before hitting thirty. We all wondered why. I rather hoped there'd be some local gossip about him.'

'I live in Hexham.'

'Of course; sorry—'

'He's a total recluse,' said Frances, leaning in between them. 'Turned his back on the world. Why, he isnae even on Twitter!'

'Nearly there, Doctor Hell,' said the driver. Five times they had surmounted what Torben took to be the final crest, only to find another summit before them, pressed about by fir trees. The road rose, dipped, writhed, and Sara had reported that she was feeling sick.

'Look, call me Torben,' he said. 'And thank you, Mr—?'

'Mr Hasan Roy,' said the driver. 'And please, do not thank me yet: I cannot take you past the gatehouse; the road surface is poor and I should not risk my car.' He pulled over to the side of the road, where a gap in the woods was barred by a pair of wrought-iron gates, flanked by buff stone pedestals. Ferns and fallen pine needles mingled with brown bracken. A square stone cottage, its windows blank, was just visible beyond.

Hasan helped Torben with the luggage. 'I will carry these for you to the house,' he said, holding up two of the bags. 'It's included in the fare.'

'Oh, I'm sure that isn't—' began Torben. But then Frances pushed the gates open, and he saw the rutted track winding up into the trees. 'Actually, that would be a great help, thank you, Mr Roy.'

'We'll take these two,' said Frances, grabbing their handbags, and she and Sara set off up the path, bags swinging, arm in arm and giggling.

As they trudged along behind for what seemed like forever, Torben found himself telling Hasan about the old woman on the platform. Hasan's laughter did him good – more good, certainly, than the climbing, scrambling, bag-juggling assault course that was this potholed and interminable driveway.

'The moral, I suppose,' said Torben, growing hot from exertion despite the winter cold, 'is not to overread simple situations.'

'I am, of course, a mere taxi driver,' said Hasan. 'But it would seem to me the moral is not to pick up old women at train stations.' He paused. 'Which is what I seem to spend half my life doing!' His chuckle rang through the wood. Then he stopped again. 'By which I do not mean—'

'We're here!' called Sara, from somewhere ahead of them. The trees had opened out into wide, rather scrubby parkland, where the two women were gazing, still uphill. 'Christ, Anthony really did make a mint, didn't he? It looks like Castle bloody Howard. Halloo!' And, waving at a score of empty windows, she set off again towards the mansion towering ahead of them, grey against a greyer sky.

Torben took in the high rows of windows, the austere geometry, the sharp-edged pediments that hinted at two further wings, tucked out of sight. Bastle House was showing them its best face, a serene impression, with all such concessions to reality as entrances, outbuildings, space to park, hidden round the back, the way the path was leading them over this last shoulder of hillside. It looked – oh *for fanden*, it looked *perfect*.

'Thank you so much, Mr Roy,' said Frances. 'We can carry these from here.' Taking hold of a case with one hand and Torben with the other, she tugged him on up the drive almost before he could say goodbye. The sight of the place had her all but jumping with excitement. 'Yaldi! I think we're going to have fun, what do you reckon? Panelling? Suits of armour? Oddly cruentating floorboards? Now tell me, *Doctor Hell*, in your professional opinion, when d'you think the house was built?'

Torben gave in, adopting a persona to match her own. 'Well, Ms Adair, if pushed, I would say that the façade betrays a strong John Nash influence without any of that neo-Gothic affectation that crept in afterwards, so no later than the 1830s, but of course the name "Bastle House" hints at a far older origin …'

Beside him, Frances was small and warm. The air smelt of pine, sheep dung and the coming snow. They were abandoned on a hill in the middle of nowhere at the whim of a millionaire hermit whom he had not seen in years.

Yaldi indeed!

2

SATURDAY, ONE-THIRTY P.M.

Ruth caught the flash of movement, doubly distorted by the crown glass of the windowpane and the tears in her eyes. Wiping away the latter, she crossed the frankly vast guest bedroom that Anthony had assigned her and peered out. Surely that was Sara, just cresting the ridge? That walk – quick, birdlike, always giving you the sense there was someone she'd rather not let catch up somewhere behind her – was unique. So. The others were arriving.

Really, she could have done with more time to herself. Coming on top of everything else, her recent chat with Anthony had left her reeling. Thankfully Leyla, who had swept in almost immediately afterwards, had gone straight to her room to freshen up; probably Sara would do likewise. She hadn't been prepared for this, mentally or emotionally; of all the crises she was currently compartmentalising, this was suddenly the most unlikely and the most insistent. It turned a weekend away into a mission, against the clock, and she just wasn't sure she had the strength for it. If she could only clear her head, then maybe with a moment's reflection – a little prayer – the right course of action might present itself.

But now more figures were appearing. She could spot Frances' hair from here, the brightest thing in this drear northern landscape – and there, unmistakably, was Torben. No, she would have to go down. This would all need managing, which meant she had to be there from the start. Carefully, calmly, Ruth gathered up the crumpled tissues, and placed them in the fireplace where, later, they might even do some good. Her troubles, too, could be tided away. For now.

Sara was waiting for the others at the top of the drive, breathing hard. Torben sympathised: despite the freezing temperatures, he could feel the perspiration on his own brow, colder still in the biting wind. What had happened to his hat? Oh. Still in the footwell of the taxi. Of course.

'Tor's been – been telling me about the house,' said Frances, too tired to remember to say 'aboot' or 'hoose'. 'Well, making it up, anyroad. How'd he do?'

Sara fished in her bag for her phone. 'Um … name "Bastle House" derived from the original building, sixteenth century, of a type characteristic of Northumberland – tum tee tum – thick walls, fortified against the Scots – that's you, wee Frances – lands granted to one of Charles II's yes men in the Restoration, much extended, distinctive long gallery et cetera, before it forcibly changed hands again after Culloden … remodelled soon after Waterloo with a lot of money from spinning jennies and things, so classic blood-of-the-workers stuff, plus probably ill-gotten gains from the slave trade in there somewhere … anyway, east wing added and the whole thing made symmetrical … architect a pupil of John Nash. Original family lived in it till the sixties, at which point – oh, at which point my phone has failed to download the final drop-down section – still, hurrah for Wikipedia.'

'Full marks!' said Frances. 'Well done, Tor.'

'You've got signal up here?' said Torben.

Sara shook her head. 'Looked it up on the train and left the tab open. Hence the cliff-hanger ending. Anyway, I'll have to turn it off now. In his invite, Anthony specifically requested—'

'No phones,' said Torben. 'I'm not sure if that's ironic, given his career, or exactly what you'd expect of a repentant geek who sells up. No tech, back to nature – maybe it's a hipster thing?'

'Mystery: check!' said Frances. 'C'mon, let's find out. Perhaps he's got himself an Amish wife.' She led them across the gravelled drive, skirting a trio of elegant, bare-limbed trees at its centre.

Torben was about to point out the flaws in her last suggestion, when a blur of motion to his right distracted him. Two figures, indistinct and silhouetted, stood at one of a run of four achingly beautiful sash windows on the ground floor and, as he turned, one of the figures vanished with startling rapidity, followed – more slowly – by the other. The first person had seemed, from what he could tell, quite astonishingly tall; they had taken up much of the high Georgian window space, which now gaped, vacant, unreadable.

He paused, but mostly to drink in the crumbled pointing on the narrow grey bricks, by which time the others were up the front steps, Sara plying the lion's-head knocker with gusto, Frances hanging back, her body language suddenly reluctant.

He could hardly blame her for being intimidated. From here, at the foot of cracked stone steps, they stood between the house's paws. On either side the wings stretched out, their height exaggerated by the double rows of windows. He could forgive the English a lot for the sake of these old sash windows, their glass panes rippling like cool water, their proportions so elegant – and, yes, their insulation so meagre. But in Denmark, it seemed like every old house had decided

21

at the same instant – some time in his childhood? – to shed its lovely windows, which grew again as soulless, double-glazed excrescences that, he had to admit, saved a ton on heating bills. Those of Bastle House, by contrast, were capped by pale stone lintels, set in the sort of mellow brickwork that, if encountered in the right mood, literally made him go weak at the knees. One day, he feared, he would go down before one of these houses like – like Kevin Costner kissing the sand in *Robin Hood: Prince of Thieves*. Needless to say, this was not something he was about to admit to Frances and Sara. But it all reinforced the growing impression that Anthony Dodd, the digital-startup success story, had turned his back on the twenty-first century.

At last the door opened, and Torben braced himself to meet his host – but the face behind it was that of Ruth Thompson, immediately engulfed by Sara and Frances, who dropped their bags and pounced upon her in delight. Torben, just managing to achieve eye contact before Ruth disappeared, shot her a wonky grin.

Ruth had been his best friend in first year. They saw far less of each other these days – especially, he had to admit, since her marriage, far too young, to Jon, who numbered a controlling jealousy among his many enlivening character traits. Even so, the sight of Ruth made the whole thing – strange house, strange summons – less intimidating. Finally dropping the luggage inside the door, he joined the general scrimmage.

'Hello, Torben,' said Ruth. She was as tall as he was, and he got in a large wet kiss on each cheek before she let him go, nose wrinkling in embarrassment. But there was something else in her face – a tiredness, a lack of focus.

'You got in OK last night then?' he said.

'Evidently,' she said. Her smile was warm as ever and, unlike his own, perfectly even – it just took a fraction longer than usual to arrive. There was no sign of their host. Not that anyone else seemed to notice.

'How *are* you?' said Sara. 'Still at the Met? You were heading up that anti-harassment campaign, last I heard.'

'I got moved,' said Ruth. 'Apparently I'm naturally better suited to knife crime prevention.'

'Seriously? Let me guess, it's because you're Black?'

'Yup. They asked if I knew anything about drill music. Sure, I thought, my dad brought me up on that stuff, trooping the colour and everything – so I said yes. Turns out drill music doesn't mean "The British Grenadiers".'

Torben half suppressed a snort, and Ruth gave a shamefaced laugh. 'Yeah. Still, I think I'm doing some good. It's East End, mostly, so close to home. But it's – it's hard, you know? Some of these boys are so young.'

Sara put a hand on her shoulder.

Ruth grimaced. 'Sorry. Look, we're weekending at a country house; shall we just forget about the existence of things like real life – work and the rest of it – for a bit?'

'Er, quite right,' said Torben. '*Ingen ko på isen* and all that.' He had been on the point of asking after her husband – purely out of a sense of duty; he couldn't stand the man who was, he suspected, the chief reason he'd seen so little of his good friend over the past few years – but pivoted swiftly on Ruth's cue. Clearly Jon came under the heading of 'the rest of it'. Glancing around for inspiration, he improvised. 'Work, pah! Strictly speaking, for something like this we should all have private incomes we're far too civilised to mention.'

'Along with honorifics that we dispense with among ourselves because it's all a bit infra dig,' said Sara, catching the mood.

Frances was looking round the hallway, awestruck. A Persian rug into which whole worlds seemed to be woven ran away from them over herringbone parquet. To either side, a flight of limewashed wooden stairs rose to a mezzanine landing, honeyed banister rails gleaming with polish. Against bare walls, chest-high Doric pillars were topped with tastefully naked statuary. 'I should take off ma boots,' Frances said, to no one in particular.

A woman appeared in the archway opposite, absently wiping her hands on an apron. 'Would you?' she said to Frances. 'That'd be a great help, thanks.'

'Oh, this is Kirsty,' said Ruth. 'Housekeeper, cook—'

'General dogsbody, aye,' said Kirsty. Her accent was the sort of thick Geordie that somehow reminded Torben of Danish, and he began to like her at once.

'I'll just pop your things in the cloakroom for now,' said Kirsty, making for their luggage, and they all dived in to help. 'Your rooms will have to wait till later – lunch is about ready. It's a mercy you weren't held up longer, not with the weather we've got coming. Mr Dodd's been following the forecast all week; he's been dead worried about it. Had me cancel this tree-surgeon he had coming round yesterday for fear of him getting stuck in the snow – at least that looks like holding off till you're all here … um, anyroad, where was I? Oo yes, lunch! It's this way.'

As the others followed Kirsty down a long, airy gallery – 'panelling: check!' muttered Frances – Ruth held Torben back in the entrance hall.

'Ruth,' he said at once, 'are you all right? I thought you looked—'

'Not now,' she whispered. 'That can wait; it's you I'm worried about.' She glanced round. 'Leyla's upstairs. She arrived a bit before you; she'll be down in a minute.'

Torben raised an eyebrow – or tried to; it was harder than it looked.

24

Ruth held his gaze. 'I just wanted to check you were ready. You still haven't seen her, have you, not since—?'

He shook his head. 'It'll be fine,' he said. 'That was nearly a decade ago; we're proper adults now. She's probably got a partner and—'

'No,' said Ruth. 'No, she hasn't. Oh, Torben.' She sighed.

He had never been able to hide his emotions from Ruth. At her 'no', something had happened inside him, a sudden vacuum, a glorious disembowelment – the reawakening of a pain, a quickening, that had lain dormant for years. He had not noticed its absence, until now.

'Well, maybe she's got fat,' he said, trying to recover.

'Maybe who's got fat?' came a voice from above their heads.

And Leyla Moradi descended the stairs.

Kirsty led the two women along the passageway, fielding their questions as best she could. It was the sort of bright chatter that flew past you like little birds; she'd never got the hang of it. With their talk and their wide eyes, they seemed much younger than her – or rather, they made her feel old – but they couldn't be really, just a few years … Was it just that she'd got so used to it being only the two of them in the house, so accustomed to each other that there was little need for conversation? No, it was more than that: these people were different, you could see it in their gaze. This sort, they looked at things differently, like they were seeing things that weren't visible. And the world that lay behind their words, it felt wider than hers, in a way she didn't entirely like. That was what London did to you, she supposed; London more than Oxford maybe, because Anthony was never like this, so quick it was almost impatience.

Strange, really, that none of them had ever been invited before. She'd have liked a bit more practice, a dummy run or two, before doing this for real. Even with all the preparation, she hadn't counted on feeling so exposed. Open to judgement on grounds she couldn't anticipate or understand. They all *seemed* nice enough, but how could you really tell, when half of it went right over your head?

Wait, what had she missed now? *Focus*, Kirsty. This was it, after all. After practically a whole year twiddling her thumbs, demeaning herself, treading water, this was their chance. Make or break. A full house. Just keep it together for a few hours more.

Torben blanched. He had written her a poem! Nine years ago, granted, and in the madness that ruled the last weeks after Finals, but still – a poem. What kind of way was that to declare your love for someone? Rather than face Leyla directly, Torben had left it in her pigeonhole: an act at once both rash and cowardly, gauche in its affectation – hah, gauche and maladroit indeed – and infinitely less excusable than a drunken declaration. They had spoken at length only twice after that, on unavoidable occasions like Ruth's wedding – and never alone. In the years since, it had been less a case of active avoidance than … drifting, he supposed. He'd stayed on at Oxford, she went to London. By the time he arrived in the capital they had lost touch completely. Though two years ago, he had kept away from the Gaudy – the wilfully eccentric name, he had learnt, given to formal college reunions – mostly because he had feared she might be there.

It was not as if it had been a *bad* poem, considering that it was written in his third language. Fifth, if you counted Norwegian and Swedish, which he didn't. He remembered most of it; it had form, rhyme, meter. But the detachment afforded by even a few months had shown him it was … problematic. Orientalising. Leyla was, by birth, an Iraqi, and he had rather overdone the imagery.

The thing was, he thought, as he watched her coming down, that her eyes really *were* like gemstones; her lips *did* wear the curve of a Parthian's bow; and she *did* trail the scent of summer nights 'neath garden walls. It was the *way* she moved, too – Leyla never 'walked'; she slunk, sashayed, swayed … But it was her way of being, not her appearance, that really quickened his emotions; he should have written about *that*. The knife-edge of her wit, forever pressed into the small of your back, so you never knew whether to expect a caress or the point jabbed home – and all of it a front for what lay behind the words: real principles, emotional and political sincerity, unswerving loyalty …

Oh, hell. All the things he had spent nine years trying to forget.

And here she was, slim as ever, with a bloom to her skin that her younger self, tired and overworked, had never known. Gone too were the hoodie and drainpipe jeans. She wore a casual suit of midnight blue, Nehru collar, trousers wide at the knee and tight at her waist and her ankles, above small yellow slippers, and with each step towards him his spirit rose in counterpoint. Her hair was up, exposing *that* neck, and at her throat – he blinked – an amber necklace, the sort they sold on Nyhavn. Surely he had once bought her that? Then—

'Lunch,' muttered Ruth, vaguely, and she was gone. Torben opened his mouth. That's what you did, wasn't it, to make conversation?

'I bought your book,' said Leyla, and hugged him. That scent, Le Labo 'Oud 27' – she still wore Le Labo! – the case for his defence was strengthening by the minute. God she smelt good.

'Leyla I'm sorry,' he said in a rush.

She stepped back, appraising him, and picked a curling red hair from his shoulder, one that clearly belonged to Frances. She raised one arched eyebrow. Maybe she could give him lessons in that …

'Oh, don't be sorry, I had a discount code,' she said. 'And bits of it were quite interesting. Lovely pictures.' She took his arm before he could explain himself. 'You look well. I bet the others don't. Anyway I'm ravenous – I think it's this way.' And, keeping up a light but insistent flow of chatter, she led him towards the smell of fresh coffee.

Torben realised something important. *He* was ravenous too.

The long gallery gave on to a cavernous dining room, unearthly in the failing light that swam in from high windows. Sara and Frances were already seated at a long, low table, their backs warming at the hearth. Its ancient stone surround was topped by a dark beam of oak, on which a heap of conkers and pinecones jostled merrily. Torben half-remembered a short story that began with a couple gathering pinecones for fuel … or had they perhaps been brother and sister? Anyway, the effect was charming.

At the far end of the room, Ruth seemed to be wrestling with Kirsty, who was inching through one of a pair of double doors with a large tray, shaking her head.

'Trying to help, as usual,' said Leyla. 'Ruth never learns.' Slowly, she turned on the spot. 'This place though …'

He knew what she meant. It was not just the scale of the house; they all knew Anthony had Made It. No, it was—

'When did he get so *tasteful*?' he said. It was, Torben thought, nothing like he might have expected of Anthony – which would have been, what? Heavy carpets, gold brocade, reams of flock wallpaper … Instead, the interior decoration of Bastle House was all bare boards, exposed plaster, mere highlights of paintwork in shades he could probably name, at a pinch, from the Farrow & Ball archive – or possibly even Rose of Jericho. Distemper paint cracked across half-height panelling. In a bay window, a rough wooden sill housed stoneware jars from which sprouted teasels, seed-heads, spiralling bare branches … A long, low refectory table, weathered and pitted; ladder-back chairs in age-darkened elm – and the other rooms, too: he could swear he'd not seen a stick of furniture that looked even slightly comfortable. It was perfect.

Leyla laughed. 'You don't think he did it himself, do you? The Anthony Dodd *I* remember couldn't have less taste if you tore his tongue out. No, he'll have hired an agency, got someone in from one of those trusts …'

But Torben had stopped listening. Kirsty had laid the tray on the table. It contained an enormous pie.

'Are you sure we should start without Anthony and the others?' said Ruth.

'Yes!' said everyone else. Sara made a pretence of interest in the accompanying salad. Torben had already taken its measure and found it wanting – frisée and iceberg lettuce, fridge-cold tomatoes, and a vinaigrette straight out of a bottle – incongruous, almost an after-thought, and hard to believe the same genius that had created the main attraction had laboured to produce this – this mere *garnish*. But plainly, salad was not where the estimable Kirsty's talents or interests lay. You didn't ask Turner for a portrait, did you, or go to Rembrandt when you wanted a seascape? But give her pastry, rabbit, bacon and root vegetables, and Kirsty was capable of wonders. Substantial as it was, his portion of pie was swiftly disappearing. He made a quick calculation based on who was missing. Anthony, Tom Goring, Wilson, and some for the cook – they would in all decency have to leave half the pie. Was he capable of that much self-control?

Leyla reached across him for more. 'Wilson's a vegan these days,' she said, reading his mind.

'*Hold kæft!*' he swore. 'How do you even know that?'

'Well, he was at the Gaudy, wasn't he?' said Ruth, who – disgracefully – had not even finished her slice of pie. 'You remember those dietary preference cards, so the servers could spot who needed a different meal? They still have those, you know.'

'I remember "fish-eating vegetarian",' said Torben. 'It always sounded like the description of a dinosaur.'

'Nah,' said Frances. 'It's us carnivores who are the dinosaurs these days.'

'Anyway,' said Ruth, 'don't get Anthony started on *that* subject.'

'"It's political correctness gone mad,"' said Leyla, in an accent that Torben, if he were feeling charitable, might just about term 'generic northern'.

'So, the Gaudy,' said Ruth. 'Anthony wasn't there, just like you three. I know he'd been *meaning* to go – in fact, he even Facebooked me beforehand, asked if I knew who else was going. This was when he still had Facebook, of course. He seemed particularly crestfallen that you weren't coming, Torben; I think he was hoping for a rapprochement—'

'Hoping to show off, more like,' said Leyla. 'Half the people who *did* make it were at pains to demonstrate the fruits of their stellar career success, and Anthony would have trumped them all. So why wasn't he there, lording it up?'

Ruth's eyes flickered, first to the left, then down at the remains of her pie. After a moment's hesitation she replied. 'Not feeling well, I think. So in the end it was just me, Leyla, Wilson and Tom, out of us lot. Wilson was very much one of the "showing off" crowd, busy trying to network with media types, and Tom just seemed really gutted that *Anthony* hadn't shown up, and went to bed early. Basically, you didn't miss anything.'

'But *I* did,' said Leyla. 'Some bastard stole my best necklace while I was asleep. I suppose, having read *Brideshead*, I should have known better than to leave a ground-floor window open.'

'"The wines were too various,"' Sara quoted. '"It was the mixture."'

'Sara, I can't imagine *what* you're suggesting,' said Leyla, with a smile. 'But yes, I *was* rather conspicuously sloshed, or I might not have slept through a burglary. Clearly, the security arrangements haven't improved since our day.'

'Mm,' said Sara. 'There was that spate of thefts in our second year, wasn't there? The mysterious cat-burglar of Peck Quad. Maybe they invited the thief back specially for the Gaudy, you know, for old times' sake?'

'Glad I didn't go then,' said Frances. 'I still remember the hell of having my laptop nicked. Turned out my mam had got me contents insurance, but I had, like, *all* my work on there. And the tutors really didn't like the "some dog stole my homework" excuse.'

'That was pre-cloud, I suppose,' said Ruth.

'Oh, I had everything backed up to an external hard drive,' said Frances. 'Only the fucker took that too. Oh, sorry, Ruth—'

'Ruth's a police inspector, dear,' said Sara. 'I'm sure she's heard worse.'

'Actually,' said Ruth, 'it was that experience that first made me think about police work. Practically everyone we knew lost something that year. Just studying the law seemed pretty useless when no one was doing anything to enforce it.'

Torben was still stuck on the first part of the story. Leyla's *best* necklace? Heigh ho; so much for the string of amber he'd given her.

'So you two didn't go to the Gaudy then?' he said, in the silence that followed Ruth's last remark.

The others shook their heads. 'Deadline,' said Frances, just as Sara said 'Conference.'

'What're the other two up to these days?' Frances went on. 'Tom and Wilson, I mean. If you tell us now, it'll save us having to ask them when they arrive. I could do with not asking a man about himself for once.'

'Wilson's getting some TV work at last, I think,' said Ruth. 'Swore he'd never do a radio play again—'

'Though I heard him last month playing a Japanese gangster in some Radio Four thing,' said Leyla, through a mouthful of pie. 'Is that typecasting?'

'For someone from Hong Kong?' said Sara. 'That's practically yellowface. I'm glad he's still acting. If an excess of good looks and ego can't get you anywhere even in drama, what chance do the rest of us have …'

'Remember that anonymous writeup someone gave Wilson in the theatre column, back in third year?' said Leyla. 'How did it go—?'

'"A promising actor who invests Hamlet with all the *Weltschmerz* and self-doubt of a matinée idol,"' quoted Torben. '"If he can add the emotional range of a mere mortal to his indisputable physical presence, this boy will go far."'

'You have a suspiciously good memory,' said Ruth.

'It's a fair cop,' said Torben, 'I wrote it. But he took it as a compliment!'

'I bet he's still got the press cutting,' said Sara, with a tolerant smile. 'And what about Tom Goring? Did he make it at the Bar?'

Leyla smiled. 'Of course not. Not many lawyers are ruthless and arrogant enough to hack it, only the likes of me.' She, Ruth and Tom had all read Law together. 'He went back to Coventry or wherever and is now the very model of an old-fashioned country solicitor, complete with paunch.'

'Daventry,' corrected Ruth, though Torben didn't think her heart was really in it.

'Five pounds, please,' said Frances to Sara, who rummaged for her purse. 'I bet Sara that Tom wouldn't stick it out,' Frances explained, pocketing the note.

Sara shrugged. 'I clearly overestimated the power of the system,' she said. 'My reasoning was that Tom had everything it takes to make it in a high-powered profession – namely, a private education and an inflated sense of his own entitlement.'

Ruth stifled a noise, and Leyla turned to her. 'Ruth, was that literally a tut?!'

'Well,' said Ruth, 'I can't help thinking you've all been so hard on Tom Goring. It's not like he went to one of the *big* public schools – and, well, there are other things than upbringing, you know. It wasn't easy for him, always being in the background, not having Wilson's looks, or Torben's wit, or Anthony's willpower ...'

Leyla laughed. 'And you say *we've* been hard on Tom? Seriously, Ruth, if that's how you rate your friends, then—'

She stopped. No one was listening. Ruth was the first to rise. 'Anthony,' she said, and Torben turned to see his host.

When Torben had first met Anthony Dodd at the age of eighteen, he had had no frame of reference to make sense of him outside of the English books he had read. Widmerpool. Gradgrind. Dursley. He had thought these were caricatures – or, at the least, anachronisms. And then he had met Anthony, the first of many to prove him wrong: the first, and the foremost. A stocky boy from Darras Hall who, as far as Torben could tell, actively chose to subsist on a diet of chocolate digestives, Warburtons white bread and Lucozade, with a complexion and a disposition to match. Anthony had worn black 'sensible' shoes and a Royal Grammar School hoodie, which Torben had taken to mean that he had gone to a state school not unlike his own – a point on which Anthony, affronted, had soon put him right. And mostly it was the scientists who wore hoodies, not humanities students, so before long Anthony had adopted a new uniform of blazer and chinos.

They had been given adjacent rooms in first year and, since they had shared some options – Torben reading History of Art and Anthony, History and Economics – they had even been tutorial partners in their first term, forcing the sort of uneasy friendship (well, bit strong, call it an entente) that would never have formed without those circumstances, and could not hold even with them. It turned out that the one thing that brought them together, the study of history, only epitomised their differences. Torben had been genuinely astonished to discover that Anthony, who had chosen for his degree the two subjects he had done best in at A level, regarded his studies as an extension of school homework, a necessary evil to be borne in pursuit of a degree. Torben, who was by that point hopelessly besotted with the history of European culture, was made to feel somehow naïve for his enthusiasm, lightly patronised by Anthony for the excitement with which he approached each tutorial – right up until the point at the end of their first year when Torben aced his Prelims exams and was rewarded with a scholarship and a first pick of college rooms for second year, while Anthony scraped a 2:1. The nagging suspicion that there was a way of thinking and talking about things that he on some level just didn't get, and that 'they' were punishing him for it, must have crystallised in Anthony's mind at that point.

Somehow their relationship struggled on, sustained primarily by a shared love of an indie music scene that, by 2007, was already fragmented and faltering. After the disappointment of his exam results, Anthony began to replace his worldly tone with an acquired roster

34

of grievances: against intellectualism, champagne socialism, art for art's sake. Anthony, the white, male, well-off Oxford undergraduate, had found a way of casting himself as the plucky underdog struggling against the system. Torben, who despite himself remained the product of essentially Marxist parents who had divided up the world for him in terms of wealth and power, had been entirely wrong-footed by this. Anthony had even altered his accent, allowing the Northumbrian back into his received pronunciation – and actually sounding much better for it, whatever the motivation. Looking back, Torben was just grateful no one had yet coined the phrase 'metropolitan liberal elite'.

The things Anthony had gone on to achieve had not surprised Torben exactly. He had always been both competent and dispiritingly determined, fascinated by minutiae but utterly uninterested in the distractions of wider university life. Torben, by contrast – after spending his teens in the sticks – had thrown himself into sport, theatre, student journalism, with such abandon that he'd probably ended up spending more hours on his 'hobbies' than his actual degree. Anthony had been infinitely more single-minded, merely switching his focus from scholarship to STONi as soon as the first route looked like being a dead end. He had never made a secret of his ambition.

Rather than envying Anthony, Torben had soon found himself doing something much, much worse – he had judged him. He had let the guy irritate the hell out of him, and responded with unspoken critique: of his plodding scholarship, his gracelessness, his politics – which were of the meritocratic, pull-yourself-up-by-the-bootstraps sort that Torben was starting to observe in so many of his privately educated contemporaries, half of whom had their own trust funds. Increasingly, he found Anthony ridiculous. A walking cliché. He could not even find it in himself to be envious of Dodd's growing fortune, as any decent human being would have been; instead he had dismissed it as just the sort of thing he *would* do. '*Dodd*,' he had once said to Leyla. 'Only four letters in his surname, and three of them are "D" – how singularly unimaginative can a person be?' And Leyla, quite rightly, had kicked him in the shins.

Anthony Dodd, in short, brought out the worst in Torben and, naturally, this made Torben, who realised this, resent Anthony even more. He knew no one else who made him feel like such an awful snob, at the same time as reinforcing that snobbery. He suspected that Anthony felt the same – or rather, the inverse. It was sort of their thing. Now, confronted with the astonishing interior of Bastle House, Torben had begun to harbour some hopes of a change in his host – but he was not exactly prepared to bet money on it.

He had not expected *this*.

The man before them – categorically *not* a boy – was gaunt, his cheeks hollow, a scarf at his neck. He carried himself as if afraid of breaking. It could not be clearer that something was terribly wrong with his health. It was a look that compelled attention. But you had to hand it to him: it didn't half work.

'Anthony,' said Torben, surprised to find that he too had risen from his chair. 'You look like a bloody film star!'

'I feel more like a headmaster,' said Anthony, and his voice, flat and bluff, was the same as ever. 'I come in and you all go mum.'

He greeted the others. 'Is that a phone, Sara?' he said. Her bag was still open on the table.

'Guilty as charged,' she said, getting it out. 'Er, "see me after class"?'

If Anthony got the joke, he didn't show it.

Kirsty reappeared. Amazing how she could just pop up like that.

'I've got Ms Moradi's phone already,' she said, smiling at Leyla. 'Inspector Thompson didn't bring one—'

'Neither did we,' said Frances, gesturing towards Torben, 'like you asked. Fine by me – it's quite nice to leave the modern world behind for a weekend. But I'm sure you needn't take our word for it.'

Anthony smiled slightly, and nodded. Then, raising his voice, he spoke precisely: 'STONi override eight eight four three two find all.'

Immediately, Sara's phone began to ring loudly, as did two more, one of them presumably Leyla's, from the kitchen beyond the double doors. Torben and Kirsty both started, while Anthony looked suddenly very, very tired. 'STONi stop,' he said, and the noises ceased.

'*Det ved jeg sgu ikke,*' muttered Torben. Everyone else seemed to know what was going on.

'It's his app,' Leyla said.

'Oh.'

'Not my app anymore,' said Anthony. 'Sold it, didn't I? Anyway, thanks for humouring me with my little request,' he added. 'Your phones will be waiting for you down at the lodge when you leave, safe and sound and fully charged, courtesy of Kirsty. I'll explain later.'

'He's got his reasons,' Ruth said quietly to Sara, who was looking mutinous as Kirsty took her phone.

'I'm with Anthony on this one,' said Torben, brightly. Better, after all, to indulge a sick host. 'I travelled up this morning in the quiet carriage. Quiet carriage indeed! There were phones going off all the time. They wouldn't stand for it in Denmark. You know what happens there if you so much as whisper in the quiet carriage? It's literally the worst thing. The guard comes up to you and smiles. Then he says quietly – it's always a he – he says, "Excuse me, perhaps you were not aware. This is the quiet carriage."' Torben shuddered. 'It's basically the modern equivalent of being put in the stocks.'

The mood broke. 'So I guess you all liked the pie?' Anthony said, grinning. 'Good, I see there's some left. I won't have any but we can save it for tomorrow. Tom Goring's driving up now and I told him to pick Wilson up at Doncaster, but Kirsty tells me the A1's at a standstill round Darlington so they'll have their tea on the way if they've got any sense. I suppose they could take the A68, go Bishop Auckland, Consett, but … no, no, not in this, better sit tight and have tea at the Barton Park services …'

Perhaps he hadn't changed so much after all.

Although actually, that down-to-earth affectation – 'tea' indeed – was new. To balance out, perhaps, the ownership of a stately home.

'Well, I'll show you newcomers to your rooms, shall I?' said Anthony, into the silence. 'You can all freshen up, dress for dinner. No point catching up properly till we're all here.'

Ruth pushed her chair in. 'I'll stay here and help Kirsty—'

'*No*,' said the housekeeper. Her face ran through half a dozen expressions before settling on Dignified Professional. 'Really, Inspector Thompson, I work much better just left to myself.'

'Let's tag along, Ruth,' said Leyla. 'Have you *seen* how many bags Torben's brought? We can carry them up the stairs.'

On the verge of protesting, Torben caught Leyla's eye and fell silent. He had unlearnt the rhythms of her teasing. No one since had been quite as good at slipping under his guard.

Ascending the stairs for the second time – but, unlike on the first occasion, unencumbered by a suitcase and by thoughts of why the hell Ruth was acting so weirdly – Leyla was at leisure to drink in her surroundings. She had to admit it, the upper floor of Bastle House was every bit as beautiful as the lower, with the same long gallery running either side of the landing, high and brilliant in the light of many windows, with lawn beyond those windows. On a clear day, the view was probably stunning. Today, that stretch of greying grass was giving way to mist. No wonder Anthony was wearing a scarf. Somehow, amazingly, it suited him; it put her in mind of Jeremy Irons in *Stealing Beauty* – only not half so hot, obviously. Speaking of which, hot was the last thing any of them could be feeling right now. Yes, the scarf was a good look – but it was hardly to the credit of his central heating.

'These rooms are only twin beds,' Anthony was saying, nodding stiffly to either side of the staircase. 'We'll leave those to the latecomers. Always thought Wilson needed twin beds – him in one, his ego in the other. And if Tom's got too porky for a single, he can always push 'em together.' Chuckling at his own wit, he led them left along the landing. 'Frances, I'll put you here, the corner room. Two doors. Best room in the house! Well, that's just my opinion of course.' Was Anthony's face glowing for a reason, or was it just the exertion of a palpably sick man who had carried bags halfway around a country house?

'And there's no en suite,' he continued, standing just a little too close to Frances, 'but you can take your pick of using that bathroom' – indicating the room they had just passed – 'or sharing the one up here.'

Wait, thought Leyla, *isn't that* my *bathroom?* There was a door leading into it from her bedroom – but also, she now saw, from the corridor. By the looks of things, she was going to have to share with both Sara and Frances. Well, perhaps age had reined in their exuberance when it came to ablutions – but it was unlikely to have done much for Frances' propensity to moult.

A memory rose before her, so that for a moment she saw another, quite different bathroom – small, institutional – the one on their first-year staircase. Heard again the stifled sobs, felt the dread of indecision. But only for a moment. Still. She hadn't thought about that in years …

A rush of feet and a sudden squeal from within Frances' new room brought her back to the present. Peering in, she saw Sara and Frances actually jumping up and down on the enormous four-poster, their heads practically bumping on its high canopy. She smiled. Let them moult all they liked. And then she put out a restraining arm. 'No, Torben,' she said. 'I fear that any more would break the bed.'

Thwarted from joining in the romp, Torben contented himself with extracting Frances' case from among the several he was balancing. Her room – painted a deep forest green, and furnished in light oak – was palatial, with windows on two sides, wrapped around the sort of colonial-era canopied bed, fully loaded with cushions – a tester, was that what they called it? and if so, why? – that he would have thought ridiculous, if it hadn't been so deliciously inviting … especially, he conceded, in its present, if over-occupied state. He tried not to imagine himself in Sara's place, beside a bouncing Frances. But his hopes of an opulent weekend had just risen considerably.

'I'm the next door along,' said Leyla, in a voice that sounded, to Torben, more like a warning than an invitation.

'And then Sara at the end,' Anthony finished, which brought the pair on the bed to order.

Torben couldn't help giving Leyla a defiant look as they offloaded every item of Sara's luggage.

'As for you, Herr Doktor Helle,' said Anthony, when only they and Ruth were left, 'you and Ruth are in the west wing with me.'

40

Impressively, he said 'in the west wing' without the faintest trace of either embarrassment or irony.

'I gave Ruth the only en suite – apart from mine, of course,' Anthony said, when they had retraced the length of the long gallery. 'She got here first, after all.'

Torben looked at Ruth, imagining her torn between self-denial and a desire to make things easy for her host.

'I'm still a terribly light sleeper,' she shrugged, 'and it's at the end, away from everyone.' So, that was how she had reconciled herself to the luxury.

'Good luck when it comes to having children,' Anthony chuckled. For a moment almost too fleeting to catch, something twisted in Ruth's face.

Torben spoke quickly. 'So this is me then?'

'Aye. Pretty bare, mind, but it's the upstairs of the original bastle house. Walls nigh on a metre thick; that's Tudor mortar that is! I thought you'd appreciate it, being a fellow historian and all.' Anthony pushed open the oversized door, revealing a large, dark room – and almost wholly obscuring the single bed tucked in the corner behind the door. Between the windows on the far wall was an ancient wardrobe – he'd guess French, and seventeenth century, if pushed. The only other pieces of solid furniture were a desk and chair of the same sort in the corner across from the bed, dwarfed by the enormous fireplace that dominated the room. The rest was bare, save for a wastepaper basket, a reading lamp, a couple of indifferent portraits in muddy oils, and – in what must have been another nod to their host's new-found old-tech principles – a pad of writing paper and a fountain pen, neatly squared off on the desk.

Anthony sniffed the air, which was so cold it seemed ready to solidify. 'Oh, sorry,' he said. 'I'd get that fire lit if I were you. Just call

41

if you need any help.' Was it Torben's imagination, or was Anthony struggling to suppress a grin?

Left to himself, Torben tried to sublimate his irritation into efficient unpacking. Finding a place for everything, taking ownership of the room. He put the book about Decamps on the desk, Anthony's invitation peeking out from between its pages: a reminder that he really needed to finish it soon if he were to get the review in on time. That left his washbag, which he would move to the bathroom later. Next, he lit the fire with a minimum of both fuss and matches – take that, Dodd – before crossing to one of the windows. He could see … nothing. A nothing that moved in massy drifts.

The snow had started falling.

3

SATURDAY, SIX P.M.

Torben had seen enough art exhibitions to know that every display of good taste, no matter how carefully curated, must contain at least one lapse. He was amused and almost touched to find that Anthony's first sign of weakness was a gong. At six o'clock precisely, a coppery clangour rang through Bastle House. Cursing the lack of a mirror, Torben made a last few hurried adjustments before heading to the drawing room.

Everyone else was there before him. The room was cosier than most in Bastle House, and seemed crammed full of things and people. Several sofas lolled about, relaxed enough to show a peep of stuffing. Velvet drapes, a hat stand, a long-case clock … candles flared in sconces beneath the twinkling glass of a chandelier, dancing in firelight. The only trace of the house's general austerity came from the clean stone lines of the mantelpiece and the bare wall above it. The din of the gong had been replaced with some really excellent, smoky jazz, emanating from – what else? – a hipster-retro vinyl player, reminding him that music had always been Anthony's one point of contact with normal human culture. Frances was conducting elaborate experiments at a cocktail table. Slowly, they all turned towards him.

Leyla was the first to speak. 'Torben, your tie's got under your collar,' she said. Sara giggled.

'Oh *for helvede!*' Torben tore the bow tie from his neck. 'Ten minutes that took, with no mirror. Your letter said *dress for dinner*, Anthony!'

No one else was in black tie. Anthony was unchanged, while Leyla had merely swapped her shoes. Sara and Frances had changed into dresses, but dresses didn't count, and Ruth was in slacks and a jumper – albeit a fantastic jumper.

Even the two latecomers, whom he hadn't seen till now, were smirking at him. Wilson sported a pure white roll-neck and tight selvedge jeans, neatly paired to emphasise his height and physique: always sleek and handsome, Wilson had evidently added muscle tone to his acting CV. Only Tom Goring, small and shabby at Wilson's side and also more filled out than of old, albeit in the wrong direction, was wearing a formal suit – a regular, ill-cut suit – and Torben had never known him without one. In fact, it might well be the same suit he had worn as an undergraduate. Torben himself was wearing an outfit he'd scarcely thought about for ten years, after all. He remembered the incredulity with which he'd first greeted the information that he was expected to wear black tie for formal dinners, so swiftly assimilated into the bizarre sub-culture that was an Oxford college. Of course no one did this in the real world. But, he'd thought, a reunion, surely that meant … ?

'Oh you bunch of bastards!' he said, and now the laughter was general.

'Um … vodka martini, Mr Bond?' offered Frances.

'I hate you all,' he said, and grinned. 'You two got here all right then?'

'Evidently,' said Wilson, and hugged him – the sort of proper hug that has no time for petty concerns like ribs and breathing. 'I've missed you, buddy.'

'You too,' Torben said, and meant it. With the physical contact came the realisation of how much he'd missed his old friend, for all his flaws. In academia, it didn't do to be so nakedly self-interested; but then, a scholar's subject was never themselves, whereas Wilson Ho's narcissism could just as easily be justified as dedication to his art. So what if that art was his own career and the body that carried it? Not for the first time, Torben wondered if he had a very slight crush on the other man, or if it was just that Wilson allowed him to indulge a different side of himself – the sports-playing, back-slapping, uncomplicated side that he hated to think of as 'manly' for a range of ideological reasons that would interest his academic colleagues far more than the sports themselves.

And then there was Tom Goring, so often the odd one out in this company. But then, you didn't *actually* get to choose your friends, did you, any more than you got to choose your family? And even if Tom was their group's equivalent of his uncle Morten, who smoked at the table, made off-colour jokes, and voted for the *Dansk Folkeparti*, hadn't he always tried to get on with Onkel Morten? Well then. Time to make an effort.

'How're you, Tom?' he said, smiling.

'Ben,' said Tom, inclining his head.

Torben, who had always hated being called Ben – a fact Tom Goring doubtless remembered – was consoled by the sight of Tom's bald patch, well in advance of his own. And for all that, Tom seemed genuinely pleased to see him.

'Glad I didn't miss this,' Tom said. 'At one point, it looked like we'd have to give up, everything snarled with the weekend traffic, and some of the roads up here, Christ … Wish I'd got here sooner, in time for some decent time one-on-one before the party started. Still, we made it in the end! I don't mind telling you, Ben, if this weekend hadn't come off, after the no-show at the Gaudy and the radio silence since, I'd be – well, disappointed doesn't come close, try "royally fucked off"—' and he stopped, flushed, looking like he'd let on more than he'd meant to.

Torben was flattered. 'Tom! I'd no idea you found my company so desirable.'

Tom stared at him. 'I meant Ant, of course.'

'Of course,' said Torben. Smiling more fixedly now, he tried again. 'So, what're you—?'

'Don't ask him,' hissed Sara, at his elbow. 'Not before *they* ask *us*. We made a pact.' Her gesture took in the other women, who adopted innocent expressions.

'I don't get it,' said Tom. For a moment, no one said anything.

'Oh, for fuck's sake,' said Leyla, and downed her Negroni. 'Right, everyone listen carefully, we're not doing this again.'

She began to point at each of them in turn. 'Ruth is now a Metropolitan Police inspector and also wife, achieving both of those things disgustingly fast. Frances is still a sculptor. She makes beautiful objects that I don't understand. Sara's about to finish a brilliant PhD at King's whilst holding down about a million other jobs, and Torben is an art historian at the Courtauld on a fellowship that seems to let him get away with doing bugger all. You should all buy his book, it's great. Me: barrister, representing too many bloody charities who pay me next to nothing but save orphans and rainforests so I let them take advantage. Anthony is … OK, I don't really know what Anthony is now but I'm sure he's going to tell us later, and we covered you two earlier' – pointing at Tom and Wilson – 'so unless anything truly momentous has occurred since the Gaudy I think we're done here and can talk about something *fun*.'

There was a pause. If you looked hard at Wilson, you could see him actively suppressing the need to monologue – either that, or trying to decide which of his recent castings, anecdotes, encounters, did *not* count as 'truly momentous'.

'I got married,' mumbled Tom.

'Good for you,' said Torben.

'We're expecting a baby actually,' said Tom, but no one was listening.

'For once, I think it's reasonable to talk about the weather,' Ruth was saying.

'It's gonna get much worse than this,' said Wilson. 'There was a special report on the radio. We left Tom's car down at the lodge where the road's still OK for now, but even so, I hope they have good snow ploughs or whatever in this part of the world, or you'll have us on your hands well into next week.'

Anthony nodded. 'I'd be delighted. A proper holiday, why not? Skittles in the long gallery, badminton in the ballroom, all that. It'll be jolly.' Jolly was the last thing he looked, thought Torben. 'Just worried about Kirsty,' Anthony went on. 'She's got to get back down to the lodge after dinner.'

'Driving?' said Tom. Anthony nodded.

'What's her vehicle?'

'We use a Land Rover Defender, just on the estate,' said Anthony.

'Trying too hard,' Sara whispered to Torben.

'Good suspension on that,' Tom said. 'Should be fine if you fitted decent tyres.'

Torben would never understand what it was about car-talk that made a certain type of man so happy.

'You know, I was thinking of putting my name down for a Tesla,' said Wilson. 'The last shoot I did, they picked me up in one every morning and *man*, it was smooth.'

Both Tom and Anthony looked at him as if he'd just announced his intention of butchering a human baby.

'So, the snow's really meant to set in overnight?' said Ruth, coming to Wilson's rescue.

He nodded. 'The press has even got a special name for it, which can't be good.'

'You're very good at melodrama over here,' said Torben. 'Even the weather gets top billing as a villain, preferably a foreign one. It's certainly more interesting. The Swedes will look at a metre of snowfall overnight, the Gulf of Bothnia frozen solid, and they'll shrug and say, "*Nåja*, I might put a coat on in a bit."'

'Don't get me started on you Scandis,' said Anthony. 'Never did any good business with the Nordics. Sweden was the first place to get out a rival to STONi. All those too-cool-for-school startups, couldn't stand them at conferences. Truecaller, iZettle ... then there's bloody Pirate Bay – and as for Spotify, well! Streaming's killing real music.' He laid a hand on the record player; it seemed to anchor him. 'Do you remember making mix tapes? I reckon we were about the last year who ever knew what it was to make a proper mix tape. Don't you miss all that? The hours you'd spend with the tape recorder, swapping the CDs over or recording straight from the radio ... working out exactly how many tracks you could fit on each side, squeezing out every last second. Getting your calculations just right, cos if you didn't, your side one show-stopper cut out halfway through the final chorus. Meticulous, it was.'

'You remember that Belle and Sebastian song, "Simple Things"?' said Torben, giving in to the nostalgia despite himself. 'I must have put it at the end of about a dozen cassettes, just because it was only—'

'One minute fifty!' said Anthony, and Torben felt an unexpected wave of affection, until Anthony rather ruined the moment by adding, 'Bunch of Scottish mimsies though, weren't they?' He looked up to check that Frances wasn't listening. 'Got away with that one, I think. She can be a bit feisty, can our Fran. Leastways, she always was in the old days.' He rubbed the bridge of his nose ostentatiously. 'I'm sure I'm not the only one to bear an old war-wound from my encounters with young Fran.'

Now what on earth did *that* mean, Torben thought. And for that matter – setting aside whatever Anthony was literally alluding to – what did *any* of this mean? Alarmingly, his host was apparently trying to be nice to him, in something of a world first. He wondered again why he'd been invited. For Anthony to arrange all of this on – on a whim? It looked like hard work. Albeit, mostly for Kirsty.

Torben sighed, slipped away, began to refill drinks. For a group of incredibly similar people, he reflected, they were really quite dissimilar. Sharing a staircase in their first year, living in the leaky brutalist building that the college kept hidden away from the tourists, a space they shared with mice and mould, they had been united above all by the suspicion that they were being unfairly ghettoised, which went some way to explaining their relative diversity. Well, diverse for Oxford, a phrase at least as loaded as 'normal for Norfolk'. He remembered Tom grumbling at being 'thrown in with all the ethnics and foreigners' in a tone that had been only half-joking – and his adamant insistence that, as a Northumbrian and a Scot, both Anthony and Frances naturally fitted into that category of 'misfits'. The fact that a viscount and an honourable had somehow ended up with the best two rooms in the eighteenth-century quad had done little to shake this general belief in their outsider status.

Only Anthony had seemed genuinely proud of the institution after the initial excitement wore off, his disappointment over his first-year exam results being directed at the department and the fellows rather than their college, which the rest of them adopted the habit of referring to as 'Slytherin'. And though they had quickly assimilated the language of 'battels' and 'collections', said 'noughth week' to refer to the week before teaching began and 'scout' instead of 'cleaner', most of them had forgotten those habits since leaving Oxford. It was as if that world – where dons circulated snuff after High Table, where a faulty bathroom window let you sneak out into the deserted starlit meadow at midnight, where someone had built an actual cathedral in the middle of the college, where punting was a thing you did unironically – had taken on the status of a fairy story, something from another life. A year or two ago he had even caught Ruth saying to someone 'when I was at uni' as if they had gone somewhere normal, which if not strictly dishonest was, by her standards, an act of rank duplicity. Certainly time had accentuated their differences, perhaps because most of them – unusually, he thought – seemed to have worked out who they really were. Well, he knew who he *wanted* to be, and that was the joker from the past, the one who got people drinks and listened to their stories. He glanced at his watch: twenty minutes till dinner. He loved these people – most of them, anyway – and he'd seen far too little of them. Time to reconnect.

'Why do you think Tom didn't invite any of us to his wedding?' said Leyla, who had switched to water. 'I mean, I wouldn't expect an invite, but it sounds like not even Anthony and Wilson were there. Why not – embarrassed of the bride, or embarrassed of us? Maybe he had our best interests at heart, and wanted to spare non-natives an encounter with the delights of Daventry.'

Maybe now was not the best time to talk to Leyla.

*

Wilson resisted the temptation to knock back the Old Fashioned that Fran had mixed him. As his personal trainer had made very clear, on this side of thirty you had to pace yourself. It wasn't so much his stomach he was worried about – the gym took care of that – but his face. Ever since a blogger had compared his eyes to Ron Ng's, he'd been taking special care. Give it another twenty years and you could let it go, do the raddled, fleshy look that Colin Firth was currently rocking. But not yet. Besides, he should really watch his mouth this weekend – he didn't want to risk a diplomatic incident on what was basically enemy territory.

Well, 'enemy' was putting it a bit strong, no? Antagonist? Too dry. This was the problem with real life: people existed in three dimensions, they kept resisting the label of supporting actor – or, as he more often thought of them, as NPCs – by doing something unexpected or contradictory. So what role was Anthony Dodd playing now, as far as he was concerned? Judas? Mephistopheles? Maybe the cocktail was the right idea after all.

He looked up from a glass that was, respectably, only half empty, to see Torben coming over. He was looking good, if you got over the entry-level tux – you could see he'd aged since their early twenties, but in the right kind of way. Torben, Fran and Leyla were definitely in the 'improved' column – besides himself, of course. The others all seemed to have let life get to them to a greater or lesser extent. Which was poetic justice in one case, of course – but he was glad to see Torben still on point. He was one of the good guys. 'Torben!' he said. 'Guess who I was working with last week? Only Olivia bloody Colman, that's who!'

Torben admired how completely and sincerely Wilson inhabited his luvvie persona. 'Do you remember what you said when you first told me you wanted to act?' Torben asked, when Wilson seemed to have run out of ways to describe how wonderful 'Olivia' was.

'"I want to be a movie star,"' Wilson self-quoted. '"I want to hang out with Brad Pitt and Beverley Hills!" Man, I was a stupid kid.'

'We all were,' agreed Torben. 'Stupid and beautiful!'

'Hey,' said Wilson, emptying his glass, 'that sounds like you've been reading my resumé. No one should knock beautiful stupidity; those assets got me *this* close to a supporting part in *Crazy Rich Asians*. Still, there's always the sequel, right?'

'Always the sequel,' said Torben. 'A good motto, that.'

'To second chances,' said Wilson, and frowned at the empty glass. It seemed to remind him of something. 'Another reason why movies are better than real life: you can always film another take. God. Want to know the stupidest thing I ever did?'

'I would love to,' said Torben, noting the shift in his friend's mood, and setting about mixing him another drink. 'Though I suspect I could top it.'

Wilson was clearly dying to vent. 'Of course, I shouldn't say anything, not here. But, if you really wanna know … I mean, you know it was me who actually invented Anthony's whole STONi thing, right?'

'I did not,' said Torben. Nor did he entirely believe it. Wilson, though a dab hand with an Xbox controller in their youth, had never struck him as the tech type. 'Do you mean the name?' he hazarded.

'The *name*? Hell no – actually, I think *that* was Ruth,' said Wilson, 'she being by far the best Christian among us. Anthony Dodd, Saint Anthony, patron saint of lost things, Saint Tony, Stony, STONi, see? Kinda genius. It wasn't a serious suggestion, more of a play on "Sony" at a time when Steve Jobs was putting a lower-case "i" at the start of every damn thing he invented – but it sort of stuck. I reckon it suited Ant; he's, well, he's a pretty stony guy, right?'

'I must've missed this at the time,' said Torben, handing Wilson a full glass. 'When did this whole eureka moment actually happen?'

'Yeah, well,' said Wilson, scratching the side of his nose. 'The three of us were staying up playing *Settlers of Catan* in Ant's room, some time early in first year. That was the year before I lost the whole of my free time to *Call of Duty* – I would so have gotten a First if that game was my degree – but between that and constant rehearsals ... Well, Ant's room was a tip, of course, and at the end I couldn't find my phone – one of those old Nokias, whatever happened to them? – and we ended up using Ruth's mobile to call it. And *then* I couldn't find my room key either, and I said, wouldn't it be great if we could call that, too? So I guess that was me, the basic leap of reasoning. Five minutes later, we had the whole idea worked out. Name and everything, like I said.'

Of course, Torben thought, that was why the voice-activated app had confused him earlier. When Anthony had first launched STONi back in their early twenties, it had been based on old tech: the product was a unique microchip attached to a tiny speaker, that you could stick to your wallet, keys, anything really, and call from your phone when you couldn't find whatever it was. The speaker went off, and all you had to do was follow the sound. So long as you had your phone, or even a landline, you could track down anything in earshot. The app must have come later once Torben had stopped paying attention to Anthony's success, as a sort of inevitable extension of the idea: using more contemporary, voice-activated tech so you could find your own phone without having to use another one – increasingly useful in a society of one-person households with no landlines.

'It was just a joke, really,' said Wilson, 'though we got quite excited at the time. Ant said that first evening that if he ever made it happen for real, we'd each get a proper cut, me and Ruth. But I think it might be time to remind him of that promise, since so far I've never seen a goddamn penny ...'

He paused, looking down at his drained glass. Torben supposed he had remembered whose hospitality he was enjoying: poor form to bad-mouth your host whilst downing his drinks. Whatever the reason, Wilson's tone was breezier as he went on – 'Which is cool, I was never serious about it, but it taught me a lesson. These days I make damn sure my agent gets every contract double checked.'

Interesting. Torben moved on to Ruth, intending to corroborate Wilson's story. He loved Wilson dearly. But take him at his word? Not so much.

Ruth forestalled him. 'I'm worried about Sara,' she said. 'Does she seem a little – tense – to you?'

'She seems fine,' he lied. 'A bit quieter than usual, maybe.' In truth, Sara looked exhausted and on edge, but he didn't feel comfortable making that sort of observation to a third party. Face to face, he had no such qualms about getting personal, and he let Ruth have it. 'What about you? That moment earlier, when Anthony mentioned having children?'

'Oh, it's nothing,' she said. 'At least, it's not about children exactly, it's ...' She tailed off.

'Jon,' supplied Torben. 'What, he doesn't want them, or—' but his courage was unequal to the look Ruth was now giving him. 'OK, we can do this another time,' he conceded. 'But it wasn't just that; you've been looking worried all day.'

'Oh look,' she said, 'Frances is sending out distress signals. One of us should help her.'

'I'll do it,' he said, resigned to the dismissal, and made for the corner where Tom Goring was waving his drink about and saying something in which the words 'modern art' figured ominously.

*

54

He had, Tom thought to himself, made his case rationally and succinctly. Not to Anthony, worse luck, that would have to wait till later. Turning up late with Wilson hadn't helped; when he'd tried to buttonhole his old friend just now, Ant had been busy talking to Sara and seemed not to notice Tom's hand gestures. It had been like this for a couple of years now. One minute he had Ant lined up as his best man, a dead cert to bankroll his wedding. Then the perplexing silence, the emails that came back with 'address not found', and the scramble to do on the cheap what he had promised his fiancée would be her dream day. At least he'd kept this lot from seeing that particular fiasco ... And now, just when he needed some alone time with Ant more desperately than ever, he still couldn't get him to himself. So he had had to make do with the next best thing: baiting Frances.

It wasn't often this crowd let him get a word in edgeways, they'd always been too chatty for their own good, but for once he'd had his say and said it well. It had started with him asking Fran if people still got their portraits done as statues – might be a nice little earner for her, that – and she'd come out with some crap about 'representation being an impediment to truth'.

You couldn't blame her, to be fair – all that theory crap had got her good and proper – but really, *someone* had to remind her that, at the end of the day, people bought art either as an investment, or to stick on their wall. And what you wanted on your wall, if you had any sense, was something that was nicer to look at *than the bloody wall*. 'And if a picture says a thousand words,' he finished up, 'then the last thing you want is something that takes another thousand *actual* words to explain what it's on about.'

'But that's the whole point,' said Frances. She was flushed now, her cheeks reddening in just the way he remembered. Which, if Tom was honest with himself, was the whole reason he'd started this argument. Frances in a temper – especially when wearing a low-cut dress – well, it hit the spot.

'It's only "art" at all if you can find something to say about it,' she continued. 'You dinnae look at some – some Tupperware – and say "that's crap". You can only *say* "that's crap" *because* it's art!'

Her accent was back in full force: she was rolling her r's. Yes, this was the stuff. Raising his eyes, Tom found that Torben had come over to join in the fun. Of course he had. Hypocritical bugger, coming across all right-on, but everyone knew that, where Fran was concerned, if you gave him a chance … Still, despite himself, Tom found himself caring about this argument, and any ally would do.

'Oh come on, Ben, back me up,' he said. 'Art, real art I mean, like Constable or whoever, not your Tracy Emins – well, it's for looking at, not talking about, isn't it?'

He'd meant to express himself better than that – he had a half-formed idea about paintings being like extra windows in a room, giving precious views onto other worlds. But he was buggered if he could put it into words.

'You did hear Leyla tell you that I am *an art historian*, yes?' said Torben. 'Talking about art is literally my job.'

'Yeah, but that's all attribution and dates, isn't it? Proper technical stuff?'

'*Dit svin,*' said Torben, secure in Tom's total ignorance of Danish. He took a deep breath. 'OK. Why not think of it more broadly, not just sculpture and pictures but all of it: music, books, the lot. How about saying there are two kinds of art – call them high and low, if you like, because those words are short and simple. The low stuff is *just* there to enjoy. To dance to, to read by the pool, to look at and think, "that's pretty". The other stuff might be that too, maybe, but mainly it's a machine for producing conversation. All those people who claim to hate "modern" art, who want it to look nice, not "stimulate a discourse" – they never realise that stimulating a discourse was the whole point of, say, Giorgione.' Halfway through this speech, Torben decided not to have another cocktail.

'Hmm,' said Tom. 'All sounds a bit bollocks, frankly. Which is Frances, high or low?'

'I've got a few pieces in a show on Columbia Road next month,' she said, before Torben could answer. 'Come and decide for yerself.'

'That in London, is it?' said Tom.

'Aye,' said Frances, refusing the bait. 'You'd like it. I've got really interested in foam lately; it's such an ephemeral medium, don't you think? I film myself in the bath with a load of bubbles. It's dead hard stuff to sculpt in but it really speaks to the idea of *transience*, if you know what I mean ...'

Tom fled. Torben tried not to picture Frances in nothing but soapsuds. It was a heroic failure. 'Do you *really* work in foam?' he said.

'Nah,' she said, 'I just made that up to piss him off. Isn't half a bad idea though, not that you'd be interested. You're all about Friedrich and that Romantic landscape bullshit, amiright?'

'Darling,' said Torben, striking an attitude, 'I live and breathe the avant-garde. Why, the first word I ever spoke was "Dada".'

'You've been saving that one up,' she said.

The crash of the gong interrupted them, and Torben realised the music had stopped. Well, speaking to four friends out of seven wasn't bad, but Ruth had got him worried about Sara, he'd have to catch her later—

'Ladies and gentlemen,' said Anthony, 'dinner is served.'

Torben scrutinised his face. Nope, not the slightest flicker of irony.

4

SATURDAY, SEVEN P.M.

The table was covered in candles. Lit only by these and the roaring fire, the room shrunk in upon itself. Darkness crept across the walls, lapping at the corners. Without sight of windows or ceiling, the shifting, flickering space seemed lost, vulnerable. Frances felt the group huddle together; found herself still beside Torben, who took a step to give her space. 'Well,' he muttered, 'it's not exactly *hyggelig*.'

'Places, places!' said Anthony, evidently the only one not unnerved by the spectacle. 'I've done you all little name cards.'

Well of course he had, thought Frances. And no prizes for guessing where she would be sat. She had been prepared for this, of course; she had worked through scenarios, ways of coping, keeping past and present separate. But still. It was going to be a long evening.

Torben found himself at the centre of the table, facing the fire. Pulling in his seat, he squirmed his shoulder blades. Given the choice, he would not have turned his back on that darkness. At his left, he saw Leyla do likewise. Frances, on his right hand, seemed especially unnerved by the swallowing dark – or was she just annoyed to be sat opposite Tom Goring? Ah, no, it was because Anthony was insisting on drawing back her chair, making a show of gallantry of the sort that would irritate any woman. She positively flinched from his hand at her shoulder, and Torben's eyes flicked to the cutlery: much more of this, and he could see one of the forks ending up embedded in Anthony's flesh. Their host, seated at the table's head beyond Tom and Frances, had indeed done that 'matchy-matchy' thing, so that Sara was across from Torben, then Wilson on Sara's other side, with Ruth as the nearest thing to a hostess at the foot end. It was something from another age; Torben was almost surprised they hadn't been asked to pair up first, to take each other in, arms linked.

'I wanted,' said Anthony, 'to try an idea Torben and I once had for the History subject dinner back at college: a meal in monochrome. Black as night, white as snow – seemed appropriate. Something special to remember the weekend by.'

Torben frowned. As he remembered, that idea had been his alone. Maybe Wilson was right, and Anthony did make a habit of taking others' credit.

'Shall we toast, then?' said Anthony. 'To the old gang?'

'The old gang,' they echoed, taken by surprise. Torben looked at his flute. Black velvet: stout floated over champagne, the dark and the light. As he raised the glass, the two opposing elements began to mix. His frown deepened. He wasn't sure he liked drinking anything so crashingly allegorical. Plus he hated Guinness.

Wilson looked along the table. 'Well, Anthony, didn't you have something to tell us?'

'Later, later,' said their host. 'It'd spoil your appetites. Dig in.'

'Whereas that comment really takes our minds off it,' said Leyla, none too quietly, contemplating the three small blinis before her, each glistening with tiny black caviar.

'Fish eggs help prevent dementia,' said Ruth, and ate a blini.

Torben, who had already finished his dish, eyed Wilson. 'I thought you were a vegan?' he said.

'Me? Nah,' said Wilson. 'What gave you that idea?'

Torben turned to Leyla. 'I will never trust you again,' he declared. Somehow, spoken amid so much darkness, it sounded more serious than he had meant it to.

At this moment Kirsty slipped back in, carrying any potential awkwardness away with the empty plates, and returning to the table with four bottles of Riesling – the sort so refined that it scarcely had a label – alongside a frothy white soup that proved, upon tasting, to be milk, elderflower, and completely delicious. Maybe when Kirsty was less run off her feet he could ask her for the recipe …

Leyla, meanwhile, was refusing to look at Torben. 'So, Sara,' she said, 'tell us about your PhD.'

Sara felt the table's focus tighten around her, the ratcheting of a lens in a microscope. Waving the question away with an automatic gesture, she very nearly sent her glass flying; recovering just in time, she sipped it instead. Really, this was the *last* thing she wanted to talk about, which was especially unfair considering she had promised not to raise the one subject she was burning to discuss. 'Oh it's – it's really intensely boring, not the stuff of sparkling conversation. I'd much rather hear about some of your cases, Leyla.'

But they were not to be dissuaded; the others were chiming in now. She glared at Torben, who was leading the encouragement, despite the fact that *he*, with his state-funded grant, had completed his own doctorate five years earlier, while she was still self-funding 'part-time' – which essentially meant in the evenings after work. Still, it *was* nice to be asked.

'Yeah, so basically it's a distant reading of the Sherlock Holmes stories,' she said. 'Meaning, more or less, the opposite of close reading? Data analysis, maps, patterns. Statistics as a form of literary criticism.' She took another sip of the mysteriously unlabelled wine. It tasted of money. Well, whatever it was, it was helping. 'It's surprising how quickly you build up a – a competence, a sort of expertise in the mechanics of murder. As filtered through the lens of Conan Doyle, of course. There are fifty-six Holmes stories plus the four novels, so you get some pretty reliable conclusions.'

'Such as?' said Wilson.

'Um, like the fact that most of the crimes aren't where you think they are,' she said. 'Someone says Sherlock Holmes and you picture East London – seedy slums, docks, street markets – but mostly it's about rich people's houses. The West End, leafy suburbs, remote country mansions.' She smiled. Actually, this was quite enjoyable, talking to people with no skin in the game. 'Statistically, Anthony, you'd be way more at risk than me or Ruth in a Holmes mystery.'

Something in the room stretched thin. There was just a little too much of the uncanny in the strange meal, in the circling dark, for her comment to sit comfortably.

Torben decided to rescue her. 'Those stories have never quite clicked for me,' he said. 'It's the clues: they only ever point to one thing. Surely, for any given clue, there are any number of equally likely explanations.' He made an expansive gesture. 'If I wished to outwit Sherlock Holmes, I know what I'd do. If I smoked, I'd *stop*, at least while actually committing the crime—'

'I've got a special pie chart for cigarette ash!' said Sara.

He inclined his head. 'Next, I'd *borrow someone else's boots* before leaving any footprints. Why does no one ever do that? And third … I need a third. I'd—'

'Oo,' said Wilson, joining in. 'I know. If I ever met Sherlock himself, I'd wear a pair of shorts, then he couldn't analyse the knees of my trousers!'

'Or,' said Sara, sipping her Riesling, 'you could just … be a woman? Then even if you got caught, he'd probably let you go.' Her expression was inscrutable.

By the next course – a cuttlefish risotto, black with ink – the conversation had moved on, but somehow they kept circling back to the subject.

'You've never been tempted to switch to the detective side?' Leyla asked Ruth.

Ruth shook her head. 'I didn't join the police to punish crime, I want to prevent it. Why would you concentrate on getting people locked up if instead you could stop them going wrong?'

'More fun though, isn't it?' said Wilson. 'I remember when I played the opium den owner in "The Man with the Twisted Lip"—'

'I've always thought of history as a form of detecting,' said Anthony, speaking over him. 'With the archive as your field of investigation. Sifting the evidence, deciding which witnesses to believe, building your case.'

'With the minor objection,' said Torben, who had heard this sort of rubbish before, 'that no historian has ever secured a definitive verdict. There *is* no solution in history, only conjecture.'

'Actually though,' said Tom, 'what about all your old paintings? Aren't they always full of clues?'

'Sometimes,' said Torben. 'But it's Holmes all over again: normally they're all put there to point the same way, there's no mystery to them.' It was part of what he loved about Friedrich as an artist: he had a genuine sense of the enigmatic. 'Anyway,' he went on, 'I'd never make a convincing detective, especially not one of the modern Danish ones. I *don't* smoke, I like women, and – worst of all – I get on pretty well with my father.'

'Exactly,' said Ruth, who was growing – by her standards – unusually heated. 'Fictional detectives have such a bleak worldview. I'd hate to go around suspecting people all the time. I truly believe that there are no evil people. Only intolerable circumstances.'

'It amounts to the same thing though!' said Anthony, leaning in, his face flushed. 'There's evil in us all. You see it every day, Ruth, you must do in your line of work. Good people do bad things all the time. *Ergo*, taken to extremes – in the right circumstances, as you say – *anyone* can be driven to crime. To murder, even.'

At that moment, Kirsty entered with the main course.

'I could certainly murder this poussin,' said Leyla, her laughter forced. A few mouthfuls, washed down with the last of the Riesling, restored some of their good humour. The chicken, poached, was impossibly moist, the easy give of its white flesh answered by the crunch of blanched almonds. Torben dragged the last of his accompanying white asparagus – from a jar, he supposed, but full of flavour – through the cream and morel sauce with something approaching reverence.

Frances, draining her own glass, gave Torben a nudge. 'OK, I've got one. How did Hercule Poirot solve the problem of the overcrowded prison?'

He thought for a second. 'By using ze little grey cells?'

'Got it in one,' she sniggered, and clinked their glasses. Each was surprised to find theirs empty. Frances turned to Anthony, who shook his head.

'Time for a change before the pud, while Kirsty clears up all this mess,' he said. 'Ladies and gentlemen, I give you: the famous black wine of Cahors!'

'I mean,' said Leyla, as they sipped, 'it's just a Malbec.'

'I'll have yours then,' said Torben.

'Piss off,' she said. But the look she gave him made his stomach do that swooping thing again. Her profile was *perfect*. And it really was an excellent wine.

Dessert was a white chocolate parfait with too-cold blackberries – the first misstep at the final hurdle, thought Torben, almost managing to align his metaphors. With this wine, and snow outside? Still, it had the virtue of simplicity; assuming Kirsty had plated these earlier, there was a chance she could get on top of the washing up. A place like this had to have industrial-sized dishwashers, but still, it was a lot of work …

Something about the quality of the sudden silence told him that Anthony had said something awkward again. God, the man was looking straight at him, as if expecting a response. 'Sorry,' he said. 'I was lost in this delicious pudding.'

'It was the pud I was apologising for,' said Anthony. 'What with the latest health reports about the evils of sugar. I said, *dextrose* is pretty *sinister* these days, isn't it?'

The joke almost worked, Torben supposed, if you had an inattentive schoolboy's grasp of Latin. Which, to be fair, they both did. He had never quite got the place that Latin occupied in the English class system – Classics had been compulsory at his *Gymnasium* – but he did know that those who had a bit liked to show it off where possible. 'Dextrose – sinister – right and left – very good,' said Torben, still a little puzzled that Anthony had felt the need to repeat a bad pun.

'Knew you'd appreciate it,' said Anthony, dabbing at his chin with a black napkin. Perhaps it had been the confidence boost he had needed, for now – at last – he rang his spoon against his wine glass. The gesture was quite unnecessary: everyone was already looking at him. Kirsty, who had cleared their plates for the final time, was at Anthony's side, pulling back his chair. And now Anthony was levering himself to his feet.

'Friends,' he began, 'the time has come. In a few minutes, we will withdraw to the room that is named for that purpose. Oh, which reminds me—' and he murmured a few sentences in Kirsty's ear. Torben, who was starting to lose track of things, half expected their host to announce that they were getting married. But then Kirsty hurried off.

'She's just getting the room ready,' said Anthony. *Lort*, thought Torben, was the whole speech going to be like this?

'But before we withdraw, I've got a couple of things to tell you all. I'm sure you've all been wondering why I summoned you all here this weekend' – *summoned?* the nerve of the man – 'after not seeing any of you for so long. You're probably also wondering why I sold the company last year, and bought this old pile instead. Well, here's the reason.'

'Christ,' said Wilson, a little too loudly. 'This is beginning to sound like that bit in *Peter's Friends* where Stephen Fry tells them all he's got HIV— oh, shit.'

Torben felt dizzy. They all stared, first at Wilson, whose hands were now clapped to his own mouth, then back at their host.

Anthony's face did something strange that might just pass, in this light, for a smile. 'Not quite, Wilson, not quite. I'm afraid it's a little bit worse than that. You see, what I've got is a rare form of what's called Creutzfeldt–Jakob disease.'

So long as he lived, Torben would never forgive himself for his first response. Before the horror, before the shock, the pity, the very first thing he did was wince at Anthony's pronunciation.

'I won't bore you with the details,' their host pressed on, 'but it means my days are numbered. They can't say when. If I'm lucky, I'm looking at three years. Could just as easily be three months. But the signs are good. I'm on all the painkillers they've got. The insomnia's kicked in, that's the first stage. Eventually there'll be memory loss and – and other things. At last I'll slip into a coma, and that'll be a blessing, I dare say.' He held up his hand. 'That's all I want to say about that. You can all say how sorry you are in a minute. First I've something else to say.'

There must have been a drawer in the end of the table. From it, Anthony took a large manila envelope. 'This is my will,' he said, and again Torben saw desperation in his face. He looked pathetically eager, as if wanting something from them. 'Most of what I have goes to family, of course, and then there're donations to CJD charities. I've got a hunch it's all those years working with mobile phones that brought it on, too much radiation exposure giving me prions, so I want them to do proper research into that. Wish I'd never heard of the bloody things, but … anyway, that's why I won't have mobiles in the house.'

He breathed deeply, and shook his head as if to clear it, before continuing. 'But you lot are the closest thing I've ever had to a real group of friends, and I suppose I owe you for dumping this news on you tonight.' He paused, his gaze roving the table, and Torben was conscious again of that new-found charisma he had sensed at lunch-time. 'Each of you gets fifty grand. No arguments.' He passed the envelope to Tom Goring at his right. 'Here, Tom, you're a lawyer, you can see for yourself.'

Tom's face was a blank as he automatically scanned the page before him. He nodded. 'This all looks – er – looks legit, Anthony. Fifty thousand each, absolute. Bloody good of you.'

Anthony returned the will to the drawer. 'Well,' he said. 'Everyone lost for words again?'

Torben's head was spinning. What the hell were they meant to say? It was awful – simply *awful* – for Anthony, that was the main thing. You couldn't blame him for trying to deal with it like this, of course you couldn't. But first to – how had he put it? – 'dump' it all on them, and then try to buy their sympathy like that? All evening he'd been wondering why they'd been asked here, himself especially. Why Anthony was trying so hard. Well, now he had his answer. It was an act – not of atonement, in fact far from it; he didn't think Anthony felt he had anything to atone for – instead … he tried to frame it in the language his host might use. An act of – legacy management? A marked man, using the little power he had left to try and dictate how his friends would remember him.

Not that Torben wasn't grateful, of course he was, incredibly, that was half the point. They could all use the money more than Anthony, he was sure of that. Most of them were groaning with student debt, Sara was working several jobs to finance her PhD, both Frances and Wilson must be living hand to mouth, reliant on the next role, the next commission – and hadn't Tom said something about a baby on the way? Well, in which case, why not a gift, now, rather than an unreliable bequest? For the sake of dodging a bit of tax? No, it was a power play, that's what it came down to. Throw in the charities, though even that sounded a bit crackpot, and his will became perhaps the one generous act of Anthony's life – and even then, he had contrived to stuff it up. *For helvede.* Still, none of that mattered now. A dying man deserves his send-off, even if he feels he has to pay for it, and if no one else could think of anything to say …

'Anthony,' he said, his tone measured. 'Given what you've told us, I feel bound to invoke an ancient Danish tradition. It's a rite that's been carried out in cases like this since Viking days.'

'Oh aye? Is it complicated?'

'Not really,' said Torben. 'It's a time-honoured law that simply states: we have to get very, *very* drunk.'

Anthony's smile widened. 'Be my guest.'

5

SATURDAY, TEN-THIRTY P.M.

A few people slipped off to bathrooms straight away, Torben among them. Leaving the table, he saw Ruth linger to talk to Kirsty, who was on her way out. Wilson hovered nearby, perhaps wishing to thank her for the meal, and Torben was about to do the same when Anthony brushed past him, holding the will. 'Must just give this to Kirsty before she leaves,' he said. 'Won't see her again till Tuesday – provided this snow doesn't get worse. Rations tomorrer!'

Faced with a queue, Torben gave in to more pressing urges. Exiting the bathroom, he was momentarily nonplussed when, tugging on the exquisitely turned oak handle of the pull-switch that controlled the light, the room was almost instantly lit up again – but from outside. Of course. A crunch of snowy gravel and a low purr reminded him: that was Kirsty, heading for bed, and taking with her – if Anthony's pessimism was justified – both their phones, and their only means of travel. Though really, he thought, they were still all being rather melodramatic about a little bit of snow.

Once again, he was the last to get to the drawing room. A rowdy shaking of piano and strings that he recognised as Antony and the

Johnsons was crackling from the record player: dark music, late night music.

'Remember this?' Anthony was at his side. 'I asked Kirsty to put it on specially.'

Torben paused. He did remember, actually – an EP of beautiful but undeniably morbid songs. A new, slower track was just starting, and that inimitable, tremulous voice swam out over the conversation and the crackling fire. Lyrics about a murderer; about sending someone to the slaughterhouse.

Could their host really be so tone deaf? Or did he simply want them all to wallow in his tragedy, now that he had bought them? Despite himself, Torben felt compelled to rile this man.

'You know she changed her name?' he asked, nodding at the record.

'She?'

'Anohni. The artist formerly known as Antony Hegarty,' said Torben, keeping his tone light. 'She's "Anohni" now.'

Anthony looked genuinely stunned. 'You mean he's a real … ? I thought it was just an act.' And he hurried off to change the music.

Leyla had been listening. 'I wonder,' she said. 'Are the terminally ill the same as the very old? Do we just – forgive them?'

'What we do,' said Torben, 'is drink.'

Frances was back at the side table. 'I cannae decide,' she said, 'which'll help me digest it better. The news, I mean.' A bottle of reassuringly dusty port, unopened, stood beside a full decanter. Next to these, several bottles of Tokaji jostled for attention.

'This takes me back,' said Leyla. 'Port *and* Tokaji – a hangover like no other.'

'Both are my friends,' pronounced Torben, 'and they can do me no harm. Old Danish custom, remember?' He began to pour.

'You want to watch that combination, especially with your record under the influence.' Anthony had reappeared. 'And we're none of us as young as we were.'

Everyone looked uncomfortable; Frances actually crossed to the other side of the room. Torben glared at Anthony, and drank a glass straight off. 'My body is a temple,' he said. 'It just happens to be concentrated to Bacchus.' He frowned. 'Consecrated.'

Things got a little fuggy after that.

Ruth – lovely Ruth – she would make it better. But where was she? Skulking, positively *skulking* by the window. Surely she'd be the first to want to comfort Anthony? Instead, they all seemed to be pretending it wasn't happening.

She twitched the curtain back as he approached. Nice thick velvet, that curtain, nice shade of – well, he'd remember in a minute.

'Snow's getting worse,' was all she said. And suddenly he understood.

'You knew!' he said. 'I thought you were out of sorts because of work or, or something to do with Jon? But it's Anthony, isn't it? You've known since – since when?'

'This morning,' she said. 'Right before Leyla arrived. Over breakfast, actually.'

'*For helvede.*'

She looked close to tears, and he hugged her. 'He shouldn't have done that to you,' he told her jumper.

'It's OK,' she said. The only sort of lie she allowed herself, he thought. 'Torben, you're getting Tokaji on my shoes.'

'Sorry,' he said. 'I'll get us some – some more.'

'Actually I was thinking of heading to— oh, I'm not sure that's very safe.'

He turned. Anthony and Wilson were talking near the fire, looking at something above the … Mandelbaum? Mantelpiece, that was the word. Wilson was impressively animated for this stage of the proceedings. And now their host was reaching up, taking down a pair of – of pistols. And where the hell had *they* come from?

Everyone was looking now.

'I'm glad you asked,' Anthony was saying. 'I'm rather proud of these. They're a matching pair of pneumatics – airguns, that is, Wilson – made by Joseph Contriner of Vienna. See the monogram here?'

'They look ancient,' said Wilson, turning one of the guns in his hand.

'From the eighteen tens,' Anthony agreed. 'Your period, Torben,' he said, raising his voice. 'Want to pass that one around? It's all right, Ruth, it's not loaded.'

'How do they, um, work?' said Wilson, passing the gun to Tom with what looked like great reluctance.

'I'm glad you asked,' Anthony said again. 'Chuck us that case by the sofa – well, not chuck, of course, it's dead expensive.'

Torben drew nearer, steadying himself on the arm of the sofa. Everyone was fascinated. Sara was examining the pistol now, her expression intent and impossible to read – though Torben had to admit that was probably just down to the wines.

'It takes a while,' said Anthony. 'That's why more weren't made, that and the price. You unscrew the handle, like so – see, it's hollow – and thread it on to this pump.' He held up what looked like the world's most beautiful bicycle pump. 'So. Stand on the footplate, grip these handles, and – pardon me, ladies – pump away.' There was something manic in his face as he did so. 'Reattach the handle to the pistol … like so. Then the bullets – pass us some bullets, Tom – pop in the magazine here.'

'I thought all those old handguns were single-shot until they invented revolvers,' said Tom.

'Not these!' said Anthony. 'See the springs? Gravity does the rest, drops them into the breech. You have to cock it, of course – that would activate this little valve here. And there's enough air pressure in this handle for, oh, about ten shots before you have to do it all again.' He looked down at the loaded weapon. 'Mayhap I'll leave it like this, in case of burglars. I swear I saw some gyppos on the road last week.' And he leered as he replaced the gun on the wall.

'You couldn't really kill someone with it, though, could you?' said – said someone.

'Oh aye. It was guns with this mechanism that the Lewis and Clark Expedition took into Indian country to impress the natives. They thought it were magic. Practically silent, and killed redskins at a hundred yards. Sorry, that's not PC – shouldn't say "yards" anymore.' Anthony chuckled.

Ruth, taking the other gun from Leyla, passed it on to Torben at once with disgust. Torben looked down. It really *was* beautiful, in an ostentatious way. Burl walnut, old leather, gold plates etched with those – why did he want to say Martine McCutcheon? Escalopes? Escutcheons!

'I'd better have that one too,' said Anthony, and Torben looked up, startled to find the gun gone from his hand. 'You're pretty sloshed, man,' laughed his host.

'My tribute to you,' said Torben. 'Although actually, I am feeling fresh as a fish.' And he went back for more port.

'I don't remember ever having been this drunk,' said Torben.

'No, you don't,' said Leyla, flopping down on to the sofa beside him. 'We do though.'

'Aye,' said Frances, squishing in on his other side. 'Twice.'

'D'you think it'll happen again?' said Leyla, talking across his increasingly recumbent body.

'Mebbe,' said Frances. 'That was years ago though. If his melato— 'scuse me – metabolism's slowed down an' so on …'

'*Hold op*,' said Torben. Their words were flitting about his head like, like little butterflies. 'What're you talking about?'

'We've told you before,' said Leyla, 'and you didn't believe us then.'

'You go – well, you went – sort of crazy,' said Frances. 'First time was after Cardinal's Cocktails at the Union. The night you took to introducing yoursel' to people as "Torben Lamborghini". You said you were off for a wee lie down. Next thing we knew—'

'You were on the roof of the debating chamber,' finished Leyla. 'You'd found a bugle or trumpet or something and you were playing the "Last Post".'

'*Hold kæft!*'

'It's true,' said Tom, who had overheard. 'God knows where you learnt it.'

'Wait – who knows this stuff?'

'Well … everyone, really,' said Leyla. 'Sara!' she called. 'Remember Torben's second "incident"?'

'Sure,' said Sara, coming over. 'Second year, the classicists had just finished Mods, and we were helping them celebrate. Everyone thought Torben had sloped off to bed, till someone spotted him running around with a bag of golf clubs. Threw them down in the middle of Peck Quad and swore—'

'That he could hit a ball into Mercury in three attempts,' said Tom. 'It was me who went to check. Did it in two.'

'But—'

'Yup, the corner of the library, plus Fell Tower, both in the way. And that's got to be a good four hundred feet, hitting blind.'

'But—' Torben tried again.

'Of *course* you cannae remember,' said Frances. 'That's the whole point. I put you to bed after that, you were quiet as a lamb.'

'But,' he managed at last, 'I don't even *play* golf.'

Anthony chuckled. Where had he come from? 'You don't need to tell *us* that,' he said. 'You tried the first shot with a driver!' He and Tom both laughed. Apparently, this was a funny thing to say for some reason?

'If we've got on to golf,' said Ruth, 'I'm off to bed.' Her face wore an expression of … oh what the hell, thought Torben. No point pretending he could interpret expressions anymore.

She left, pressing Anthony's shoulder on the way out. One by one, the others got up too. Traitors! Non-observance of the ancient custom!

'Oh, it's Leyla,' said Torben. She was going to her bed. Her lucky, lucky bed. '*Jeg elsker dig*,' he said.

'I love you too,' she said, kissing his forehead. 'Be good.'

'I'll make sure he gets to bed,' said Wilson.

'Let's leave the gentlemen to their port,' said Torben, somewhat at random.

'Actually, old feller, I need a word with this one,' said Anthony, taking Tom's arm. Tom was grinning like a – like a creamy cat? – practically dragging Anthony out of the room. 'Just make yourself comfy here if you can't manage the stairs,' Anthony added, over his shoulder.

'*Fuck dig*,' said Torben, forgetting that some words are the same in different languages.

'Actually,' said Wilson, 'I think I'm gonna be sick. Night, Torben. It's just one flight of stairs, I'm sure you'll manage.'

It was later. Or earlier. Or something. All his old friends were gone, dry, empty. No more bottles. No more for Torben.

'I love the phrase "a flight of stairs",' he said. 'In fact, I can think of no everyday idiom more purely poetic. Not in English, anyway.'

'That's right,' said Wilson. He rose, displaying impressive mastery of the upright position. 'I'm going now.'

'I mean, just think of them,' Torben went on. 'Forever poised upon the brink, ready to take off.'

No one answered.

'Oh,' he said. 'All alone.' Even the fire had gone away. He hauled himself up. The mantelpiece – *see?* he knew all the words – the mantelpiece made an excellent handrail. Clever to have thought of it.

Hold op, nearly fell over there. He put out a hand to steady himself. What a pretty pistol. Its barrel so smooth. Like a duckling's bottom.

'Stairs,' he said.

Cold! Cold room! That *svin*, to give him a cold room! He nestled his back against the door. Bed on the left, table on the right. The homing instinct that had carried him this far was stuttering. Cold in his hand, something cold, something precious, let's just put it here on the table. Very good. No, spoke too soon – ah well, tidy that up in the morning. Now. Shoes. *For fanden*, why had he let the pixies tie his shoes? Get off, little bastards! And stay off. Bed.

Bed.

B …

And now it was morning. Light like snow. His world was glass, brittle-thin. If he moved, his head would shatter.

They might at least stop screaming. What kind of person screams 'he's dead, he's dead' over and over like that, when someone in the next room has a hangover?

Rude.

6

SUNDAY, NINE A.M.

The screaming had stopped. But now there were shouts and running feet. He'd have to tell them to be quiet. Piece by piece, Torben lifted himself from the bed, assembling the heavy limbs and curdled organs that once had been his body. He tried to leave his head till last, but that agony had to be confronted, and he swayed so badly that the flimsy construction of his self nearly tumbled back upon the sheets. And it was cold. True, homecoming cold. Squinting, a mass of shivers, he bleared at the windows. Snow mounted on the sills outside. Beyond, the sky danced white. There was no sign of the pine forest that had closed in so enticingly the afternoon before. The wind was a living creature now; the house lay in its talons as it moaned and tore.

He had to get out of this room or he would freeze. Pulling open the rickety wardrobe, fingers fumbling, he dragged a jumper on over his rumpled shirt and trousers. What time was it? He glanced automatically at a bare wrist, the movement sending renewed pain shooting through his skull. More cautiously, he checked his pockets. Empty. The desk was a mess of papers – had it snowed in here as well? Surely he hadn't left it in quite so bad a state – but still, no watch. *For Satan*. That watch – a classic Georg Jensen Koppel, white dial, steel case, tan strap that he should really replace, if only because of the smell – had been a gift, his twenty-first birthday present from – well, from everyone: friends, family, they had clubbed together … he would find it later. Must get out, get warm, find a dark snug silence to curl up and die in. To die in …

Torben carried himself out into the corridor. His bones felt hollow, like a bird's. People were pressing round Anthony's door, craning necks. The door opened, and there was Ruth, and – oh, mercifully – silence. A couple of them looked round as he approached. '*Morgen*,' he whispered. 'You lot look as bad as I feel.'

'Torben,' said Ruth, 'it's Anthony.'

Sara was crying quietly into Frances' hair.

He understood before he saw. 'Who – er, who found him?' he said.

'We did.' Ruth nodded at Sara. 'We were first down for breakfast. I was making tea – there's a big pot, it'll be stewed now …' She pulled herself together. 'We saw the state of things outside and thought, if we're going to be snowed in for days, maybe An— … maybe he wasn't joking about rationing. So we came up to ask. Knocked; waited a bit. The door wasn't locked.'

She took a deep breath. 'Of course, suicide's not a crime anymore, but I have to call it in. Look, there'll be an inquest, we can't touch … It's bad enough that Sara and I even went in, we should have—'

Tom and Wilson were here now, jostling to see; there were too many people squeezed into the corridor. Torben knew Ruth, a mild claustrophobic, always hated that. 'I have to find a phone,' she said. 'You know, a landline, since all our mobiles are down at the lodge. And confirm if we can leave, I suppose …'

Was he missing something? He would have expected Ruth to shine in a crisis, the epitome of the professional policewoman. But she was strangely disjointed … It couldn't be a hangover, she'd hardly drunk a thing. If he could only set the pain aside and focus.

'I'll stay here, keep an eye on … on the body,' he volunteered. 'I'm no good for anything else yet. Leyla, would you wait with me?' He didn't fancy a lonely vigil. 'The rest of you, can you help Ruth look for the landline? Split up?' For one wild moment, he thought about asking them to keep an eye out for his watch. Not quite appropriate, he decided.

For some reason, they obeyed. Maybe immense physical suffering lent one authority? Like Anthony's aura of the day before.

As soon as it was just the two of them, he put out his arms to Leyla. Her hug practically shattered him, but it was worth it. Neither of them spoke.

And then, because after all he had not *precisely* been told not to, and he was only human, he gave in to the inevitable, crossed the threshold, and looked at the body.

Anthony might have been sleeping. He lay in bed, half propped on a pillow, left arm cradled on his stomach. He was turned to the right – towards the door – his right hand stretched off the edge of the bed. Just beyond his fingertips, the air pistol lay, still beautiful. But its owner was grey in death. Blood matted his hair and head, stained the pillow, the mattress. But there was less than Torben had expected: the wound was a neat one. Above the bed, a wan light trickled through shutters, scarcely brightening the room. It was a space as austere as its owner, its pale walls unadorned with pictures. There was one faded patch above the bed where something had once hung, with an ugly little hole where a nail must have been wrenched out, its symmetry with Anthony's death-wound almost too much for his artistic sensibility. The whole thing seemed strangely familiar. Torben's eyes went to the bedside table, saw the scribbled piece of paper, weighed down by a fountain pen. Anthony's cheek was mashed into the pillow, his expression unreadable. Not beatific, not sad, not even tired, just – not there. In death, his features had ceased to signify.

Above all, it was that dangling hand that affected Torben. A person's hands were so much a part of their essence – more so even than the face – that to see one inanimate, reduced to the status of mere meat, troubled him far more than the stricken head. Without meaning to, he stretched out his own hand to Anthony's, and gave the fingers a gentle squeeze. It was an intimacy he would never have contemplated in life.

'I suppose I shouldn't have done that,' he said, stepping back.

Leyla put a hand on his shoulder. She had not cried, and her voice was rich as ever when she spoke. 'Maybe it's for the best?' she said. 'I mean, by the sound of things, he died before the worst.'

What had he thought, as the train passed over the Tyne? 'It's the way I'd want to go,' he murmured aloud. And yet …

'But it's wrong,' he said, not yet knowing what he meant. 'It's all wrong.'

Her eyes widened. He thought he saw there a glimmer of an understanding he did not himself possess – oh but for his *head*, his broken head – but now there were footsteps, and Ruth coming along the corridor, trailed by Frances.

'You should *not* be in there!' Ruth said. 'I thought I told you … Out! Out … oh, at least get away from the bed.' She seemed exhausted, bedraggled even, dreadlocks coming loose, wet and shivering.

'Sorry Ruth,' they said, together, hastening away from the body.

'Any luck?' said Torben.

Ruth shook her head. 'Two landlines,' she said. 'One in the room beyond the kitchen, sort of a utility room thing—'

'Scullery?' Leyla offered.

'Fine, scullery. Next to the back stairs anyway, at least I assume that's what's behind that locked door. And one in the library, east wing, ground floor. Must be – must have been? – Anthony's study. About as far apart as you could possibly get, predictably enough, hence the delay. And – guess what – they're both down.'

'England,' Torben said. 'No idea how to handle a bit of snow.'

'Not exactly helpful,' said Ruth, and he couldn't tell if she meant the phone lines or his comment. 'OK,' she went on, 'we are literally snowed in, with no means of communication. Forget "a bit of snow", I had a look outside and couldn't get across the courtyard, let alone think about tackling that drive, which was bad enough even getting up here before the snow started. Tom's car is stuck down at the lodge and no use anyway unless they clear the roads; remember how steep that hillside is? Kirsty's not scheduled to come until Tuesday and I very much doubt she'll make it even then if things carry on like this. The one shred of a positive is that Frances brought along this very professional-looking digital camera,' she said, and Frances held up a bulky black object, 'so we can document the b— ... the scene, before it, um, deteriorates at all. Beyond that, our main responsibility, so far as it remains possible, is to keep the room undisturbed. As it is, forensics will probably kill me— I mean ...' She took a breath, pulled herself upright – then slumped again. 'Oh, *poor* Anthony – just to have to leave him like that ...' And Ruth stifled a sob.

She was, Torben thought, the only one in the room who had been at all fond of Anthony, and yet, just because of where she worked, she was the one expected to act professionally. What had she said yesterday, before lunch – can't we just forget about work for the weekend? Yet here it was. It was deeply unfair on her. Luckily, something about the situation – maybe he had an unreconstructed nervous system that responded to distressed damsels – was affecting his hormones. Adrenaline was just what his hangover needed.

'Here's a handkerchief,' he said, 'and it's even clean. Use it. As for the body, if we open the windows just a little, the air temperature will look after it. When we're done, can we lock the door? Yes, there's a key – you'll have to keep that, Ruth. But we must read that note – his *suicide note*, Ruth, surely no one can object to that if we're careful? – and if we've taken photographs beforehand?'

Ruth shrugged. 'There's certainly no way we'd be expected not to read that note … Oh, what harm can it do? This is a tragedy, after all, not a crime scene. Just – just be really careful, OK? No one touches anything with their bare hands. And, well, try not to breathe too much.'

Minutes later, they had taken every shot from every conceivable angle, and Torben was feeling sick. 'Tweezers?' he suggested, realising he sounded incongruously like a surgeon. 'Frances, you've got the deftest touch, plus you're already wearing gloves – could you lift off that pen and pick up the note?'

Frances carried the note over to the desk, laid it down carefully, and lit a lamp. It read:

Dear friends,

I have chosen to end it now because I cannot face what I know is coming. You know what they say, go out in style! They say a problem shared is a problem halved. Well this way you each have 1/7 of a problem which is better than putting it all on Kirsty. Thank you all for coming. Sorry and goodbye. A.D.

There was silence in the room. Frances took a picture of the message, the camera's artificial click making them all jump. Torben realised that, in order to read Anthony's final words, they had turned their backs on his corpse. Looking round, he half expected the body to be gone, or rising up, in – what? A joke? A nightmare?

Leyla was still regarding the note. 'He died as he lived,' she breathed, and he thought her words were for him alone. 'In cliché.'

That was callous even for her, but he supposed they were all erecting what mental barriers they could.

'Um, are we done here?' said Frances. 'I'm a wee bit freaked out, and I'd like to check on Sara …'

'We should all have breakfast,' said Ruth. 'Eat something. Drink some tea. Tea is stage one of dealing with the bereaved, I don't see why it wouldn't work on us.'

'Come on,' said Leyla, putting her arm around Frances. A year younger than the rest of them, Frances seemed younger still in her state of what had to be shock, spots of colour high on her cheeks. She hugged her camera to her chest as they went, like a child with a favourite teddy bear.

Torben made to follow them.

'Actually, Torben, would you wait a moment?' said Ruth. 'I need you to do something for me.'

'Something procedural? I'll try.'

'Not exactly. I just want you to sit with him for a moment, can you do that? I'm going to pray for his soul.'

'Oh,' said Torben. All his pain, all his shock, his discomfort, all gave way in that moment to an excruciating embarrassment as Ruth bent her head over the body. But for all he knew, this was really important to her – for Anthony's sake. Raised in a secular household, he had only the vaguest notions of the Christian view on

87

suicide. From Ruth's point of view, his 'soul' might be in very real danger.

Loth to bow his head or close his eyes, Torben settled for looking at his dead host. So still. For the first time, he really *saw* the bullet wound itself, in the centre of the broken-in forehead. Such a small hole, to wreak such damage, the body untouched, at rest. The hands, one folded, one outstretched. The hands ...

Torben rubbed his eyes. What had he said to Leyla? 'It's all wrong.' And it was. It *was* all wrong.

7

SUNDAY, TEN A.M.

The kitchen must be part of the original – what had Torben called it, a bastle house? – thought Leyla; it had astonishingly thick walls, the original Tudor stonework. The side facing the courtyard had two recessed alcoves corresponding to the corridor upstairs: little larders, their shelves crowding in around the high Georgian windows, incongruous against this rougher, older room. For the most part, it had none of the rest of the house's beauty. Clearly this was Kirsty's space, off-limits to guests, its walls lined with cupboards, fridge-freezers, a cork noticeboard. Granite worktops, a big double sink, and one of those supersized gas-fuelled Agas that the English seemed to fetishise. Leyla found the others hunched on bar stools round a central island, cradling large mugs of tea. Sara and Frances had done best as usual, getting nearest to the Aga. Tom Goring's mug had 'Sports Direct' on the side and a large chip to its rim.

Wilson got up to pour Leyla some tea. Most of them still weren't dressed, with jumpers or coats pulled over nightwear, and she realised that her own eyes were red-rimmed, encrusted with sleep. She felt seedy, unclean, and that seemed about right for the situation. 'Thanks,' she said, as Wilson passed her a cup.

'Frances has caught us up to speed,' he said. 'As in, we know we're kind of stuck in a dead man's house. Poor bastard. Where are the others?'

Leyla shrugged. 'I think Ruth wanted a moment with the, the body. Probably a Christian thing.'

'Quite right,' said Tom. 'And what about us? Do we – we should say a few words. Or something?'

'I still can't take it in,' said Frances. 'Sorry, I know it's an obvious thing to say, but it's all so sudden. I've barely realised that he was even ill, and now he's *dead*? I just …'

No one spoke for about a minute.

'I think the great thing is to be honest,' said Leyla at last. 'I mean, it's no secret that I didn't like him. Anthony. Let's say his name, shall we? And whatever any of us felt, there's no point pretending to some deep grief when we're all still in shock. Wait a minute, Tom – I'm actually working round to saying something nice, honestly! Something real, anyway. But what I find really sad about the whole thing is how little of himself Anthony's decided to leave behind. As in, this is something he's done more or less on purpose, erasing traces of himself. It's not as if this house exactly sums him up, it's not his taste at all. And last year, when he did whatever he did – sold his company, retired from the world – he really did *remove* himself. It's all very well deciding the digital is inauthentic or whatever but the real tragedy is that he's undone every sense of his shared past with us. Every photo untagged, every thread deleted, even getting pictures taken down …'

Leyla drew breath – looked around – and, since no one seemed minded to interrupt, went on. 'You know, when I got his invitation for this weekend, I did that nostalgic thing of going back through Facebook, and he might as well have not existed. Literally the only thing I found was this nice shot of Ruth at some formal dinner that

I use as her profile picture on my phone – you know, it comes up when she calls – and on one side, you can just see his arm, his hand. I could only tell it was him because of that awful shirt he used to love … sorry, what was I saying? Yes, all I have that is tangibly Anthony is a handwritten invitation and a photo of his arm. He's deleted himself. And I wonder, when he did all that, *did he already know*? Had he already been diagnosed, or whatever – is this just a cruel irony, or was he already sort of, I'm not sure, turning his back on life? Walking away? It seems so sad.' She looked round. 'Sorry,' she said, 'that's all I've got. No one ask me to speak at the funeral, OK?'

'One second, Ruth,' said Torben. More than anything, he needed to clear his head. Ducking into Anthony's bathroom he found, as he had expected, an apothecary shop's worth of pills crammed into a cupboard. Among the foreboding-looking boxes like poodles in a pack of wolves, he found what he was after. Two paracetamol seemed a pointless gesture; the third was the charm. He had a great respect for the placebo effect. There was endless water in the bathroom tap, could he drink it all? And some for his face. It was ice cold. Or rather, *almost* ice cold, he told himself, since it was still flowing. He felt the first traces of ironic detachment stealing back to him. Since waking he had been raw, exposed, all nerve endings and palpating flesh. He welcomed the return of something like intellect; it armoured him. All right, so he still felt like a gutted fish. But he was *thinking* again. And he should have seen it earlier.

'Ruth,' he said, returning to the room. 'Can I just check – when you said we couldn't get out, that wasn't just you being English? I mean, I know it's blowing half a pelican out there and everything, but is it really impassable? We're all trapped in together?'

'Yes,' she said slowly. 'Or I wouldn't still be here. Torben, when you say *trapped in together*, you mean … you just mean by the storm, or—?'

He held up a hand. '*Klap lige hesten*. For now, can I just, just make a couple of observations about Anthony's – Anthony's death?' He was so, so tired. But Ruth was listening, her face grave. And the hangover almost helped. It forced him to speak slowly and deliberately, each word exacting its little toll of pain.

'Firstly, the suicide note,' he said. 'From what Anthony said last night – or rather, from what I can remember' – Ruth shot him what he believed was called a speaking glance, but he pressed on anyway – 'Anthony said he sold the company and bought this house *because* of his diagnosis. At the same time he wiped his own social media presence. Frances mentioned this on the taxi up here: he disappeared from the internet, practically overnight. As far as I'm aware, he cut ties with all of us at the same time – even Tom, who was telling me before dinner how much he was hoping to catch up with Anthony for the first time in years. I can understand that desire to erase yourself. And it's really sad. But it's also the *opposite* of what he says in— of what the note says.'

Ruth turned back to the desk and read aloud. '"You know what they say, go out in style! They say a problem shared is a problem halved." Hmm. It seems he changed his mind at the end; that's not unreasonable, is it?'

'Maybe not,' said Torben. 'I just mention it as an inconsistency.' He found that he was framing his sentences differently, speaking more like he wrote, aiming for precision. It came surprisingly easily.

'My second observation is speculative,' he admitted. 'But it feeds into the third one, which isn't.'

'Go on,' said Ruth.

'Why shoot himself?' said Torben. 'Why the gun, when his bathroom – as I've just confirmed – is full of the sort of drugs that, taken as an overdose, would presumably not only kill, but do so painlessly, as a – well, as an extension of sleep? It is a significant coincidence that he should die by means of a gun that his guests had learnt how to fire only hours earlier, whereas they might not be so sure about administering an overdose of unknown drugs, even if they somehow found the opportunity.'

'Torben,' said Ruth, 'that's not an observation, that's – well, legally I'm not sure exactly what it is, not libel, but … but, Torben, are you implying that—'

'Thirdly,' he said, and she let him say it. '*Thirdly*. The gunshot itself.'

'Which no one heard? Yes, I noticed that,' said Ruth. 'But it's an airgun; not only would it leave no residue of powder or scorching or whatever, but it's practically silent. A suitably private sort of weapon, I'd've thought; tactful, even.'

'No, not the *sound* of the shot,' said Torben, 'but its location. I have two problems with the gun. Anthony was shot in the centre of the forehead. Who shoots themselves in the *centre* of their forehead? It's an unnatural position, it puts strain on the wrist. In the mouth, yes, or else at the ear, the temple – the side of the head nearest the gun, in other words.' He was about to mime the action, then realised what poor taste that would be. 'Do it yourself,' he said instead. 'You automatically put the "gun" to the side of your head.'

Cringing, Ruth did so, first raising two fingers to just in front of her ear, then deliberately contorting her wrist round to point at her own forehead. She shrugged. 'You're right.'

'And that,' said Torben, 'is my final problem, the really big one. Anthony, the evidence of our eyes tells us, shot himself with his right hand. *But he was left-handed.*'

93

It was not the mic-drop moment he had meant it to be. His listener did not gasp or faint. Instead, Ruth scratched her head. 'Was he though?' she said. 'It's not a thing you really notice. Is this the sort of thing that three degrees in Art History teach you to spot? Or wait – I suppose you *were* Anthony's tutorial partner in first year, weren't you? You must have seen him taking notes. Still, that's impressive recall.'

Actually, Torben thought, it probably *was* because he was an art historian. He certainly didn't think he'd ever paid the slightest attention to Anthony's penmanship; he had always been far too caught up in the discussion for that. No, it more probably came from his training: from comparing prints with paintings, from knowing about the number of processes that involved mirrored images, and a paper he'd once heard about a celebrated one-legged fiddler in Regency London, whose wooden leg switched from left to right in different caricatures by the same artist.

'What's the Sherlock Holmes line?' he said. 'Sara would know. "You see but you do not observe," something like that. Think back to the dinner, Ruth. Anthony raised a toast: which hand did he use?' And Torben's mind returned to the moment when their host had called for silence, ringing a spoon against his glass.

'I was at the far end of the table,' she said at last, very slowly. 'And what with the dark, and the candles … but I do remember this sense of somehow looking in a mirror. A reflection, my glass and his, the way we held our cutlery … Gosh. He really *was* left-handed.'

'Of course,' said Torben, 'it is not impossible to shoot yourself with your "wrong" hand. But would you? Remember: this act, for Anthony, meant taking control over his disease. Asserting his own agency, choosing to die *by his own hand*. You can't tell me that you'd use your right hand, if you were left-handed.'

He paused. It was vital that the point went home. 'But if someone else were involved? If someone needed to make it *look* like suicide, but was in a hurry, or panicked, or hadn't been paying enough attention ... if that were you, Ruth, then what would you do? You would shoot him in the centre of his forehead, because that is the natural way for one person to shoot another: from straight on. And, just as naturally, you would put the gun by his right hand.'

This time, it worked.

'Leyla, I take your point about Ant's retreat from the world,' Tom was saying. 'No one knows that better than me, this last couple of years. But – but he wanted us here at the end though, didn't he? Those were literally his last words, after all.'

He gestured at Frances' camera in the centre of the island, its viewfinder still open. 'I mean, we've all seen the pictures of the note, it's no secret.'

Leyla was surprised without entirely knowing why. She hadn't thought Ruth, in her capacity as Inspector Thompson, had exactly meant everyone to see them. But then again, why would Ruth worry who saw the photos, unless—?

Meanwhile, Tom had gone rather red in the face. 'And it feels bloody hard right now, but at least we were here for him, yeah? Gave him a good send-off, even if we didn't know it. We did our bit?' He sounded like he was pleading, though with whom and for what was unclear. Leyla wondered if Anthony made everyone around him except her feel guilty – even those like Tom, his closest friend, who presumably had nothing more on his conscience than the injustice of being alive, when the other was not. Well, wasn't that enough?

'Oh!' said Sara, jumping up. Everyone stared at her. 'Croissants!' she said, and dashed to the Aga. Opening the upper hatch, she drew out a tray of charred pastries. 'Sorry,' she said. 'They were left out on the table and I thought ... and then I forgot ...'

'Rookie error,' said Wilson. 'You want a lower shelf for croissants.'

'I more meant – oh, never mind. At least they're hot.'

Leyla understood. There was something indecorous about eating a dead man's croissants, bordering on the indecent, that would not have been true of, say, porridge.

'Good jam,' said Wilson, a minute later. 'Oh, does anyone want coffee?'

'Oh God yes!'

'Great idea.'

'Shall I put on some toast?'

Outside the windows, the snow still fell. The drifts would reach the bottom of the sills before long; the windows onto the central courtyard showed nothing but a churn of white. If you didn't think about it too hard, it was almost cosy.

'So does this mean we can all see thestrals now?' said Wilson. 'Like in Harry Potter?'

'I think you have to actually see the death happen,' said Frances. 'A body doesn't count.'

'I've often thought,' said Sara, 'that Harry should *always* have been able to see them, since he was in the room when Voldemort killed his mum. Or is it different for babies, if they don't understand what they're seeing?'

Leyla glanced at the camera again; thought of the scene above them. No one else seemed to be wondering what was taking Ruth and Torben so long. And though she'd sat through some long prayers in her time, not even Ruth could still be … so what were they—?

'Hey, d'you remember,' said Wilson, 'that Harry Potter quiz Anthony set for Freshers' Week in our second year? The one with all those riddles in?'

'And how pissed off he was when Torben got full marks – especially since the last book hadn't even come out in Danish yet,' Frances chuckled.

'Ant was *obsessed* with that final book,' said Tom, smiling. 'I mean, who wasn't – but he didn't even try to hide it, pretend to have grown out of it – just kept going on about how awesome the whole reveal was, that Dumbledore had it all worked out, what was going to happen, masterminding it from beyond the grave.'

'All very mathsy, wasn't it?' said Sara. 'His quiz, I mean. The way he conceptualised things – fuck, actually, that might've been when I started thinking about distance-reading literature. Don't tell me I have to credit Anthony with inspiring my thesis. I still remember that one question, fill in the blanks … Dumbledore, McGonagall, Dumbledore, *blank*; Dumbledore, McGonagall, *blank*, McGonagall – genius!'

'Argh,' said Frances, 'now I want to work that one out … hang on, isn't it about—'

Leyla placed her cup down on the table. She knew what they were doing, this stitching the world back into place, their need to fill that grey void with humour. But her need was quite different. There could be only one reason why Ruth and Torben were taking so long. Seized with an overwhelming sense of being in the wrong place, she slid from her stool. As unobtrusively as possible, she reached for Frances' camera, as if in idle curiosity, and quietly slipped out of the kitchen. Enough of this little group therapy session. She had to be in the room where it happened.

'If you're right,' said Ruth, 'they'll never forgive you.' She paused. 'And they'll never forgive *me* either. The Force, I mean. Look, before this goes any further ...' Averting her eyes from Anthony's silent figure, she crossed to the window furthest from the bed. Torben followed. It looked south, like those in the gallery, but even the garden was gone now. Flurries of snow were whipping past from left to right. All was white, and noise, and motion.

'No one could overhear us with this wind,' she said, as if that, and not the insistent corpse on the far side of the room, was why they were standing at a freezing window.

At the bottom of the pane, flakes of paint were coming away from the frame; the wood beneath was slick with damp, and spotted with black mould. He resisted the urge to run his finger along it, to scrape and scrape till the whole shell of paint peeled off.

'Tor, you do see, don't you? This isn't some abstract problem you're analysing anymore; there are implications. If what you say is ... well, it means that someone, one of *us*, is the, the—'

'*Gerningsmand*?' he said.

'Sure,' said Ruth. 'That.' She sighed. 'You're right though, people *do* aim for the centre of the forehead in real life, or rather, kids who don't know much about shooting do. It's a stupidly hard shot unless you're right up close, but it's what happens in films, and head-shots score highest in most video games, so anyone used to playing first-person shooters ... besides, they *would* have been right up close ... oh, Tor, it's too much, it's too – too personal, to think that one of us can have done this. I can't believe it yet, I just can't.'

He held her for a moment, leaning his forehead into hers. Her smell was comforting; the light fuzz at her hairline brushed soft against his brow. But that small word, *yet*, had not gone unnoticed by either of them. 'Neither can I, Ruth,' he said. 'And each of them probably *didn't* do it; I mean, it's seven to one against each of us … sorry. Can we – can we think of this as an exercise? Start with what we can be objective about? There's no point worrying about who might have done it before we know for certain that someone *did*.'

'That's … that's terrible grammar, Tor.' She smiled, and sniffed. He remembered, twelve years ago and new to the country, asking her always to point out any mistakes in his English. She had really *hated* that. But she had done as he asked.

'I admit that I've been thinking too,' Ruth said at last. 'Two things, both entirely circumstantial. The rest of you aren't exactly religious, you wouldn't've thought about it, but Anthony was – as an under-graduate – a practising Catholic. We spoke about it sometimes. I remember asking him why he didn't go to Holy Rood, just across the bridge, as it was the closest church for him on a Sunday. He always trekked up to the Oratory, you know, up by Somerville? I think it was because it was so much posher … Anyway, if he still had his faith, then suicide would be self-destruction, a mortal sin.'

'Meaning, straight to hell?'

'And no Catholic burial. Actually the official line these days leaves room for manoeuvre, but I'm pretty sure most Catholics still believe that suicide means damnation.' Something in Ruth's manner gave Torben the idea that she shared that belief.

'But I thought Catholicism was all about salvation,' he said. 'You make suicide sound like a greater sin than murder; that's – that's abhorrent!'

She shook her head. 'You're forgetting the importance of contri-tion,' she said. 'A suicide dies unrepentant and unforgiven. As long as a murderer remains alive, there's the chance to atone.'

Torben shook his head. 'Like that bit in *Hamlet* when he won't kill Claudius, because Claudius has just been praying?'

Her smile was weak, stretched thin across her face. 'Always with the Danish example, Torben.'

'Hmm. So, if Anthony was still a Catholic, that makes suicide even less likely. And the second thing?'

'Oh,' she said, looking away, 'it's nothing really. I mean, it's just so sad, I'd almost rather she hadn't said it—'

'She?'

'Kirsty. At the end of dinner, I had a word with her. To say thank you.'

'Yes, I saw. I meant to do the same.'

'And she said ... oh, the worst thing she could have said, really. She said not to worry, because she thought he was getting much better.'

'Getting better?'

'I suppose that's not possible, is it? Unless, maybe, the doctors got it wrong? Or remission or something – at any rate, she said that when she first started working for him, when he first came here, he was already displaying some really bad symptoms. But that these had been slowly improving for a couple of months – almost disappeared, in fact.'

'What symptoms?'

'Poor coordination, lack of motor control. The main thing she mentioned was meals. He dined alone, so she only came in to clear up, but apparently he used to take ages, and he'd get food all over the table – but recently his appetite had noticeably improved; he was eating more, but he was also eating faster, and his plate, the table, they were far cleaner. And he seemed so much happier along with it.'

'So Kirsty thought he was getting better, not degenerating—'

'And that his spirits were improving.'

'He seemed pretty buoyant yesterday too. Unless that was just because he'd made up his mind to end it, of course.'

'Tor, that's conjecture again.'

'Sorry. Let's leave that there then: we have the gun, the history of Catholicism, and the … how would a real sleuth put it? How about: the general inconsistency of conduct, as evidenced by the reason given in the note versus his wider reclusiveness, and by the negativity of suicide versus his improved morale and physical condition.'

'You almost sound as if you know what you're talking about.'

'*For fanden* do I know what I'm talking about.'

'You know I still know it's blasphemy if you say it in Danish?'

'Sorry.'

There was a pause before Ruth spoke again, filled only by the howling of the wind. When she did, she was quieter, hesitant. 'Tor?'

'Yes?'

'A moment ago, when you thought I was calling suicide a worse sin than murder. I haven't seen you look that angry in years, and over a point of theology of all things. You looked positively … I almost want to say zealous.'

He sighed. If only there were something to look at from this window.

'I think it's exactly *because* I'm not religious,' he said at last. 'You lot never credit us atheists with real sincerity when it comes to having morals. But as I see it, death being final makes killing someone far, far worse than it would be if there were an afterlife. You are annihilating someone forever. No, it's worse than that.' He was working this out for the first time as he spoke. 'As far as that person's concerned, if you kill them, you destroy the entire universe. Each murder is the destruction of *everything* for that person: of "Existence", not just their existence. Is this making sense? To choose that for yourself I can understand. But to wipe out someone else's entire universe – friends, family, culture, beauty, nature, history, the lot' – and he was actually making himself breathless as he took in the real enormity of it – 'I mean, *lort!* That is just so unbelievably arrogant, you know?'

Ruth hugged him, and did not let go. And Torben realised that this, exactly this, was what he needed. What they both needed. And that it had taken a death, and a decade, for them to recapture the closeness, the bond, that had been lost when … when, exactly? When Ruth had got married.

He thought of the man he had filed, erroneously, as Jon Thompson, never having been able to quite remember his actual surname. Thought of *that* East London wedding – his surprise at seeing a guitar band in a church – his consternation when the entire congregation except for his pew, reserved for Ruth's Oxford friends, had sung the songs swaying, arms in the air. His dismay at a sermon, at speeches, that seemed calculated to eradicate the individuals involved, their rhetoric focused instead entirely upon proselytising for the Church and its mission. To him – as they had just established, a life-long atheist from a Lutheran culture – it had seemed like stepping into a cult. Worst of all, Ruth had seemed so happy with it, her ecstasy palpable, like a fever, like a drug high, and he had thought, *this is when I lose her*. All for a man with a too-quick smile and an assumption of moral certainty that must have been, for Ruth, a haven, but that felt to Torben more like the walls of a prison. That man would never have stood for Ruth hugging him like this. So maybe, just maybe, Ruth had grown weary of her self-imposed sentence.

'All right,' she said, when at last they broke apart. 'We're both thinking the same thing. So what do we do now? Given our suspicions, the proper thing would be to leave well alone. Lock the room, wait for the weather to change; hand the whole thing over to the local police.'

'I know,' he said. 'But think about it a minute, Ruth. If we're right, then this snowstorm is our best chance. With everyone still on the scene; without the time for the killer to cover their tracks, straighten their story – get away, even. And we can do this, I know we can. Between us, we have everything we need to clear this up. We can be of *use* – of much more use than if we were held as witnesses by some local plodder who probably won't even be convinced it wasn't a suicide.'

He saw this last remark hit home – at least, it made her knit her brows.

'Please, Ruth,' he said. 'We need to investigate this ourselves. For Anthony. For our own peace of mind. We've been walking like the cat around hot porridge for too long already; imagine being shut up here for days more with the thought that, all the time, one of us … Oh, Ruth. *We have to know.*'

In the dozen years they had known each other, she had never yet been able to resist a direct appeal. He held her gaze, imploring.

Nothing happened for perhaps ten seconds. And then someone knocked on the door. It was Leyla.

For a moment the three of them stared at each other. Leyla took in their expressions. 'I was right then,' she said at last. 'Anthony Dodd was murdered.'

8

SUNDAY, ELEVEN A.M.

'I thought,' Leyla went on, before either of them could muster a reply, 'that in the circumstances you might be needing this' – holding up Frances' camera – 'and this.' And she held out her washbag – wishing, for the first time, that its Liberty print was less ostentatious. It seemed, somehow, inappropriate.

Torben, who took it, clearly thought so too. Well, pardon her for not bringing her weekend-away hair shirt. But she couldn't help smiling as he unzipped it and saw the makeup. His baffled expression took years off him.

'No offence, Ruth,' she said. 'But I thought you might need mine. I know you don't use much – if I had skin like yours, I wouldn't either.'

She glanced again at Torben, who was now squirming a little. As the self-aware embodiment of the white patriarchy, comments on skin colour were off limits, and she almost felt bad for teasing him. Almost.

'Then why—?' Ruth said.

In answer Leyla rummaged, bringing forth a wide, soft brush and a couple of compacts. 'One's a lightish face powder, one's a heavy bronzer. For contrast,' she explained, flipping them open.

'Fingerprints!' said Torben, rather too late in the conversation to save face.

'It's all right,' he said five minutes later, in tones of consolation. 'I'm sure a lot of people don't manage it the first time.'

Ruth shot him a thoroughly un-Christian look. 'I *can* dust for fingerprints,' she said. 'If you want to persist in this irresponsible investigation, then why don't you try testing the pen? Use the foundation this time. *Carefully.*'

Torben ignored the last word; he was actually surprisingly nimble at this sort of thing. Dust on, brush off, apply tape, remove … no, why hadn't it worked? Unless—

He looked up. 'Are we saying that neither the suicide note, nor the pen it was written with, has a single distinguishable fingerprint anywhere on its surface?'

'Just this blank smudge at the edge of the page,' said Ruth, holding it up. 'Gloves, and the pen was handled either with gloves or wiped.'

'Bloody hell,' said Leyla, from behind them. Neither commented on her choice of language.

'That clinches it, don't you think?' said Torben. 'No suicide ever left a note written in gloves, then disposed of the gloves before settling down to do himself in.' His mind was functioning properly now. 'If that was even the pen that was used. If we're going to call it a forgery, it would have been written beforehand, surely, rather than on the scene? And we've all got pens in our rooms, haven't we? At least I have; there was one laid out when I arrived. I'll bet that either this *is* Anthony's pen, but a different one was used to write the note, or this is someone else's pen – but then theirs would be missing if we searched the rooms, which seems an unnecessary risk, so probably it *is* Anthony's … Look, we took photos, you've both witnessed this, right? So I can just—'

And before Ruth could stop him, he unscrewed the pen. It was – well, it would be – a classic Mont Blanc Meisterstück; slim, black, taking a cartridge … He squinted at it. 'Is there a pack of these cartridges on the desk, or in the drawer maybe?'

Ruth muttered something exasperated in which the words 'hanged', 'sheep' and 'lamb' figured prominently – but she produced the cartridges.

'Pass me one?' said Torben. He held them up, side by side. 'It's hard to be sure, but the one in the pen seems completely full to me.' He crossed to the desk. Anthony's pad of writing paper, identical to that in his own room, looked pristine. 'Second opinion, please,' he said. 'Has one of these been torn off?'

Ruth hesitated. Torben began thumbing through the pad. 'I make that … actually, no, you count them Ruth.'

She did so. 'Forty sheets exactly.'

'That's what I came to as well. Suggestive, isn't it?' Putting the pen back together, he began to doodle on the topmost sheet.

'Torben!' Ruth protested.

'Hah!' he said. 'Let's have the note. No harm in touching it now, not with three witnesses to the lack of prints.' He laid the two side by side. 'One's indigo, one's royal blue. A subtle but unmistakable difference in colour. And for my final proof' – he copied out the first line of 'Anthony's' note, his mind now supplying the sceptical inverted commas – 'the width of the nib is very slightly different. Whoever wrote this note, they didn't use this pen, or this pad of paper.' He flushed, smiling at his own small triumph, before remembering the implications of the discovery. 'It's definitely murder, I'm afraid,' he finished up.

Ruth exhaled. Then she took up the original note once more. 'What about the handwriting?' she said. 'I mean, is it even *like* his? It'd be a pretty short-lived cover-up if the two hands didn't match.'

'Wait there,' said Torben, and rushed to his room. The unmeditated speed reawoke the pain in his head, but it was lessening now: background music, not a fanfare. His own desk was a disgrace, he must have knocked into it last night … Anthony's invitation was no longer marking his review copy of the Decamps book, lying instead a little crumpled beside it. He snatched it up. Then, as an afterthought, he grabbed the pen too before heading back.

'Let's see,' he said to Ruth, laying the invitation beside the note. Together, they pored over the scripts. On one sheet, the short missive:

Dear friends,

I have chosen to end it now because I cannot face what I know is coming. You know what they say, go out in style! They say a problem shared is a problem halved. Well this way you each have 1/7 of a problem which is better than putting it all on Kirsty. Thank you all for coming. Sorry and goodbye. A.D.

On the other, Anthony's equally brief invitation – worded identically to each of them but laboriously handwritten, an act that Torben could only think of as quintessentially Doddish:

Bastle House, Northumberland
17th December

Dear Torben,

I am writing to propose a grand reunion. All the old friends from Staircase Two, back together again, in the suitably grand

surroundings of my new home, Bastle House. Whilst I can't
promise you quite the splendour of the old place, I think it will
prove worth the long trip north! So how about it, a long weekend,
spent in style, the last weekend in February?

I realise this is all a bit out of the blue, but I promise all will be
revealed when you get here. If you don't drive then the nearest
station is Bastlehaugh and taxis should be no problem if ordered
in advance. Come ready to dress for dinner but please note,
mobile phones are not allowed in the house. Looking forward to
seeing you soon I hope and trust.

Kindly RSVP.
Yours ever,
Anthony Dodd

'The writing's very similar,' Ruth said.

'Hmm.' Taking up the pen that he'd brought from his room, Torben began to note down letters and numbers.

'I don't know if this helps,' he said eventually. 'But neither letter includes a lower-case j or z – all other letters are common between them except x, which is only in the invite – and the capitals in the note – A, D, I, K, S, T, W, Y – are all present in the invitation. So are the numerals 1 and 7 – see, he dated the invitation 17ᵗʰ December? There are lots of duplicate words that could be difficult without this example to copy from – "problem", "style", "friends". So assuming they had access to one of these invitations, the forger hasn't had to invent anything, not even a single letter, that's not in the genuine piece of writing. Hmm. Except that in the invitation he – the real he – signs off with 'Anthony Dodd' rather than A.D., and in a much freer hand, it's almost a signature – no wonder they didn't try to copy that.'

'It *is* a forgery then?' said Ruth.

'I think so. See, they've made a mess of the r's that don't join up. And would someone who writes "17ᵗʰ December" with that superscript "th" go on to express a fraction as "one slash seven" rather than "a seventh"?'

Ruth was looking at the letters Torben had jotted down with the second pen. '*That's* the blue!' she said.

He nodded. 'Looks like the right nib too.' He looked more closely. 'And a *right-handed* nib; that Mont Blanc will have a left-handed one. I imagine we all have one of these – what is it, a Waterman – in our rooms, with a standard royal-blue cartridge. You can't expect even a multimillionaire to go about sticking Mont Blancs in all his guest bedrooms. Whoever wrote this note surely did so in their own room, in advance, and cribbed it from a copy of their invitation.'

'My pen certainly looks like that one,' said Ruth, contemplating the Waterman. 'I suppose we could search the other rooms to check they're all the same, but I'd rather not go public yet, not when we're all equally likely to have access to the invitation and a means of duplicating it. But we should check for any more evidence in this room before moving outwards … What haven't we done yet?'

'Well, for a start, we haven't dusted the murder weapon,' said Torben. The enormity of the task was settling now; it was like the snowfall.

'Oh, but that won't help us,' she said. 'Don't you remember? We *all* handled that gun. No wonder they used it!'

Torben made an effort of memory. 'I'll take your word for it,' he said at last. 'In that case, I think our forensic examination is at an end.'

'Does that mean I can have my makeup bag back?' said Leyla, from behind them.

They both jumped.

'*For helvede!*' said Torben. Then he began to laugh.

'I take it I'm not exactly suspect number one?' said Leyla. She sounded almost affronted. 'You know I thought he was a bastard, right?'

'I don't think we've started a list yet,' Torben said. 'But you won't be on it.'

'I won't?'

'No. It would prejudice the investigation.'

'Because I've heard too much already?'

If only Ruth weren't in the room. To be fair, she was doing a very good job of pretending she wasn't. 'Because,' he said at last, 'I have no wish to live in a world in which *you* of all people could commit a murder in cold blood. I'd be actively looking to exonerate you; the whole thing would be messed up.'

He pressed on quickly before anyone could speak. 'Much better to exclude you from suspicion at this stage, in fact discount all three of us – we can be added back in if it becomes necessary later. Besides, I think you two are probably the only ones who have any experience of violent death – surely that makes you less likely to proliferate it.'

There was a smile playing, not exactly on Leyla's lips, but somewhere nearby. 'A purely impersonal piece of reasoning, then?' she said.

'Cold hard science,' he said. 'Are you OK with that, Ruth?'

'Ideally,' Ruth said, 'I'd discount everyone. And you did come to us in the first place, Leyla. I'd never have thought of makeup for fingerprints by myself – and clearly, neither would Torben.'

'So,' said Leyla, 'does that mean I can play? I'd much rather be inside the tent, you know.'

'I don't think we could stop you,' said Ruth, with a rather exasperated laugh.

'But three's the limit,' said Torben. 'Or it gets silly.'

'I don't think there's much risk of that,' said Leyla. 'Sorry, Ruth, I'll take it seriously now. Given how awful his illness sounded, I'm OK that he's dead. I'm not so comfortable with the thought that someone killed him.'

Ruth nodded. 'Frances was very helpful with her camera,' she said. 'And of all of us, I suppose Sara's the most knowledgeable about murder investigations, if only from a literary standpoint – but I think it's more sensible to treat her as an expert witness, than let anyone else in on our thinking. We have to face up to the reality that, while they can still be our friends, we can't fully trust anyone else from now on.'

'That's why I brought the camera,' said Leyla. 'It seemed unsafe to leave it lying around. In fact, that's when I knew it must have been murder: I instinctively thought someone might tamper with the photos, and there was only one logical reason for that.' She paused. 'Plus, I suppose, I'm a lawyer, and when a man shows up dead the morning after he's told everyone they'll gain fifty thousand pounds *by* that death, my next thought was always going to be: follow the money. So I brought the camera up here, where it – and I – get to be on the side of the angels.'

'So,' said Torben. 'We have a team. What's next – like Ruth said, check the room?'

'The problem,' he concluded, what felt like quite a long time later, 'is that, not being Sherlock Holmes ourselves, we have no idea what might constitute meaningful evidence. As it is, stuff is just – you know, stuff. There are pills in the bathroom: well of course there are. Are they suitable for an overdose? We don't really know, it depends how seriously you take the small print. Conclusion: bugger all. There is a pair of leather gloves exactly where you would expect it to be in that chest of drawers: so what? I imagine we *all* have gloves with us. I don't even know if you can use normal gloves like that – shouldn't they be latex or rubber or something? Either way, we've poked about in a dead man's intimate space and found nothing that looks like being something. I feel grubby, that's about it.'

'I can't help feeling that something's missing, though,' said Ruth. 'Something I expected to find when we started, but—'

'Hah! Here's another blow to the suicide theory, as if it needed it,' said Leyla, emerging from a wardrobe with a sheaf of magazines. 'His stash.'

'Stash?' said Ruth.

'What used to be called "literature",' Leyla elaborated.

'Porn,' said Torben. 'The downside of not having internet, I suppose. Leyla, put it back, I don't want to know.'

'*Playboy … Lovely Lassies … Rampant Redheads … Nuns in the Sun …* There's nothing especially … esoteric,' she said, with a note of regret in her voice. 'Still. Embarrassing.'

'As embarrassing as this?' said Torben, who had unearthed Anthony's certificate from Mensa. 'This takes me back.' He remembered his incredulity, first at learning that such a society existed, and then that the teenage Anthony had been so proud of joining its ranks.

'Hmm,' said Ruth. 'Or maybe, Torben, seeing that you actually laughed in his face when you had it explained to you, it might be you that should be embarrassed?'

'Ruth,' said Leyla, 'he had it *framed* on his *wall*. Anyone who does that deserves everything they g— deserves all the mockery, I mean. It's almost as bad as the British citizenship tests, which, let me tell

113

you, is saying something.' She paused. 'Anyway, my point was, if you were planning to kill yourself, you'd hide your dirty magazines a bit better. Or better yet, get rid of them entirely.'

'So,' said Ruth, her discomfort palpable, 'we keep producing circumstantial evidence amounting to the same thing. I don't think we can keep on interrogating an empty room. We know *how* it was done. We need to move on to people.'

There was silence. Leyla fiddled absently with objects in a drawer; opened a cheap-looking locket containing a wisp of coppery hair, grimaced, snapped it shut. Watching her, Torben realised they were both avoiding meeting Ruth's gaze. This was the point where it tipped over from the abstract to the personal, and she was right, they had been putting it off for too long.

'I suppose,' Ruth went on, in a slightly firmer voice, 'we could start with each other? As practice? Does any of us know anything – what's the word?'

'"Germane to the enquiry"?' said Leyla.

'Right,' said Ruth. 'For example, starting with me ... Yes!'

They stared at her.

'Last night,' she said. 'Torben – you came to bed around one o'clock, yes?'

'Probably,' he said. 'My watch is— oh, never mind.' Again he felt an entirely selfish pang of loss, and swiftly suppressed it. 'Anyway, one o'clock sounds about right. Sorry, did I wake you?'

'No,' she said, 'I was still reading at that point.'

Something about her manner caused him to interrupt. 'Ruth?'

'OK, I was waiting till I heard you come to bed; I was worried about you. But I must've drifted off almost immediately after that. Because I next woke at two seventeen exactly – I always check when I wake, it's a bad habit – and I realised that I had heard a door opening, somewhere down the corridor. And I *think* I remember footsteps. I'm not sure …'

'Coming or going?' he said.

Ruth took a second to think about this. 'No, no idea, sorry,' she said. 'There was the wind, too – it was the door noise that registered; that rough, metallic sort of sound, it stands out, you know? And at two twenty – I was nearly back to sleep – I heard a door close. Definitely a shutting noise. And – I *think* – there were footsteps again? But I'd only swear to the door. Anyway, at the time I assumed it was you, going down the corridor to the bathroom and coming back again. Then I slept through.'

'But I didn't,' he said. 'Go to the loo. One moment, I was falling into bed. Next, I was awake and Sara was screaming "he's dead".'

'You're sure?'

'As sure as I can be.'

'Then,' said Ruth, sounding excited, 'it must have been *this* door I heard, and that must've been the murderer, entering and leaving!' She paused. 'Could you do all this in three minutes?'

'Easy, I should think,' said Torben. 'If you'd got the note already written. Door open, two or three steps in, shoot … place the gun, place the note, move the pen, and out. The quicker the better. You'd probably avoid touching the body.'

'Because of the blood?'

'Because it's a dead body, frankly.'

'Hang on,' said Leyla. 'Ruth, you said you heard a door open, and then a door close. Which you mistook for Torben going to relieve himself of about a full mixed case of fine wines?'

'Yes …'

'Well,' she said, 'wouldn't the door have opened and closed both times? Surely if you were going to shoot someone, you'd want to close the door behind you first?'

'Well, maybe they forgot?' said Ruth. 'In the heat of the moment?'

'I don't think so,' said Torben. 'If you take Anthony at his word, that the gun is almost silent – we should check that, by the way, maybe we need a to-do list … anyway, assuming it is silent, and if it has ten rounds – maybe you'd test it out of your own window first, or in a safe place out of the way downstairs …'

'Tor,' said Leyla, 'get to the point or there will be a second murder in this room.'

'OK, OK! Assuming or knowing the gun to be silent, especially with that wind outside, a closed door wouldn't be necessary on the grounds of noise. You'd have your back to an open door, which would be unnerving. But worse, surely, to spend even a second with your back turned *to the bed* when coming into the room in the first place? If you're the murderer, for all you know Anthony is awake, or will wake up the moment you open the door. The important thing is to take your shot as soon as possible, before he can move or make a noise. It's crucial that he doesn't cry out, and that he remains *in the bed*. So you step in as you open the door, make it to the bed double quick – two steps, as I said – and fire. Maybe you'd keep the gun hidden in a pocket or behind your back till you were next to the bed, but you'd have it in your hand, cocked, with your finger on the trigger. The last thing you'd have time for – or the nerve for – would be delaying in order to turn and shut the door.'

Leyla shuddered, rather deliciously. 'I feel like I was there.'

'It's convincing, anyway,' said Ruth. She seemed happy that her vital evidence had not been discredited. 'So we have a time of death? Two seventeen? Which we'd only be able to confirm—'

'If we had a medical team, and a coroner, and all the people who can tell things about dead bodies,' said Torben. 'I feel hopelessly inadequate. All I know is that rigor mortis is notoriously unreliable as a means of determining time of death. Is that the only sign?'

Ruth gestured helplessly. 'As I think we've thoroughly established, this is not exactly my field.'

'And I've no idea,' said Leyla. 'But Sara might have.'

'Sara?'

'She's got a whole chapter of her thesis on the relationship between clues and medical symptoms. Apparently it's mostly metaphorical – like, murder clues are the symptoms of societal diseases, that sort of thing – but there's a chunk about the actual medical side of dead bodies too, at least in terms of how it shows up in fiction.'

'When did you find this out?' he said.

'After dinner, of course,' said Leyla. 'I'm willing to bet there's a lot of relevant information from those hours that *you*, for some reason, are unable to recall.'

Torben had a go at raising his eyebrows. 'Well, let's lock up here and gather the others. We can't put off telling them any longer. Then we can start by asking Sara to examine the body.'

They locked up. Torben smiled. 'We are in danger,' he said, 'of turning a PhD in literary criticism into something objectively useful. If Anthony here were already buried, he'd probably be turning in his grave.'

9

SUNDAY, TWELVE-THIRTY P.M.

'Actually,' said Ruth, 'can you two wait here a minute? I need the loo.' Rather than using the bathroom opposite, she headed back up the corridor to her own en suite.

At the corner of the gallery outside Anthony's room, the passageway jutted out towards the garden, forming a private – albeit chilly – alcove. Torben drew Leyla into it.

'Look,' he said, 'I'm sorry I sort of forgot you were there for a minute. I didn't mean … I just got a bit … rapt up?' Sometimes the finer points of English still confused him.

She ignored all of this. 'I never told you I've seen people killed,' she said.

'No,' he said, surprised. 'But you told me what part of your childhood you spent in Iraq. And I know roughly where your family—' he hesitated. The choice between 'live' and 'lived' seemed tricky. 'Where your family comes from,' he said. 'I checked the dates. You must have been caught in the uprisings. I've always assumed you'd rather not talk about it.'

She looked out of the window. If anything, the snow was increasing; it was practically a blizzard. 'I actually like you better like that,' she said. 'Absorbed in a challenge; you're very dynamic. It suits you better than this mooning thing where you're haunted by some bad poem you once wrote me. Instead it's like you're playing the role of amateur detective in a TV drama. One of the new, slick ones, I mean, where they match the clothes to go with the wallpaper. It makes you very … I mean, it suits you.'

So, she had thought it a bad poem. 'Is this the game where you always answer the question before last?' he said.

'No,' she said, 'it's called a grownup conversation. And I feel bad about Ruth. I think she preferred it being just the two of you.'

'That's sweet,' said Ruth, from behind them. Leyla literally jumped; Torben had never seen that happen before. Ruth went on. 'But really, this is more important than my feelings. I love you both – just don't distract each other.' She *did* sound a bit hurt.

'Sorry,' said Torben. 'I think we assumed you were giving us a tactful moment.'

'What?' Ruth seemed almost angry. It was unfamiliar. 'No! I'm not some wise mother figure. I needed the loo.'

'OK, OK – sorry,' he said again.

'Shall we go downstairs?' said Leyla.

'Good plan,' he said.

They began to walk.

'I had three cups of tea!' said Ruth. 'Big ones.'

Torben didn't answer. But it had proven one thing: these floor-boards didn't creak. And neither he nor Leyla had heard Ruth's foot-steps over the sound of the wind.

'Drawing room,' said Torben, opening the door.

'Why?' said Leyla.

'Because of this.' He took up the beater and rang the gong. His headache had practically cleared. In his relief, he rang it again. The noise was curiously satisfying.

Within three minutes, everyone was there. Perhaps it was something about being summoned – the last person to ring that gong had been Anthony; there was something spectral in the renewal of his call. Perhaps it was the sound itself, the harshness of metal, hard-edged clangour in a place of softness, snow and mourning – whatever it was, they seemed on edge. Torben contemplated them all. Leyla and Ruth off to one side, Leyla fidgeting, Ruth pensive and lip-bitten. Wilson tense, alert, perched on the arm of a sofa and leaning in, a glass clutched tight between his hands. Sara like a startled falcon, all sharp points and ruffled feathers. Frances beside her, still somehow diminished, frightened. And Tom, his face a question, his rumple-suited body brimming with the promise of righteous indignation. The last ripple of the gong had faded away, leaving only the howl of the gale beyond, so constant now it might as well be traffic noise, accepted and forgotten.

Torben's throat felt dry. He was on a threshold, the next step irrevocable, the other side unknown. Still, the time had come to shave the goat. 'I have something to announce,' he began.

Thirty seconds later, and Torben could not decide which of the two storms he would rather be in: the one outside, or the one he had started. Apparently he was seven kinds of shit, a know-nothing foreigner, a wilful wrecker of peace and fraternity.

'I mean,' Sara was saying, 'the thing that *actually* killed him, that was what he told us yesterday, wasn't it? When we found out what – what was wrong with him. But doesn't that mean *this* is more …

more like release? Catharsis? For God's sake, it was in his note, he wanted it this way. We have to accept it! Have to … have to have an open mind! Yes, poor old Anthony was killed. But by his *disease*, not by—' She was leaning for support on a small side table as if winded, thin wrists braced, quivering, against the veneer.

'Bloody idiot,' said Tom. 'Torben, I mean,' he added, as if anybody could be in doubt.

'I don't know if any of you have read the Father Brown story "The Absence of Mr Glass"?' Sara was restless, unable to leave go. 'I only mention it because it's a satire on a self-important detective who works up an elaborate deduction of blackmail and attempted murder from a scene where no crime has actually taken place.'

Wilson seemed not to have heard any of the argument around him, but he had been swirling a non-existent drink round the bottom of an empty glass for at least a minute now.

'I just think it's actually a really insensitive thing for Torben to say,' concluded Sara at last, very quietly. 'Insensitive and unhelpful.'

'Well, he's said it now, hasn't he?' said Wilson, finally breaking his silence. 'In the full knowledge that we're all stuck here together for what might be days. I can only assume he's still drunk. We *are* stuck here, I suppose?'

'Afraid so,' said Ruth. 'I tried to get out earlier, and it's only worsened since. I don't think in all conscience I could allow any of you to try and leave even if – even if this hadn't happened. It wouldn't be safe.'

'"Even if this hadn't happened",' said Frances. 'You mean – you mean we're under *suspicion*, just cos Tor has got some notion into his daft wee head?'

'Idiot,' said Tom again. He made a movement towards Frances as if about to put his arm around her, and she pulled away at once.

Torben felt his cheeks reddening. It was like being back home, accused of upsetting his sister, told he was in the wrong when he knew he was right. If he entrenched, that always only made things worse.

'You *do* see what you've done, don't you?' said Frances. 'We *were* staying in this gorgeous country house. Now we're trapped in Bentham's pan-thingummy.'

'Panopticon,' said Sara, automatically.

Wilson looked blank.

'It was an idea for the perfect prison,' said Sara. 'Built in such a way that every prisoner knew that, at any given moment, they were potentially under direct observation. Total round-the-clock surveillance, or more accurately the *possibility* of it. The point being that people would behave accordingly. A self-policing prison.'

'Basically the worst idea ever,' said Ruth. 'No privacy, no trust, no chance of self-respect or self-redemption. A really hellish idea – I mean that quite literally – and entirely coercive.'

'Prisons sort of *are* coercive,' said Wilson.

'I agree,' said Ruth. 'That's part of my problem with them.' Her voice was hard.

'We're kinda straying from my point,' said Frances. 'Which is, I don't want to feel like I'm under surveillance. Now we'll all be suspicious of each other. Fuck that. I mean, why would any of *us* want to kill Anthony?'

At Torben's side, Leyla gave a sort of start, and her cheeks flushed – with embarrassment at the question, he presumed. And it struck Torben forcibly that he had not yet begun to consider this rather important point. He was simultaneously convinced that Anthony had been murdered, and that none of these people, his friends, could be a murderer. But he was forced to conclude not only that these positions were incompatible, but that, if *he* felt they did not know *him*, he must necessarily concede that *he* no longer knew *them*.

He thought for a moment. Sara seemed a harder, more harassed person than the girl he'd known at twenty. They all knew what a difference a sizeable inheritance would make to her life. Tom, once so complacent, now came across as thwarted, almost at bay. What had he been saying about being abandoned by Anthony? Frances appeared to be unchanged from the girl he had always known – but then, that was strange enough, like she was performing an old version of herself. Like Leyla, she even smelt the same, still wearing CK One, its strong scent indelibly associated, for him, with the younger, simpler Frances – surely, after so long, she'd have moved on? What was the point of this whole front, and why was she the first to seem so frightened? And though he liked Wilson very much, a whole lot of that was admiration of how well he played the *part* of Wilson Ho – he'd never seen him, so to speak, backstage. Unless you counted that moment, the night before, when Wilson had sipped his Old Fashioned and talked of an old debt Anthony owed him. It was only Ruth that Torben really felt he knew, and even then the part of Ruth he knew was not the wife, the church-goer, not even the policewoman. One of them *could* be a murderer, then. Had to be.

He realised he would have to relearn these people he used to know: wake himself to their changed patterns, their habits of mind. Maybe this was something all friends should do over the years, to shake themselves out of complacency? Or maybe the act was purely destructive, a stripping away of everything that had grown them together? Well, he supposed he would find out.

He was about to try and explain all this, when it hit him. Frances was right. In going through with this, he had created a climate of suspicion, and that worked in two directions. It could almost be put as one of those Sherlock Holmes axioms: just as the murderer risks exposure to the investigator, so the investigator must avoid sharing confidences with the murderer. The price for carrying on was constant self-censorship. And he had to think like this – not as a friend, but like his cold, academic self – if he were to stand any chance of 'solving' the 'problem'. Make use of the tools of his trade.

So all he actually said was, 'I've always thought the phrase "it's academic", meaning irrelevant, was grossly unfair on academia.'

Their reaction of complete incomprehension reassured him that at least no one was reading his mind.

'It's too soon,' Ruth was saying in answer to Frances, 'to talk of motive. I can confirm that Torben's correct: we're definitely dealing with a murder. The method seems clear: as we all know, Anthony was shot in the head with one of his own pistols. But until we establish a few more facts we shouldn't start speculating, or throwing personal accusations around.'

'*More* facts?' said Tom. 'You mean you've got something solid to back up this bollocks with?'

Torben and Ruth exchanged a glance.

'What?' said Sara. 'All of a sudden we're beyond the pale, are we? We just have to take you at your word, while you won't trust us at ours?'

Frances was frowning. 'I've just noticed,' she said. 'Why is Leyla standing over there with you two, and staying – no offense, Leyla, love – uncharacteristically silent?'

'Out with the facts!' said Tom, belligerent. And now everyone began to talk at once.

Torben hit the gong again and they stopped. Maybe he should always have a gong. 'I'm afraid you're all just going to have to accept that it's gone beyond the point where we can share everything.'

'Except between the three of you,' said Sara. 'Like Frances said: when did that become a thing?'

Ruth spoke up. 'We've got proof that Leyla's in the clear, all right?'

Torben almost stared at her, then controlled himself. But they had no proof. Had Ruth just *lied*? And for whose sake – his or Leyla's?

'What sort of proof?' said Tom.

'Tom,' said Wilson, looking painfully disappointed, 'they've, like, literally just said they can't share things with us mere suspects anymore.'

'Secret proof,' said Frances, in a hoity-toity voice.

This was better. But it wasn't exactly helpful. 'Don't make me hit the gong again,' said Torben. 'And I am so, so sorry. I know it sounds ridiculous. But I think, logically, the simplest thing is to ask: does anybody in this room want to … confess?'

It was like asking a new seminar group of undergraduates – well, asking them anything, frankly. Everyone shuffled about, darted their eyes. It was obvious that no one was going to speak, or look anything other than intensely uncomfortable.

Tom Goring half rose from his seat. He looked very red. Then he sat back down again. By now, people were looking at him.

'Well,' he said. 'It's obvious, isn't it? Why are we going through this pointless bloody charade? Talking about pan-watchums and worrying about accusing each other? Is it just a political correctness thing?'

Everyone else looked as confused as Torben felt.

'Oh, come on!' said Tom. 'It's that woman, Kirsty, isn't it? "The butler did it." Well, she must've done!'

'Now, Tom,' said Ruth. 'You can't just pick on the one person who isn't here—'

126

'The easy target,' said Frances. 'What did you say, "that woman"? Aye, the domestic in the subordinate gender and class position, of course she must've done it.'

'I miss having a butler,' said Wilson, very quietly. 'It's different in Hong Kong.'

Everyone suddenly seemed more comfortable now they were arguing about an outsider.

'The butler,' said Sara, 'never does it. Actually no, there's "The Musgrave Ritual", but even then he's only a thief, so the point stands: servants are never likely suspects. Unlike the guests, the staff can literally produce a good character, or they wouldn't be hired in the first place – but more importantly they're there all the time, not turning up just at the fatal moment, and there's no reason for them to develop sudden homicidal tendencies. It's the people who show up just before the murder that you have to watch out for.'

'Also,' said Frances, 'Kirsty's the only person who looks like they've got an alibi, right? She left the house, we heard the car.'

'Did we?'

'*I* did.'

Torben had. At least, he'd heard it turning in the driveway …

'Plus we'd have heard it returning too.'

It all sounded genuine, which it probably was …

'*If* she came back by car.'

'She didn't come back at all!'

But then, if someone was acting innocent, wasn't this exactly how they *would* behave … ?

'Have you even looked outside? All that snow. You'd have to be a husky!'

'Practically everyone has servants in Hong Kong.'

The safest thing would be to play to type. So, was atypical

behaviour a sign of guilt or of innocence … ?

'Except, presumably, the servants themselves?'

'She could've parked up just out of sight and crept back in.'

'You clearly have a very high opinion of Land Rovers.'

Once you went down the bluff/double-bluff line of reasoning you were lost …

'Wait, what did you mean, Frances, the one person who's got an alibi?'

That stopped them short.

'Are you saying,' said Wilson, 'that *none of us* has an alibi?'

'And of course all our prints,' said Sara, 'will be on the gun …'

'Fuuuuuck,' said Frances. She made it take a really long time.

People were shouting again. As far as Torben could tell, the consensus was that no one had an alibi and everyone had a motive.

'Fifty grand each though,' Frances was saying. 'It's just enough to kill for, isn't it? That isn't a confession by the way. Like, theoretically, it's conceivable.'

'*Just enough* …' said Leyla.

Torben looked around the room. What might fifty thousand pounds mean to each of these people? Impossible to tell from the outside, but he was willing to bet that, for most of them, it could be life-changing. He thought about his own position: renting a shoebox in central London, student debt, temporary contract coming to an end … the security that much cash could buy him—

Tom was glaring at Frances. 'Why are you wearing gloves?' he said.

'It's a wee bit nippy, you might not've noticed.'

'For fuck's sake, Tom, we've *all* got gloves,' said Wilson.

'I haven't.'

'Then you're an idiot,' said Sara. They all seemed to have latched on to the idea that gloves were significant, but no one had been told about the lack of prints on the pen, on the note. Oh it was toxic, thought Torben. In a climate of suspicion, any hint of deviancy became grounds for accusation. He hit the gong again, and kept hitting it until they shut up.

'I love this thing,' he said. 'Look, if we're going to maintain any sort of order, the only thing to do is assume that we are each, individually, almost certainly innocent. Including Kirsty. That isn't me getting cold feet, it's statistics: the probability is strongly in favour of any given person being innocent, so don't let's go attacking each other. Apart from everything else, we're stuck here until either this snowstorm clears or Kirsty *does* make it back in the car. It's not only good manners to be nice to each other, it's probably safer as well.'

That got their attention. He didn't think any of them had considered the possibility that the murderer might still be a source of danger now that Anthony was dead. Neither had he. Well, if it made them behave a bit better, that was fine by him.

Tom was still muttering belligerently. 'Safer indeed. I tell you, the killer's down in the lodge with a mile of Himalaya between us, congratulating herself on a suicide well-staged. No one's in any danger.'

Everyone ignored him. 'Surely,' said Frances, 'we're not in any danger *now*? If Anthony was killed for his money – it's not like bumping anyone else off means you get their share too, is it?' She paused. 'Is it?'

'The laws of this country leave much to be desired,' said Leyla, 'but take it from me: no, they do not offer financial incentives for serial murder. Quite the reverse in fact.'

Ruth looked at her gratefully. 'The most dangerous thing we could do right now is to panic,' she said. 'This isn't one of those Agatha

Christies where the killer works through the whole house, like – what's it called, Sara?'

'*Ten Little*— um, I mean *And Then There Were None*,' said Sara.

'Exactly,' said Torben. 'You might hope to get away with one carefully planned murder. To improvise another one when everyone's on the alert would be madness. Much safer to sit tight – which sounds perverse, the investigator advising the killer, but then, I don't much want to be bumped off either.

'And speaking of safer,' he added, conscious that the tension in the room really needed releasing somehow, 'it's about time we tested the pistol that's still hanging on that wall. Find out if they really *are* silent.'

And, he added in his own head, find out just how much damage they can do.

'You know,' he said, a few minutes later, 'this is the sort of thing this long gallery would originally have been used for, in the Jacobean version of the house. Conversation, exercise, fencing practice – well, why not target practice too? Even if a stray shot ends up in the panelling, the bullets are antiques. It'll add character.'

'It's certainly a comfort,' said Sara, 'when we've all been practically accused of a murder and a mad Dane is wielding weapons, to know that the situation is historically accurate.'

They were all clustered at the western end of the long gallery, just outside the drawing room. Some twenty paces away, Leyla had arranged some of last night's empties on a demi-lune table, pivoted away from its original spot by the wall.

'You know,' said Tom to Ruth, 'that even if there hasn't been a murder, it's actually a crime to damage someone else's property.'

Ruth shrugged. 'We need to know,' was all she said.

Torben levelled the pistol; squinted down the beautiful long barrel. The butt in his hand felt strangely natural, almost like he knew what he was doing. He took aim at an empty bottle of Tokaji. What had he called these bottles? His friends, that could do him no harm? Well, how much harm was *he* doing to his friends?

The bottle exploded, almost before he realised he had pulled the trigger, cold steel beneath his finger. Behind him, he heard a short burst of applause, and turned to see Frances flushing guiltily while Sara glared at her. Leyla was smiling. 'Practically silent,' she said. 'And undeniably a lethal weapon. I assume you weren't aiming for that bottle in particular?'

Torben glared at her. 'Pick one,' he said.

'All right. Since the gun's still pressurised, I take it? That port bottle, the one on the left end of the table.'

'This takes me back,' said Tom, as Torben raised the pistol once more, and the port bottle shattered. About half of them applauded this time. 'You were exactly this much of a show-off last time we went shooting.'

'You've done this before?' said Ruth. 'Where? With whom?'

'The four of us boys, ages ago,' said Torben, distracted by Tom's accusation. He hated the thought that he might be parading his skill in front of the others. 'Look, does anyone else want a go? How about you, Wilson; you've always been a fiend at a first-person shooter.'

Wilson looked reluctant. Hadn't he been the keenest of them all around the guns last night? Or was Torben getting his facts muddled? Anyway, Wilson was now accepting the proffered weapon.

'Show him how it's done, Ho,' said Tom. 'That gin bottle on the right, the green one!'

Wilson took aim almost carelessly, and Torben braced himself for the smash. But the only sound was the little *pfft* of air, and a dim *thwock*, as the bullet embedded itself in the door at the far end of the corridor.

Wilson shrugged. 'Whoops,' he said. 'I'll tell you what it is: there's no sight on this thing, that's the trouble.' And he sounded annoyed enough as he handed the gun back. Still, was it just Torben's long-standing respect for his friend's physical prowess, or had Wilson Ho, that unparalleled self-promoter, just missed a shot ... on purpose?

Well; what had Tom been saying? 'This takes me back'? Yes, it certainly did: about a dozen years. A shooting range in Snowdonia; a private session for the four of them – him, Anthony, Tom and Wilson. Both Anthony and Wilson had worn new Barbour jackets and taken pains to scuff them up at every opportunity. Torben remembered a sort of covert, half-suppressed eagerness around the guns, an almost fetishistic attitude. Which of them had it been? Notwithstanding the embarrassing fact so recently alluded to that he, Torben, had turned out to be by far the best shot, better even than Wilson, who apparently had done this at his private school. What had they been using? Those little biathlon rifles, of course; they had all managed to laugh off his success as being down to a Nordic affinity with winter sports. Though the others had treated him with a new and wary respectfulness that had taken some days to wear off.

If only he could remember more about the guns. Not just that far-away Easter, but last night. That whole song and dance around the pistol was lost in a fog of fortified wine. What had Leyla said – there'd be all sorts of relevant evidence that he wouldn't be able to remember? Torben had to restrain himself from taking the gun back, from revenging himself on more of those treacherous glass bottles and their former contents. He felt sure he'd missed something vital from those lost minutes ...

132

'Well,' Ruth was saying, covering for Wilson's embarrassment, 'we've tested the gun and it confirms what we thought. A silent murder weapon, to which everyone had access. I think that brings us to the end of our investigation into method, I'm afraid.'

'Agreed,' said Torben, coming back to the present with an effort. 'From now on, everyone, if you don't mind, we go full Poirot. Generally I try to avoid clichés like the plague, but I think we're going to have to do this by the book. Interviews with each of you – as witnesses, of course, not as suspects,' he added, forestalling the immediate clamour. 'And one at a time! I can't cope with this thing where we all talk at once.'

'Piggy's got the conch!' said Frances.

'Wrong genre,' said Sara, causing Frances to stick out her tongue. Sara made as if to cuff her ear.

'That,' said Torben, cutting them short, 'is exactly the sort of thing I mean. And we agreed who our first expert witness should be. Sara, could you come upstairs please?'

Sara looked terrified.

'We think you might be able to assist us with the time of death,' he added. It didn't seem to help.

'What about the rest of us?' said Tom. 'Since you're apparently convinced there's a killer among us, rather than safely stuck down at the lodge. Do we get locked in our rooms or something?'

'If you like,' said Ruth, who seemed happy that this bit was nearly over. 'Alternatively, there's most of Bastle House at your disposal. Why not try to relax until we talk to each of you? Have lunch, if anyone feels like eating, that sort of thing. We could all do with taking it down a few notches.'

'I need a shower,' said Wilson.

'Assuming there's still hot water,' said Frances.

'Well, let's keep the boiler going and then at least the pipes won't freeze.'

'And isn't there a games room? With a pool table?'

'Plus the library.'

'Someone needs to sort out supper later.'

'Has anyone found the wine cellar, that's what I want to know.'

'I found a backup drinks cabinet.'

'Isn't it a bit early for a drink?'

'There's no yardarm, no sun, and a dead body – who cares how early it is?'

Sara was still sticking close to Frances, who gave her a little squeeze. 'Sure, and we'll all get a turn in the interrogation chamber,' said Frances. 'Go and do your stuff, tell them all about the cutting edge of Edwardian criminology, I assume that's what they want you for. I'll see you later.'

Leyla had already slouched off. A minute later she reappeared, brandishing a meat thermometer.

'From the kitchen,' she said. 'I just really hope we don't have to use it.'

10

SUNDAY, TWO P.M.

Sara was slow to mount the stairs. It had all changed so swiftly since she and Frances had boarded the train at King's Cross. Back then, she had been looking forward to this weekend, to the escape it seemed to offer, her hopes high for the one thing she really wanted to get out of it. Then had come the revelations of last night, irrevocable facts she had not been prepared for intellectually or emotionally, and to which her response had been – well, regrettable, to say the least. She hated facts; they were so lumpen, hard, unwieldy. You couldn't think them away; you had to act, respond, feel. And right now her feelings were threatening to overwhelm her. Part of her wanted shot of the whole thing, to be back safe among her books, buoyed by the prospect of fifty thousand little golden lifelines that would make everything so much easier. Part of her just wanted yesterday back: the country house, the party atmosphere, the world on hold and everyone an innocent. Even Torben's absurd dinner outfit, so redolent of a cosier time and place. But – as any two-bit crime novelist might put it – there was no undoing what was done.

One thing was certain: no part of her whatsoever wanted to be dragged into *that* room; to be forced to confront the too-real result of her theoretical work. In her ideal world, murders were done, not just planned, on paper only. They did not involve … *this*. She blanched as Ruth opened the door; there was ice in the draught that came from within.

'Am I really necessary here?' she said. 'Surely I don't know anything that Ruth—'

'Sorry,' said Ruth. 'I'm an ordinary plodder, not a detective. I've tried to learn how to prevent crimes, not solve them. Unfortunately' – and Sara heard the little catch in her voice – 'it doesn't always work out that way. So I think your years of scholarship beat that one training day I had nearly a decade ago.'

'Still, do I really have to go in … in there?'

'It's just that it's easier to see the body once you're inside the room,' said Leyla, deadpan.

Was she enjoying this? thought Sara as, bracing herself against the cold – and the rest of it – she shuffled past. 'It's like a morgue in here,' she said.

'Well, that's good, isn't it?' said Torben. 'We cracked the windows open to prevent putrefaction.'

Putrefaction. Sara clung to the technical term, welcoming the detachment it afforded. 'Mm, but that rather cocks things up.' She still hadn't looked at the bed, the – the body, but she was starting to get a hold of herself. She began to marshal her references around her, the thin armour of articles and monographs. Ruth was right. This was her chance to play the expert.

'You shouldn't have opened that window really,' she said. 'There are four stages of death before putrefaction, and room temperature's a pretty big factor in most of them.'

'Well, is there anything we *can* learn, from a … what, a

medico-forensic-literary perspective?' said Leyla. 'With apologies for excessive hyphenation.'

'And why don't you sit down?' said Ruth. Sara realised she was actively shivering. God, she must look awful.

'Thanks, Ruth,' she said, and closed her eyes. For about a minute, she allowed herself the luxury of abstract thought; it was what they wanted her for, after all. It might even end up helping. 'OK,' she said at last. 'Keep in mind that I'm no Sir Bernard Spilsbury – you can google him once we're out of here – but I *have* just been mugging up on this stuff for the thesis, so … of course I've mostly focused on the medical understanding of the time, which is a century out of date, and my fact-checking of how much is accurate hasn't been rigorously scientific …'

'Never mind that,' said Ruth. 'Hopefully, a proper forensic pathologist will still be able to give a definitive verdict. This doesn't make you … responsible … for anything.'

'Right,' said Sara, not entirely convinced by either of Ruth's assertions. 'Plus this whole field's notoriously inaccurate, I assume you know that? But that said, I think we'll be able to get a rough fix. So. The first stage of death is pallor mortis, which is only much help with white people really – which he, I mean Anthony, is, obviously – but also it's pretty immediate, and he's been dead a while now. So stage two is algor mortis, which is the temperature of the corpse. Over time, before putrefaction sets in, body temperature gradually nears the ambient room temperature. This one never really comes up in the fiction, at least not in detail, because it basically requires taking the temperature either rectally or by inserting a thermometer into the liver.'

Their eyes all went to the meat thermometer in Leyla's hand. She made a face.

'I'd rather not move the body,' said Ruth. 'The experts will want it untouched as far as possible.'

'Don't worry, Ruth,' said Sara, who was if anything comforted by Ruth's pretence of professionalism. Evidently, they were every bit as squeamish as she was. For the first time, she almost felt like smiling. 'It wouldn't really help anyway. There's actually quite a reliable equation here – if I could remember it – but it assumes a stable room temperature. Which you've kind of screwed by opening the window.'

'Sorry,' said Torben. 'That was my fault. But the ashes in the grate suggest he had a fire in here when he went to bed, which will have gone out at some stage during the night – I think we were always doomed to fail on this one.'

'Fair point,' said Sara. 'And he was on medication, wasn't he? So his body temperature might've been higher than normal anyway.' She paused. How serious were they about this? 'Look, I really think we should just leave all this …'

'You said four stages,' said Leyla.

'OK, fine. Three is the famous one, rigor mortis. All the great detective writers loved that one. About as much as they loved exploding it as a theory. In *The Unpleasantness at the Bellona Club*, Dorothy L. Sayers has the solution partly hinge – quite literally – on a leg-break that could only have occurred *after* rigor— sorry, do you not want spoilers?'

'I think,' said Ruth, 'that what we want is to focus on how this helps us find out what happened to Anthony.'

'Of course, of course – sorry, where was I? Yeah, so it wears off eventually – but not yet, I imagine – and it's affected by loads of things.'

'Such as?'

'Um, let's see: it's cold – which would slow rigor mortis down, actually, which is a bit counter-intuitive. Even Christie gets this one wrong in *The Body in the Library*, but of course it's a chemical thing, not about muscles stiffening with cold, so the low temperature would inhibit its onset. As would a relaxed, rested state at time of death.'

'Well, he was in bed,' said Leyla.

'Right. Against which, since he was ill – I mean, he blatantly *was* terminally ill, wasn't he? – that might speed things up a bit, though maybe not enough to counter the rest. Basically if he— if the body is completely stiff, it's safe to say the time of death was at least eight hours ago. And of course any obvious discrepancies – the position of limbs, unexplained breaks, that sort of thing – would suggest he's been moved since it set in.'

'Well, we wouldn't expect that,' said Ruth. 'I suppose he *is* completely stiff?'

Sara shrugged. 'I'll check,' said Torben, going over to Anthony's body. For the first time, Sara willed herself to look at … at it. The position seemed entirely natural – innocent, even – but when Torben steeled himself and laid a hand on Anthony's covered legs, torso, left arm, it looked like he was adjusting a shop dummy. He nodded. 'Rigor seems universal,' he said, in what Sara recognised all too well as an attempt at a detached tone. 'What's the fourth stage?'

'Livor mortis,' she said.

Torben frowned. 'Liver?'

Sara flushed. She had never had occasion to say it before; she hadn't presented on this stuff yet. "With an "o",' she clarified. 'Meaning blue, or something. Maybe it's "lie" like "liver bird"; I don't know, I didn't do Latin. Is that really important?'

'No,' said Torben. 'Sorry. I was just worried about the thermometer thing again. So – "blue" – you mean, referring to these purple patches on the skin?'

'Don't make me look, please.'

'All right, all right, just give us the theory.'

'Once the blood – I'm generalising here – stops circulating, it follows the gravitational pull, settling in the lowest parts of the body. It's another way of telling if the body's been moved since it set in. Bit forensic, this one, so it doesn't come up much in the classics. Again, the cold will slow it down – those lower parts of, of the body go red first, after a few hours, and return to skin colour when subjected to pressure. Eventually they go purple, and don't respond to pressure. There might be some speckling in the lowest extremities; those are Tardieu spots. It'll all wear off, but not any time soon.'

'Can you say how long it'd take to reach full … full whatever, lividity I suppose?'

Sara shrugged. 'Anything from eight to twelve hours, twelve at the most. Nearer to twelve actually, given the cold. You – you can check that yourselves, yes? That's the limit of my usefulness, for what it's worth.'

'You've been *incredibly* helpful, thank you, Sara.' Surprisingly, this came from Leyla. And it sounded genuine to Sara. If this was all there was that they could find out, then maybe – just maybe – this was the end of the ordeal. Nothing to be scared of, not anymore. The past dealt with – justice served – and no one made to suffer for any of it. Closure, in short, for all concerned. And now she could go, and get warm, and not have to think about any of this again until the inheritance – call it blood money – landed in her overdrawn account—

'Sara,' said Ruth, 'while you're here – and Leyla's right, this has been extremely useful, thank you – is there anything else you can tell us? About last night?'

Ah.

*

140

Torben turned from the body to Sara. She was shaking her head, her lips tight.

'Nothing you saw, overheard? Nothing that struck you as odd?'

'No.'

'Could you tell us,' said Torben, 'what your movements were between leaving the drawing room and waking up this morning?'

'I went to bed, obviously.'

'Right away?'

Sara paused. 'Yes,' she said at last. 'I mean, I went to the bathroom first. The one between Frances and Leyla's rooms. I've no idea what the time was, probably about midnight? Quarter to? I was pretty tipsy. I ... I didn't see or speak to anyone after I went up. And then I slept right through!' She hesitated, a sort of smile forced on to her face. 'My room's furthest off, anyway, I wouldn't've heard anything even if I did wake. Not that I did. Can I go now?'

'Yes. Thank you again.'

At the door, Sara stopped; turned. 'I can see where you're heading with all this. There's another Sayers novel, *Unnatural Death*, where a terminally ill person makes a will. In theory, it grants a form of licence, a get-out-of-jail card for your conscience that lets you ... hurry things along? But theory and reality aren't the same. You'd still have to pull the trigger on someone you knew. Just remember how hard it must be to do that, before you start throwing around accusations.'

White-faced, she left them. Torben closed the door.

'Well,' said Ruth.

Leyla made as if to speak, then didn't. Her body language was curious, Torben thought; brimming over with the urge to say something, yet there was a reticence there too. Conflict raced across her features. He had never known her to look so irresolute. Well, it could wait, whatever it was. They had to finish this part first.

'Come on,' he said, 'before we forget. Let's check this discoloration.'

'Definitely purple,' said Ruth. She whispered something to herself that sounded like a prayer – whether for Anthony or her own career prospects, Torben couldn't tell – and then set about prodding at the patches: the right hand, ear, cheek. Together, they folded back the bedding in sections. Too much of it, Torben thought; all these old-fashioned English quilts rather than a decent down duvet, and no fitted sheet, just hospital corners that always came undone. At his side, Ruth raised and lowered Anthony's pyjamas. They were striped, sexless, ageless. But they made for better viewing than his body.

'It all fits,' she said at last. 'His back, buttocks, calves – all purple, and none of it changes colour. He's pretty cold, too, even under the bed clothes.' She checked her watch. 'Coming up for half past two. If we accept Sara's estimates, and I don't know why we wouldn't, that means he probably died no less than eight hours ago, and far likelier more like twelve.'

'We can do better,' said Leyla, who looked relieved to be concentrating on the mechanics of it again. She was flicking through the images they had taken earlier on Frances' camera. 'These are time stamped between 9:39 and 9:48. Tor, you're the colour expert, back me up – this is nowhere near the same, is it?'

Together, they peered at the small, unsatisfying screen. 'Red,' said Torben at last. 'Nothing like this. And I've remembered something else: I squeezed his hand, a few minutes before that. Call it half past nine. I can't swear to it, but I'm almost certain it went white. That's five hours ago – it'd be a little more than seven hours after you heard that door, Ruth. That all works, doesn't it?'

'I *think* so,' said Ruth. 'It's certainly all consistent with what Sara said and what I thought. Which is nice and neat, and makes me want to distrust it on principle.'

'I know what you mean,' said Torben.

'The really useful thing,' said Ruth, 'would be to examine his intestine. We know when he ate dinner; if only we could check the extent of digestion – but we'll have to leave that to the pathologist ...'

'I suppose we just have to swallow that particular camel,' said Torben. 'What? Don't look at me like that, it's a perfectly normal idiom. So in summary: the evidence of the corpse matches our hypothesis as well as it could in the circumstances. We're almost certain he couldn't have been killed before one a.m., and this all matches the timings we're working with from Ruth's watch – doesn't it?'

Leyla made a non-committal noise.

'Maybe,' said Ruth. 'At least our time of death seems ... plausible.'

'What about Sara then?' said Torben. 'I know, it was cold, she was queasy, I don't want to judge, but ...' They could decide for themselves how he might have ended the sentence.

Leyla put her hand up. 'I really, *really* need to say something,' she said. 'But could we be overheard? We need somewhere more secure.'

'And warmer,' said Ruth.

'I could certainly do without the company of our silent fourth partner,' said Torben. 'So, a big, lockable room, out of the way, and ideally comfortable. Somewhere we can use as a – well, the word that comes to mind is "headquarters", which sounds absurd.'

'The phone's in the library,' said Ruth. 'I'd like to monitor that, see if the line comes back on. And I think I spotted a reference section. If we're as ignorant of everything else as we seem to be of pathology, that could come in useful.'

'Library!' said Leyla and Torben, together.

'Like in *Buffy Vampyrernes Skræk*,' Torben added. 'It's where the magic always happens.'

II

SUNDAY, THREE P.M.

As they passed the main entrance hall, Torben paused. 'No offence, Ruth,' he said. 'I know you've already tried. But I've rather more experience of snowy conditions than you' – he reached the main door – 'and while you, quite rightly, do not want any old idiot risking themselves in unfamiliar weather' – he turned the handle – 'I think I might just be better equipped to—' and the rest of his sentence was lost in a flurry of snow.

'*Lort!* Fuck fuck fuck it's bad,' he said, getting his back behind the swinging door and forcing it shut against the blizzard. 'Z-zero vis, visibility,' he shivered, 'and I think even dear old Anders Celsius himself might need a bigger thermometer to gauge that cold. Not even a Swede would go out in that, not even a Swede.'

'Well, it's good that you double-checked,' said Ruth.

'Which is Ruth-speak,' said Leyla, 'for *I told you so, you bumptious arse.*'

Wilson and Tom Goring were playing snooker in the games room. Green baize, parlour games ... ugh. It reminded Torben of the

Oxford Union, of braying young men in chinos and tweeds sipping bad beer and wishing they could still smoke pipes. After the first term, most of them had stopped going, except to catch the odd celebrity speaker. Not Wilson, though, who'd made a decent fist of taking part in debates because, he claimed, it 'got his face out there'. And not Tom, who blended right in to the place, a perfect match to the carpet and the shooting anecdotes. He'd been on the fringes of that whole public school crowd who went to the Hunt Ball and insisted on calling the game in question 'billiards' rather than snooker, even though, someone had once told Torben, the two were quite different, because then they could pretend they were in a gentlemen's club, not a glorified pub where you could get a subsidised pint. No wonder Anthony had one of these tables in his house. In fact, for all he knew, this *was* an actual billiards table – it would be of a piece with his late host's mania for authenticity. Torben frowned. He didn't like not knowing things.

'Look out,' said Tom. 'Here comes the inquisitorial squad.' He missed his shot.

Wilson flashed a perfect, leading-man smile at them. Leaning back against the table, he looked born to the role: the rich playboy, the merchant-aristocracy dilettante. 'Come on, Tom,' he said, in a louder voice than was strictly necessary. 'You know the rules: a shot missed is a shot downed. What'll you have this time?' Tom grimaced, and, not for the first time, Torben wondered about their friendship, and its inequalities. You could sum it up by their physical appearances – did Wilson, tall and chiselled, simply enjoy having someone like Tom around to provide a flattering contrast? Surely not. But then, that worked both ways: Tom had always shown a tendency to idolise – first Wilson, for his charisma, then Anthony, for his success ...

The library doors opened silently. On the other side of the

book-lined room Frances and Sara were talking in low voices, intent on something they were huddled over. He just had time to catch the words 'the gun, in the dining room' before they noticed the intruders and looked up. Hastily, Sara sought to hide whatever it was they were looking at.

Torben blinked. Surely this wasn't what it looked like?

'Seriously?' Ruth was striding past him. 'You two *seriously* think that's appropriate right now? How you could—'

'All right, all right!' said Frances. 'I thought you told us to go do something fun.'

'It's, like, a coping mechanism?' said Sara. 'Catharsis. After what you just put me through, I needed to destress.'

'It is in the most appalling taste to—'

'OK, OK. We'll be buggering off then. Come on, Sara, time for a drink.'

Ruth watched them go. Torben and Leyla watched Ruth. She looked like she was counting to ten. 'Well,' she said at last, 'I suppose *that's* not a bad idea. I'll go and make us some tea.'

'What was all that about?' said Torben, once she too had left the room.

'This,' said Leyla, and held up a battered *Cluedo* box. 'Unless I'm very much mistaken, they've just accused Professor Plum. I'd watch out if I were you.'

She shut the double doors, checked the phone – 'still dead' – and hesitated. 'Torben?' she said.

'Yes?'

'You know that phrase, "the truth, the whole truth, and nothing but the truth"?'

'Of course.'

'What do you think of it as a principle?'

He considered this. 'Less than you, I imagine. As a vow goes, it gives the promise of being all-encompassing, but it leaves aside the tricky little matter that "the truth" as such doesn't actually exist, only each individual's sense of it.'

'Exactly!' She seemed keen to seize on this. 'It's subjective. Take just now, for instance – *your* truth might have been that you over-heard Frances and Sara discussing a gun in the dining room. But if you gave that under oath, it might seriously misrepresent what was actually going on, yes?'

'Yes, naturally. Look, Leyla, what's all this—?'

'Oh,' she said, 'nothing. I mean, let's wait till Ruth gets here. I *mean*, let's keep going with empirical evidence for now, shall we, not hearsay? Take this desk, for instance – Anthony's desk, maybe it has something to tell us.'

He let it go. If it really mattered, he thought, she would tell them when she was ready.

Meanwhile, Leyla had crossed to the desk. 'It's unlocked,' she said, pulling open the drawer.

'But – let me guess – empty?' said Torben.

'Well, aside from a book of stamps, a pencil … a two-pence piece … a business card for a tree-surgeon, whatever that is, presumably a glorified lumberjack – anyway the card looks pretty unprofessional for any kind of surgeon, like it's been done on a home printer – and an elastic band, rather slack … yes, that's it. Unless there's a secret compartment?' She held the home-made business card up to the light as if it might somehow be a clue. The most you could say about it was that, if this was a representative example, the tree-surgeons of the Tyne Valley were not to be hired for the sake of their production values.

Torben pulled himself together. 'There's never a secret compartment. Go on, pull the whole thing out. See? No decent post-Chippendale cabinetmaker worth his salt would waste good mahogany like that. It would spoil the classical line.'

'Oh, shut up, Torben. You sound like a daytime antiques show.' Leyla's poise was fully recovered by now. 'Anyway,' she went on, 'where *is* everything? I thought this was meant to be his office.'

'Typical hypocrisy, at a guess,' he said. 'Anthony renounces technology, goes practically off grid – but I bet you anything you like that down in the lodge, Kirsty's got three iMacs synced to the cloud with fibre broadband. That will be where the actual work gets done, he's just outsourced it. You said it yourself, this place is a sham. But we have to concede that Ruth was right,' he added, as another howl from outside set the sash windows rattling, flinging another deluge of white up against the sills. 'In this snowstorm, the lodge might as well be on the moon, for all the good it does us. What were you looking for anyway?'

'Oh, I don't know. A birth certificate revealing that one of us is actually his next of kin, a secret love letter leading to a deadly rivalry – something insane like that. I suppose that sort of thing only really happens in detective stories.'

'Hmm,' he said. 'Although, have you noticed, no one in the real world actually ever says "that sort of thing only happens in books"? Except you, for some perverse reason. People *in* books say it all the time, I think authors think it's "meta". But in real life, when something turns out like a piece of fiction, no one's really surprised, if anything it's sort of what we expect. We're always acting under the influence of culture, we find it a natural state of being.'

'You're acting under the influence of *something*, all right.'

'I mean it! Books, films, even video games – life imitates art, especially low art. Ruth said the same about the gunshot: people act in life like they've been taught to when playing Xbox. We all know this.'

Leyla narrowed her eyes at him.

'Oh, I'm not saying that violence in video games actually creates murderers, I'm not the *Daily Mail*,' he protested. 'Just that if you *were* a murderer, then you'd most likely follow the examples you'd picked up from gaming, or from watching films – or, to come back to my original point, from reading. The only people who don't think that things happen like they do in books, are people in books.'

'Torben?'

'Yes?'

'Shut up.'

'All right.' He had been enjoying this exchange; it was the closest thing to flirting he'd managed so far. 'What shall we do until Ruth gets back then?'

Leyla eyed him wryly. 'Much as it pains me to say it, the most helpful thing might be … to look at the books.' And she began to examine the bookcases, pulling volumes from the reference section, skimming contents pages, putting them back. Sublimating her … well, her impatience, he conceded. Still, her movements were efficient, meticulous … fluid … graceful. Like a cat. A lovely, sexy cat— OK, he had learnt his lesson. No more comparisons. But he couldn't help but see the pattern of her shifting limbs. How the arches of her brows knit in concentration. The way she bent to the lowest shelf, the snug curve—

Torben turned away hastily. Books, books, books. The cases looked original; they had stood through two centuries. And there was something so patently undisturbed about the shelves that struck him as sad. Realistically, Anthony could not have handled more than a tiny fraction of the volumes, let alone read them – he had never been one for novels – and besides history and fiction, here was poetry … theology … agriculture. Clearly a job lot, they might have come with the house. You had to fill this room somehow. *Books do furnish a room*, where had he read that? It made him wonder what Anthony had done, day after day, if he wasn't in here, reading. He had a momentary image of Dodd playing endless games of billiards against himself, and turned back to the books, shutting off that depressing line of thought.

It was practically an affront, this library, to the flippancy of his generation. He felt almost ashamed. Stack upon stack, bound in calfskin, superannuated, impenetrable. It spoke to a dignity, verging on pomposity, that someone of his era could never honestly assume. This was a good thing on the whole, obviously – but a little more sobriety, a little less ironic self-awareness, would be useful in this sort of situation. Maybe that was the real reason for the death of the super-sleuth: not the march of technology, but the extinction of earnestness. Impossible to 'sink into a brown study' when that very phrase, 'brown study', made you instantly self-conscious … Oh look, he was doing it now. *Books*, Torben. Check the books.

By the time Ruth returned with the tea, Leyla had a mixed stack of medical treatises, books of psychoanalysis, and works of criminology. Torben added a single slim volume, *A History of Bastle House*, evidently published by a vanity press. The double doors of the library had an ancient lock with a rusty key – a rusty key! – and they locked themselves in.

There was a loose arrangement of well-upholstered chairs around a coffee table in a corner furthest from the door, next to the fireplace. The room was heated by an iron stove rather than an open grate, presumably to protect the books from sparks, and a couple of minutes' poking about produced a satisfying glow. They were insulated from the cold by centuries of calf bindings and paper pages; the crackle of the fire played against the ceaseless buffets of the winter wind. A French window faced north, swagged in faded linen. The disconnected landline had a table to itself, one of those vintage phone tables that were starting to crop up again in certain East London boutiques. Outside the east windows, snow mounted in great drifts upon the outer sills, and more snow fell beyond. It was – well, it was perfect.

'Headquarters: established,' said Torben. 'Now out with it, Leyla, you said you had something to … divulge.'

She nodded. Now the moment had come, she looked less than comfortable with what she was about to lay before them. 'Well,' she said, 'I think I can confidently state that we've been told our first lie.'

'By whom?' said Torben, as Ruth said, 'Lie, or discrepancy?'

'To adopt the phraseology of this room's previous occupants: Sara Courtenay, in the bedroom, with a big fat whopper! You remember she told us she went straight to bed, pretty much? Well, she didn't.' Leyla sighed. 'She went to Frances' room.'

'When was this?'

'Around when she said, I suppose – it must've been after she used the bathroom, because I remember there was a wet toothbrush next to mine in the mug thingy, and the hand towel was all ruched.'

'Ruched?'

'I wanted to sound period appropriate; used, anyway. The towel is immaterial! Anyway, *I* was in the bathroom – it's got two doors, one on to the corridor, and one that leads into my room, which I suppose might also lead to embarrassment, but I don't think Anthony's the sort to pay much attention to that kind of nicety. *Was* the sort, I should say. Point being, I used the door from my room, and was being especially quiet, because I knew Frances had gone to bed already, and her bed – as I'm sure you, Torben, remember, from your transparent desire to bounce on it – her bed was right up against the bathroom wall. So they wouldn't have known I was there. Even so, they were speaking pretty quietly.'

Torben was flicking through *A History of Bastle House*. 'There's no fireplace in that bathroom, is there?'

'No—?'

'That room's not on these older plans. Must be a … what do you call it in English? We call it a *stud væg* but now I think about it, "stud wall" sounds like nonsense.'

'No, no that's just English for you. Stud wall is correct,' said Ruth.

'A thin wall anyway, which they wouldn't be expecting.'

Leyla practically growled. 'Do. You. Or. Do. You. Not. Want to hear what they sodding well said?'

'Sorry, Leyla,' they said together.

'I … I didn't catch much. It was just a few stray phrases that I took in without meaning to. It was the tone that really caught me; one of them seemed really upset, there were a couple of what might have been sobs. And whether it was suspicious or not, they definitely sounded like they were arguing.'

'What did they say?'

Leyla seemed gratified. 'Just snatches. One of them was saying "no, not tonight", the other said "why not?" and then I heard "is in the way" or maybe "*he's* in the way". Then something I didn't catch at all – and then something that ended "do it tomorrow?", the reply "maybe", and then, "once Anthony is out of the picture". I couldn't tell which speaker was which, it was too sibilant. If that's the word.'

Ruth let out a long breath. 'Well, that's quite the conversation, in the circumstances. But to only have half of it! Leyla, is that absolutely all you heard? You can't remember anything more that might give us a handle on what that all meant?'

Yes, thought Leyla. Yes, she could. Because the conversation had not, in fact, ended there. *The truth, the whole truth, and nothing but the truth*. Torben was right. It was a stupid code to live by.

The thing was, the words she had just reported really could mean anything. Even the bit about *once Anthony is out of the picture* – that could mean murdered, dead from his illness, gone for a walk – who was she to put a construction on it? But what she had heard next had been a little less equivocal.

Sara had said, 'What's Anthony got to do with it?' – her voice rising loud enough for Leyla to tell who was speaking. And then ... and then Frances had told Sara about The Thing.

The Thing had happened ten years before, and until last night – the night of Anthony's murder – Leyla was pretty sure she was the only one Frances had ever told. And now she saw again that other bathroom, a decade earlier: the mean, windowless, breeze-blocked shower on the second floor of their first-year staircase, with its manually operated extractor fan and automatic motion-sensor light, its refusal to compromise between extremes of scalding heat and stinging cold, its mouldy wooden pallet to keep your feet from the verruca-inducing floor. Remembered the summer night that she had sat outside its door, patient and a little scared, waiting for a trembling Frances either to come out, or to let her in.

Those were the days when no one spoke out. After a couple of hours and several brandies, Frances herself had insisted that Anthony had made no more than a clumsy pass at her – had misjudged the situation – that she'd probably led him on. None of which had washed with Leyla for a second, even then. But she'd gone along with it, and kept it secret, that being what Frances claimed she wanted. But

Leyla had seen Frances flinch, only the night before, as they had sat down to dinner. And she had listened, ears straining now, in the shared bathroom of Bastle House, as Frances, her voice rising louder with the heat of it all, told Sara much more than she had ever told Leyla. Told her of being pushed against the wall; of Anthony's grasping hands and his foul breath on her face. Listening, Leyla had felt doubly sickened, both with The Thing itself and her own voyeurism. She had not waited for Sara's response: coming to her senses, she had slipped from the room, tried to sleep. But she could imagine the fury it might arouse. She had felt it herself.

But it was like the *Cluedo*, wasn't it? Things heard out of context could sound awfully damning and in fact be wholly innocent. And Leyla knew, now, that she had to keep this truth to herself. She had told the truth, a truth; a partial truth. And that was enough. Because either Frances, or Sara, or Frances and Sara together, might well have murdered Anthony Dodd for the money. And if so, that was a terrible crime for which they should pay, and in reporting what she had first overheard, Leyla had done her part in gathering the evidence that might convict them.

But there were alternatives. They might both be innocent, Anthony dead by another's hand, in which case the last thing the three investigators needed was a highly circumstantial red herring, she told herself.

Less palatably, either Frances, or Sara, or Frances and Sara together, might just as well have murdered Anthony Dodd for revenge. It was all too easy to imagine: Sara as avenging angel; Frances with her past stirred up, taking the open invitation to get her own back before it was too late. In cold blood or hot, they could have hastened the demise of a horrible man with a sentence of death already over him, put him out of his misery, in retribution for what, to Leyla, was an unpardonable and abusive act that had gone unpunished for a decade. If so, if the three of them uncovered enough evidence that this became the clear solution, then and only then would Leyla give up her secret. In the meantime, she would pursue the practicalities of the case against them without – what was that stupid phrase? – without fear or favour. But she was damned if she was going to bring up a man's abusiveness as a reason to heap suspicion on the survivor, or on the survivor's friend.

There was such a thing as the sisterhood, after all.

'Leyla?' Ruth prompted her again. 'Nothing more at all?'

'Sorry?' said Leyla. She looked like she had been miles away. 'No, nothing. Circumstantial as hell, really. I just offer it as proof that Sara was lying to us when she said she went straight to bed. I heard her going past the bathroom a minute later, so that must have been that, but then I fell asleep almost immediately.'

'Let me write this down,' said Torben. '"No, not tonight." "Why not?" "He's in the way." "Do it tomorrow?" "Maybe." "Once Anthony is out of the picture." Hmm. Certainly adds colour to all the times they've been huddling in corners.' He paused. 'But as you say, it could mean anything.'

'We're just collecting data,' said Ruth.

'Not putting a leading construction upon anything,' said Leyla.

'Still,' said Torben, 'shall we interview Frances next?'

Frances twirled her red hair round a finger like spaghetti on a fork, and Torben realised that he must be getting hungry. 'You can keep the camera, of course,' she said, 'until the whatsit – the inquest?'

'Thank you Frances,' said Ruth, as if this really was a free choice Frances was making.

Torben sat in a corner, *A History of Bastle House* open in his lap. He was letting Ruth do this, as seemed only right, this being their first formal interview and her being a police inspector. Still, that was not his real reason. He felt deeply uncomfortable questioning Frances – because she was a close friend. Because the power relations of the situation felt artificial and wrong. All right: above all, because of that one time in second year – following the first fancy-dress Bop of Michaelmas Term – when they had slept together.

And also that other time.

The last of the (several) times had actually been shortly after he had written Leyla the poem, at the end of third year – long enough afterwards to conclude that Leyla was avoiding him, but too soon to pretend to himself that the two things were unconnected. Which made him feel doubly guilty about that time. No, three times as guilty – because on some level, he'd been dishonest to himself as well as to Frances and Leyla.

He thought Leyla knew about the first time, perhaps the ones in the middle, hopefully not the last. He knew Frances *didn't* know the details of the Leyla situation in that final summer term, but she must have suspected. Ruth probably understood more about the whole thing, emotionally, than Torben – but lacked the crucial detail that Torben had kept from her: namely, that he and Frances had had sex at all. Both the sex and the secrecy had been Frances' idea. Hadn't they? At least the first time?

For helvede. A murder investigation he could cope with. But the intricacies of a (long dead) love life were more than he could ever hope to understand. Best he kept right out of it. That was not what they were here to scrutinise.

It had been *good* sex too. The first good sex of his life. He smelt again the sharp, fresh notes of her CK One; remembered the glow – and the ache – the morning after the first time, feelings warm enough to insulate him against the knowing looks as he endured the 'walk of shame' – why shame? – back to his own rooms. He had had to cross half the college, conscious not only of his incongruous costume but of the unholy concoction of scents upon him – hoping the traces of Frances' powerful perfume were enough to mask the less savoury odours – running into first Anthony and then, of all people, the chaplain – with whom he occasionally played squash – who was on his way to the Sunday service in the main quad. The man of God had, disgracefully, winked at him; it was Anthony who had taken him to task, displaying his uncanny ability to manifest the most censorious parts of Torben's own conscience. But it had been worth it, a hundred times worth it. He had learnt important things about sex, about relationships even; about talking and reciprocity and how laughter had its place. About asking without shame. Would you—? May I—? Like this—?

Certainly he knew enough to tell that, unless she had changed out of all recognition, Frances was not herself right now. Her body language was diffident, almost supplicatory. She was normally so natural, her edges either soft or else alight with confrontation. Her self right up against the world. Where now was the indignation, the challenge, that combative quality that he had come to think of – having nothing to compare it with – as her Scottishness?

This was, thought Frances, very much like a nightmare she had once had. Three of her oldest friends, sitting in judgement upon her – and instinctively she glanced down, to check if she was wearing clothes. She might as well not be, the stare Leyla had on her. This couldn't really still be about *that*, could it? Her and Torben? Seriously, what was it with these people; first Anthony, now Leyla, and – to judge by the way Tor was hanging back – maybe even him too? The last thing she wanted to think about – no, the *second*-last thing, she corrected herself – was sex, especially as it related to her own too-scrutinised body.

It was how people saw her, how they thought of her. It didn't matter how she acted: shy, friendly, angry, amusing, it always somehow got categorised as flirtation. So fucking *reductive*. Oh yes, they asked Sara all about her thesis, but the only person interested in *her* work was Tom bloody Goring, who wanted to pick a fight, and even then she had to come out with some bollocks about soapsuds, just to get a rise.

And why had she done that – because he was looking at her breasts? When they go low, we go lower? Frances Ottilie Adair, she told herself, you are your own worst enemy. Why couldn't she have talked about schist and gneiss, the disciplined violence of turning that which was hard and lumpen into that which was fluid and animate? Maybe, if she'd talked to Tom about attacking an obtuse rock with sharp objects, it wouldn't have reminded them of all *that*, and Anthony wouldn't've put his hand on her bare skin (and *why* had she worn an off-the-shoulder dress?), and she wouldn't have remembered The Thing – and she might just have been a friend, among friends, having a ... how had she put it, a lifetime ago? A holiday? Too good to be true, Frances. And now they were asking her to think about the *actual* last thing she wanted to discuss. With the rest of it lurking right beneath the surface.

Oh Christ, maybe *that* was what Leyla's look was about. She'd forgotten that Leyla knew. Fuck. Fuckity fuck. She was a lawyer, too.

How the hell was she meant to play this? But then, it had been ten years ago. Maybe Leyla didn't remember?

'No,' she said, 'I'm sorry. I really don't think I saw anything helpful.'

Torben snuck another look at her. So subdued. Was it just that the sobering fact of Anthony's death – his murder – had finally sunk in? Or was she still cowed by Ruth's unusual harshness over the *Cluedo* thing?

'I've no clue, frankly,' Frances said. 'If that note and all was a setup … I can't imagine any of us doing something like that.'

Or was she protecting something? Someone? Acting unnaturally because it was not herself she was afraid for?

'OK, Frances,' said Ruth. 'Don't worry. Your camera's been the most useful thing anyone's contributed so far.' Her voice was calm, familiar. Almost apologetic. Ruth's anger never lasted long. And now she smiled at Frances. 'Before you go, could we just run over your movements last night? So we can build up a clear map of where everyone was?'

Just too much, thought Torben. Never justify your question, it attracts attention. He turned a page of *A History of Bastle House* idly. But something had shifted in the room, Ruth's false note still in the air. Across from him, Leyla had sat up a little straighter without knowing it.

'I … OK, I went upstairs just after Ruth, before Leyla. Sara came with me. I peeled off – I'm sharing a bathroom with Wilson and I wanted to get in there first. Then I went to my room. None of the boys had come up yet, from what I could hear.'

She seemed to hesitate. Twirl, twirl, went the finger.

'I'd just got into bed when the door knocked, and Sara came in.'

160

Torben turned another page.

'She was upset, she wanted to talk. I budged up. We must hae chatted for, I don't know, ten minutes maybe? Then she left. This would be around midnight? After that I tossed and turned a wee bit – Anthony's news, and then my room's got all those windows on the stormy side, it was starting to batter about. I tried to read, but I couldn't concentrate. Probably I dropped off after an hour, or it might have been more?' This sounded like a question. 'Next I knew, it was morning.'

'Might I ask what you and Sara talked about?' said Ruth. It came out a bit stiff.

Frances stared at her for a second. 'Sure,' she said, and her eyes flicked at Torben, then at Leyla. 'But I'd have thought that was obvious: this whole setup, Anthony's illness.' She paused. 'We actually got a mite cross about it. She was just sorry for him; I said it was unfair him loading it on us all like that. That … that was all.'

'Of course,' said Ruth. 'Thanks, Frances.'

'It's weird, you know?' Frances seemed keen to carry on, to take the conversation somewhere else – somewhere safe? 'We're staying in a dead man's house. Like we're trespassing. You'd think it'd be like walking around inside someone's mind. But instead this place is more like a hotel. Or like being in a play. Isn't that sad? Like, it's not "Anthony Dodd's house" but "the house that, coincidentally, once contained Anthony Dodd".' She swallowed audibly. 'Or, even, it's that he bought this place to die in. The man had a death wish, and Bastle House was part of it. Like a great big tombstone. And tombstones, I can tell you, never have much to do with the person they're commemorating.'

She rose. 'Oh, if I were you, I'd hurry up with those two boys out there. You know they're playing some sort of drinking game?'

'Good point,' said Torben, speaking for the first time. 'Would you get Wilson straight in here? And – and see if you can do anything to keep Tom sober? Sorry to ask.'

'Suppose I shouldn't have said anything,' said Frances. 'Oh well, that'll teach me. Aye!' And she went out, leaving one door open.

The three of them barely had time to exchange a glance before they heard her say: 'Wilson Ho, the dentist will see you now,' and then, in a quieter voice, 'Want a game, Tom? Forfeits, my rules …'

Wilson's head popped round the door. 'Yes?' he said. 'I hear it's time for my truth extraction.'

Wilson was only too happy to help. 'I should warn you guys that I've been drinking with Tom,' he said, 'but don't worry. I chose sherry, he chose port – hah! – actually it's a very good Fino after a few minutes chilling on a windowsill, dry as hell, and I'm kind of an ace at snooker, so I've only had a tiny glass or two. So hit me. Whadaya want – motives, movements, libellous theories about who dun it? "Where were you at such and such a time on the night of the twenty-fourth?"'

'Slander, not libel,' said Leyla.

'And you can start,' said Ruth, 'with an account of what happened after *we* left the drawing room, until the next morning. I don't count him' – she nodded at Torben – 'as a reliable witness.'

'And I seem to remember you promising to look after him,' said Leyla. 'Given his history of bizarre behaviour when – what's the legal term I'm looking for? – pissed out of his mind.'

For the first time, Wilson looked embarrassed. 'Yeah, about that,' he said. 'You were last of the women to leave, I think, Leyla? Us guys all stayed on a bit. After that, Anthony took Tom off for … I think he said "I need a word with this one" – and then something about Torben making himself comfortable on the sofa. Tom seemed delighted to go off with Anthony, he couldn't get out soon enough. So those two went out the other way, back into the dining room, and I stayed for one last drink – only so I could keep an eye on Torben, obviously …'

'Did you see Anthony and Tom come back in?' said Ruth.

'Nuh-uh. I assume they went round the other way, they'd said good night already. Then I was gonna take Torben upstairs, only … OK, so I'd had a bit too much myself. There was a loo next door; I rushed in to – you know. Afterwards I felt kinda vile, so I headed up to brush my teeth. From there it seemed natural to go to bed. I guessed Torben had gone up himself by this time, but I – I didn't check, sorry. I was on autopilot, you know how you get … well, maybe you don't, Ruth. Anyway, I didn't see anybody. Fran must've used the bathroom before me, there were things everywhere.'

'Things?'

'Products, you know? A facial cleanser, wipes – also her hair gets *everywhere*. After that, bed. My watch said one something, I think, last I looked at it; I can't do better than that. I made sure to drink about a gallon of water too, so I had to get up once in the night. All I can say about that is that "it was a dark and stormy night", sorry. Might've been four a.m.? Five? But that's just a guess. And I woke early too, maybe seven, but I just lay there for ages, trying not to make any sudden movements. Had a shower, read over a script – sorry, is this still relevant?'

'Not really,' said Leyla.

'That's all we wanted,' said Ruth. 'We're just getting the practical side sorted. You didn't see or hear anything else suspicious at any point?'

'I … no, I suppose not.'

163

'Well, I think that's it then. Thanks, Wilson.'

He looked crestfallen. 'Was there something you wanted to add?' said Torben.

'Um, not – that is, no … Sorry, I guess I was preparing for my big moment and now I find my lines have got cut. You're sure *you* don't want to ask *me* about anything else?' And Wilson looked hard at Ruth.

She didn't blink. 'No, I don't think so. If it's all right, I'd rather get on to Tom while he's still sober.'

'Complete the set,' said Torben, smiling. He was pretty sure he, Ruth and Wilson were all thinking of the same thing. But none of them was going to say it.

'Right – I'll send him in then. See you at dinner, I suppose.' Wilson went out, deflated. Torben did not think it was quite the exit he'd had in mind.

Tom was red in the face, his forehead slick. He sat down with an audible sigh of relief.

Leyla, inimitably, raised her eyebrow.

'Never,' said Tom, 'agree to forfeits with that little ginger minx.' Unlike the rest of them, he managed to use words like 'minx' without a trace of self-consciousness, a trait he had shared with Anthony. 'Started off with downing pint glasses of water. Water! Soon we were doing laps of the table if we missed a shot. Which I only agreed to because I thought, well, not so bad to see Frances'— I mean, which I was a fool to ever agree to. I'll say one thing for artists, they can have bloody good hand-eye coordination.'

That they had heard nothing of this boded well: the library was clearly better soundproofed than Leyla's bathroom.

'Well, you're safe now,' said Torben. 'This workout will be purely mental.'

Tom frowned, possibly wondering whether to take offence.

'We're just accounting for everyone's movements last night,' Ruth said. She hesitated. 'From what we've heard so far, you were the last person to ... to see Anthony alive. So obviously it'd be great if you could be as precise and as detailed as possible.'

'Wow,' said Tom. 'I hadn't thought of it like that before. But I must've been. Poor, poor Ant ... oh, right. Um. So I should start with the point when you girls' – hypocritically, Torben judged his choice of word – 'went to bed? Leaving the four of us chaps. I remember Ben here swearing at Ant; I reckon he was properly plastered by then. Anthony took me back to the dining room for a minute, checking the fire was out in the grate. We had a few words.'

'What did you talk about?'

'I'm not sure that's strictly relevant.'

'Even so.'

Tom looked like he might try blustering, then thought better of it. He was no match for Ruth's brand of politeness and, to give him credit, he seemed to know it. 'He – he wanted to apologise,' he said. 'For the will. Bloody good of him, actually. Said in the natural way of things, he'd have asked me to draw it up, only of course, as I pointed out at once, that'd be a conflict of interest, seeing as I was mentioned as a beneficiary.'

'Had you carried out any legal work for him before?' said Leyla.

'Well, no,' said Tom. 'But that would all have been commercial stuff, business, not in my line, whereas this was personal, so he thought it could've hurt my feelings. Very big of him, I thought.'

'Since you've brought it up, what can you remember about the will?' said Torben.

'Uh, not much, I'm afraid. You see, I only had sight of that one page, where we were listed – I wasn't exactly going to go through the whole thing there at the table. By candlelight too. But it all seemed in order. There was a paragraph naming his parents as executors, that was really sad.'

For once, Torben found himself in agreement with Tom Goring.

'Anything about the estate proper?' said Leyla.

Tom shook his head. 'Small bequests only on that page,' he said. 'If you can call three hundred and fifty thousand quid small, which to be fair, I reckon Ant could. But look, I've been thinking about that.'

'Yes?'

'*This house*. Assuming he paid cash for it after he sold up STONi. Which he could have done easily – that deal must've netted him, oh, twenty mill? More? So forget the fifty K for each of us, that's small beer next to the big prize. We're talking murder here, we should keep our eyes on the prize! Well?' He looked at them all expectantly. 'The house! Think about it. Even with death duties and all the gubbins, getting this place would be quite the motive, wouldn't it? It must be worth millions!'

'Tom, we're not really in a position to—'

Torben cut across Ruth. 'Why do you mention the house in particular?' he said.

'Because,' said Tom, and his face regained some of its former redness, '*it's going to that Kirsty woman*, that's bloody well why!'

12

SUNDAY, FOUR P.M.

Tom wished his face wouldn't always do this in moments of emotion, he knew how it looked – he'd even heard someone using the term 'gammon' recently, which was a new one on him. Partial as he was to a proper bit of pork, he'd rather not be compared to one. Especially by people who were probably vegans. Anyway, he'd promised himself not to lose his cool, because it was imperative that, right now, he sounded convincing. Rational. Someone giving an honest statement, not – what was it? – sticking it to the person in the subordinate gender and class position.

And how bloody ironic was that, if only they knew? So what if she'd had to do Ant's housekeeping – she was living in this place, wasn't she? And probably minting it all the time, without a care in the world. Whereas life in the Goring household right now was … no; no need to worry about that. Not anymore. Fifty K, Tom, fifty K. It was just enough, just in time. All right, in an ideal world, he wouldn't have got his hands on it this way, but then, beggars can't be choosers and all that crap. And when it came down to it, that's what he'd been for years now, a bloody beggar, going cap-in-hand to a guy who turned his back when the going got really tough. So: subordinate gender and class position, his arse.

Breathe, Goring. Rein it in. This was important. He had to make them believe him.

'Kirsty again?' said Ruth. 'Is this more of what you were saying in the drawing room?'

'I thought you said you only saw the small bequests?' said Leyla.

'I'm not talking about the will. This is something I heard. Or aren't you interested in my witness testimony?' Tom glared at them. He seemed ready to make a speech about having had enough of experts.

'Go on,' said Torben. 'Please.' He raised a pen conspicuously above his notebook.

Tom looked gratified. 'It was right before Ant's big revelation, so it went clean out of my head straight after – if I'd been thinking straight then maybe I would have insisted on reading over the whole will. Christ, I might even have been able to warn him, poor sod.' Tom's face wore an ambiguous expression that Torben tried to read as regret, though he had to admit it looked more like self-importance.

'Yes?' said Torben.

'Do any of you remember, when he rang for silence – you were right, Ben, it *was* his left hand, I can picture it now – he said something to Kirsty, before she hurried off? Well I was pretty close to them, and though he was whispering, I distinctly heard him say that she wouldn't have to worry with all this running about for him when *she* had the house to herself! Then *she* said something I couldn't hear, but she was definitely frowning. And he said – these were his exact words – "Remember, you *are* my sister." And she went off right away, hiding her face from him. But *I* saw it, and she looked awful. *And,*' he finished up, 'where's the will now? Gave it to Kirsty to take away, didn't he? There! How about that!' He slapped his palm down on the table and sat back, soaking up the effect of his words.

No one spoke. Then Torben asked Tom to repeat both direct quotations, and added them to his list of evidence. After a moment's thought, he drew a large question mark beside them. But only lightly.

'Well,' said Ruth, 'it's certainly something to consider. I think Anthony *did* once mention that he had a sister—'

'Yeah,' said Tom. 'He did. Never met her though.' He paused. 'If you ask me, our Ant was always a bit embarrassed of his family. I mean, he came to stay with my people once or twice in the long vacations, but I was never invited back to his, and they never came up to take him out for dinner or anything. Started to seem like a bit of a shameful secret. I got the sense that his parents, his sister – well, that they were everything Kirsty is, you know? So it all fits!'

'"Everything Kirsty is"?' said Leyla. 'Care to expand on that?'

Tom caught the expression on Leyla's face. 'Um, actually, I'd rather not, if it's all the same with you.'

'Good!' said Ruth, a little too brightly. 'So, have you got all that, Torben? Great. Thank you, Tom, that's really helpful. Could I – could I ask you to complete your account of the evening from the end of your later conversation with Anthony?'

'Well,' said Tom, clearly irritated to be moving on from his big reveal, 'I went to bed, didn't I? Anthony headed to the kitchen first, said he'd check that the side door was shut and everything was off – always was a bit anal about these things – and I toddled off up. I could hear you and Wilson still chatting in the drawing room, Ben, some crap about flying staircases. I had a slash, brushed my teeth, and went straight to sleep. Slept like a baby. Always do after a big night.' His eyes hardened. 'And more's the pity, or I might have heard that ungrateful bitch come back and murder her brother. But she'll have been quiet, won't she? She knows this place. I suppose you've checked the back staircase, the one by your room, Ruth?'

Torben started, and quickly flicked through the book he had laid aside. Tom was referring to what was marked as the servants' staircase, at the end of the west passage. It led both up and down from their bedrooms – up to the second floor where the staff would once have lived, down to what they were now calling the scullery – and presumably down further still, to what must have been the original kitchens and pantries of a house this size, a whole lower level that, according to this book, had been sealed off years ago due to a pleasant-sounding combination of rising damp and exposed asbestos. To avoid the guests and staff coming into unnecessary contact with each other, this service staircase was hidden behind a door on every floor. If anyone *had* returned to the house at night, by way of the kitchen door, then that – and not the main, central staircase – would be the obvious route to take to Anthony's room.

'Of course,' said Ruth, in answer to Tom's question. 'Doors locked on both levels, and no sign of a key when we searched the house for a landline earlier. Anthony told me on Friday it's no longer in use; that's why he put me next to it, so I wouldn't be disturbed.'

'Which proves bugger all,' said Tom. 'Sorry – but really, do I have to point this out? It's Kirsty who'll have all the keys!'

This was certainly true: the row of key hooks in the kitchen had been conspicuously bare. Torben had dismissed this second, back staircase on the grounds of Ruth's testimony: as a notoriously light sleeper, who *had* heard a door open and close that was perhaps five times further off than the staircase door – which would, moreover, need to be unlocked as well as opened – it seemed unthinkable that she had not heard, or had forgotten hearing, the nearer door. But – and this was something he had literally never asked himself before – just how reliable was Ruth?

'We'll need to discuss all this,' said Ruth. 'But this is really invaluable, Tom, thank you.' She smiled at him. Even Leyla seemed pleased.

'I should bloody well hope so,' said Tom, rising. 'Just hurry up and close the case so you can arrest her and be done with it, all right?'

And he left, leaving both doors juddering behind him. Torben really wanted to call him back, to come out with a classic 'just one more question'. But he had nothing.

It was like looking into a mirror. Doubt rang clear on both Ruth and Leyla's faces – what to believe, how to react, where to begin.

Torben got up. 'There's a thing detectives do in old books at moments of crisis. I've always wanted to try it. Can you two just sit here for ten minutes and, I don't know, make notes? Great.' And he was through the door.

On his way to the kitchen, he passed his – could he still call them friends? suspects? really, what *was* he doing, this was monstrous – and every face turned away. He felt marked. A pariah of his own making.

Deserted, the kitchen was no longer a place of warmth. Reduced to signifiers, he saw only the key hooks, mostly bare – and surely there would not be so many hooks if there were not more keys somewhere? – along with one of those heavy-duty Maglite torches, the size of your arm; a spare pair of wellingtons, presumably Kirsty's, by the side door; the cork board, incongruous and banal, its pinned schedule – *Wednesday 12pm: nurse (palliative) / Thursday a.m. Corbridge Cleaners, p.m. gardener / Friday 11am: Waitrose delivery (car to lodge), 3pm tree-surgeon* – indescribably sad. He tried to lose himself in mechanical action, the slice, the spread, the pour. Where were trays? Were these the best plates? Seriously, who kept tomatoes in the fridge and open mustard in the cupboard? Actually, that was some good mustard ... *for helvede*, he should *not* have licked the spoon, now his mouth was burning ... Returning, preceded by a merry jingle of crockery, he met no one.

He used his elbow to lever the doors open, jeopardising the whole enterprise. He considered the fact that this manoeuvre came off to be a good omen.

'Of course,' he said, 'in the books they always *send* for beer and a plate of sandwiches, which is even better. These are chicken, these are rabbit, these just cheese. And you can take the beer to be symbolic if you like, I've got water too.'

Leyla sprang up. 'This,' she said, 'is the best idea you've had all day.'

Once more, the door was locked. Torben, Ruth and Leyla sat around a mass of crumbs and paper. His stomach full, Torben found it easier to withstand the pincer attacks of doubt and conscience. Angst was as nothing in the face of a good lunch.

'Can we start with what we actually know for certain?' said Ruth.

'Amen to that,' said Leyla. 'The crime is murder. The method – we're not disputing this, are we? – is a single shot to the forehead. To continue the running thread: Anthony Dodd, in the bedroom, with the air pistol.' She paused. 'Sorry, that's wrong, isn't it? Unlike Frances and Sara, I've never actually played *Cluedo*. Just in the bedroom, with the air pistol, then. And time of death, between two seventeen and two twenty ... wait, is that a fact?'

'No,' said Ruth.

'After one o'clock but within a few hours of that time, we can probably say,' Torben amended. 'With a working hypothesis that matches the time to what Ruth heard. Before we turn to suspects, I want to note something else about the crime itself. We know that this was a murder disguised as suicide. So far, I think our assumption has been that it was therefore premeditated. Based on our plausible time scale, we've been taking it as read that the killer arrived on the scene with the note already forged.'

'You're not seriously suggesting that someone faked that letter in under three minutes?'

'No, but there *are* two alternatives. One: that the sound of the door closing at two twenty was actually the killer shutting themselves *in* – safe enough, who was going to disturb them at that time? – and settling down to write the note in Anthony's room. All that done, they then took pains to leave silently, some time later – by which point, Ruth was fast asleep.'

'What about the ink?' said Ruth. 'And the nib. We've established that they didn't use Anthony's pen.'

'Well, fair enough, but it's just possible they had their own in a pocket by chance, or that Anthony had a second pen lying around that they took away with them or that we overlooked in our search. The Mont Blanc's cartridge appeared to be full; maybe he saved that for best, or for show, and used another? Anyway, the second possibility is that they left the scene at two twenty, went back to their room to forge the note, and returned silently later on to set it up.'

'Hmm,' said Leyla. 'But since no one was apparently awake or in the corridor until four o'clock at the earliest – that's according to Wilson's testimony – I don't see that it makes any material difference what order they did it in.'

'No,' said Torben. 'But psychologically, it might make *all* the difference. We've been looking at this as calculated, premeditated – as a killing in cold blood. But if it arose from something that only happened – or that the killer only discovered, maybe? – last night, and the cover-up was only thought of *afterwards*, out of panic – which I admit doesn't really fit with the precise forging of the handwriting, but run with it for a moment – then I think we arrive at something more …'

'Forgivable,' said Leyla, with unexpected warmth. Since when had she been the charitable one?

'Well … let's go as far as understandable. Bear in mind that the whole plan had to be concocted fairly quickly, within the space of a few hours at most, once we all heard about Anthony's illness and the will. None of us except Ruth knew before his announcement, did we? A hot-blooded action retrospectively disguised seems far more plausible to me than something completely mapped out in advance.'

And *wasn't* that more forgivable, he thought? All right, the murder of even an already-doomed man was indefensible, but once done, disguising it as suicide – no perpetrator, no victim – was practically doing the decent thing. Why cause more trauma and recrimination than necessary, when it could be presented as an almost merciful tragedy? In a way, he, Torben, had caused more harm than the murderer, in stirring everyone up like this …

'Unless,' said Ruth, whose thoughts had evidently centred on the hot-blooded aspect, 'it was Kirsty, in which case she might have been planning it for far longer—'

'Wait wait wait,' said Leyla. 'I'm trying the stick-to-the-facts thing – and much as I hate to say it, we simply *can't* set up this dichotomy – Kirsty as long-term versus us lot as spur-of-the-moment. How do we know for sure that, even if it *is* one of us, they hadn't been planning it for longer, since getting the invitation even?'

'Ugh,' said Ruth. 'What a horrible thought.'

'We can't, I suppose,' said Torben. 'Sorry. What with Anthony giving us all such a glaring motive last night ... but you're right, Leyla. We can't exclude the possibility that one of us showed up here with – what's that phrase?'

'Malice aforethought,' supplied Leyla.

'Yes, that.' And immediately, he thought of Wilson, whisky glass in hand, sounding off. Of Tom Goring, desperate and delighted to get Anthony on his own.

'I can't pretend that doesn't make a sort of sense,' said Ruth. 'You have to admit the whole thing is unbalanced. Whoever it was clearly had a precise idea of the mechanics of murder, as if they had been thinking about it for a long time, but sloppy execution – sorry, sorry, I didn't mean that as a pun but ... anyway, sloppiness when it came to the more human side of it. To prepare the note, to leave no marks, to time things so exactly – but then to get the wrong hand, to aim for the forehead like a child playing *Grand Theft Auto* ... and it would have been so easy to press the pen against Anthony's fingers once he was dead. The fact that they didn't looks like squeamishness, and I don't blame them.'

'Hmm,' said Torben. 'So what you're saying is, top marks for theory, but they fluffed the reality? Yes, that's all true – but as far as last night goes, I can't see that it makes much difference. Since none of us has been here before – which I think we can assume based on our reactions to the place, and the wording of the invitation – there'd be no way to plan ahead even if the motive *does* go further back. You could show up with murder in your mind, but the mechanics would have to be worked out on the spot.

'For now I just want to have two possible interpretations of the murder in play: the version that is prepared in all particulars, and the more or less spontaneous act that gets covered up. For all we know, Anthony could've taken the gun to the bedroom himself; no

175

one saw him go up. For, I don't know, protection against "gypsies", like he said. That goes for any of us, I suppose – easy enough to nip back down once the house was quiet and dark – but easier still for Anthony, who knew the terrain. Someone came in to see him, they argued, this person snatched up the gun and – *bang*. Or rather *pffft*, as we've conclusively established. In any case, while this last spin on things sounds, now that I say it out loud, the least likely of all, we have to admit its remote possibility.'

'Fine!' said Leyla. 'So the crime is murder in blood of a temperature yet to be determined. What's next? Suspects? Or motive?'

'Suspects,' said Ruth, 'or we'll just keep on dreaming up ways to avoid having this discussion. Motive depends on suspect, after all.'

'Whoever said it earlier was right. No one has an alibi; everyone's a suspect. Let's take them in the order they were interviewed,' said Torben. 'If only because that seems arbitrary enough to guard against too much prejudice on our part. Which means we start with Sara Courtenay.' He paused. He had not meant to use her surname. The formality felt like a form of distancing, and that distancing felt like judgement. Well, why not face it? For better or, almost certainly, for worse, they were here to judge.

'Let's be scientific. I think Sara would like that,' said Ruth. 'Opportunity?'

'Yes,' said Torben. 'By her own account she was in bed by midnight. Leyla, you'd agree, give or take? Then she'd have had a clear run. In fact I think we can take "opportunity" as read for everyone.'

'Not all to the same extent though,' said Leyla. She sounded as if she were talking to herself as much as to them. 'Her room's the furthest away, with the most doors to pass. And there's only me between her and the nearest bathroom, so she'd have no obvious excuse for being out of bed if she met Frances, Wilson or Tom Goring, all of whom were also en route. After that dinner, I don't think "feeling peckish" would wash, and it would be hard to hide that pistol in a dressing gown, it's too bulky. Yes – so really, when you think about it on the grounds of opportunity alone, Sara becomes the *least* likely of our suspects!' She sat back, looking rather pleased with her own logic.

'OK, opportunity: relatively low,' said Torben. 'Set against which, she's the only person whom we definitely know to be lying. What you heard was circumstantial, but it still sounds bad.'

'Motive?' said Ruth.

'Money,' said Torben. 'Fifty thousand pounds. What do we think? *Would* you kill for a sum like that?' He paused. 'You know, I think if you asked anybody – even in private, in total anonymity – pretty much anyone would say "no". Anyone living in a stable western democracy, supported by a functioning welfare state, I mean,' he added. Much as he hated the phrase, he had recently started trying to check his privilege. 'The basically comfortable conditions of our lives – all seven of us have families, friends, places to live … you just wouldn't feel able to articulate that kind of amorality, I don't think, if you had it put to you; it would sound obscene. But … but in the quiet dark of your own thoughts? Alone, perhaps in bed? It's the kind of thinking that creeps in with the night. Fifty thousand. Enough for a deposit, to clear your student debt, to start a business. A useful sum of money; nothing fantastical, but more than any ordinary person is ever likely to come by without outside help. It's the sort of amount that lets you think … well, he's going to die anyway, and he wants me to have it. It's not really hurting anyone.' His voice was getting gradually softer as the idea unfolded. 'Phrases like "a clean death" start to do their work, and then, beneath it all, that thought: what would I do with that sort of money? You can't tell me you wouldn't start making hypothetical plans for the future. And once you've let that possibility in ...'

'In one way,' said Leyla, 'it's just money, and people are greedy. But in another way – I can't believe I'm saying this, I'm a barrister for God's sake – in another way, it's a license to dream. Yes, Torben, in answer to your question. I think fifty thousand pounds *would* turn a lot of people into killers, if the dreams it might buy, the problems it might solve, looked so very much more important than the hellish-sounding final months of a terminally ill man.'

Ruth shook her head. 'I don't want to believe it,' she said. 'But everything I've seen these last few years – you're both right. There's nothing a desperate person won't do if they think it will get them a way out.'

A way out, thought Torben. For Sara – even for Frances, Wilson, himself – hell, maybe even for Tom – that meant a way out of debt, stress, uncertainty. Only the women beside him seemed immune from this motive. Anthony had offered them all a panacea. Was it any wonder that someone had taken him up on it?

Of course, you'd still have to be the right sort of person, to make the leap from thought to deed. If you were naturally timid, or pragmatic even, then news of Anthony's terminal illness might deter you from action – safer to let nature take its course. Alternatively, it might make your mind up for you, if you had been hesitating – a sort of moral green flag to give you the go-ahead. But only if you had a catalyst, some pre-existing motive; especially if you were, what, a born narcissist, or had sociopathic leanings – either that, or entirely desensitised to killing by your experiences or your habits ... and in the absence of ulterior motivation, he didn't think that six years' work on Sherlock Holmes was going to do the trick.

Leyla flushed. 'Well, Sara needs the money more than any of us, that much we can say for certain. It's no secret she's self-funding her PhD, and working crazy hours just to scrape by. Job prospects must be low—?'

Torben nodded. 'Which is no slight on her research, just the state of academia.'

'So, horrible as it sounds, fifty thousand pounds would make a real difference to her – if it came through soon,' said Leyla. 'For all we know, Anthony had several years left to live, by which time, without a job ...'

'Quite,' said Torben. 'It's the difference between a scholarly career and giving up on her dreams. I'm afraid Sara's definitely on the list. Also, didn't you notice, Tom's been the only person to mention the inheritance? And that was only because we asked him about the will first. For the others to ignore the hippo in the room—'

'Elephant,' said Ruth.

'Really? Shame, I like hippo better. Tom reckoned the house was the main motive, which would make Kirsty our suspect number one, but I'm not convinced. Something on that scale, when you know it's coming, you can afford to wait a few years, surely? It's almost too big to rush for – or to jeopardise by doing anything rash. And it certainly wouldn't solve any short-term problems, quite the opposite – there'd be death duties for starters. But the lure of fifty thousand – as you say, Leyla, that's the sort of sum that would be life changing only if it came *at the right time*. Anyway, the point is that everyone's actively avoided the subject of the money, which seems unnatural to me.'

'Sara's been very helpful,' said Ruth.

'So has everyone,' said Torben. 'It would be dangerous not to be. Conspicuous, even. Besides, she was well aware no one else would have had an alibi at that time of night – that came up earlier, didn't it? – so surely it would have been in her interests to help pin down

179

the time of death, to maximise the pool of suspects. If you've picked a moment to commit your crime precisely so that anyone could've done it, you want the detectives to get the time right. In fact, I'm sure Sara could point us to a novel, probably something unnecessarily longwinded by Sayers, where the whole thing turns on the murderer committing the death at a specific time to fit an alibi, and the detectives getting the time wrong, or something. She's bound to be alive to that sort of detail.'

'I hate this,' said Ruth. 'Sorry.'

'I'm sure it'll get easier,' said Torben. 'Which is hardly a consoling thought. Anyway, if that's all we've got for Sara, we should move on.'

'Frances Adair comes next chronologically,' said Leyla, sounding brisk. 'Opportunity: marginally greater, but still at risk of discovery by the boys in the intervening bedrooms.'

'Motive?' said Ruth. Leyla hesitated.

'Honestly, it's personal gain all round, isn't it?' said Torben. 'And if "gain" sounds too petty, then try "desperation". We don't know anything for sure about *anyone*'s personal finances. If one of us has some major debt that's getting called in soon, then that person immediately has a first-class incentive. As for Frances in particular – well, she's a sculptor, that makes her part of the precariat. Anyway, it's a classic motive, even if it lacks psychological interest.'

'Hmm,' said Ruth.

'What?'

'Well, it's just … look, I know we said to stick to facts, but …' Her eyes flickered to each of their faces, then down at the table. Then she sucked in her lips. Torben, looking on, was mystified.

'Well, since we've started on Frances,' Ruth said at last, clearly hating every word of what she was saying, 'don't we think she might have been trying to cover for Sara?'

'But their stories didn't match,' said Torben.

Ruth shrugged. 'Maybe she realised that Leyla could have overheard something? Or she decided on a safe amount of the truth to tell – admitting they had talked, which would be dangerous to deny in case Sara had been spotted, but not the substance of that talk, which was likelier to be private?'

'What happened to sticking to facts?' said Leyla.

Ruth threw up her hands. 'Frankly, if it comes to *facts* I'd put her down as likelier to have carried it out than Sara – from a detached, practical perspective, I mean,' she said. 'You saw Sara today, the way she carried on this morning, and then her queasiness later. Set against which, Frances is a professional artist. She'd have no trouble imitating Anthony's handwriting, nor in staging the whole thing.'

'In which case,' said Torben, 'you might as well ask why she didn't make it look *more* convincing. The wrong hand, the shot in the centre of the forehead, the ink, the lack of prints – these are *aesthetic* details.'

'But would even an artist think of those things half drunk, scared, in the dark?' said Ruth. 'And here's another objective fact. Frances owns the supplest, most beautiful pair of gloves I've ever seen. I imagine most of us have thicker, more practical things – more practical for keeping the cold out, I mean.'

'That's a fair point,' said Leyla. 'They really are gorgeous. And they certainly helped when it came to picking things up earlier – so useful, in fact, that we forgot to be surprised that she was wearing them indoors.'

'I might observe,' said Torben, 'that that's probably because she doesn't like to have all her chisel scars and calluses on show.' He thought back. Even a decade ago her hands had been marked with cuts. He had had ample opportunity to study them. 'Or I don't know, poor circulation? It could be anything. But of course I wouldn't want to get involved.'

Leyla let out a – well, you could only call it a snort. 'Maybe we should wrap up Frances,' she said. 'One other thing did occur to me though: if she *was* covering for Sara – if they were in it together or if one was masking the other – surely they'd have concocted a mutual alibi?'

'For quarter past two in the morning?' said Ruth.

Torben laughed. 'All right,' he said. '*Så er den ged barberet*. Let's bracket them both as possibles. But we've nothing definite against either of them.'

'Wilson Ho then,' said Leyla. 'Opportunity: slightly better again. Have you noticed we're inching closer, bedroom by bedroom? It's almost like we're heading somewhere.'

'Not helpful,' said Ruth, whose patience was – in another first – apparently finite.

'Sorry,' said Leyla. 'Well then. We all remember – actually, maybe Torben doesn't – that Wilson was the one who first asked Anthony how the pistols worked? Though he didn't turn out to be a very good shot, did he?'

'Yes, I wondered about that,' said Torben, ignoring the jibe. 'I swear he was a better marksman than that when we were on that stupid boys' holiday. Or maybe I'm just getting muddled with all the *Call of Duty* he used to play. What about motive, then?'

'I assume,' said Leyla, 'that as a jobbing thesp, he's in the same boat financially as Frances and Sara? Though his career seems to be picking up at last – and isn't his family pretty well off? We all heard him carrying on about servants and butlers.'

'That needn't mean he's well supported,' said Ruth. 'Especially if his parents were unhappy at his choice of profession. I always had the impression he was reading PPE because he was expected to go into banking or something; they might have cut him off when he turned his back on a respectable career. On the other hand …' She faltered.

Torben regarded her. 'On the other hand,' he said, taking over, 'Wilson also has a second motive. One that – rather like those sandwiches – is best eaten cold.'

'You knew?' said Ruth.

'He let it slip before dinner, yesterday,' said Torben. 'It's true then?'

Leyla actually growled in frustration.

Ruth sighed. 'This is ancient history, Leyla, but Wilson has … well, a pretty legitimate grievance against Anthony.'

'So do you, in that case,' Torben said.

She waved this away. 'STONi,' she explained. 'The original idea – the entire premise, the ability to locate a missing object by calling it with your phone – it all came from Wilson.'

'And Anthony "stole" it?' said Leyla. They could both hear the scare quotes she put around the word.

'Oh, you're quite right,' said Ruth. 'Nothing that would stand up in court. And obviously having ideas is nothing compared to seeing them through. Wilson's often said as much himself; I never thought he really *blamed* Anthony. And yes, the STONi *name* was my idea – but again, it was all just talk. Late-night dreaming. It's not like we even wrote anything down – and I was more proud than anything else when Anthony made something of it. You all remember how quiet he went after undergrad – none of us heard from him for, what, two years? It must have consumed him, turning that idea into a viable business, getting investors, the advertising – it went global in no time, suddenly everyone had STONi chips on speed-dial – next to that, neither of our contributions stacks up to much, not really. *I* certainly never begrudged him his success. But perhaps …'

'There was certainly *some* resentment there,' said Torben, 'based on his attitude last night. And then, when the will came out – maybe he'd expected some extra recognition, or something?'

'It wouldn't surprise me,' said Ruth. 'In that case, a legacy of fifty thousand wouldn't be a temptation so much as a provocation ... Oo, and don't you remember, Leyla, at the Gaudy, two years ago – before Anthony sold up? Wilson was fuming because Anthony had offered to back this production he was slated to star in, but was insisting on slapping STONi advertising all over the programmes and posters. I think Wilson turned him down in the end.'

'Something at the Arcola, wasn't it?' said Leyla.

'Yes, Jon and I went to see it,' said Ruth, 'which was a mistake – too much nudity and cross-casting for his taste! Yes, it's coming back to me, sort of an experimental take on *As You Like It*.'

'"Blow, blow, thou winter wind"?' said Torben. 'Hmm. I can see why, in the circumstances, Wilson would've thought Anthony was being rather tactless.'

'So that was it,' said Leyla. 'I couldn't quite make sense of it at the time – surely that's just how theatre financing works – but if Wilson felt entitled to the credit, or the intellectual property or whatever, then being patronised like that must have been unbearable. I know *I* certainly wouldn't have stood for it.' She shook her head. 'And of course that explains all his posturing this afternoon – he thought you were going to bring this up, and he wanted the chance to defend himself.'

'Which we didn't give him,' said Ruth. 'Maybe that was unfair. But you know what he's like with a monologue, once he gets started ...'

'It would have thrown us,' said Torben. 'And we wanted to get on to Tom. You did the right thing, Ruth. Wilson always wants to get the last word, I sort of love him for it—' And he broke off. That phrase, *the last word*, had reminded him of something.

'What is it?' said Leyla.

'After dinner!' said Torben. 'Ruth, what was it you told me this morning? You spoke to Kirsty before she left, just to say thank you,

184

and she told you that she thought Anthony was getting better? Well, I've just remembered something: Wilson was standing right behind you. He'd have heard the whole thing.'

'Which would have spurred on someone who really needed the money right now,' said Leyla, 'but doesn't fit the revenge narrative quite so well.'

'Well, Wilson's always struck me as the sort of person who runs up debts,' said Ruth. 'Which is shameful of me. But—'

'He's also the sort of person who can't keep a secret,' said Torben. 'So if Wilson had that information, he might have shared it with anyone by the time we all went to bed.'

They all let this sink in.

'That puts him top of the list, anyway,' said Ruth. 'And, as an actor, he might back himself to brazen it out.' She blinked. 'And we're back into speculation. Sorry. Let's move on – Tom Goring.' This formality at least sounded natural. He was the sort of person that you thought of by his full name.

'Opportunity: best of all,' said Torben. 'The last one to see Anthony alive, with only a bathroom between them in the corridor.'

'Motive, though,' said Leyla. 'Compared to the others, he must be the best off.'

'Hmm,' said Torben.

'What?'

'Oh, nothing – nothing I can put my finger on, anyway.' He sighed. What was it that had made him think Tom was in pressing need of cash? 'We know so little of anyone's private circumstances, and it's not like we can ask them … We could ask Wilson about Tom, I suppose, they're still close, but Wilson has a pretty highly developed sense of – what would you call it? Loyalty? Honour? It seems the one sort of secret he'd actually be able to keep …'

'Tom also seems to have actively enjoyed Anthony's company,' said Leyla. 'And to have kept way more in touch with him than the rest of us – until recently, at least. He was so disappointed when Anthony wasn't at the Gaudy. And it doesn't sound like Anthony was at his wedding.'

'Interesting,' said Torben. 'Before dinner yesterday, he was saying something about being desperate for a "decent one-on-one" with Anthony.'

'Which is more than can be said for most of us,' Leyla said. 'We're just a bunch of spongers, really.'

'Well, we are now we've been made beneficiaries,' said Torben. 'I had the impression we were all just naturally curious to see what this place was like, and then Anthony went and turned us into parasites.' And he felt a faint aftershock of the fury that had seized him the night before. Let it go, he told himself. 'Tom seems keen to exonerate us all, anyway. According to him, fifty thousand is chicken feed – you know, I almost think he's protesting too much? – and we're just the sideshow in this sordid tale of profit.'

'Yes, what about his story?' said Ruth. 'If we take him at his word, it's pretty damning.'

'We need a new heading,' said Leyla. 'Kirsty … Kirsty what? Dodd?'

'Kirsty X,' said Torben. 'And frankly, I can't believe Tom's evidence that Kirsty is Anthony's sister. Or rather, I believe Tom heard *something*, and got confused.'

He thought about Kirsty. Her homely accent. Her deferential struggle to keep Ruth from getting under her feet, and into her kitchen. The sumptuous dinner. That pie – that glorious pie. Surely nothing evil could come from the same hands that had concocted that masterpiece? Well, except the frozen nightmare of a salad that had accompanied it, he supposed. That had been pretty malicious.

'It's a hell of a lot of interpretation to put on a few chance phrases,' he said, striving for a more scientific basis for his defence of her character. 'Just the sort of thing we were trying *not* to do with Sara and Frances. But here we seem to have gone from some mumbled line about houses, to a secret return in the dead of night, the use of a mysteriously silent staircase, and a crime committed at great personal risk of discovery in the midst of a house full of potential witnesses, when she had him to herself every other day – with total control over what went into his meals thrown into the bargain. Why would someone who cooks for a man who's practically her captive wait until the house was full of people in order to *shoot* him? She could have killed him whenever she wanted, with no witnesses.'

'But don't you see?' said Leyla. 'That's coming at it backwards! We're not a house full of potential witnesses, we're a house of potential *suspects*. At literally any other time, Kirsty would be the prime, practically the only suspect in a case of murder. Her only chance of getting away with it would be to do it when there were other people around to take the blame. It's logically perfect. *You* just feel uncomfortable trusting the word of an offensive, public-school bore over that of a working-class female carer. Torben, I'd love to agree with you, but in my bitter legal experience, it's the crashing bores – the counsels who make Latin quips with the judge, the clients who play golf with them on Sundays – it's just that sort of person who tends to be in the right, technically if not morally. And surely, setting ethics to one side, it's easier to accept that a total stranger might be a murderer than one of your oldest friends. Which isn't grounds for complacency, or bigotry, or anything – I just think, in this particular instance, that it makes more sense.'

'I have to agree,' said Ruth. 'I liked Kirsty very much. But what you said, Torben, about the hot-blooded option? Well, if it was one of us, it *does* seem pretty rash, or at least impatient. I mean, killing him just hours after finding out about the will, in a house full of people? I can't make that square, in my head, with the calm forging of the note; it seems so … self-possessed. Is any of us that *efficient*? On the other hand, what Leyla says fits perfectly. If Kirsty had always been planning to do it last night, when we were all here to take the blame and the attention, then of course she'd have the note all worked out and ready to go. She knew Anthony was going to announce the will, she was in the next room when it happened; why, he even gave it to her to take away! The perfect red herring was literally in her hands. I'm sorry. She's got to go top of the list, even without this story that she's Anthony's sister.'

'Which is a pretty monstrous thought,' said Leyla. 'Not just the idea of murdering your sibling, I mean, but the whole situation. Can you imagine being in that position? Waiting on your own brother hand and foot – and having to keep it a secret from his friends into the bargain? I'm sorry, but a person who could put up with that … or, put more fairly, I can easily imagine finding that situation literally intolerable. The resentment would be crushing. What did you say last night about "intolerable circumstances" leading to crime, Ruth? Throw the prospect of inheriting this place into the mix, and it starts to look pretty bad for Ms Kirsty X. It doesn't matter that we sympathise. In fact, that only makes it more plausible.'

'And she *definitely* thought Anthony was getting better,' said Ruth. 'If she thought her promised windfall was in danger of being snatched away, or indefinitely postponed …'

Torben shook his head. 'Using that information against Kirsty is perverse, don't you see? It was Kirsty who told you that in the first place! What soon-to-be murderer confides one of their key motives to a police inspector just before committing the crime? Oh, make her suspect number one if you like. Ignore the fact that, if this is in fact just a job for her, she'd get her inheritance either way in the end – assuming she's written into the will at all – and that she has a not unenviable position of security in the meantime. Ignore the half-dozen other inconsistencies that arise when you make it an outside job. We're tired. I know we all feel morally soiled by now but I've just realised that physically I am also extremely dirty and wearing yesterday's clothes. Can we knock this on the head for today? No one's going anywhere, all our evidence is circumstantial, and I'm incapable of any more thought until I've had a bath. I *need* a bath. That at least is undeniable.'

He saw their nostrils twitch, perhaps involuntarily. And neither of them denied it.

While the bath reminded Torben, once again, a little too much of David's *Death of Marat* for comfort, it was nonetheless hot, foaming and capacious. One of those freestanding copper baths that you saw on house programmes – with the added virtue of being dignified by age, as witnessed by the creep of verdigris across its dulled exterior. Still, it conducted the heat superbly. Across the room, a fire danced in the grate. With only a single window facing north into the sheltered courtyard, the din of the storm was mercifully silenced. He was alone with his thoughts, and that was company enough. His eyes closed.

When he awoke, the water was tepid. But he knew two things he had not known before. There was a third possible motive in play, besides gain and revenge. For, when you put it all together, hadn't Anthony practically been *begging* to be killed? Stressing the pain that was in store, whilst dangling the reward before them? If he *was* still a Catholic, mightn't it just be possible that he was looking for an easy way out, one that wouldn't cost him his soul? Some sophistic loophole in the theological rules against self-destruction, a sort of sin-free euthanasia? Which meant, rather unflatteringly, that Anthony by this theory considered at least one of them capable of murder – but, on the other hand, it also made that murder a little less cruel. Almost an act of ... an act of mercy.

This was going further than his earlier thought – that, by disguising the murder as a suicide, the killer was doing the decent thing. It framed the whole affair as something that could be carried out with the best of intentions. And wasn't it often the case that terrible things were perpetrated by people convinced they were in the right? If the murderer thought themselves to be acting mercifully rather than from self-interest, however disingenuous that thought might be, then it opened up a whole new sphere of troubling possibilities.

And, secondly, if you extended to its natural extreme the logic that the safest course of action for the murderer would be to act naturally, to respond to each fresh revelation just like the innocent majority, secure in the knowledge that the available evidence was diffuse and circumstantial, and that so long as they didn't draw attention to themselves, the chances of being found out were a hundred to one against ... well, where did you end up?

What was that English phrase about poachers and gamekeepers?

Torben grimaced as he watched the water swirl away. At least he was clean on the outside now.

13

SUNDAY, EIGHT P.M.

Somehow, they all arrived in the kitchen at more or less the same time. Torben, his stomach actually rumbling, found Ruth and Sara laying out plates, each giving the other a wide berth around the central island – and when he tried to join in, Sara set down her stack and slunk back to lean against the Aga, arms folded. It was too small a space to sustain this hostility, but evidently, no one fancied the prospect of returning to the dark cavern of the dining room. He resolved to eat his portion of leftover pie swiftly – no problem there – and retire as early as possible.

Just as they were all sitting down, however – Torben, Ruth and Leyla squeezed absurdly on one of the four sides – Tom Goring spoke up. 'Hey, guys, are we seriously—' He stopped; coughed. 'What I mean is, I think the least we can do right now is have a minute's silence. A minute's silence where we think about Ant, and then do our best to share our favourite memories of him over dinner.'

Torben looked at Tom Goring – who, standing, his face purpling, was still scarcely taller than Wilson, sitting at his side. Somehow there was a dignity to Tom, a moral force, that impressed him. And it solved the question of how they were to get through dinner in a civilised fashion.

At last, Frances broke the silence. 'Och, why not?' Her voice was bright, with the false jollity of a children's television host. 'Though I suppose,' she said, reverting to type, 'the last thirty seconds of us all looking at you mutely doesn't count? We have to begin again?'

'Well yes, Frances, obviously we have to begin again,' muttered Sara.

Tom sat down. Point won, he looked suddenly sheepish.

'Actually, shouldn't we all stand up?'

'Who'll time it?'

Torben looked down instinctively at his own wrist, the slightly lighter skin that showed where his watch should be. Raising his eyes, he met Tom's, who had followed his movement. 'Er, I suppose I'll do it,' Tom said, hastily looking away. 'Yeah, let's … let's stand.' They shuffled to their feet. 'Starting … now.'

Torben closed his eyes. The last thing he wanted was anyone thinking he was trying to read their mind.

Traces; images. Little flits of thought, half-grasped, to chase or to flee.

Sara struggled to focus. It was like being back at school, always unable to concentrate on the thing she was meant to be commemorating. Yes, it would help appease her conscience, to honour Anthony now that his retribution had been delivered. OK, 'honour' was the wrong word; it was those assemblies again, poppies and prayers, fidgety eyes, the terrible year she'd needed to cough, tried not to, and ended up more or less choking— there, she was doing it again! Wandering off. Stick to Anthony, the good bits rather than the recently revealed sex pest: the generous host, the expert organiser, the boy who'd once taken one look at her revision schedule, snorted, and produced a seamless workflow diagram in fifteen minutes flat. Which only reminded her of next week's crunch, those two extra shifts refusing to reconcile with her imminent chapter deadline ...

Tom found himself thinking, not of the Anthony of yesterday, or the deep-pocketed tycoon he had gone begging to with increasing regularity over the past decade, nor even of the sudden stranger who had cut all ties a year ago, casting him adrift and re-evaluating what he had always thought of as a real friendship, but of the boy of eighteen. Whatever had passed between them of late, he couldn't let it sully his memories of that boy in those more innocent days. Nervy, a bit awkward, a bit overawed. A natural ally. It had helped, having someone like that, had really steadied him that whole first year, the one good year before things had ... no, not that; think of Ant. The dirty jokes, the pints they had shared. The evenings they had spent side by side in simultaneous essay crises, scribbling their wrists off, trying to keep the spill of facts from tumbling out of their fuggy brains. The reassurance of having someone to glance at, to back you up that yes, you were the sane one, and that whatever nonsense Torben or Leyla was spouting was exactly that: nonsense.

Ruth knew that, if she relaxed her guard for even half of this minute, she would almost certainly start crying. She tried to fix her mind on where Anthony might be now, on her hopes for his salvation. For some reason, the image of her husband, Jon, rose before her – the last thing she wanted to think about. In her mind's eye, he looked like she had seen him last: face contorted with a petulant anger, so jealous of this other life of hers, so disapproving of these old friends, atheists and artists. Why oh why did she have to think of this now? Probably it was the way they were all standing round the same table in silence. She had met Jon in just such a circle, felt his hand upon her head, the sudden warmth, the intimation of a presence – been unsure whether this was really the Spirit moving through them or something more earthbound; either way, she'd asked him for a coffee at the end of the session – could still remember his start of surprise, the nagging implication that she should have let *him* make the first move – could remember, too, the point a year or two ago when she had looked again, as ever, for that inspirational energy, and failed to find it … She frowned. Grace is infinite, she reminded herself.

Despite himself, Wilson was back there, in Anthony's untidy room, *Settlers of Catan* spread out on the standard-issue coffee table. He could even picture the layout of the pieces. That damn ringtone, going right through his head, just as it had done nearly every night for eleven years. He'd hoped that his actions this weekend would silence it once and for all. But then, it turned out the curtain hadn't fallen yet – perhaps, after the funeral, it would finally shut the fuck up, give him the closure he had sought? It had come up on *QI* once, the Nokia ringtone, turned out it was a waltz by some Spanish dude. They hadn't paid *him* a penny either – but then, he had died in 1909. FFS, Wilson Ho, he thought, his mind sounding out the initials. How could you have been so stupid?

It was a pity, thought Leyla, that – having gone to the trouble of reheating the pie in the Aga – they were now giving it the chance to go cold. Maybe they should have warmed the plates.

Forty-nine, thought Frances. Fifty. Fifty-one …

'I was just thinking,' said Wilson, as they finally tucked in, 'how he would have loved that. You know Anthony – always wore a poppy, always bowed his head for grace at formal hall, always loved a speech … so yeah, basically: nice one, Tom.'

Tom beamed.

'D'you remember,' said Sara, also smiling, 'that speech of his in second year?'

'That's not exactly specific,' said Ruth.

'Oh, come off it, we all know the one,' said Leyla, smirking. She'd seemed much more herself ever since they'd made the case against Kirsty, perhaps because it allowed her to feel she was safely among friends again. '*That* speech. He got us all along to that special talk for the History Society, because he'd secured this big name in Anglo-Saxon studies or whatever it was. God knows why we all went.'

'The drinks were free,' Frances reminded her.

'Oh shit, wasn't that the one where—?'

'Yup,' said Sara. And suddenly they were staring at Torben.

'What?' he said. And then he too remembered. 'Oh, yes – look, I told you at the time, it was an honest mistake—' He was aware he was blushing now.

Anthony had made a great show of introducing the distinguished speaker – going so far as to speak from flash cards – and he had earnt the moment, the result of weeks of email chasing. But his introductory speech, dwelling on the scholar's contribution to the understanding of heredity and succession laws in pre-Conquest English society, had featured the word 'lineage' no fewer than five times, at each of which, Anthony had pronounced it—

'"Line-idge",' said Ruth, shaking her head. 'I remember now.'

'And then he paused before his closing words,' said Wilson, barely able to suppress his laughter, 'and there was this silence, and *you*' – pointing his fork at Torben – 'just came out with, in, like, the loudest whisper ever, "Isn't it pronounced "lineage?"' And finally his mirth spilled over.

'Ant dealt with it bloody well, I thought,' said Tom. 'Went a bit pink and dropped his cards, but he got the thing done, didn't he?'

'It was certainly more memorable than whatever old professor what's-her-name spent the next hour talking about,' said Frances. 'Thank Christ for the champagne.'

'I never meant—'

'It was hilarious,' said Sara. 'And actually, I liked Anthony a whole lot more after that.'

'You had to sympathise with the guy,' said Wilson. 'I mean, seriously. If I ever got a heckle like that …'

Torben hid his face in his hands. He still couldn't tell if they really understood how he'd spent more than a year grappling with the idiosyncrasies of English as spoken in Oxford: how half of them said 'Charwell' instead of 'Cherwell'; being introduced to people with surnames spelt Featherstonehaugh or St John, who called themselves Fanshaw and Sinjen; realising how many Americanisms had slipped past his guard; the number of idioms he still misused. And above all the fact that, like the idiot he was, he had thought this was all about not being a native speaker, rather than about subtler, more insidious forms of distinction, of class and of region. Certainly Anthony had not understood, had taken it personally … Well, too late to make amends now. If anything it sounded like Anthony should be thanking him, for endearing him to the rest of them. And he felt again the familiar flare of guilt, of resentment, at how Anthony Dodd was there at the heart of his greatest embarrassments, every time. If the bastard had only practised his speech to someone beforehand, but oh no, he had to keep it to himself—

He looked up. Leyla was nudging him. 'Tor,' she said. 'If you're not going to eat that …'

Everyone seemed slightly subdued as the dinner broke up, which was at least appropriate. And no one was jumping down Torben's throat anymore – perhaps Tom's rather clumsy idea had actually done the group some good. Well, that was something. It had not improved Torben's own mood one jot, however. Enforced thinking was bad enough – enforced thinking about Anthony, even worse – and extended reflection upon their own shared past, worst of all.

In a gesture of – what, atonement, irritation? – Torben declared that he would wash up, and chivvied them all from the room. Inevitably, Ruth lingered. He wished, for once, that she wouldn't. He suspected something was going on. And, just as he had got the water temperature exactly right, his suspicions were confirmed.

'That minute's silence,' she said, scraping crumbs from a plate into the bin. 'Could I, could I ask—?'

'You could,' he said. 'But I have the right to remain silent.'

'It's just,' she said, undeterred, 'you had your eyes shut – but your jaw was all … oh, Torben, what *were* you thinking about, to make you look like that?'

'I was trying *not* to think,' he said. He did not need to add, *and I failed*. His mood must have been legible, then.

'Mm,' she said.

He passed her a clean plate. 'The drying rack's pretty capacious,' he observed. 'It's probably more hygienic just to let them …'

'Fine,' she said. 'Fine.' And, flinging down her tea towel, she stalked from the room.

The problem was, he thought later, as he manoeuvred a morose Oral B toothbrush around the contours of his mouth, the particular memory of Anthony that had arisen, insistent, during those sixty seconds, was ten times worse than 'line-idge'.

Ruth was waiting for him outside the bathroom. Longing for bed, for oblivion, he couldn't help but feel collared. Typical, he thought, that she had chosen the bathroom rather than his bedroom for her attack: whatever was going on in her marriage, she clearly wasn't ready to revert to undergraduate levels of intimacy.

'I just think,' she said, 'that it would help if you got it off your chest.'

'Ruth,' he said, 'please. I need to sleep. If it puts your mind at rest, I can confidently state that this information is not germane to the enquiry.'

'I mean,' she said, 'that it would help *you*. It's something awful, isn't it? And it makes you feel guilty? Look, I'm no Catholic. But I think ... I think you could use a confessor.'

For helvede. How did she always know?

Leaning up against the lip of the bath, he eyed Ruth warily. Admittedly, perched on the edge of the loo seat, her rimmed eyes full of worry, she could not have looked less like a chair-straddling, lamp-shining, inquisitorial copper. But that was half the problem. She was Ruth. And there were details about this particular memory that he didn't want to share with her of all people.

'It will help,' she said. 'Getting it out. All of this – I honestly think it will make the rest of it a lot easier.'

She was almost *too* sympathetic. And in that moment, Torben realised something that Ruth had probably known ages ago. This whole hornet's nest that Torben had kicked – how much of it was about atonement? Or rather his desire to lay the ghost of his guilt about Anthony; that, by solving his murder, he might cancel out the resentment, the snobbery, all the least edifying parts of his own past?

'It's about the old days, isn't it?' she said. He must have been silent for longer than he'd thought.

'Mm,' he said. 'I've been thinking a lot, since this morning, that if I could have that time again ... or, or if there was a moment when it tipped, that broke me and Anthony forever. And during that stupid minute's silence, there was, I don't know – it must be like that phrase "don't think of an elephant" – honestly, it's always elephants in English, isn't it? – I mean, the one thing I *didn't* want to remember, sort of forced itself upon me. Sorry, is this— this is boring for you.'

She shook her head; smiled. 'I'm all ears,' she said. 'Like an elephant.'

He grimaced. 'I'm not sure we've ever had the whole Anthony conversation, not properly. All this talk of commemorating – and I still can't get past how much I've always resented him. At first I thought that whole persona was an act – the bluff northern thing, the cynicism, it seemed so ... so dated ... and that beneath that there was a real person I could get through to, you know – maybe he was just shy? It was interesting. I think it was when I discovered it *was* serious that I stopped taking *him* seriously. I've never met anyone with such a total lack of any sense of humour – and considering how many Swedes I know, that's saying something. He had no ability to laugh at himself. That seemed inhuman to me.'

'Inhuman?' said Ruth. 'Implying there's some objective set of prescribed human characteristics? Hmm. But you're right about one thing, he was never exactly ... self-aware. He had such a chip on his shoulder after first year, and he worked so hard to keep it there ... maybe that grievance was what he needed, I don't know – the excuse he needed to give up on academic achievement without losing face, the grudge he needed to fuel his energies in developing STONi. And it got more toxic by the day. There was a time in second year, when he'd developed his whole grievance against "The Man" and the Oxford system, that he kept telling me how hard it was to be an outsider. Telling *me*, Torben!'

'That's – that's taking solipsism to a whole new level. I don't know how you stood for it. Well, I suppose I do; you're Ruth Thompson. But it just made it very, very tricky, you know?' Torben sighed. 'And never more so – to finally get to the point – than on this one occasion that's been playing in my head non-stop since dinner. It was the morning after the Freshers' Week Bop in our second year – otherwise known as The Year We Wore All The Scarves. Technically I think they called it a "Re-freshers' Ball" … You and Leyla weren't there, were you, or Tom for that matter – you'd been hit by that really harsh early dead-line by one of your Law tutors …'

It was, he thought, precisely *because* Leyla hadn't been there that it had all happened. In her absence – and the absence of Ruth's civi-lising influence – he had spent rather too much of the party dancing with Frances. He closed his eyes, remembering the night: the resid-ual heat of an Indian summer, the close-pressed bodies, the music, her scent. It had been Disney themed, of all things; he had gone as the Beast, and Frances … Frances had of course been Ariel. In hind-sight, what ensued had probably been inevitable.

Despite himself, scenes from that night flashed through his mind. Those sea-shells … that tail. Frances had a room in Meadows build-ing – so as to be near the Art Room, she claimed, but probably for the sake of the first-floor balcony looking out over the Meadow itself. At night, that whole vast space was deserted, every gate locked until morning, and they had – they had spent some time out on the bal-cony. Frances had draped herself over the stone parapet—

'Anyway,' said Torben, taking the night itself as read, 'obviously I wish it hadn't happened. But I don't think I've ever been more blissfully happy than the next morning. I mean, you know, drunkenly, stupidly happy. Like a bee stumbling about in a load of honey.'

'Sticky,' said Ruth.

'Sorry,' said Torben. 'But the context is important – the point is,

I was on top of the world. Anyway it was very early when she kicked me out; there was a mist rising from the Meadow, and the light – such light! I had got back into my Beast's outfit, I had no choice, but I was sort of proud too, I suppose. I just wanted – wanted to be alone with my thoughts. Happy thoughts.'

'Mm-hm.'

'Wait, I'm getting to the point.' He had started, so he'd finish. 'Because it was right then that I bumped into Anthony of all people just coming in through the Meadows gate. Must've been out for a dawn walk by the river. He looked rough as hell – he'd stayed dancing longer than us, I suppose – and obviously he was the last person I wanted to see right then. I remember that he literally wrinkled his nose and sniffed, which was rich considering the state of him – I mean, I must've smelt pretty ripe, but still, the way he reacted … Anyway, he walked halfway back across college with me and, you know what, he chose *that* moment to pick a fight? About my costume of all things!'

He had been wearing, he remembered, the blue mess jacket and breeches of a Danish guards regiment – God knows which one – picked up in a vintage store on Strøget over the summer. In the low light of a disco, you didn't notice the moth-holes. For some reason Anthony had taken issue with this, going from the understandable incomprehension of *where do you find those clothes?* to the outright aggression of *what gives you the right to think you can dress like that in public?* in a few short sentences. It was, apparently, disrespectful to armed forces everywhere. But that hadn't been Anthony's real problem, he thought.

'He got fixated on the idea that I found everything so *easy*, that it all came naturally, my – I think he called it my pretentiousness. Which was accurate. It was a sort of affront to his whole industrious, head-down ethic I suppose; he was so hung up on the idea that things just fell into my lap, that I took things for granted … and for the space of a single second I was so totally, utterly pissed off at him standing there and going on at me – and at the same time so, I don't know, I felt lighter than air after, well, you know – that I just looked at this preposterous, flat-footed person, standing like a blot in the way of my sun – yes, I think I really did see him like that, I know it's awful, and it's no excuse but he was *literally* blocking the light … but obviously, I couldn't say that – you just can't say "I don't want you in my life" to someone unless you're, I don't know, married – why is it that it's socially acceptable to unilaterally end a romantic relationship, but not a friendship? And it was then, I think, that whatever had held between us, the ties of social obligation, whatever we had in common – it was then it snapped, for me. I could never think of him again as anything but a burden. He was just this person in my life, making it worse, and if I could have clicked my fingers and have him vanish I'd – I'd have done it.'

Torben took a long breath. 'It seems, from the fact he invited me this weekend, that he got over that break between us. I … well, clearly, I never did. I'm still judging him, even now. And it appears I'm trying to solve his murder, not because it's the right thing to do, but to get him off my back. It's … it's a hell of a thing to realise about yourself. Here you are, Ruth, doing this for the sake of justice, and I'm … doing it in order to be rid of him?'

Ruth looked away. 'It sounds,' she said, 'like he was just … well, jealous. For all his disdain for your way of looking at the world, there must've been something there that he envied. Would that have been so hard to forgive?'

'Well of course, I see that *now*! I'd like to think that I was too humble back then to think for a minute that anyone could envy me, but, at least that morning, I was feeling pretty damn cocky. I was …

I was just young, and full of opinions, and – and incapable of *seeing* him properly. Neither of us was capable of that basic leap of empathy. I hope I'd have handled it all better if it happened now. But given how little I seem to have changed, I'm not so sure. He certainly did a lot more growing up than me in the time since.'

'We *were* teenagers. Just children really.' It was almost as if it were Ruth who was pleading now, making excuses – for Torben? For Anthony? For herself, so close back then to both of them, with all this happening under her nose? 'None of us really had any sort of control over our emotions. Each of us in a private hurricane of feeling, our eyes turned in. We were constantly being taught to think only about ourselves, first at school, then at university – it was always our studies, our careers, our needs …'

'I know, I know.' Despite himself, Torben found himself responding to her argument. 'Nineteen! At that age, we just sort of guess what bits of life to take seriously – of course we get a lot of it wrong. Or maybe I should use the past tense? Some of my students seem so much more informed than we were at their age, on – on the climate, on consent … but still, they make mistakes. Nineteen!'

He shook his head. Weren't they straying from the point? She was trying to offer him a way out, he could see that. To show him that somewhere a distance was opening up, between the boy he had been and the man he was now. Did it help? He still felt the guilt. But he was starting to hope that the arrogant, disdainful boy he had been – the boy that Anthony had brought to the fore – might just have died along with Dodd.

He looked at Ruth, desperate after all for the forgiveness in her gaze. But either she had given up on following his train of thought, or something else was going on. And now she rose, with infinite care, and placed a hand over his mouth. 'Hear that?' she whispered.

And he did. Beyond the door, the sound of hurried feet and raised voices, coming nearer. Silent as Ruth now, he stepped to the door, easing it ajar.

Frances and Sara, at the head of the stairs. By the uncharacteristic sound of their step – clumping, irregular – at least one of them was drunk. When Frances spoke, he could hear the tears behind her voice, the words ragged. When Sara spoke across her, he could hear the anger.

'—of *course* if it'd happened today or, well not today obviously but like, a year ago, of *course* I'd've said—'

'—still can't get my head around the fact that you *never*, in all this time, thought to tell me; why in the world you chose last night of all nights—'

'—thought I'd put it behind me, but being face to face with him again—'

'—not that I'm saying it wasn't the right thing to do, but if anyone gets wind of—'

'—I mean, if it'd happened a year ago I'd just've sued the fucker for every penny—'

At the word 'penny' it was as if Sara came to her senses; realised where they were. 'Frances,' she said.

'Still,' said Frances, sniffing, heedless, 'it's finished now, isn't it? So long as—'

'Frances,' Sara said again, her voice hard. 'Frances, for fuck's sake *shut up. Now.* Someone could hear us.'

Behind him, Ruth leaned closer, and the bathroom door gave a creak that echoed down the cold corridor, breaking through even Frances' tear-streaked protestations. There was a hiss, a gulp, and the muffled sound of what might have been a blow. And then their footsteps, faster now and fading, and the slamming shut of a bedroom door.

14

MONDAY, EIGHT A.M.

She could get used to this, Ruth thought. Waking up alone. How was it that she slept better here, in a snowstorm – in the middle of a murder enquiry – in the middle of the *countryside* – than she did in Limehouse? Without the comfort of Jon's body beside her, gym-hard and yet, at least when he was still asleep, so well fitted to her own; of the murmuring traffic that reminded her (she liked to imagine) of sand and shore. Was it the bluster and rattle of wind and window, the sense of connection with something bigger – or higher – that loomed beyond, ready to take her in its billows, enfold and girdle? The sensation, despite it all, of holiday? Or, just maybe, the freedom afforded by a clearly defined problem with a neat solution …

Of course, this sense of freedom could not be about being away from Jon himself. The thought was absurd – after all, he was her husband, not her keeper. *Definitely* not her keeper since he'd quit his job in accounting to become a full-time youth pastor, quite the reverse in fact. But it wasn't that she was feeling the lifting of the pressure – the quite natural, unavoidable resentment that any man might feel at no longer being the breadwinner, especially a man as … traditional, that was the word, as traditional in his values as Jon. And even that was unfair on him; after all, there was nothing traditional about him marrying a Black girl, was there? Well then. And certainly, the pressure she had been feeling was nothing to do with his unlooked-for enthusiasm for the new Charismatic programme that had advertised at their church, his keenness that she should come along … should speak in tongues … His *un*spoken disapproval of her switch in jobs from harassment to knife crime, of the dangers he thought it wrong she should be exposed to. Of the fact that she had kept her own surname.

Above all, she told herself, she was absolutely not using the problem of Anthony Dodd, a problem she demonstrably had the tools and the moral certainty required to set right, as a welcome distraction from the one question she hadn't yet found a way of answering; the one underneath all of it. Was it worth it, her marriage to Jon, was *he* worth putting up with, however controlling and fanatical and unreconstructed and inflexible and, in the final analysis, just downright *disappointing* … if it meant that she could have a child?

And there it was, the morning guilt. Hello, old friend. How was it that no matter how many good deeds she did, how many sacrifices she made, the guilt was always there? Well, she knew exactly how it was, it was basic Sunday School stuff. No good easing the burdens of others if you refused to examine the state of your own soul.

And here she was, trying to set a house in order, when her own was falling apart. At least, she thought, anyone who could see inside, see the sacraments she was risking, the commandments she was prepared to break, would understand why her actions thus far this weekend had been so slapdash, so shoddy. Oh look. Now she was feeling guilty about *both* sides of the coin. And Torben thought he had it bad. That boy had no idea.

Maybe she should start a blog. Anonymous, of course. A modern

206

policewoman seeks to reconcile principle, profession, domestic duty, desire and altruism. Tries not to die in the attempt.

Well anyway, at least the guilt had woken her up. Only half reluctantly, she dismissed those first dreamy, almost lyrical thoughts, and focused the entirety of her mind upon her current difficulty. It all seemed different today. Anthony's – what should she call it? Release? No, best to remain objective: Anthony's *death* was a historical fact now, no longer happening but happened. Until Torben's petulant halt to proceedings the afternoon before – but then, he *had* been tired, and still hungover, she reminded herself – until then, it had been a moment they were inhabiting, acting only in relation to the death. Now, they had washed, eaten, remembered, confessed, slept, the sleeping especially an acknowledgement that, immense as it was, Anthony's death was still only an event. Enormous, but comprehensible.

Maybe Torben had been right. Tom too. They had all needed a break.

Gosh but her room was cold this morning. Not for the first time since arriving at Bastle House, Ruth really wished she could let herself swear. It seemed to help other people …

'Holy *fuck* it's cold!' Leyla practically shouted to herself as she sat bolt upright, duvet, quilt, jumper and scarf sliding off her, and causing her to dive again, to bury herself in their comfort. What kind of unthinking brute puts his female guests in the bedrooms on the windward side when there's a storm coming? She had a hat … but it was downstairs. Or – Ruth! She could bunk up with Ruth, it would be warmer there. Was Ruth any good with fires? What time was it? And was it permissible, in the circumstances, to take this duvet for a walk?

Having decided against it, on the grounds of its tripping her up every other step, Leyla pulled herself together and set off – meeting no one – until Torben's door opened.

His hair was a mess, which she liked. Improbably, he was fully dressed, apparently as some sort of fisherman, but – but in a good way? This was confusing. Thick wale cords, very 70s, if she had that right; anyway they hugged his thighs almost distractingly. She recognised the subtly ribbed indigo jumper; it would be thick and warm; remembered him showing off the label with a self-mocking laugh – *Made for Sailors, Hunters and for looking good* – his flush of mingled pride and shame at having spent so much on an item of clothing, in some just-opened Copenhagen boutique. *It will last for years*, he had said, and she had sensed his underlying fear at spending a hundred pounds in one go – but to be fair, it *had* lasted. His shoulders had been slighter then, his beard less full. But the hands – long-fingered, powerful, surprisingly competent – the hands were the same. She fingered the velvet of her dressing gown, glad she had abandoned the duvet.

'Did you – want me?' he said. That trace of the un-English in his accent, yet so very different to her own.

'I … actually I was going to see Ruth.'

Was that a smile, or a wince? 'Of course,' he said. 'Me too.'

Ruth's head emerged around the corner, her dreadlocks disordered. 'Well?'

Leyla had not anticipated having to explain herself. She hesitated.

'Key,' said Torben. 'After what we heard last night, well … there's one last thing I have to check in Anthony's room.'

'OK,' said Ruth, producing it almost at once. Once he was gone, she came to Leyla. 'You must be freezing,' she said.

Ruth always understood.

'Budge up,' said Torben, squeezing onto the edge of Ruth's bed. They were falling into old undergraduate patterns after all. The shapes, the frames, that made things easiest.

'Ruth's told me what you – what you overheard last night,' said Leyla. If anything, she was the one who looked most ill at ease with the situation.

Torben nodded. 'Any idea what that was about?'

Leyla hesitated. 'Best not to get carried away,' she said at last. 'You know Frances, she's pretty ... intemperate. She was probably remembering one of Anthony's more spectacularly un-PC moments, something hurtful he said. Remember what we decided in the library: words taken out of context get misconstrued, and we end up worse off than if we'd never heard them at all.'

'Maybe,' said Ruth. 'But you *didn't* hear them, Leyla – not this time, anyway – they were pretty wound up.'

'As if they'd been ... drinking?' Leyla suggested.

'Fair point,' said Ruth. She turned to Torben. 'Did you find anything to make it more likely?'

Torben shook his head. 'Inconclusive,' he said.

'OK,' breathed Leyla. 'Good. Subjectivity alert over. In that case, maybe we should turn to a rather stronger grievance against Anthony. I've been thinking this over, and I want to get Wilson back in – have it out. The STONi motive ... what did you say, Torben, about the psychological angle? It's the strongest thing we've got.'

Ruth fidgeted. 'Leyla, we covered this yesterday – Anthony really has no case to answer for there. One idle conversation when we were teenagers for Heaven's sake – no one would feel justified in resorting to murder over a thing like that, surely?'

Leyla waved this away. 'Look, *I'm* the lawyer here, and there's absolutely no correlation between the legal status of a grievance and how much it matters to people. Unless it's an inverse correlation – you'd feel more thwarted, surely, if you had no means of redress – and then the person you blame looks like dying before you can take any sort of revenge – wouldn't it, I don't know, act as some sort of catalyst? If he sees Anthony's act as dishonourable, that's had years to fester. Never mind that we're talking twenty-first-century tech here, this kind of thing is – it's practically biblical! I say we question him again.'

Ruth was looking increasingly uncomfortable. 'But Wilson's a professional actor. I just don't see how a direct confrontation would help matters – it would be—'

'It would be picking a battle on his terrain,' said Torben. He hated seeing the two of them at odds. This was precisely what he had wanted to avoid – and that went for the rest of the house party too. 'And I'm just not convinced. Killing someone over – over an *app* – it just sounds, well, silly really. Motives are meant to be, say, a famous diamond, adultery, a noble title, not something you can download from the Google Play Store ...'

He sighed. 'Besides, this frontal approach we've adopted has got us nowhere. I'm starting to think I should never have made my suspicions public in the first place. The whole thing should have been more ... more subtle, somehow. All we've achieved is to alienate our friends, suspect everyone, exonerate nobody, stir up all manner of tensions and bad blood, and prove ... well, nothing, really.'

'I think it's been helpful,' said Ruth, a little pointedly. He remembered last night's conversation; the scouring of his own soul.

'Important,' said Leyla. 'Not something to give up just because it involves a little unpleasantness. That's your problem, Tor, your actual work seems to be mostly quite enjoyable; ours isn't. We were expecting this.'

'Maybe you're right,' he said. 'Sorry, I'm … I mean, it's like we were saying. When you think about it with any rigour, you stop believing that there are things like facts – or, even if they do exist, you stop believing that they're the things that matter. Nuance, diplomacy, intuition – these are the things you can actually rely on.'

'So what do you propose? Fact-free detection?' said Ruth.

'Well, I suppose it's hardly an unprecedented concept,' said Leyla.

'Messy stuff, that's what we need,' said Torben. 'Casual conversation, stuff that takes time to digest … If anybody, in theory, *could* have done it, then we need to be more sensitive to minutiae. Whose actions – the small ones, not their headline movements – have been inconsistent? And of all our old scores with Anthony, which are the ones that still really rankle? Is there anything that might have led to someone arriving with murder already in their mind? And what about the present? How are things for people at home? Is anyone going through a crisis, that might seem unrelated but …' He thought of Sara's palpable unhappiness; of Wilson's flare of resentment over drinks; of Tom's threadbare suit and ingrained sense of grievance against, if not Anthony in particular, then certainly the modern world in general. 'And we need more details about money and credit, not just who has it and how much, but how important it is to them, how they react around money, are they rational or passionate—'

'We can't ask people those things!'

'No,' he said. 'We can only look, and listen. I think it's worth a go.'

'Anthropology over criminology?'

'Exactly! Tom of all people gave us the steer, with his wholly reasonable request that we share our memories. Time to stop investigating,

211

and do what we probably meant to do this weekend anyway – get properly back in touch with our friends.'

'If,' said Ruth, 'any of them still *are* our friends.'

'And chief suspect number one, otherwise known as Kirsty?' said Leyla.

'Can wait,' said Torben, 'since we can't exactly observe *her* until this storm lets up.' From the fact that they were all speaking louder than normal over the constant howl from outside, a din that had if anything only increased since yesterday, this didn't seem like it would be an option any time soon. 'Maybe once we eliminate the impossible, she'll be all that's left. And if her plan was to implicate *us*, she's hardly likely to do a runner or anything. I still think the solution's somewhere in this house though – not lying hidden somewhere, but animate, legible … is this making any kind of sense?'

'Not much,' said Leyla.

'Good. Because sense has more or less failed us.'

'What you're saying,' said Ruth, 'is that we need … inspiration?'

'Yes!' He beamed.

'Art historians,' said Leyla to Ruth, in a stage whisper. 'Mad as coots.'

There were eggs, there was bacon. Torben's mood was rising by the minute, and he began to hope that his talk with Ruth had really done him good, a sort of therapeutic cleansing that would leave him more objective, more at peace. He hunted out a round of black pudding the size of a dinner plate, and as thick – he observed aloud – as an Elena Ferrante novel. An encounter with the Aga did wonders for the cold tomatoes. While he would never understand why you couldn't get decent mushrooms in England, even in the countryside, the addition of butter, dried herbs and a splash of soy sauce might just redeem the regulation chestnut variety he had found at the back of the fridge. Salt, fat, and freshly ground coffee thickened the air, so much warmer here than elsewhere, and the erstwhile sleuths demonstrated their penitence by serving the others breakfast.

'And not a bloody avocado in sight!' said Tom, mashing butter into his toast.

Leyla summoned an appreciative smile, then quickly erased the expression – perhaps that would be overdoing it. But the plan seemed to be working.

'We admit it,' said Torben, 'we've got nothing sticky on anyone in this room. Viewed as an intellectual problem, it's a touch disappointing. But as a human being I am extraordinarily relieved. Tom, you were right – our immediate priority is to remember Anthony, not to avenge him. To pay tribute. He wanted this to be a party, after all.'

'Friends again?' said Ruth.

'Hell yes,' said Wilson. 'As long as you keep cooking like this, obviously. A general amnesty, then?'

'Yup.'

'So,' said Sara, 'we just … wait for a change in the weather? What happens when the snow stops – can we go home?' She seemed as keen as any of them to move on, grateful perhaps that the contretemps at the top of the stairs had apparently gone unobserved.

'I don't see why not,' said Ruth. 'Obviously we'll have to get the local police in first. They might want our prints and do some swabs as a matter of routine, but once they've got our details I'm sure we'll be free to go.'

Torben busied himself with his plate. It seemed highly unlikely to him that any of them would be allowed to leave before the inquest took place – was Ruth lying again? She was worryingly good at it for a beginner. Still, anything that helped them all relax.

'I was meant to be at work today,' said Tom. He sounded almost happy. Like a schoolboy playing truant.

'I used to love snow days,' said Frances, who was apparently on the same wavelength. Besides a little redness round the eyes, she too seemed back to her usual self. 'Course, we didnae get so many of them in Scotland.'

'I'd have thought it would snow more, not less,' said Wilson.

'Yeah, it does. Enough that the councils have to have a basic level of competence, unlike you Sassenachs.'

Torben glanced at the window, white with the glare of the mounting drifts beyond. 'Speaking of which,' he said, 'I should also apologise about the weather. I remember thinking what a fuss the English made about a few flakes. But this – this, I admit, is some actual snow.' And in spite of the blazing fires, the Aga, the woodburners, the cold was starting to penetrate. Before long, they would no longer be besieged by this blizzard: they would be … what was the English word? Ha, yes – stormed. Time to shore up their defences. Was there a log store somewhere, outside, or in an outbuilding? There had been two full baskets by every fire, and a stack more in the recess under the servants' staircase, but if this kept up—

'If this keeps up,' said Leyla, 'we might want to think about evacuating the bedrooms in the east wing.'

'Evacuate the east wing! Man the barricades!'

'Refugees to the great hall!'

'I'm happy to share with someone,' said Tom, looking hopeful.

'You should be so lucky. Aren't you married?'

'It's a twin room!'

'I still wouldn't risk it,' said Torben. 'He snores.'

'How would you know?'

'Oh, like Tom was saying yesterday when we tried out the gun, we boys have holidayed before,' said Wilson. 'Unsuccessfully.'

'One of those outdoor adventure things, in Wales,' said Tom, as if the choice of country had been the main problem.

'I rather liked it. Apart from the snoring,' said Torben, determined to remain amenable. 'And the smell. Four boys in a bunkhouse. It was like—'

'Being back at school,' said Tom and Wilson, together.

'I was going to say like a pigsty, not having been subjected to a single-sex education, unlike the other three occupants. But I suppose it amounts to the same thing.'

'You're not wrong,' admitted Wilson.

'Other three?' said Leyla. 'I don't think I realised Anthony was there too.'

'Oh yeah, it was his idea. No wonder it went wrong,' said Wilson. 'And to be fair I think *his* school went co-ed, just not till after he'd left; I remember him ranting about it … Actually, didn't we almost get snowed in in Wales as well? Seems to be a running theme of our gatherings.'

Torben noted the ease with which Wilson had swerved what he still liked to think of as the hippo in the room. Was that significant, or just tact? Too early to tell. He let the conversation flow around him while he studied the sus— … the others.

Wilson's clothes and haircut looked carelessly expensive, too much so for an actor still on the verge of his first real break, especially one who had to rent in London. *Crazy Rich Asians* indeed – was that the world Wilson felt he belonged to? Had once belonged to, before he had been, as Ruth had speculated, cut off by his parents? If all that wealth might have been his on merit, were it not for what Wilson clearly regarded as Anthony's betrayal … And then there was the way he talked – had always talked – about wine, spirits … maybe even stronger stimulants? And now, apparently, Teslas. Torben knew next to nothing about cars and cared less, but even he had gathered that they were not exactly a budget option. Take it all together and Wilson seemed the archetype of a man brought up to the good life, now living beyond his means.

Was all this more or less suggestive than Tom's appearance, bursting out of a ten-year-old suit, dressed down today with the addition of a moth-holed V-neck? No belt, the sort of shoes that schoolboys wore … Not for the first time, Torben regretted his imperfect grasp of the English class system. There were pitfalls here; sometimes a dilapidated appearance was apparently meant to be a mark of status rather than the reverse … But he had the nagging feeling that Tom had said something, back before 'it' all happened, that had made him think this might be more than affectation. No, it was gone. Wishing, not for the first time, that he had stuck to just one of the after-dinner drinks, Torben shifted his gaze.

Sara seemed to be positively cheering up after the rows they had overheard the last couple of nights, especially whenever the weather was mentioned. There was something in all this, sealed off from real life in such a setting, that must be appealing to her sense of nostalgia – for Oxford, maybe, but also, he was beginning to think, for the books she must have read as a child. He felt something of that too. You could imagine Andersen writing a fairy story about a place like this. And Frances was hamming up the accent again, and flicking her hair.

He thought of what he had found in Anthony's room that morning, a little wisp of copper nestled even now in his trouser pocket. *Inconclusive*, he had said. Which was true.

Well then, what about that adventure holiday, over a decade ago?

Until now he'd almost forgotten it, or had thought of it, with a rare plummet of his insides, only as the shameful occasion on which he had managed, somehow, to mislay his iPod – at the time by far his most valuable possession, both financially and emotionally, and something over which he had taken an almost paranoid level of care, making sure to know where it was at all times, whatever his own state of mind – an attention he had subsequently transferred to his watch. He had thought his system foolproof. The iPod had always been carried in a left pocket, of the trousers if he wore no jacket – just as the watch was always on his left wrist during the day – and laid carefully on his bed-side table at night, a practice he had also continued with the watch … so perhaps, after two inexplicable losses, it was time for a better system? Momentarily, he felt a pang of regret that he had always been too proud to invest in an original STONi chip himself, to attach to his watch. Before reflecting that, thanks to Anthony's own recent eccentricity about mobile phones, this was the one place he would not have been able to make use of it. But maybe, once they were out of here, hopefully having found his watch, he'd finally embrace what was now only slightly outdated technology. There had to be STONi chips on eBay at least. And what with his hat, not to mention the umbrella, he seemed capable of losing anything these days.

Torben blinked. This was not what he was meant to be thinking about. So, what else could he remember from that holiday, apart from the shame, and the shooting range? It had been the Easter of their first year, back when he was new enough to England, to Oxford, to the whole baffling nonsense of it, to make the effort to hold on to any friends that came to hand, however unpromising. New enough to think that deliberately single-sex holidays might be a reasonable thing.

A question, there: was there a sex angle to any of this? It was hard to think of Anthony in relation to sex: he'd never had a girlfriend as far as Torben was aware – but then, there were the magazines, which seemed strong evidence of a hetero appetite, even to the point of cliché. In which case, it was just possible … But how to broach such a delicate subject under their new, oblique approach? He'd have to ask Ruth if there'd ever been anything between Anthony and one of the others. Then again, these were deep waters – what if the magazines were simply evidence of trying too hard … especially if Anthony had been an old-school Catholic … in which case, what, some suppressed homoerotic tension? All right, his mind refused to put Tom Goring and homoerotic in the same hemisphere, even – but Wilson, maybe? Or – or himself? The talk on that trip, or 'banter' as the others had termed it, had certainly been phallocentric enough …

'More coffee?' he said, in the next break of conversation. He was ashamed to admit to himself that his mind had got to coffee by way of Grindr. Still, the general mood in the room had improved so much that his suggestion was met with actual cheers.

Irritating, then, that the grinder in question wouldn't start. It was, inevitably, expensive, with a precision burr mill, but at least it wasn't some enormous all-in-one machine that no one could operate. And German, rather than Italian, which he felt left him with little excuse for failure. Too many beans, perhaps? He squinted into the aperture. More light would help. He found a switch.

Oh.

'I'm afraid,' he said, emptying his words into the happy babble, 'that we've had a power cut.'

Seven people raced through the house, flicking switches. 'No,' they shouted, from room to room. 'No,' and again, 'no.'

And all of them were smiling.

Sara was first to find the candles, two hundred at least, in a scullery drawer. Tall, tapered ivory candles, the same as had been used at what one or two of them had taken to calling 'the last supper'. 'Got them!' she sang out, happy as the rest of them with this new adventure, so much more innocent than the last turn of events. It made it feel much more like a holiday, somehow. And they were doing the thing properly now the power was out, not like in Ngaio Marsh's *Death and the Dancing Footman*, which she'd always seen as a bit of a cop-out. It felt sort of … authentic.

Leyla helped her with the boxes, unloading them onto every available surface. One set displaced a thick, bound magazine, which toppled heavy to the floor. Sara picked it up, handing it to Leyla. 'The *Blizzard*,' she said. 'Huh. Appropriate title.'

Leyla glanced at the cover. Surely not more of Anthony's stash? No. For one thing, it featured a line drawing of someone in a cap pushing a lawnmower, which was unlikely to titillate even the most warped of appetites … She moved to the window, and the context of the image – some sort of sports stadium – revealed itself. She read the subtitle to herself: 'The Football Quarterly, Issue Twenty-Seven.' Strange. Anthony had not, as far as she knew, shown any interest in football beyond a token allegiance to Newcastle United. She flipped it open, saw it was based in Sunderland, and knew just enough to appreciate the irony. Certainly this seemed to indicate a level of absorption in the sport that ruled out Anthony's ownership. Besides, why would it have been left *here* – suggesting Kirsty – oh. It would, of course, be Kirsty's – why had she automatically discounted that? Because she was a woman, and women couldn't like football? Annoyed with herself, Leyla replaced it on the worktop, knocking aside a bulky Zippo cigarette lighter. She picked it up. It was in chrome, emblazoned with a crest featuring two fish-tailed horses and, in place of a motto, the words 'Newcastle United'. Presumably this too was Kirsty's – though she had not seemed the type to smoke, especially in a kitchen. But of course, it would be for lighting the candles. Well, at least she'd found something useful.

A change in the light made her look up. Sara was gone, distributing candles, and the bare scullery felt at once too large, too still. Its pale walls and the snow outside made the light somehow spectral, too white to be quite earthly. And there it was again, a flicker of shadow, a sudden darkening, as something or someone passed by the window.

Despite herself, Leyla gave a start, letting the lighter fall from her hand; it hit the table with a thunk that echoed round the empty room. 'Sara?' she called. But why would Sara have gone outside? And she thought again of Tom's irrefutable evidence, of all the reasons to suspect Kirsty – Kirsty, who knew the terrain, who had a Land Rover, who had access to whatever gear you got in the lodge of a country estate – including, as likely as not, such pleasant things as knives, axes, shotguns …

Like most of the large, square rooms, there were two windows on the western side, facing a little huddle of outbuildings and the path to the kitchen – and it was these windows where the light had changed. But really, was it anything more than that? A bird, maybe, flying low?

She had form, she told herself. There was that time at the start of second year, when she'd been working on an essay while the others had gone to the Bop. Looking out of her Meadows window, she'd been treated to the wholly unwelcome sight of Frances and Torben 'cavorting' on a balcony – and somehow the combination of that unedifying horror-show and her own over-caffeinated, sleep-deprived state had led her to hallucinate the shape of a man where no man could be, standing by the trees in the locked, deserted meadow, looking up at the balcony from which her own eyes were averted – a sort of avatar, she had later speculated, for her own unwanted voyeurism … the fact that the same shape was in the same place ages later, when she'd finally finished her essay, had convinced her that it was, in fact, an actual tree. On that occasion – as now – she had been looking through ancient glass in strange light; it had a distorting effect, like those mirrors at fairgrounds … Well, if she could mistake a tree for a man when nothing more than her *amour propre* had been affected, then surely she could mistake a bird for a murderer when someone had actually died. Maybe it was Anthony's ghost, diligently showing up to haunt his own murder-scene? She laughed, the sound ringing hollow round the pale space.

'Found any candleholders?' said Sara, behind her.

'No,' said Leyla, returning to reality with relief. Whatever her private knowledge about what Sara knew, she felt safer with her in the room. 'No shortage of matches though, plus this lighter. And we were never going to find a hundred holders. We're just going to have to make a mess.'

'Sounds good,' said Frances, coming in.

Leyla smiled, shrugging off her momentary distraction.

Everyone got to work, prepping bedrooms and bathrooms, the kitchen, the drawing room. Candle bases were held above a flame till the wax melted, then thrust onto surfaces or into nooks, pressed in place until set. There was some debate over the corridors – Leyla's view that the slight through-draught would be enough to keep blowing them out eventually prevailed – and no one even suggested going near the locked room.

221

Soon the house was bristling with pale little stalagmites, ready to be lit. It made the place seem older and somehow wilder, like a cavern or an enchanter's cave. Whorls of warped and melted wax sketched curlicues on sills and stairs.

Wilson meanwhile had unearthed what he called 'an actual, authentic coffee grinder', all brass and walnut with a little handle, and launched into his task with an enthusiasm that rapidly dwindled.

And at least they still had the Aga.

15

MONDAY, TEN A.M.

In every downstairs room a fire blazed. The snow still fell, but now it flurried, inconstant, hinting at respite. In ragged gaps they glimpsed a world beyond the windows: falls of white, like tablecloths, stretching to the treeline. Something about so many firs, their boughs laden, smacked inescapably of Christmas.

'It's like all the best bits of *The Lion, the Witch and the Wardrobe*,' said Sara. 'Narnia meets Professor Kirke's house.'

This was better, thought Torben. It was just as he had hoped. Sara especially could be unreachable in the wrong mood, and she had certainly been in the wrong mood last night. But in this … what had they called it? Snow day. In this snow day, she was thawing.

'Nae word of a lie,' said Frances. 'I have found crumpets *and* chestnuts. There'd bloody better be a toasting fork.'

Ruth began to hum a carol.

Wilson ran up, breathless. 'I've found—'

Torben turned. His mind raced through a dozen macabre scenarios before he realised that Wilson had finished his sentence.

'—a badminton set! Four racquets, a net, shuttlecocks. Didn't Ant … didn't Anthony say something about badminton and skittles?'

I thought we could set it up in the ballroom, chalk out a court. You know, as a way of keeping warm,' he added, a little disingenuously.

Well, why not?

'You're on,' said Torben. 'Mixed doubles? A tournament?'

'*Badminton*?' said Tom.

'Yes,' said Torben, 'just one of the many sports the English may have invented but have never understood. But we Danes know how to take it seriously.'

'Denmark,' said Wilson, 'is by far the most successful European nation at badminton. Someone once told me that, I wonder who it was? Whoever they were, they kinda forgot to mention that the Danes always end up losing to East Asians in the finals. I googled it.'

'Wait a sec,' said Tom. 'Isn't Torben some sort of champion – didn't he get a blue or whatever?'

'Uh – I think you got the wrong end of the stick on that one,' said Wilson, and sniggered.

'No,' said Tom, 'I remember this now. Me and Ant were in the Undercroft, nursing a couple of pints, when a bunch of you in tight white shorts burst in carrying Torben on your shoulders and singing "We Are the Champions". He was definitely waving a badminton bat – racquet – thing … You bought him champagne!'

'That was, um, inter-college, not university level,' said Torben, aware his face was colouring fast.

'Didn't stop you going on about your record achievement, did it?' said Tom. 'Ant couldn't take it; he went off in a huff, muttering something I shouldn't repeat in mixed company, and I can't say I blame him.'

'What Torben's not telling you, mate,' said Wilson, 'is that we'd just come rock *bottom* of the competition. With Tor here achieving the unprecedented feat of not scoring a single point on his own serve in any of seven matches. One of which was against *Pembroke*. It was quite something. Of course we had to get pissed after that.'

'Oh,' said Tom. He looked much happier. 'In that case, count me in. I've never played in my life, but I can't do worse than zero out of … well, out of however many you go up to in this game.'

'I've been practising since then,' Torben warned him. 'I might even win a point.'

Leyla regarded them. Was this all part of Torben's plan to put the suspects at their ease? After her fright in the scullery, she could do with that herself. 'I can co-represent Asia,' she said. 'I mean, I'm used to squash, how different can it be?'

'Oh, my child, you have much to learn,' said Wilson. 'But sure, pan-Asians for the win. We can have a round robin. Ruth, you play, don't you? You'd better partner Tom, it sounds like he'll need to be carried.'

Ruth shrugged. At school, the sort of rough inner-city comprehensive that had attracted enough headlines to be thrown an awful lot of money in the Blair years, she had actually reached county level for her age group in both badminton and hockey, two activities improbably unlike the rest of her life. She'd given both up after school, too afraid to own up to such esoteric talents. It might as well have been lacrosse, or that thing on ponies … anyway, she wasn't going to admit it.

'I'll referee!' said Sara, who had clearly seen where things were going. 'Since there are seven of us. I'm hopeless with spatial awareness.'

'Umpire,' said Ruth, automatically.

'I guess that makes me an honorary Viking?' said Frances. She looked up at Torben, her eyes full of mischief. 'It's like tennis, right? Scots are great at tennis these days.'

'Why do I have a bad feeling about this?' said Torben, who didn't. This was falling out perfectly, each of them paired with a potential suspect. The only problem would be keeping focused on the others, rather than on the game ...

The ballroom was perhaps Torben's favourite space in the whole house. Discreet, crumbling cornicing in milk-white stucco, about a mile above their heads. A series of floor-to-ceiling windows with built-in wooden shutters. The whole place – both panelling and plaster – in that complex pale blue, now flaked and peeling, that the Georgians had excelled in. A plain fireplace in simple stone. And furnished with a handful of antique Gustavian chairs, backs like lyres, set at slender half-moon tables around the edge, the better to allow for dancing ... or, he supposed, for badminton. It was also, of course, incredibly cold, which is where historic properties tended to let you down. Time to get to it.

As Torben and Wilson marked out the court, bickering over dimensions – 'who measures things in *feet*?' – Ruth gave the others a crash course.

'I keep hitting the feathers,' grumbled Tom. 'The feathers get in the way!'

Leyla stepped aside to talk to Sara. She couldn't help but notice the look of alarm that flashed across Sara's face as she approached. But then, lots of people did that when Leyla tried to corner them. Still, after what she had learnt on Saturday night, and the row that had apparently followed yesterday evening, it was astonishing that Sara was keeping up any semblance of normality. Had Leyla been exaggerating the whole thing? If so, then perhaps, in keeping silent, she really was doing no more than keeping things in proportion, avoiding starting them on a false track, rather than covering up a potential motive? After all, how angry would you really be, finding out about something done ten years ago by someone who'd just announced they had a fatal illness? Wouldn't you consider the karmic score to be more or less settled without feeling the need to intervene? If so, it would be a great weight off her own mind, if Sara really *was* feeling more or less at peace. Time to do a little digging.

'Everyone seems so *happy*,' Leyla said, as if at random. 'With all that's happened – and now being cut off here for who knows how long, with jobs, families, everything …'

Sara rolled her eyes. 'You wouldn't get it,' she said.

'Try me,' said Leyla.

'You have a good, secure, well-paid job. You own property. Basically, you've got it sorted. For some of us, stress and uncertainty more or less define our existence.' Sara picked absently at a hangnail. 'Frankly, I'm starting to find this therapeutic. You know that the whole murder-mystery weekend thing is big business among millennials, right? Sorry, does that sound callous?'

'You're asking the wrong person,' said Leyla. 'I didn't like Anthony either.' No reaction. She tried again. 'It's not as if he led a blameless life.'

Sara turned to her, suddenly pale, her mouth open.

'Oi!' said Wilson. 'No conniving with the umpire. Come on, Leyla, we need to talk tactics. I'm not getting beaten by a Danish beefcake.' And Sara took the chance to slip away.

Leyla glanced at Torben. He must have heard this last remark: he looked delighted. *Beefcake?* She could sort of see it, she supposed. If beefcakes came in low-fat versions.

It was, thought Ruth, ridiculous. Tom had opted to slide around in socks, rather than clump it in his work shoes; she at least had a pair of Converse. But this meant the game mostly involved negotiating her way around a slipping, flailing Tom Goring. He was soon puffing, still up for it, but incapable of small talk. It reminded her inescapably of the time she'd tried to teach Jon how to play tennis – probably the closest they'd ever come to breaking up. And Tom wasn't reacting any better than her then-fiancé had, growing redder in the face by the second. Only an improbable smash he pulled off out of nowhere seemed to save the situation. Here was someone, clearly, whose temperament was easily swayed by the superficial.

'Um, twenty … twenty-one twelve to team Denmark,' called Sara. 'Does that mean it's over?'

'Best of three games,' said Wilson. He and Leyla were loitering by the fireplace, watching the match. 'You change ends.'

Right. Ruth was going to take this one seriously. 'How about you cover the back court?' she said to Tom. Her height advantage over him hovered somewhere in the background to her words, but she was damned (sorry God) if she was going to refer to it explicitly.

'What, no more smashes?' said Tom. But he agreed readily enough, perhaps glad to retire the shot that had undoubtedly been a fluke.

Across the net, Torben grinned at her. 'Why did we never play in the old days?' he said. 'As soon as we're back in London, this becomes a thing.'

He too, she recognised, had hung back through the first game, trying to involve Frances as much as possible. Probably this was just fair play on his part.

Leyla had clearly noticed this too. Ruth saw her eyes follow Torben's, which were following Frances' rear, snug in a pair of high-waisted jeans, as she stooped to reach a drop shot. Anyone might do that once, of course. She just hoped – for Torben's own safety – that it *was* just the once.

Torben was impressed by how quickly Frances had picked this up. 'Like tennis,' she had said, which had worried him, especially as he'd never seen her on the grass courts in Trinity term. But she played feet-first, which was creditable, and adjusted her grip with surprising deftness. Strong wrists too, as you'd expect from a sculptor. Most disconcertingly of all, she played silently. He had expected shrieks and giggles.

'I'll play back,' Frances said. Interesting. He'd assumed, if nothing else, that she'd enjoyed wiggling at him when waiting to return serve. Either she had suddenly decided to be extra serious, or it wasn't him she was flirting with.

'If in doubt, hit it,' he said.

'That's my attitude to life in a nutshell, right there.'

They smiled at each other.

But what if it was?

Despite the best intentions of both, the second game degenerated into Ruth versus Torben. Watching on at Leyla's side, Wilson had clearly lost himself in the contest, keeping up a flow of light but nonetheless precise commentary. He was, it seemed, something of a nerd, and Leyla wondered how, between sports and Xbox, he ever found time to learn his lines. His life seemed to consist of nothing but games of one kind or another ... anyway, his prattle allowed her to concentrate on the others.

Sat across from Leyla in a chair someone had dragged over, separated by the flitting bodies, Sara was a study in suppressed tension. Tight-lipped, thighs clenched, a finger constantly tapping as she kept her eyes fixed, unblinking, on the shuttlecock. On the court, Frances kept flashing glances towards Sara, twice hotly disputing marginal calls when a shot she couldn't reach dropped right in the corner. Clearly, Leyla couldn't yet rule Sara out on the grounds of emotional equilibrium – but was this ongoing spat between her and Frances actually just about Sara's anger at Frances for keeping the truth from her? It seemed an overreaction – but then, theirs was a very old friendship, and to find that you had not been trusted ... Leyla knew well enough what it was like to be confronted with that sort of – was betrayal too strong a word? – disappointment, then, when one least expected it.

Inevitably, she turned her eyes to Torben. Unlike Frances, he never questioned a decision from the umpire, doing his best to keep everyone happy, which was a luxury he could afford: he seemed irritatingly proficient at this game. That enormous wingspan helped, of course, with Ruth repeatedly trying and failing to lift it over him. Leyla kept expecting the room to judder as he landed, but he was light as a cat ...

Tom Goring, Torben had decided, could safely be written off as a suspect. No one capable of that slick, efficient murder could even pretend to be this inept. Besides, Tom had never been one for sports. As undergraduates, Torben had invited him to join a casual five-a-side group he was trying to set up, assuming that all English public schoolboys were games-mad. Tom had reddened, and mumbled something about doctors' notes and poor coordination – or had it been asthma? On the other hand, under the transformative influence of enough alcohol – and how hard had the murder really been, from a purely physical perspective? No, no, Tom would surely have bodged it somehow … now, take *that*!

Leyla smiled to herself as Torben flicked an overhead backhand down to land precisely between Tom's slipping feet. Ruth, she noticed, was actually getting cross, obviously wanting to win, her patience wearing thin. These were hidden depths indeed! And she wondered what she herself was about to give away.

'Er, game, set and match!' said Sara. 'Well, no, just game and match I suppose, but it sounded so good.'

'Can we stay on?' said Ruth. 'I'm just warming up. And, Tom, find yourself a pair of shoes? We can still do this!'

Torben came over to Leyla. 'You want to watch that one,' he said, nodding towards Ruth. 'I appear to have awoken a monster.'

The difference between this and squash, Leyla realised, was that when you hit a squash ball, it always came back. There wasn't this great stupid net in the way, with its maddening strip of white tape at the top that always leapt *up* to block her perfectly judged shots.

Also, if you were good at squash, you basically got to stand still on the T for most of the game. This … this was tiring.

Fun though.

Torben would never have guessed Leyla to be the noisy one. She was hollering and cursing all over the place as she scrambled about, a curious mix of innate grace and total confusion. In time, he saw, she would become an excellent player.

'Now you get it,' said Wilson, close to Leyla's ear.

'I do,' she said, panting. She had practically forgotten her silly scare in the scullery; the game had taken over. 'And that – that *reprieve* you keep getting, thinking it's gone, and then you just get there – that's like nothing else!'

Wilson nodded, and refocused. There was no more banter from him now, just efficient movement. Leyla felt something shift between them, an almost palpable change of connection. She was, she realised, no longer Leyla, his friend, but simply a factor in play, a coordinate, a probability to be calculated. She hoped she came across as more of an asset than an obstacle.

Torben, looking on, saw Wilson's natural command over his body, and something more besides – the effect, perhaps, of years of discipline, of a schooling and an ethos that prized attainment and exactitude above all else. And his racquet moved so fast! To watch him pit his cool, finely honed will against Ruth's quite unexpected passion was – well, it was a treat, quite honestly. But it was a one-sided contest. He nudged Frances. 'When we play them for the win,' he said, 'aim at Leyla every time.'

Ruth tried to interest herself in the deciding match. But really, it was just too silly. Two posturing men bullying the space and a pair of incompetents who could barely hit the shuttlecock without it wobbling all over the place.

'Back in a sec,' said Tom, whose face had gone a more than usually unattractive shade of puce. 'Just off for a slash.'

She nodded. Well, that explained the way he'd been fidgeting about beside her, seeming to grow more restless by the minute. What was he, five? Instantly, she rebuked herself for the unkind thought. Really, this sport brought out the worst in her.

Meanwhile, there seemed to be two parallel contests going on – a good-natured one between Torben and Wilson, and an increasingly heated exchange between Leyla and Frances.

Well, Ruth could guess what that was about.

The game – or games – went on, the rallies lengthening as everyone redoubled their efforts to reach the flying shuttlecock.

Still no sign of Tom. No wonder he'd played so badly if his bladder had been this full. Ruth checked her watch. Frowned. Should she maybe—?

When it actually happened, she missed it. There was a shout, a slam, and a *'For helvede!'* Torben was on the floor, and Wilson, ducking under the net, was offering him a hand. Leyla waved him back.

'Ankle,' Torben said. 'Oof.' He hissed. 'OK, roll me up.' Wilson and Leyla eased him to his feet. Ruth came over, followed by Sara and Frances.

'Sprain,' Wilson said. 'That sucks.'

'Frozen peas? The freezer's full of them.'

'Feels like a coals-to-Newcastle situation on a day like this.'

'Yes, I would like some peas please. Sorry, Frances, technically this means we lose.'

'Bugger,' she said. 'I was hoping to kickstart my career wi' this trophy. Well, never mind, I'm off for a consolatory shower. I can't abide being all sticky.'

233

'Library?' said Wilson. 'That's the nearest sofa.'

Torben shook his head, thinking of that elegant piece of furniture, its straight back and thinly padded seat. There were circumstances, he was forced to concede, in which exquisite taste could be a major drawback. 'Drawing room, if you would be so kind. If I'm going to be lying down for a few hours, I'd like it to be somewhere comfortable.'

'Wilson, do you fancy a singles match?' said Ruth.

'Absolutely! Just let me offload this lump of Danish bacon and I'm your man.'

'Hop to it then,' Leyla said to Torben.

'Hilarious.'

'Er, guys?' said Sara. 'Has anyone seen Tom?'

16

MONDAY, NOON

'Oof,' said Wilson. He was a heavy fucker, Torben, not that you'd think it to look at him. Wilson was doubly relieved when they reached the drawing room and he could offload his cargo – now groaning what were presumably Danish swearwords – on the couch. 'I'd better find Tom,' Wilson said, before Torben could thank him. He did not add, *before anyone else does*. But behind the smile, his mind was racing.

He thought back to the chat he'd had with a slightly pissed Tom Goring, leaning up against the snooker table. What Tom had said to him about the Saturday night, his chat with Anthony – about what he had done, and the guilt of the morning after.

Ten to one Tom was acting on that guilt right now. Doing precisely the thing Wilson had warned him against, if he didn't want everything coming out. Oh, Tom, you poor, stupid, dear old bastard, now was *not* the time to give in to that weakness. To expose their little secret.

This was going to take swift, decisive action if they were going to cover it up. Quitting the drawing room, Wilson ran the options in his mind. If you broke the house into zones, where was Tom most likely to be? He tried to imagine the mansion as a level of a game, with quest markers and infra-red heat trails. Given what Wilson suspected Tom was up to, the downstairs cloakroom was the odds-on favourite. Yes, that was sure to be it – all those coats on pegs, it brought it all back. Now, there was a direct route via the main corridor. But it was critical that Wilson found him alone ... Best cut through the foyer, less risk of being spotted.

Wilson sighed. All of this should have been over by now. He hated it when people led him off-script.

Leyla was fighting down a rising panic. What was this – worrying for the wellbeing of *Tom Goring*? Was this what she'd come to? But in the moment's silence after Sara's question, it had all come rushing back. The shadowy figure flitting past the window. The sense of being under siege – but no, worse than that. Because *they* sure as hell couldn't get *out*. But if it *had* been Kirsty, and it was her out there now, armed and equipped, and driven back up here by gnawing doubts – had they all bought it? did anyone else need silencing? – well. *She* could most certainly get back *in*.

Why oh why hadn't she told anyone? Pride, in the final analysis. And then to – to play *badminton*, while somewhere in the quiet of this freezing house, Tom was being ...

They had to find him. Fast.

'I'll just – just lie here, shall I?' said Torben, to the empty room. He was cooling off fast, shivering even, and his ankle hurt like hell. No one had remembered the peas, either. At least the fire was lit. He felt, suddenly, intensely vulnerable.

He tried to focus on the sounds of the hunt for Tom Goring,

elsewhere in the house. It was hard to concentrate. After a month, maybe two, had passed, he heard a clatter of footsteps and muffled voices. Soon afterwards, Ruth entered.

'Panic over,' she said, arranging a blanket over Torben and proceeding to tuck him in. 'Wilson found Tom. He said he'd just been to the loo – which was where he'd said he was going to me too, before he disappeared – but here's the thing: they were coming out of the cloakroom. And fair enough, that's technically between where we'd been playing and the nearest bathroom, but it's an odd route to take when there's a perfectly good corridor. Something about changing his shoes, but he hadn't, and when I peeked in the cloakroom, I swear a couple of things had switched pegs since we left them … Still, I suppose it's all a fuss over nothing. But it's mucked up the plan. Now everyone's back on edge, just when we were starting to relax. Even Leyla looked worried!'

Torben refrained from pointing out that Ruth herself had hardly seemed relaxed by the game.

'How are you, anyway?' she said. 'I saw your ankle go, that must really hurt.'

'Uh-huh,' he said. 'I could put it into words, but you wouldn't approve of them. Still, maybe it was worth it; we learnt a thing or two. Listen, I think—'

Sara came in, then Leyla, looking agitated, and Torben switched tack mid-sentence.

'Sara,' he said, 'I need some advice. I can't move. I'd turn my mind back to the problem of Anthony, but like we said earlier, we're at a loss. Tell me this: what would Sherlock do?'

'You know, I've actually seen that on a t-shirt,' she said. 'Not as common as "I am Sherlocked" though. Um, what would Sherlock do? Cocaine, I suppose. Or three pipes of tobacco.'

237

'And if neither of those came readily to hand … ?'

'Throw himself into some unrelated work. Textbook displacement activity. Look, you seem to be feeling better. Can I – I mean, I need to just …' And she was gone.

'If you're really all right,' said Ruth, 'I might see if Wilson will give me that singles match. It'll give me the chance to clear up what was going on with Tom.' And she followed Sara out.

'*Et tu, Courtenay, et tu, Thompson,*' Torben said. 'They always leave.'

'Well, if you will go bastardising Shakespeare—' said Leyla. 'Look, Torben, I—'

'*Lort!*' said Torben, wincing, as another pang shot through his ankle. 'You know, Sara's advice might be worth trying after all. Focusing the mind on something else. It'll help with the pain anyway. Leyla, did I mention the excruciating pain? Look, would you be singularly lovely and fetch some stuff from my room? There's a book about a French orientalist artist I'm meant to be reviewing, and a notebook – oh, and my pen? Thank you!'

For a moment she stood there, gazing, not at him, but almost – out of the window? – with the strangest expression on her face.

'Sure,' she said at last, and went off, looking less than satisfied.

It was not, Torben thought, a nice position to be in. The invalid and his lackey. A situation both parties naturally resented. Like Anthony and Kirsty. Sacrificing your life to be at another's beck and call. Despite himself, he was starting to believe it.

Leyla soon returned with his things. 'If you don't mind,' she said, plainly as uncomfortable with the setup as he was, 'if you're going to try and get some real-life work done, I'm going to … just going to check on something. You're sure you're all right here? I'll move the gong nearer, you can bash it if anyone … if you need anything.'

'OK,' he said. 'Thanks.' He was only half listening. It had seemed highly unlikely that, what with the turned ankle and the murder on his mind, he'd be able to focus, but he found himself already drawn back into the discussion of Decamps' *Suicide*. In the circumstances, academic distraction was exactly what he needed. And hadn't he had some rather excellent ideas of his own on the train, before Frances and Sara had turned up? Ideas the author of this monograph had so reprehensibly failed to grasp … He began to jot things down.

Leyla hastened along the gallery. Check the French doors in the library first, she thought. And the latches on the windows. After the false alarm of Tom Goring's absence she no longer knew what to think, but it couldn't do any harm to make sure of all the entrance points, could it? If there was no sign of an intruder, that would settle the thing for good – and no one need know she'd been quite so foolish. Because it *had* been foolish, hadn't it? There was nothing to be scared of. And she was only leaving the scullery till last in order to be systematic. That was definitely the only reason.

Torben studied the painting again. That 'clue' of the broken mattress … Yes – what if you considered the scene as neither a crime *nor* a tragedy? For the solitary artist Decamps had depicted, was death simply a logical, dispassionate solution to money problems? On a fresh page of his notebook, Torben wrote down: *Suicide as moral imperative? As socially acceptable solution to private disgrace?*

Interesting. Yet still his ankle nagged away. The clean, bright pain had subsided into something duller, a throb that, if anything, was harder to ignore. His eyes continued to follow the author's argument, but his mind was drifting. Why had he agreed to review the book in the first place? It did you no favours. It was only that the journal's editor had asked him personally – at a urinal, of all places! Hard to say no under such circumstances. Oh, concentrate, Torben!

No, it was hopeless. So what if the review was a bit late? *For helvede*, he was snowed in, unavoidably detained. Especially right now, stuck on a sofa. Another twinge from the ankle.

He began to cast around, ungainly, hauling himself to a kneeling position on the cushions. Surely there had to be something here that would serve as mindless distraction for a convalescent. And – yes – down behind the sofa back, a pile of dog-eared paperbacks, plainly a lot newer than the imposing volumes in the library but conspicuously more used. Recently, too. He picked one up. *Gone Girl*. Hah! So this was where Anthony – or his imagined guests – read for pleasure. It cheered him up, this evidence of normal recreation, reassurance that Dodd had done something more than simply stalk about and brood on his own mortality.

He began to go through the stack. A few Agatha Christies – *Murder in the Mews, Curtain, The Murder of Roger Ackroyd* – a Patricia Highsmith, some dubious-looking thrillers … even one called *Whose Body?* It was like any typical holiday cottage. Albeit unusually weighted towards murder mysteries.

Somehow, discovering what Anthony must have considered to be something of a guilty secret made Torben think more fondly of his late host. You could relate to this sort of thing. Smiling, he began to leaf through *Clouds of Witness*, reading pages at random. He'd always meant to get round to some Dorothy L. Sayers, but it was a long series – were they really worth it … ?

Lord Peter was asking someone about letter-writing. *He slipped a paper-knife under the top sheet of blotting paper and held it up to the light*. The prose style was maddening here, it almost looked like Sayers was deliberately trying to hide what was going on, as Peter pocketed the piece of paper. Hah, alliteration. Torben was willing to bet this ended up being a vital clue—

Oh.

Oh.

It would prove nothing, of course. But it had to be checked. At once! He was about to swing himself up, when he remembered. Damn this ankle ... Awkwardly, he inched himself more upright, looking around him. The gong was behind his head – but could he really ask someone else—?

Shoved back against the wall behind the gong, there was a tub or bin of some sort, an old barrel with a couple of croquet mallets, more badminton racquets, mostly broken, and – yes – an antique walking stick!

It would do.

Slowly, carefully, he levered himself upright. Pen and notebook slid off his lap, on to the sofa. Well, they could stay there. He needed one hand free for the doors, for the banister rail ... With an effort unconsciously similar to that he had needed for the same task on Saturday night, Torben began the long journey upstairs.

Frances' hand was on the tap when she paused. No electricity. What were the chances of there being any hot water left? Pretty low here, on the opposite side of the house from the boiler – though she was pretty hazy about how these things worked – but if there was a reserve of at least tepid water, and she was going to risk stripping off in these sub-Arctic conditions, then whose bathroom was likeliest to get that reserve? Ruth had a private one, didn't she, right above where the water would be coming from? And they were all downstairs, so …

Grabbing her towel, she dashed along the hallway. The exercise had done her good, a boost of adrenaline, endorphins, the sort she usually got from work – how she could've done with them these last couple of days. A smidge more of that, and maybe she'd not have cracked and told Sara the truth – a terrible decision, given the consequences – hey, maybe she'd even not have let that memory get to her in the first place.

Her gamble paid off. Ruth had a lovely wee bathroom to herself here – impeccably tidy, naturally – and double aspect, albeit north and west facing. Though this too was a blessing: no icy blast coming through the old sash windows. The warmth of the water on her skin was a benediction, and she opened herself to it. Let it rain down, hot and cleansing; let it sluice away oh fuck that was the last of it, oh fuckity fuck it was cold now …

Hopping out, she reached for every towel she could find, whirling about, shameless now in purloining Ruth's things. So manic was she in leaning over the towel rail by the west window in order to grab a final flannel for her face, that she almost failed to register the blur of motion below, as what looked uncannily like the figure of a man slipped out of sight, vanishing in the shadows of the brick outbuildings.

Was there anything worse, thought Ruth, than being cold *and* sweaty at the same time? Well yes, plenty, obviously, but that knowledge didn't make her feel any less clammy. She started to shiver. But she had triumphed – narrowly, the best sort of victory – over Wilson, and triumph was sweet. Cold comfort for her failure to find out exactly what Tom had been up to, but comfort all the same. *Something* was up, that much was clear: Wilson had looked shifty and started talking about the gentleman's code of honour when she pushed him on what Tom had been doing in the cloakroom. But all he actually came out with were excuses – Tom was having a hard time at work, a client was filing for compensation for mishandling of a case, his wife had been unexpectedly laid off halfway through pregnancy, he had a lot on his mind – all deeply distressing stuff, but nothing about where he had gone or what he was really up to. So now she had to feel sorry for Tom without advancing her aims one jot. Typical of Wilson, the schoolboy covering for his chum when something was actually at stake … Hold on.

Ruth did a quick calculation. Pride (in badminton, of all things!), duplicity, resentment, on top of all the rest – she was racking up sins like no one's business. So this was what getting caught up in a murder investigation was like. Maybe Jon had been right all along: stick to women's issues, the anti-harassment campaign. No knife crime. No detective work. No death and danger. Well, she wanted no more of it in her future. Never again, Thompson. Never again.

She was still shivering. Would there be enough hot water left to justify a shower? Or should she check on Torben? What she really wanted to do was to curl up beside the fire and close her eyes, but that was hardly the sensible option. And the fire here in the ballroom left much to be desired. Neglected, it had burnt almost out – and there were precious few logs left in the basket.

Hmm. Was this the case everywhere? Ever since the heating system had cut out along with the power, they had been burning through firewood at a rate that now looked reckless. If they were stuck here beyond tomorrow …

She was on her way to the scullery before she realised where she was going, following a trail of bark scraps and dirt. There had been a stack in there, beneath the staircase, from which they had been refilling the baskets – it had looked substantial at first glance, but …

At the foot of the main stairs she met Frances, running down, double-jumpered now but with her hair up in a towel that tried in vain to keep the red locks from spilling free. Nice to know that some-one had felt entitled to use up what little hot water was left. Anthony had evidently provided his guests with matching towels too, or she could have sworn that was hers. 'Frances,' she said, realising that she sounded for all the world like the head girl she once had been, 'would you help me for a minute? I think we're running low on wood.'

'Aye, sure,' said Frances. 'But listen, Ruth, I think …' She clammed up, looking uncertain. Ruth held her tongue. 'Is this going to mean – to mean going outside?' Frances said at last.

'Maybe,' said Ruth. 'Look, just come along, and we'll see.' She was in no mood to brook argument.

'That's what I'm afraid of,' said Frances. 'Ruth, I thought … oh, forget it.'

She seemed off-kilter, unnerved by something. But she came, sticking close to Ruth's side. Together, they surveyed the stack beneath the scullery stairs.

'We're down to only one log deep,' said Ruth. 'I'd hoped for more. Still, this is a good moment to hunt for another reserve.' They both looked out through the sash windows. Though the sky remained heavily laden, only moderate flurries were currently falling – by recent standards, this counted as a sunny interval. Though even as she looked up, it was beginning to thicken again. Better hurry.

Beyond the side door, where Kirsty's spare wellingtons still stood, almost jaunty, they could see a couple of ramshackle outbuildings, mere metres away across a small, relatively sheltered courtyard. Ruth knew it was no good hoping to get *away*. But this was the side that was out of the wind – it was enclosed – and if there was more wood anywhere, it was surely in one of those sheds.

'Now or never,' said Ruth, her hand upon the kitchen door handle. The door was not locked, there was not even a night latch, and it surprised her, as she opened them up to the outside world, how firm a border this had come to seem, between the house and what lay beyond. They had all felt so besieged by the weather, so utterly trapped within four walls, that even the thought of crossing to an outbuilding seemed dizzyingly radical.

'Um, Ruth,' said Frances. 'I'm not sure this is the best idea. You see—'

But Ruth wasn't listening.

It was indeed sheltered in the little courtyard, with a wall and an old stone stable to the north, and these outbuildings close in front, the house itself a bulwark against the bitter east wind. To the south, a straggled hedge of privet blocked them from the garden. The snow lay thinner here, drifts blown in by chance rather than the impenetrable mass that had fallen elsewhere, and just beyond the door, at the foot of the three stone steps that took you down to ground level, there was a patch of bare and muddy earth. It seemed scarcely frozen, which puzzled Ruth until she noticed the vent above it, opening from beneath the floor of the room she was on the point of leaving. Until the power cut had done for the boiler, this must have been where hot air emerged, warming the ground beneath just enough to keep it damp, not frozen, so that—

'Frances,' she said. 'Shut up a sec, and look at this.'

245

Together, they gazed down at the footprints that the recent freeze had captured.

'Pass me that welly?' said Ruth. Silently, they compared the prints.

There was no question. At some point before this morning, who knew how long before, Kirsty – or someone with identical boots of the same size – had passed in and out of the house. And after that – superimposed with rare clarity – someone had laid down the mark of a heavy, out-sized boot, on their way in.

'That's a, what, size fourteen? More?' said Ruth. 'Have any of the boys got feet this big?' But she knew the answer.

'Last time I saw a print that size, I was watchin' some documentary about yetis,' said Frances. 'Which would be sort of appropriate, wouldn't you say, given the conditions?' She tried to laugh but failed.

'Not Anthony?' said Ruth. 'No, not Anthony,' she answered herself. She had recently inspected his feet, after all, an experience she'd rather not repeat. All thought of the wood shortage forgotten, she shut the door and leant her back against it. Her mind was racing. Thank God (thanks were allowed) that Frances was here to witness the discovery, or they'd all think she'd gone mad …

'This, this – person,' said Frances. 'They've been in the house then?' Ruth nodded.

'Because – I wasn't sure whether to mention this, but … but I think I saw someone outside, just now, from your— from the bathroom window. I couldn't be certain, but if this is for real …'

Ruth stared at her. It seemed almost uncanny. As if the footprint, and her thought, had conjured this person into being. She clenched her jaw, willing her brain to assimilate this new angle, to fashion it into a shape that made sense. And Frances had actually *seen* them? 'You're sure?' she asked.

Frances jerked her head. 'I mean – maybe? It was just, like, from the corner of my eye, but … aye, I think so. It looked like a big man,' she finished up, sounding rather like a small child.

'Because,' said Ruth, 'the print suggests they've definitely had access to the house since Saturday evening – since which time I can't imagine anyone either coming or going from up here without, I don't know, a snowmobile or something. Skis might get you down – but up? This hill, in this snowstorm … and there's only one road, right, the main drive? They'd have to pass the lodge gates if they had a vehicle, Kirsty would see them.'

'Hmm,' said Frances.

'Which leaves a lot of questions,' said Ruth. 'Of which, the most pressing is probably … where is this person right now?'

17

MONDAY, ONE-THIRTY P.M.

Frances stared at Ruth. 'Where *are* they? But, but they're outside, right, I saw them – him – whatever I saw, they were *outside the house*.' That division, out and in, seemed somehow absolute. Ever since the snow had set in, none of them had seriously considered going out, especially after Torben's embarrassment by the front door. Then she remembered something. 'Wait, you said "access to the house" … and the footprint's coming *in* … but, but the door's not been forced or anything—'

'It wasn't locked,' said Ruth. 'Either Kirsty left it open, or – or they had a set of keys? We're just assuming that Kirsty has all the spares.'

'But that was Saturday,' Frances objected. 'And today's Monday. I think?' She felt something slipping. That adrenaline, so welcome before, had gone into overdrive. 'That's an *old* footprint. Maybe who-ever made that wasn't the person I— maybe they had some reason, some legit—?'

'Look, let me check that planner.' Ruth went to the corkboard. 'No, nothing since Friday – it's blocked out for "party time".'

'Some party this is turning out to be.' There was an old iron bolt at the top of the door; Frances slammed it shut. 'I … let me get this straight,' she said, irritated to find her own voice trembling. Well, she could claim it was the cold. 'You reckon that after Kirsty went off on Saturday night, someone – some man, possibly a clown or an Olympic swimmer – came into the house?'

Ruth nodded.

'And – because of the weather and that – if I've just seen someone hanging around, it's the same person?'

Ruth passed a hand across her brow. 'That would be logical, yes.'

Frances glanced out of the window. The low cluster of buildings she could see were dark, shuttered, agricultural. They looked little more than sheds. 'No one's spent the past two days out in those. They'd've frozen stiff ... So, they've been in here all this time? What are they, a ninja? And when I saw them, they'd just, like, popped out for a fag?'

Ruth said nothing.

'That wasn't a rhetorical question!' Frances could feel the heat rising. 'But if they still can't *leave* ... if they planned a getaway, but got trapped by the snow like us ... ?'

'When you saw this – this figure,' said Ruth, 'which way was it heading?'

Frances thought for a moment. Into the shadows, not into the light. 'Oh fuck,' she said. 'Back towards the house.'

'OK. OK. So what have we got?' said Ruth, slowly, as if reasoning it out to herself. 'If he's the murderer, then maybe he was surprised by the snowstorm? It set in over Saturday night, after all. A while ago the snow was lessening, so maybe he risked breaking cover to check the conditions, before deciding it wasn't worth the risk. And now he's just waiting it out. Or ... or he's been deliberately waiting around in secret, to check we all accepted it as suicide?'

'Which we fucking well have *not*! Jesus, Ruth, if he's *heard* – if he *knows* – oh why did we ever listen to Torben? Ruth, I really don't like this. *What if he decides to kill again?!*'

'Frances, stop it, you're going too fast. How would he have overheard us, for one thing?'

'Hiding!' said Frances. 'Look at this place, it'll be riddled wi' secret passages!'

Ruth shook her head. 'Torben's seen the plans,' she said. 'There's no hint of a false door or a concealed corridor or anything – besides, I don't think Georgian architects went in for that sort of thing, did they? But if he *did* have a set of keys, then he could be in the parts we simply can't access. The bits that have been locked all weekend. The basement's definitely sealed off. But there's the entire attic floor. Which you access by … by *this* staircase. This staircase right here!'

Frances looked at Ruth for a long, long moment. She could almost feel, once again, the breath of an unwanted man, too close. Could sense his hand, reaching out from the shadows. For an instant, she was back there, in the place she'd thought she'd put behind her for good. Then she grabbed the nearest chair and jammed it under the door handle of the sealed staircase. 'Oh, shit,' she said.

What was that Ruth had thought about being besieged? Now, more than ever, she needed her police training to kick in. This was officially a situation – one that had emerged completely out of left-field – and it was on her to handle it. It was what they expected of her. It was, in fact, a chance to do her duty.

She took a breath. 'Frances, go to the drawing room and start whacking that gong. We need everyone in one place, so we can warn them.'

'Where are *you* going?'

'Upstairs.' Ruth grimaced. 'I'd best get the staircase blocked at that end too; it leads up *and* down after all. And … and it's right by *my* bedroom.'

'Jings,' said Frances. 'OK.' And she was off, hastening away from the foot of the silent staircase. Ruth looked at it, suddenly feeling very silly. All this, for a footprint and a glimpse of a figure? It was scarcely credible. But then, it was the first piece of actual evidence of something wrong, of someone where they shouldn't be.

She tried to reason it out as a credible hypothesis. Logically, if someone had crept in this way in the night, and assuming they – she tried not to think 'he'; it conjured visions of a hulking, half-seen monster, and emotional complications were the last thing she needed at this moment – had keys to the house … yes, that was reasonable, they could be in league with Kirsty (so Tom, at least, would back her up along with Frances – this matched his whole theory), or they could have burgled the lodge, or taken an impression of the keys some time … *or* the door had been left open, but they had found spare keys on the hook where Kirsty had left them, and taken them … In any case, with access to keys and some knowledge of the layout, they would logically have approached Anthony's room via this back staircase; the route was shorter and safer than going through the main part of the house.

But did that all hang together? After all, *she* had not heard that door open in the night.

Well, it was possible that she could have slept through it.

Or else, even more plausible, and safer for the intruder – if they had not opened that door, but instead gone on, up to the attic floor, the old servants' quarters …

She thought hard. Had there been a hatch, a trapdoor, in the ceiling of Anthony's room? In his bathroom, perhaps? In *any* of the upper rooms? A safe way down to Anthony that someone with inside information would know about. The house had been through who knew how many alterations, after all. Who pays attention to ceilings? A trapdoor was not the sort of thing you noticed without looking for it.

Feeling dizzy, Ruth put a hand to her head. She imagined herself upstairs, unarmed, passing from room to room. Looking upwards, always upwards, while overhead, unseen ... those enormous feet, moving above her, a potential killer among the eaves. Someone who knew the house, who was waiting – perhaps listening ...

And she knew that, whatever else came of this, she would not be going up there alone.

From the drawing room, the gong rang out. Breathing hard, Ruth obeyed its summons.

Leyla had made her inspection as far as the stairs before another thought struck her, and sent her hotfoot to her bedroom. Opening the door from the west-facing corridor, she almost baulked at the icy air within. Well, that settled it. She couldn't spend another night in this room, kept awake by shrieking winds and skewered by the icicles that were all but forming on the ceiling as she grappled with two mohair jumpers. Somewhere nearby there were footsteps and the sound of things maybe being shifted about in cupboards, she couldn't tell the direction. Perhaps Frances was having the same idea as her. Either that, or – or it was *definitely* high time to move her things into Ruth's room – she could ask permission afterwards. Ruth would be reasonable: it was only natural to stick together. For warmth ... and, yes, for safety.

Unsighted behind a small, hastily filled suitcase that would no longer shut, spilling over with rumpled underwear, she collided with someone at the top of the main stairs. To judge from the ensuing roar of pain she thought it might be some sort of bear, but it turned out to be Torben. Heart still in her mouth, she lowered the suitcase.

'What are you doing up here?' The shock made her sound angrier than she'd intended. 'You're meant to be crippled, Torben. You can't make me run around fetching books for you if you're not crippled!'

At another moment, she might have apologised. But her nerves were still jangling. And he *had* made her fetch that book. A book, moreover, about some French orientalist painter – which set off a series of recollections that ended in that mortifying poem he had once left in her pigeonhole: a beautifully presented, flowing, lyrical bit of objectification that had reduced her to a series of racialised body parts and if this man was no longer that boy, his ankles were presumably more or less unchanged, and she was suddenly, shamefully glad that one of them was in pain.

Torben glared at her. '*For helvede!* Leyla, that really hurt. And also I can see your knickers. Loads of them. Are you *leaving*? Never mind, just – just let me get to my room.'

'Do you need a hand?'

'No, Leyla, what I *need* is to be left—'

From below them, the gong began, a furious dinning that went on and on.

'Oh no,' said Leyla.

'You'd better go and see what's going on,' said Torben. 'I'll be down in a minute. Maybe five. Could you make my excuses … please?'

His eyes, she thought, could be very, very blue when he wanted them to be. And she needed to know what was going on downstairs more than Torben needed help. She sighed. 'Oh, all right. You certainly pick your moments to go all mysterious.'

'Thanks, Leyla. I – I think I might just have the answer. To everything.'

She stared at him. Below, the gong was still going.

'I mean, I think I know who killed Anthony. I know how it was possible, I can guess at a motive, and I even think I know why we've taken so long to work it out. It's in our pasts, Leyla, our shared histories, it's all there. We've been so confused by all these contradictions, and all the time there was a simple … oh, Leyla, I'm – I'm sorry. Go on, go down, I have to check this.'

He held her gaze. Oh fuck, his eyes were *really* blue. She had so many questions – in their pasts? Had she been on the wrong track this whole time?

'Go!' he said, turning away. And she went, suitcase abandoned, taking the stairs two at a time.

The drawing room was filling up. Leyla, rushing in, saw Frances still fitfully bashing the gong every now and then, while the others kept to the far side of the room and looked irritated.

'Tor said he'd be five minutes,' she said to Frances. 'Sorry – he's moving pretty slowly, as you can imagine; he said to start without him. Now, what's going on?'

'Oh,' said Frances, laying down the beater. 'Well, mebbe we should wait just a minute …' She looked over at Ruth, who nodded, her lips tight. If anything, the silence was worse than the clang of metal. Leyla threw herself down on the sofa, her mind in turmoil. The look in Torben's eyes – their shared pasts – and something about being on this sofa, where Anthony had passed round the gun; where they'd teased Torben about his drunken antics. It all added up to something. If only she could …

If only she could stop whatever it was digging into her ribs, for starters. She glanced down. The notebook she had brought down earlier was wedged open between her side and the crease of the sofa, open at the page where Torben had been writing. Leyla was about to drop it on the walnut coffee table when a word, underlined, caught her eye. The ink was still fresh. Feeling slightly sick, she began to scan the page.

Beside her, Ruth stirred. Leyla glanced up at her. 'Ruth,' she said, very quietly, 'has Torben – has he ever talked to you about suicide? I mean, in general – like, does he approve?'

'What?' Ruth looked nonplussed, her mind clearly miles away. 'Oh – yes, actually, yesterday when we were alone with … with the body, he seemed totally OK with the idea, said the important thing was being able to choose for yourself. Look, I'm sorry, Leyla, I really can't wait any longer.'

Ruth moved to the centre of the room. Leyla took in the change that had come over her in the past few seconds – the way Ruth held herself, her expression. This was not, or not just, her friend: this was a professional. Still, compelling as Ruth was, right now Leyla was more interested in Torben's notes. This was it, she thought. The key to everything.

'We've found something,' Ruth was saying. 'A footprint, by the kitchen door. Not any of ours – too large – and not Anthony's either. More recent than some others that we've identified as Kirsty going in and out on Saturday.'

Leyla looked up, startled.

Wilson raised his hand like a schoolboy. 'And this one you've found – going out?'

Ruth shook her head. 'Coming in.'

Sara spoke up. 'In "The Adventure of the Beryl Coronet"—'

'Not now, Sara,' said Ruth. 'I'm afraid there's more. Frances thinks she saw someone. A – a man. Outside.'

'Probably,' said Frances.

Leyla sat bolt upright now. 'You actually *saw* him, Frances? Today?'

'Yup.' She sounded scared, uncertain.

'In that case,' said Leyla, 'I think I may have seen him too.'

Ruth rounded on Leyla. 'Seriously?! But you didn't say!'

Leyla nodded. 'Outside the scullery. When I was looking for candles. I decided it was just a bird or something, but my first thought was that it was a figure outside the window.'

So she had been right all along, she thought. But, *no* – no no no, she had thought of *Kirsty*, not a man at all, in which case – oh God, Leyla Moradi, *think*. It was like being pulled apart by horses. This figure, outside, tugging her in one direction. Torben's manner, his words, the notebook, all leading somewhere else. Surely – *surely* there must be a world in which the two things matched up.

Outside, the blizzard was still raging, loud as the tumult that was growing within the room. The blizzard. The *Blizzard* … Yes. Everything was starting to take its place in what she was increasingly sure could be the only solution. A solution that was monstrous. Unthinkable. And yet here she was, thinking it.

At this point, Leyla stopped paying attention to the others. For the second time that weekend, she was seized with the overwhelming sense of being in the wrong room. If she was right, then no one here mattered. Torben. She had to convince Torben.

'So,' Ruth was saying. 'This unknown person. It could be Anthony's murderer—'

'I told you so!' erupted Tom Goring.

'No you bloody didn't,' said Sara. 'You said it was the housekeeper.'

'I said it was an outsider—'

'Meaning,' said Ruth, speaking over the pair of them, 'that the good news is, as Tom says, this suggests an outside killer. So we can all be friends again. The bad news is—'

'He might still be in the house!' said Frances. 'Hiding out on the shut-up second floor wi' the rats and that. Listening to what we've uncovered. Knowing we need to be silenced. Waiting for his chance to kill again!'

And for a moment, maybe as much as three seconds, nobody said anything at all.

'I need a drink,' said Tom. 'Wilson?'

'Hell yes.'

'Oh no you don't,' said Ruth, grabbing Wilson's arm as he turned to the drinks tray. 'You're coming up with me to block the staircase, then we go round the first floor and check for trapdoors in the ceilings. We lock up any room that has one.'

'Christ,' said Tom. 'What a bloody mess. There are only four words for this – and all of them are "fuckbucket".'

Sara laughed, like ice cracking. 'Fuckbucket, fuckbucket, fuck-bucket and fuckbucket. Sounds like a firm of solicitors.'

Frances glared at her. 'You're not takin' this very seriously,' she said.

'Well, why should I?' said Sara. 'You see one random footprint and a couple of shadows that might've been, like, a bird and a badger, and you deduce a deadly— ohmygodfuckshit! Oh it's only Torben.'

Torben had just that second appeared in the doorway. 'Have I missed something?' he said.

*

Everyone was speaking over everyone else. Leyla was obviously trying to get Torben alone, and he was just as clearly resisting her efforts. Ruth was feeling uncomfortably hot. If Sara's first thought won out among the rest of them – that she and Frances were really making something out of nothing … If so, that was not merely embarrassing, it looked unforgivably rash, a bizarre way for someone in her position to behave, like shouting 'fire' in a theatre …

Slowly, they all noticed that Tom Goring was gibbering about something. One by one, they all followed the line of his trembling finger as he pointed at the wall above the mantelpiece.

'Guys,' he said. 'Guys. When we tested the second gun – did you lock it up somewhere safe, or—?'

'No,' said Ruth. 'No, it wasn't part of the evidence, so I put it back on the wall. Why?'

'Because' – and Tom's voice cracked as it rose – 'it's gone, it's sodding gone, and so' – and their eyes all followed his down to the side of the sofa – 'so is the case with that pump … that pump and all the bloody bullets.'

And this time, there was uproar.

18

MONDAY, THREE P.M.

Either Ruth or the room was whirling. Whatever she had begun when she spotted that footprint, it had taken on a life of its own. Wilson had got to the drinks table after all. Tom Goring seemed to be in a tug of war with Frances over the sofa, trying to drag it against the door whilst she swore at him. A touch on her arm and Ruth turned. Leyla's face was in her own, practically snarling: 'Don't. Leave. Torben. Alone.' Ruth blinked. Leyla let go. 'Tor,' Leyla shouted. 'Just – just wait for me, OK? Wait for me.' And she was gone.

Where had she— and what? But now here was Torben, and Sara saying, 'Weren't they Reykjavíks?' Ruth goggled at her. The sofa's feet screeched on parquet.

'What?' she said to Sara.

'Recusants,' repeated Sara, 'back in the day. This house, we looked it up. Maybe there's a priest's hole?'

'Trust me,' said Torben. 'There's *never* a priest's hole.'

'Hey,' said Frances. 'Ruth, did I leave my ring in your bathroom? I'm missing a ring, it's got these wee garnets in it – wait, if this murderer bastard has swiped my ring—'

'What?' said Ruth, distracted. 'No, I haven't seen …' Oh, if only everybody would shut up. Where was that gong? And where had Leyla—?

Everyone had scattered. Leyla had said, *don't leave Torben*, but now Leyla was gone and no one had noticed, and anyway there was Tom gibbering to Torben about hidden doors in the library – he seemed genuinely unhinged by the turn of events. Then again, he'd clearly clocked Torben reading *A History of Bastle House* earlier, which suggested … oh, who cared what it suggested? Worrying about what Tom was up to was not her job anymore.

But she could protect people.

What would her friends expect Inspector Thompson to do in this situation?

Getting a grip on herself, she headed upstairs. She'd meant to bring along Wilson for this, but she'd given up on keeping track of where everyone had got to in this ridiculous place. Well, she knew her own role anyway. Time to get that staircase shut off. Time to look for trapdoors.

A terrible crick in her neck, a humming. Ruth felt dizzy. The staircase doors were now sealed … What if he – he! she was really starting to believe in this person – starved in there? The last thing she should be doing was shutting him in. But no, he'd just have to break cover, bang away, give himself up. Or weren't there dormer windows in the loft, could he climb down the outside? In *these* conditions? They'd have another death on their hands …

She had a moment's genuine, unexpected terror when she spotted the hatch in the ceiling of her own bathroom. But it had a bolt, and that bolt was secured. Nothing in Torben's room, nor Tom's, Wilson's, the two south-side bathrooms … Another hatch, unlocked, in Leyla's room. Trembling atop a chest of drawers, she jammed the bolt home. Rust flaked on her fingers. And where *was* Leyla?

Looking up, she saw the cracks and cobwebs. Little fault lines everywhere that let the darkness in.

Oh, man up, Thompson. You started all of this. Now see it through.

The drawing room again. Well, why not? It was familiar, it was sheltered from the resurgent snowstorm. It had two doors that actually shut, and Ruth, returning, lured by noise and warmth, was startled to be challenged, her hand on the door, with a slurred 'Who goes there?'

'Oh, for fuck's sake,' she said, shouldering her way inside.

'You *swore*,' giggled Frances, as Tom shut the door behind her. There was just so much – of everything … The room swam, and Ruth found herself on the sofa. The fire roared. From across the room, something pulsed that sounded of streets and night-time, neon, concrete … Torben was holding up a record sleeve. So, he at least was still here – good; hadn't she promised Leyla? Leyla … no, still no sign of her.

'Underworld,' Torben said. 'Turns out this record player has a battery compartment. Batteries! Genius.'

'The underworld? Yes.' Ruth could only agree: this spinning, crackling room *was* like the underworld.

Torben shook his head. 'The *Trainspotting* soundtrack. The 1990s!'

'When we was kids,' Frances contributed.

Someone was slurring the word 'lager' again and again. People were …

People were *dancing*.

Another log crashed on the fire. Tom leant in to Ruth, his forehead slick. There was a vein on his temple she had never noticed. 'What you have to understand, Inspector T, is that there is a corpse upstairs. Outside's gone all Scott of the Antarctic. And someone, somewhere, has a loaded gun. Damned if I know who. It might be me. Hey! That's a thought! It might be me!' He was manic, careering back to the little dance in the middle of the room.

Torben, awkward beside her, ankle cushioned, had found himself a bottle. 'Isn't it obvious?' he said, though she had asked no question. 'If everyone's in here, they can all keep an eye on each other. If we're all friends together, no one can pull a gun in a lonely corridor. Didn't you see *And Then There Were None* the other Christmas, sexy Aidan Turner and all that? You said at the start this wasn't like that. Well as far as they're all concerned, it is now, and the only way to be safe is to stay in the same room. Check their pockets – we're all just pleased to see one another.' He hiccupped. 'Probably we'll all have to go to the bathroom holding hands.'

Ruth's only answer was to examine the bottle he was holding more closely. It looked like beer, which reassured her, until she caught sight of the percentage.

'Is that a good idea?' she said.

'I know,' he said. 'A decent Tripel really needs a glass. One of those balloon glasses for brandy, that would do the trick. Could you just reach—? *Tak.*'

In a daze, she found herself handing him the glass. Someone had turned the record over, and Sara and Wilson were swinging each other round, bawling the words of 'Lust for Life' into each other's faces. Outside, it was darkening again. Early, too early.

'No,' said Ruth, her mouth practically against his ear. 'I mean, shouldn't you have your wits about you? There could be an armed man on the loose. This – this is all getting ridiculous.'

Dum dum dum, dum-dum du-dum.

Torben waved his free hand. 'No, Ruth. It's fine. Everything's under control.'

Somewhere, a glass smashed. One or two people jeered or whooped, and Ruth was returned, for an instant, to her school cafeteria, the deafening crow of opprobrium when someone dropped their tray. Please God, let it never be me.

'You call this under control?' she said. Someone had knocked over the fire guard, and sparks were now starting to spit out, black ash on worn parquet, an almost smoulder on the Persian rug. Ruth hurried to replace the grill, missing Torben's answer. 'Sorry, say that again?'

'I know what happened, Ruth. I know who killed Anthony. It's so simple. If we can just prove one more thing—'

'Ssh! Not here!'

'It doesn't matter.'

'What? So you *do* think it was that outsider then?'

'Look. Remember earlier, after Wilson carried me here from the ballroom? I tried to do some work, so obviously I ended up flicking through the only really readable books in the house as procrastination. Turns out Anthony has a weakness for detective stories. There was something in this one book about a writing pad and working out a message. And I thought, whoever forged that suicide note, working from their invitation – they must have done it in their room.'

'But I thought we just agreed it *wasn't* one of us—'

'*Hup*! Let me finish. All right, if it were one of us – were, was? I get confused with conditional tenses … whichever, anyway, they would have written it, as like as not, on their own pad of paper. And writing leaves an impression. Like when you get the, the duplicate or whatever, on those forms with carbon paper. If I could find the right pad, and hold the top sheet up to some light—'

'So *that's* why you were late coming back in earlier!' Her mind was racing now. 'You wanted to test the pads when the coast was clear and everyone was downstairs … yes, and you could get in all the rooms, because none of them have locks apart from Anthony's – I noticed that just now when I was checking for trapdoors – which means …'

'And I did,' he said. 'Find the right pad. It's pretty faint – especially without direct sunlight to help – but it's definitely the one on which the note was written. I suppose if you're concentrating on forging the handwriting, you write more firmly and deliberately. The slash in "one slash seven" and the "A. D." signature with its full stops came through quite deep.'

Behind them everyone was singing now, a song Ruth knew – Sleeper's version of 'Atomic'. The four of them had formed a circle, arms linked. They were starting to jump.

'Ruth,' said Torben, his eyes blazing into hers. 'The pad – it was in my bedroom.'

Four pairs of feet stamping in unison; Frances' hair a blur of red.

Ruth grasped his hands. She was having to think very fast to keep up with the situation. If only they would all just shut up. 'Right, that makes sense – what did you say straight away? The whole place is compromised … But they didn't *burn* the evidence, they tried to plant it on someone else … but you'd only do that if the murder was *suspected*, or what, as backup … ?'

'Ruth—'

'Oh, that's clever. The intruder *must* be Kirsty's accomplice, then. What was it Leyla said about her? "We're not a house full of potential witnesses, we're a house of potential *suspects*."'

It was all clicking into place, Ruth thought. Kirsty Dodd, who stood to gain the most, biding her time; setting her trap. An accomplice – her partner, someone hired? – to carry out the actual wet work, because when it came down to it, killing your own brother ... Then, with access to the hidden parts of the house, he could stay on site, planting the incriminating pad, keeping watch ... The evidence was all circumstantial, of course. But it sounded convincing. A plausible case for the prosecution.

'Leyla? What was that about Leyla?' The urgency in Torben's voice pulled her back to the present. For the first time, he sounded alert.

'Yes, back in the library, when—'

'Ruth, *where is Leyla?*'

A new song had begun, in a clatter and bustle of drums. 'Oooo-oo-oo! Oooo-oo-oo!'

'She ... Torben, I have no idea.'

'Ruth, help me up, now!'

Wilson throwing shapes to a langorous guitar line. The yearning tug of melody.

Barely sparing a glance for the dancers, Ruth and Torben left the room.

Behind them, Frances and Sara, pirouetting, pogoing ...

Ten minutes later, Torben and Ruth stood on the scullery step. The light was failing, they would have to light the candles. Two coats were gone from the cloakroom and Ruth's bobble hat was missing. By the doormat at their feet, a smear of mud was the only trace left of Kirsty's spare wellington boots.

Seriously, thought Leyla, how long did it take to walk a mile? *Walk a mile in their shoes* … It didn't help that these bloody boots were a couple of sizes too large. She thought some snow had got in over the top; one of her ankles felt damp, it was going numb. And it was still coming down. *Who cares: they're a mile away, and you've got their shoes.* Fuck knows where the path was meant to be.

'There was a torch here too,' Ruth said. 'At least she has a torch. Unless … unless she was *taken*?'

Torben ignored this. 'What the *hell* was she thinking?' he said. It was almost a shout. 'Was she *seriously* scared that—? Ruth, I need to get after her.'

The snow was falling again. Even here, out of the wind, Ruth could scarcely make out the sheds a few metres away. She looked at Torben, his weight all on one foot. And it had been the *only* torch.

'At least,' she said again, 'it was still light when she left. If she was heading for the lodge, she … she might have made it.' She couldn't get the image out of her head, the indistinct image of a great, hulking shape, with huge feet and hands. Dragging a body through the snow. It felt like her fault for starting all this. Had Leyla found him? Confronted him? But – but it made no sense.

She hadn't been stupid, had she? Like, seriously, dangerously stupid, the sort of stupid where you realise you forgot to put on the parachute before jumping out of the plane? She'd gone trekking in the Zagros Mountains, for fuck's sake, she'd been on the Dena glaciers. This was – this was *England*! Weather didn't hurt you here. Trees. At last there were trees. That was right, wasn't it? She couldn't feel that foot anymore. Still, not far now. Not far.

'Absolutely not,' said Ruth. She was literally blocking the doorway, arms folded. All signs of doubt, hesitation, were gone. The person Torben was looking at was not his friend but a policewoman.

'Ruth,' he tried again, 'We *have* to go after her.'

Behind them, the others staggered up.

'Where's ... whersh Leyla?' said Frances.

Mutely, Ruth gestured behind her, out into the darkening storm.

'Christ.'

'Running away?'

'You don't think *she*—?'

'Should we maybe—?'

'No one,' said Ruth, 'is going out there. Not until morning.' She raised her voice over Torben's renewed protests. 'Answer me this,' she said. 'Is any one of you sober?'

There was a silence.

'No? OK, next question. Does any one of you have a torch?'

A pause. 'There was one—'

'Leyla took it. Final question. Does any one of you, who does *not* have a newly sprained ankle, have extensive experience of orienteering? Mountaineering? Extreme conditions? No?' Ruth shook her head. Lit only by candles and the dim grey of twilight, it was hard to tell. But Torben could swear there were tears on her face.

'Anthony is dead,' said Ruth. 'Leyla is in terrible danger – but she has a torch, decent clothing, and a sizeable headstart on both us and on nightfall. I will not – I will *not* risk any more of my friends. I'm sorry. But there's nothing we can do.'

*

269

She could see it, or see – *something* up ahead, a greyer shape, bigger than the trees. Did you get mirages in the cold? Something – something like a humming sound, but that could be in her ears. Dark now too. Can't see the wood for the trees, a voice said. Can't see the wood for the trees. Dragged, blown, buffeted … oh fuck it was cold.

This may not have been the best idea after all.

Can't see the wood for the trees.

The snow kept coming. It was in her eyes, in her mouth; it rose up to meet her in drifts and gullies; it hid raised roots that snagged and stumbled her. Half the time she was slipping sideways and the torch zagged madly. Her cheeks, the only part of her left exposed, stung worse than if she'd been slapped. Not the best idea after all. But – but the only idea, that was right, wasn't it? The only way to …

Can't see the wood for the trees. Can't see the … can't see. Can't see the—

Oh fuck. She really *couldn't* see the wood – and that went, too, for the massive root that some absolute bastard of an oak had grown exactly … exactly where … if she could only—

But getting up, it turned out, was no longer an option. Snow-blind and nine parts drugged with cold, Leyla lay, and in a few moments she was quite, quite still. A swaddled shape for snow to settle on, lit by the soft glow of the lodge windows.

19

MONDAY, FIVE-THIRTY P.M.

'Fuck this,' said Tom. 'I'm going up to lock myself in. I'll see anyone who's left alive in the morning.' He left the kitchen. Wilson started after him, a hand on his elbow. Sara was next to slip away. Frances seemed caught in at least two minds, her gaze still on the exit Leyla had taken, but her feet carrying her ever further backwards. She was in the doorway when Torben spoke.

'No,' he said. He wasn't sure to whom he was speaking: Ruth, Frances, the pain in his ankle, the snow outside. But his mind was finally clear, his whole being seized with a total certainty that was almost exultant, except for its bleakness.

'Frances, I need you and Sara to do something for me. I know you're scared, but it will be quick, and it will help. The two of you have to go to Ruth's room. Ruth, do you have the key to Anthony's room?'

Bewildered, Ruth nodded.

'Good, give it to Frances. Now, Frances. Tell Sara to lie on Ruth's bed and shut the door. Her job is to listen. Yours is to go down the corridor to Anthony's room, open the door, close and lock it again, and return to Ruth's room. Ask Sara if she could hear you opening and closing Anthony's door, then report back here. Can you do that?'

Frances nodded.

'Then go.' She went.

'Ruth,' said Torben. 'I've got some work to do in the scullery. Can you find, and bring me, anything like rope – curtain cords, belts, that sort of thing? Also, in the drawing room, you'll find a barrel full of games equipment. We'll need two croquet mallets and four badminton racquets. Plus that wide-necked decanter with the brandy in it. No, I'm not insane, at least I don't think so. But I *am* in a hurry.' He looked at Ruth, willing her to trust him. And she, too, sped off.

In the scullery, Torben set about gathering everything else he needed: candles, matches, old rags and papers, a bottle of white spirit. Better still: a Newcastle United-branded lighter, heavy duty – and a football magazine he recognised, the many pages of which would, at a pinch, serve as further fuel.

The other two arrived back at almost the same moment, Ruth with stuff spilling out of her overladen arms, Frances looking wild and flustered. He turned to Frances first, his face a question.

'Nothing,' she said. 'Sara heard nothing.'

Torben sighed. It was the very last thing. Well, his work here was done. 'Thank you, Frances,' he said. 'Now, get back to her; that's the most important thing, isn't it?'

A light of surprise in Frances' features. But all she said was, 'Aye, it is.' And then she was gone.

'I – I don't think I'm quite ready to think about the implications of that,' said Ruth. 'But I *have* worked out what you're up to with all this gear. I really can't stop you, can I?'

'Short of knocking me unconscious and locking me up, no,' said Torben.

'You know I'm coming too,' she said.

'Of course. Hence the four racquets. Now come on, let's get to work.'

*

'Do you remember the first time we all met?' said Ruth.

Torben nodded. Neither took their eyes from their tasks: the improvising of buckles, the wadding of fuel. But it seemed natural, at what might very well be the end of it all, to go back to the start.

'At the bottom of our stairwell, on the first day of noughth week,' he said. 'I'd just unpacked and was coming out of my room. Struggling to deal with the disappointment of breezeblocks and Brutalism instead of Palladian splendour. Anyway, you introduced yourself, and *hugged* me, immediately. Physical intimacy! This was not what my cultural researches into the English had taught me to prepare for.'

Ruth gave a sort of hollow chuckle. It was the best she could do.

'Still,' he said, 'thank you. It meant a lot. And then the staircase doors swung open and this ... and Leyla walked in.'

'And minutes after that, we'd all been dragooned into lugging her boxes in from outside Meadows building,' said Ruth. 'Along with every boy in sight.'

'She had a *lot* of boxes,' said Torben.

'There,' said Ruth. 'Two pairs of ersatz snowshoes finished. Let's get them on.'

Torben set down his home-made storm lantern; pulled on the boots he had arrived in. They seemed ludicrously inadequate.

Mindful of his ankle, Ruth stooped down to lash the racquets to his feet. Eyes cast down to her task, she said, so low he could hardly hear it, 'I'm thinking of getting a divorce.' It seemed important for her to get this out, in case – in case anything happened.

'Huh.' He paused. Tried to take in, with what was left of his functioning brain, what a word like *divorce* meant to someone like Ruth, to whom it was so much more than a private matter; thought about its

273

possible ramifications in her personal as well as her spiritual life.

'Well,' he said at last. 'At the risk of you casting me adrift on a snow-swept hillside … it's about bloody time.'

Ruth groaned. 'You as well? Ugh. I'd hoped it was just Leyla. Not that she's ever actually *said* it … but she's been thinking it for years.'

And again that worry, that fear for Leyla, swept over them both, an icy draught.

'Do you … do you want to talk about it?' Torben offered.

Ruth let out something that could almost have been a laugh. 'Oh, Torben. Let's just find Leyla. Then we'll … then we'll deal with all this.'

They lashed the last remaining rope about their middles, tied together like polar explorers. Feeling at once ludicrous and apprehensive, armed with mallets as ski poles and the one flaring lantern, they shuffled back to the kitchen. Torben, in front, put his free hand on the door handle.

A sound behind them.

Frances' head, a mess of stray curls, poked round the door. 'Thought so,' was all she said, as she began to pull on her own boots. 'What? She's our friend too, you know.'

Behind her the others filed in: first Sara, then Wilson, with Tom Goring bringing up the rear. 'Hmm, do we know if there're any spare gloves?' said Sara, rummaging in her handbag. 'Mine seem to have strayed …'

Wilson sighed. 'Let's just get out there, shall we? Hurry the fuck up, Tom.'

Tom looked wary, red-faced, and kept close to Wilson. 'I'm coming, aren't I? No way am I staying in this house alone, especially after … oh for God's sake, why did she have to take *my* coat when she ran off? First things first: when we find her, I get my coat back.'

Almost smiling in spite of everything, Torben opened the door.

20

MONDAY, SIX P.M.

It was easy enough getting to the driveway, through a cobbled area and a low stone arch. Emerging on the other side, Torben braced himself for the shock of wind and snow. It did not come. Blinking in the unlooked-for half-light, he raised his lowered head.

The sky had cleared, the wind had dropped. All around, the snow shone eerie with the light of a newly revealed gibbous moon. Though the pristine drifts rose up around, formidable, he could just make out a smooth surface with rough banks delineating the start of the driveway. Their hopes rising, the six of them waded forward, as far as the northern edge of the main courtyard, the house at their backs. Still, the snow was knee-deep even here, and before them, unsheltered by the walls of the east wing, even the course of the road was obscured, melting into night. Torben chewed his chapped lower lip. He remembered the surface that lay far beneath – pitted, pot-holed, and scarcely distinguishable from the ground either side once you got away from the house, towards the wood.

'Come on,' he said, to the little column bunched up behind him. 'If she's fallen, we'll find her.'

But no one moved. And then he heard it too – the low, determined purr of an engine. A yellower glow on the horizon. A minute later, the shadowy form of a Land Rover Defender crested the hill. Snow-chained wheels crunching gamely, snowplough glinting in the glare of its headlights, it inched its way towards the house. Still, no one moved. Then a rear door flew open and a tall, gangling male figure was calling. 'Well, come on, all youse! I canna get her inside on me own!'

On the driver's side, Kirsty killed the engine and clambered out. Taking another key from the pocket of her coat, she strode, heedless of the snow, to the nearest doors – those of the library. 'Get her on the sofa in here,' she said, unlocking the French doors, and gestur-ing back to where her companion was struggling with something in the back of the car – struggling with Leyla.

Suddenly everyone was moving, flocking round Leyla and the oversized, unknown man. Torben's knees went weak. Whatever hap-pened from here, it was fine by him. Leyla was alive.

Somehow, they got her inside; relit the stove. 'Now,' said the youth – not a man, he couldn't be more than eighteen, nineteen – 'which one of youse is the doctor – what was it – Doctor Hell?'

Oh, *for helvede.*

Ruth knelt at Leyla's side. 'Torben's not a real doctor,' she said – somewhat unfairly, he felt – to Kirsty. 'But she seems all right, thank God. Still shivering a bit; I think that's a good thing. If we can get that fire going properly—'

'Shall I get some brandy?' said Wilson.

'No!' said Ruth. 'For one thing, that's a myth, and for another, we just burnt it. But if someone could heat some milk?'

'On it,' said Frances. She hastened off, one hand gripping some-thing at her waist, beneath the bulk of her jumpers.

Leyla seemed to be breathing easily enough, though she looked horribly pale.

'Any frostbite?' said Ruth.

Kirsty shook her head. 'She was well covered up. Danny here wanted to give her a hot bath, but—'

'I'm not a pervert, like!' he protested. 'I wasna going to *look* – and I said to give her some brandy too, but Kirsty said not; that the best thing was to get up here straight away.'

'Good, good,' said Ruth, a little distracted, still checking Leyla over.

'Could you … it would be helpful to hear the whole story,' said Torben.

'Of course,' said Kirsty. 'We found her in what must've been the nick of time. I was nipping out to the woodshed for a few more logs and I found Ms Moradi just outside, all wrapped up like an Eskimo or whatever, just lyin' there … anyway, we got her in between us. I don't think she can have bin there long. Danny made her some sweet tea; we got a few sips down her when she came round, though she were gabbling about her phone the whole time, kept wanting to do something. I reckon she must have been pretty confused, 'cause like I told her, we've not had reception since the storm came, nor internet neither – there's a telegraph pole down right across the main road – but I've brought her phone along anyway, since she was gettin' so agitated. Our electrics still work, mind,' she added, taking in the flame-licked gloom, 'so I assumed yours did too, or I'd've been up here earlier.

'Anyroad, I decided to bring her up here now the storm's calmed down, remembering one of youse is a doctor and the main road being out of action, only now it turns out he's not, and what the ruddy blinking hell is happening here anyway, that one of yeh ends up half dead in a snowstorm?!'

She turned upon them all with righteous anger. No one met her eyes, though Torben heard Tom mutter something about 'putting on a good act' under his breath.

They were spared the effort of an immediate answer by the return of Frances with the milk and a faint stir from the sofa. 'Phone,' murmured Leyla. A wave of agitation swept her face.

'Ssh,' said Ruth, stroking her hair.

'Can I have her phone, please, Kirsty?' said Torben, and handed it to Leyla. Far from soothing her, this only seemed to distress her further, as she immediately began poking at it with shivering, wayward fingers. A succession of random images filled the screen until, at last, Leyla calmed down, sinking back upon the cushions.

'Well?' said Kirsty again. 'Are any of yeh going to tell me what's been going on? I think I'd better speak to Mr Dodd.'

Kirsty refused to believe them until she had seen the body. Shaking, supported by the boy, she went upstairs with Ruth, who still carried the storm lantern. Torben, loth to abandon his place by Leyla's side even for a moment, waited with the others. Leyla held the milk to the blue bow of her lips. Her sips were agonisingly slow.

Tom was whispering to Wilson, something about big feet. Torben thought he knew what that was about – less clear was Tom's steady avoidance of Frances, and the way he had almost flinched when she came back into the room. Still, none of it mattered. Leyla was going to be all right.

At last the three others returned. Kirsty sat down heavily in a chair. 'Did … did someone mention somethin' about brandy?' she said.

No one looked like speaking. Kirsty seemed to be in shock; the gangly youth – Danny? – was vaguely patting her shoulder, and eyeing the new bottle of brandy rather hopefully. On the sofa, Leyla's eyes were fully open, pupils wide in the firelight, and she drained the last of the milk with a grimace of disdain that was almost familiar. The time had come, Torben thought.

He stood up. 'Well,' he said, 'the time has come—'

Instantly, Sara began to giggle, which dissolved into a cough in which the word 'mansplaining' was distinctly audible. Frances slapped her arm. 'Hush,' she said, 'I want to hear this. This *is* the denouement, right?'

Then Tom Goring sort of – exploded. 'Look, before anyone says *anything*, tell me this, Frances Adair, you … you crazy … *woman!* Why the hell did you take the other gun?'

Sara clutched at Frances. The others turned, started to speak. Even Leyla's face showed signs of shock.

Tom went on. 'And *don't* contradict me, anyone, because I bloody saw you, didn't I? When you were haring about in the upstairs corridor before we decided to go out. It's a miracle more of us aren't dead. I had to … I had to barricade myself in my room,' he finished up, in a rather quieter voice.

'She took the gun for protection. Obviously,' said Torben. 'I don't think any of us would have resorted to firepower if we were only worried for ourselves. But when the person you love is under threat – that changes things.' After the relief of the last half hour, heaviness was settling in upon him again. None of this was going to be easy.

279

'You know, Frances, Sara, it would've been easier if you'd told us straight away. Did you think we wouldn't be happy for you?'

'Oh. Of course,' said Ruth, very quietly. Tom goggled.

Frances looked at Torben. 'How long have you known?'

'Only for certain since I knew you had the gun. But I guessed on the train,' he said. 'That nonsense about happening to have booked the same carriage – why pretend? And then Leyla overheard some things on Saturday night, quite by accident. That bathroom wall is very thin. Specifically the words "no, not tonight" – "is in the way". Presumably deciding whether or not to share a bed – and Leyla's room being the thing "in the way"? Then "do it tomorrow?" and "maybe" – which meant, telling the rest of us. Anyway, congratulations.'

'Er … thanks,' said Sara. Ruth gave them each a hug.

'Cheers!' said Wilson, who had helped himself to brandy. The boy called Danny was starting to look interested.

'Oh,' said Tom, deflated. 'Yes, right. Lesbians. Hah – I knew there was a reason you turned me down in first year, Frances.'

'No,' she said. 'No, I was definitely into boys back then.'

Torben looked at the pair of them. For a moment, he was able to block out the rest of it and see only Sara and Frances, hands slipped quietly, unconsciously, one into the other, and a crackle of fierce affection between them. It was a bright, joyful, hopeful thing, a second fire in that glowing room, and in the midst of so much wreckage, he was glad it had been brought out before them.

Ruth was shaking her head. 'But … it's the twenty-first century! I just don't understand why you ever felt this was something you should keep from us.'

'I didn't want to,' said Sara. 'We're mostly out in London. OK, Frances' parents don't know, to them I'm just her … particular friend …'

'Dyed-in-the-wool Presbyterians,' said Frances, 'of a more than usually dour variety. We'll get there. I told my brother and he was pretty funny about it, I didnae expect that … which was hard. But it's not that so much, it's … well, partly reactions like Tom's, I suppose, but more—'

'She doesn't want you to stop fancying her, for one thing,' said Sara to Torben.

'Oh for fuck's sake,' said Frances, 'can we just – for once, can we just stop thinking about my sex life?' She was firing up. 'I'm talking to you, Tom Goring, and *you*, kiddo' – she pointed a trembling finger at Danny, who blushed – 'but really,' and she sagged slightly, 'it's like I'm talking to the whole bloody world. Take Anthony, for example. Back end of first year, like, a lifetime ago, he takes to pestering me, like he's somehow got a right. A red rose in my pigeonhole, that's almost cute. Stares over dinner and "coincidentally" bumping into me when I'm coming back from the shower, rather less so. After a while it's borderline stalkerish. And I'm doing *nothing* to encourage this, right – *nothing*. And then …'

She drew back her shoulders; fixed her gaze somewhere over their heads. 'And then one night in the stairwell, it's late, it's dark, we're both a wee bit drunk. Pimm's, of all things. Somehow, maybe he planned it, it's just us, and he starts in, telling me how he needs to express his feelings, talking about true love and things being meant to be. I don't want to hear any of this, obviously – I make to go – and he has the, the *temerity* to put his hand on my arm and, when I tug, he holds on.'

She was somewhere else now, not in the cosy library, but trapped and afraid in a darkened staircase. 'Both hands on my shoulders, and me back against the wall, and I can't *move*. I mean, I try, but he just slams me back, hard, and suddenly he's not a boy being too forward, he's a *predator*, and his eyes, just … Yeah. Talking like the purity or

281

the strength of his feeling or whatever gives him the right, entitles
him to … and I'm just shaking my head, trying not to cry. At last he
stops talking, like he's made his mind up, and he leans in, starts to kiss
me – I can taste the drink, Christ, I can even taste the chopped-up
bits of cucumber – and …'

'And?'

'Well,' said Frances, her face red. 'You can take the girl out of
Glasgow, but … and so I nutted him, like, this instinctive jerk of the
head, *bam*, between the eyes, and I was off. My shoulders burning. I
mean, I'm sure you've all experienced much worse,' she said, looking
at Ruth, Sara, Kirsty. 'I have too, loads of times. But that's almost
what frightened me most, how he didn't even cop a feel, just – held
me there. I felt so powerless. Like, beneath it all, all the talk of his
passion, it was the control he was getting off on … it's stayed with me
ever since. I thought I was totally over it, but he touched my shoulder
again on Saturday night and I was more or less triggered—'

'Oh,' said Ruth. 'So *that's* what your outburst on Sunday night was
about? Sara hadn't known until this weekend?'

Frances nodded. 'And if Leyla heard the first bit on Saturday
night, she must have heard the rest; we got pretty mad, almost shouting – I said I was damned if I was going to come out in front of
Anthony, give him something more to leer about, and of course that
meant explaining why he was such a problem, which meant telling
her all about it. She's been pissed about that ever since, that I kept it
from her for so long—'

From the sofa, Leyla sighed, rather like an engine letting off steam.

'—which was stupid of me, of course,' said Frances. 'I should've
told her at the time. I didn't want to make something of it, you know?
It was bad enough Leyla there twigging something was up the night
it happened. I kept telling her it was nothing to worry about, but

I'm not sure she believed me ... Anyway,' and she wheeled around on them all, 'the point is, I'm fed up with being the sexy one. It's so limiting! I attack rocks for a living, with sharp implements, shouldn't that be the headline?'

Even as she said it, Frances winced at the hypocrisy. Would she rather be ugly? No. She wore gloves to cover her calluses, she cared about how people thought she looked ... but that was common self-respect, right? It needn't always bring along with it this ... this *prurience*. Did she give off some secret pheromone, was there something innate in her body that just signalled sexuality?

The look of agony on Ruth's face – compassion? contrition? – was making her feel guilty. 'Och ... well maybe it's not so bad.' She forced a smile. 'Better the cross you bear than the bear you cross – as Leo di Caprio said in *The Revenant*.'

Sara forced a cracked little laugh. 'I like that. Could I make it Antigonus in *The Winter's Tale* for use among academics?'

'Sure, love.' Frances sniffed. 'But you see now why I didn't want to tell anyone? Not in some grand announcement, not all together – and especially not with Anthony getting off on it. I thought, this weekend, it could just be about being a bunch of friends – no romance, no complications, no awkward recollections' – and here she glanced, inadvertently, at Torben – 'just a, just a nice wee time. Which, in retrospect, is looking a touch over-optimistic.' She grimaced. 'It's *because* you're, like, my oldest friends. It's easy to introduce ourselves as a couple to new people. But you lot – you all thought you knew us. It's harder than you think, showing your new self to old friends.'

Torben winced at this. Sara looked exasperated, but gave Frances a kiss anyway.

Tom Goring glowered. 'Everything you've just said sounds like a bloody good motive for murder if you ask me. Why take the gun if you hadn't shot Ant? Or, Sara – Sara, *you* found out on Saturday night, and Fran said you were mad – what if you—?'

'—Killed a man in cold blood for harassing my girlfriend a decade before?' Sara's voice dripped with scorn. 'A slight overreaction, don't you think?'

'Speaking of overreactions, I feel I really have to add that arming yourself with a gun is the worst sort of self-defence,' said Ruth. 'I suppose that was your first thought when you left the kitchen, Frances, before ringing the gong even? But a gun never protects, it just puts everyone in more danger.'

'Rather like convincing yourself that there's a deadly assassin hiding in the attic because of one outsize footprint and a kid hanging out by the kitchen,' said Torben. Glancing at Ruth, he saw the dig go home and, instantly regretting it, pressed on. 'Oh, and, Danny, since we're turning to your role in all this, I think you left your copy of the *Blizzard* in the scullery.'

'Oh, ta. Think I'm finished with it though.'

Torben stared at him. 'You *finished* an issue of the *Blizzard*?'

'Well, I skipped some bits … Did you find me lighter an' all?'

'Oh,' said Sara. 'That big Zippo thing we used to light the candles?'

Torben fished about in his pocket, where he'd stowed it for the night expedition, and tossed it across to the youth.

'Ta,' said Danny. 'Forty quid that cost us. I was going spare when I thought I'd lost it – that and I couldn't light me ciggies. Out of matches, see. That's why I come back up here yesterday, spite of the bleeding snowstorm; I canna go without me ciggies. Took the Defender, left it just out of sight, thinking I could sneak back in mebbe—'

'Hold on,' said Ruth. 'Just, just who are you, exactly, Danny?'

'Besides being the guy with the enormous feet,' put in Wilson.

'Daniel Bellingham, at your service,' said the boy. 'Apprentice in Professional Cookery at Newcastle College.'

'My little brother,' said Kirsty.

'But *Anthony's* your brother!' said Tom. 'Bellingham? What's this Bellingham?'

Kirsty looked astounded. 'Mr Dodd, my brother?'

Torben interceded. 'I'm sorry, Kirsty. Tom was never a great student of contemporary music. If I could ask you to think back to Saturday night, before – before Anthony died – when we all left the table after that truly *splendid* meal, for which we all owe you and Daniel many thanks.'

'Oh … oh of course, you were in the kitchen!' said Ruth, pointing at Daniel. 'That's why Kirsty wouldn't let anyone else in there.'

Daniel nodded. 'Aye, I was. Kirsty didn't want it getting out, Mr Dodd being very strict about not having any extra staff about the place. I had to hide away the whole time I was here, even ducked out of sight of the windows when you lot first came up the drive. So of course, when I missed me lighter, I didn't want to be seen coming back, or she'd have got it in the neck. If I'd known he was a goner …' He flushed. 'But he ran her right off her feet, didn't he, the rich git – sorry, I know he's dead – but she needed the help! Poor big sis. And it's good practice for me catering course, so … so, you liked it then?'

'Best meal I've ever eaten,' said Torben, not quite truthfully. Daniel beamed. A thought occurred to Torben. 'Did you make that pie too?'

'Yeah. Kirsty helped with the salad and the dessert, mind – but yeah, pies are sort of my speciality.' .

'Well now I just want to hug you. Mark my words: you will go far!'

And Torben turned back to Kirsty. 'So: after dinner. Anthony asked you to put a record on, didn't he?'

'Yes,' said Kirsty, looking more confused than ever.

'What was it?'

'An EP by – by Antony and the Johnsons, I think. Called … oh! *You Are My Sister*. So, you were listenin', were you? That'll teach you to eavesdrop.' And, abandoning the last of her professional reserve, she looked daggers at Tom.

'In short,' said Torben, 'Tom heard Anthony ask Kirsty to put on a record. From which he, Tom, concocted a fantastical theory that somehow you, Kirsty, stood to inherit your supposed brother's fortune …' He left the thought tactfully unfinished, and turned to Tom. 'Even if you didn't have the wits to see the record sleeve later, you might have realised that no sister would forget that her brother was left-handed and leave the gun at his right.'

Tom began to bluster. 'Well, it certainly *sounded* … anyway, I'm sure she does stand to come into a packet. There was that other thing he said first, wasn't there? She wouldn't have to worry when she had the house! Explain that away if you can.'

Kirsty went red. 'The house goes back to its owners, of course.'

Everyone stared at her.

'Oho,' said Kirsty. 'He didn't tell you that, did he? Stands to reason, he was so keen to impress you all. No, Mr Dodd's been renting this place long term from the Borders Trust. On condition he preserves the integrity of its interiors and pays for the upkeep … I s'pose it'll revert back now, which makes my life a lot easier.'

'Kirsty's been caretaker here for six years,' said Daniel, looking rather proud of her. 'We want them to sort out the drive, do weddings and things. I could cook. There's a mint to be made in weddings. We were hoping this weekend would be a test run, like. See if we could cater and that, just the two of us. Maybe now the house won't be rented anymore, we'll get the green light.'

'That explains the state o' the place,' said Frances. 'It always did seem far too tasteful for poor old Anthony.'

'But, the inheritance,' Tom persisted.

'Frankly,' said Torben, 'I don't think we have a right to enquire whether Kirsty gains in any way from Anthony's death. He only showed us the parts of the will relating to us, after all. Fifty thousand pounds, we're all agreed, might just be a sufficient incentive.'

He took a deep, deep breath. 'Of course, we've mostly been thinking about it in terms of simple greed, when it always seemed to me that the real provocation was as an insult to someone's sense of pride – if, that is, they felt they were entitled to more. It's a funny thing, fifty thousand pounds. From some perspectives, it's a dazzlingly vast sum of money. From others, it's paltry. And as emotions go, I think anger, pride, resentment, are more powerful motivators than simple greed. Really, the will only gave one of us an especially outstanding motive for murder. I mean you of course, Wilson.'

21

MONDAY, SEVEN-THIRTY P.M.

The focus of the room shifted. Like a lens screwing into machinery it fixed itself on Wilson, who stirred in his chair, but said nothing. After a moment, he picked up his brandy glass with exact, deliberate slowness, swirling the contents. Eyeing the glass rather than Torben, he said, 'How d'you make that one out, Torben?'

'The method points to you. A headshot in the centre of the forehead – as Ruth pointed out, that's what gamers go for, and we all know you've spent half your adult life playing first-person shooters. Plus there's something theatrical about the whole setup – the antique pistol, the note, it's all classic set-dressing.'

'Am-dram, even,' breathed Frances. Sara shushed her.

'As to motive,' Torben pressed on, 'your mask rather slipped over pre-dinner drinks, that first night. Anthony made his fortune through an invention that, if the story you told me then is true – and Ruth corroborated it when I asked her – you might consider to be more your work than his. Morally if not legally, you were entitled to recognition that you never received during Anthony's lifetime. Perhaps that was part of what brought you here this weekend: a desire to remind him that, while he might have wanted to forget STONi, he should not forget his debts. That it was all very well running away from the twenty-first century; he would still be bound by far older standards of obligation.'

Wilson sipped his brandy.

'In fact, you even said something of the kind – that you were going to "remind him" of your claim? Was that what you did later that night, once he'd dealt you the ultimate insult?'

'Insult?' Wilson's voice was glassy.

'The will,' said Torben. 'No mention of his creative debt, no singling out of the one he owed the most. Bad enough two years ago, when he tried – as it must have seemed to you – to rub salt into the wound by trying to patronise your play, with money and advertising that could have been yours by right. How much worse for the injustice to go wholly and irrevocably unrecompensed when it came to settling his legacies and his debts? For a man of honour such as yourself, that must have hurt.'

'And you think my code of honour extends to murdering a sick man? That I was so enraged by Ant's refusal to play the game that I stole into his room while you were in an alcoholic stupor and blew his brains out? Or no, not like that? Maybe that we had it out, we argued, the gun was just – I don't know, lying about – that I shot my old friend in a fit of vengeance and then set about covering it up? Is that what you really think, Helle? Is it?'

Only now did he raise his eyes to meet Torben's gaze, and held it. For three seconds, four.

Then Wilson started to laugh.

Torben smiled. It was so nearly over now. 'No, of course not. Sorry for that, everyone – we were cruel to Wilson yesterday afternoon, when we wouldn't let him have his moment in the limelight. It seemed only fair to give him a chance to perform before the end.'

Wilson shrugged. 'I've never really thought you could be so stupid. Sure, I resented Ant for ignoring me. I won't pretend it didn't hurt, and especially when we heard the will on Saturday night. But to go from that to murder … because of the insult to my *honour*? Bit of a lazy Asian stereotype that one, Torben, it gave you away. Even if you believed it, you'd be too embarrassed to present it as evidence.'

'Sorry.'

'No offence taken, man.'

Torben breathed more deeply. So, Wilson had got his moment. Frances and Sara were, whether they liked it or not, outed – and, more importantly, reconciled. And the mysterious assassin was revealed as a trainee caterer with big feet. Leyla was safe. There was nothing left to do. He put a hand in his coat pocket.

Ruth looked at him, and whispered a short prayer. Despite the growing warmth of the room, Torben was losing colour. That vitality, so much a part of his character, was draining away. He took a glove from his pocket and dropped it on the coffee table. Leaning in, you could just make out a dark stain, no more than a few spots, at the tips of two of the fingers.

'Exhibit A,' he said. 'A bloodstain on a glove. Negligible. Easily missed, until you start to look for it.'

'Tor,' said Frances. 'Tor, whose glove is that?'

A log crashed within the woodburner; a couple of candles guttered. For the first time, it really sunk in that the storm was over, leaving behind a silence that stretched out around them, taut and quivering.

'It's mine,' Torben said. 'I killed Anthony Dodd. I'm the murderer.'

22

MONDAY, EIGHT P.M.

In the silence that followed, Leyla found her voice for the first time. 'Hook,' she said.

'What?' said Ruth.

'Hook,' said Leyla again, then sank back. It was all she could manage.

'Sorry, Tor, but seriously, what the actual fuck?' said Wilson. 'Are – are you confessing? This is the craziest thing I've heard since … no, it's the craziest thing I've heard.'

'Not confessing,' said Torben. 'Accusing. The case against me is irrefutable. It just so happens that I can't remember actually doing it.'

'Ruth, what's he talking about?' said Frances. She looked more scared than when they had found the footprint.

Ruth breathed hard. If she just seized the dirty, turbulent hell of it all with both hands and forced it back down, she might contain it long enough to get them through the next few minutes.

'I'm sorry, Frances, but I think I know what he means. When you came down to tell us you couldn't hear Anthony's door open from my bed – well, I've thought it through. I wish I hadn't,' she said.

'Look, let's take it from the start. Remember after dinner on

Saturday?' Ruth's voice, even to herself, sounded remote, untethered. 'We all told him about those times before when he's been drunk out of his mind. The things he got up to whilst off his head – climbing buildings, playing instruments. The golf thing. Bizarre mental processes combined with heightened physical competence – though in this case, we've all seen how well he can handle a gun even without that stimulus.' She shrugged. 'Can you be held responsible for what you do under those circumstances? I'm not a practising lawyer, but—'

'But … but why?' said Sara.

'Because,' said Torben, 'I've always resented Anthony. Worse than that – I've always judged him; found him wanting. And if any of you could have seen inside me that evening, could have *felt* … I was furious with him. Such anger. At his condescension, his tactlessness, at thinking he could buy our memories. And besides, I need the money.'

'But, your job—'

'My fellowship runs out in a few months. Do you know what I'm going to do then? No? Well, neither do I. So I had a motive. I was angry with him. And … and I must have felt he didn't deserve to live.'

He held up a hand against objections. '*And* I had the opportunity. I was in the next room. Given my past propensity to, I don't know what you'd call it, to have these manic episodes, it must have been simple. Look, I've thought about this a lot, all right? I'm not excusing myself, just trying to understand, when I say I must have been in a state of total *liberation*. Half awake, half in a lucid dream. I know that I had – have? – this, this sort of idea that Anthony *wanted* one of us to kill him – he was under sentence of death anyway, it would be an easy way out for him, the legacy was sort of a bribe, almost … and somehow, that was the catalyst for me deciding to be, I don't know, God. Above morality. Being so drunk must have given me licence, like a state of grace.'

'Like a video game more like,' said Wilson.

294

'Exactly! How easy must it be to pull the trigger when your moral framework, the world of consequence, proportion, respect, all of that just … falls away.' Torben shivered. And he remembered how, at one point, he had made the same comparison – thinking, at the time, that Wilson was the implicated party. He should have known better; known, of all of them, whom he had the most reason to distrust.

Frances was shaking her head. 'No. No! You cannae confess to something you don't remember,' she said.

'I'm not confessing' – somehow, it was surprisingly easy to remain calm, once you gave in to it – 'I'm building a case. I've proven the plausibility. Now, let me present the evidence. I'm not staking everything on that glove.'

'All right,' said Sara. 'Let's hear it.'

'Some of this you could dismiss as circumstantial, but I include it because it helps complete the picture. So. First, the crime. On Saturday night, I was left alone in the drawing room by Wilson. No, don't apologise. When I got up, I have a definite memory of going to the mantelpiece and taking hold of the pistol. And I also remember placing something cold on the desk in my room, just before I must have lost consciousness. Next: we estimate a time of death that tallies with two noises that Ruth heard, of a door opening and shutting, at two seventeen and two twenty. Because I had no memory of waking during the night, we assumed those to be the sound of *Anthony's* door being opened and closed by the murderer. But a few hours ago, I asked Frances and Sara to test what could be heard from Ruth's bedroom. Anthony's door proved inaudible. But there was another door more than twice as close: the door of *my* bedroom. Clearly, then, Ruth heard *me* leaving and returning to my room, at a time that matches the timing of the murder.'

Torben was aware of someone stirring among his audience, but he ignored it. It was important that he finish this now; he might not have the strength if he stopped. 'Now like any of us, clearly I am capable of the murder itself; as Ruth has observed, I'm demonstrably a good shot. Next comes the attempt to disguise it as suicide. I must have prepared the note in advance, since I accomplished the whole thing in three minutes. I had the means to hand: I was using Anthony's invitation as a bookmark, which was visible on my desk, and a test I carried out early this afternoon proves that the suicide note was forged on the pad of paper in my room, just as the ink matches the pen on my desk. I've got quite a bit of experience when it comes to things like calligraphy, and – being the unbearable snob I am – I've cringed so often at Anthony's turns of phrase over the years that I'd back myself to come up with a convincing imitation of his style at a moment's notice. Maybe I even overdid it a bit. All those repeated words …

'It's also just the sort of thing that would have occurred to me. For example' – why not let it all out now – 'I once wrote Leyla a rather compromising poem in a not dissimilar fashion, and left it in her pigeonhole. Clearly, I've got form when it comes to hiding behind elaborately worded documents. But I failed to replace Anthony's invitation properly once I'd copied from it – it wasn't in my book anymore – and, since I was operating more or less subconsciously, I couldn't help making the whole thing look extremely similar to a painting of a suicide I've been thinking about a lot recently, which must have been my inspiration. I should have noticed that sooner.

'And finally: whilst I had the coordination to carry out the murder, I was also apparently drunk enough to miss certain nuances that my sober self picked up on – the positioning of the gunshot, the wrong hand, and the removal of all prints from the note and the pen, when it would have been simple enough to add Anthony's prints once he was

dead. I like to think that, even so far gone, I retained enough humanity to flinch from touching his body. Maybe, deep down, I knew that
would make it real … make it real to me.'

Un – fucking – believable, Tom thought. He'd heard it all now. To
be honest, the whirl of the past hour had been a little much for him,
but what Torben had said had put the thing to bed. So all the dicking
about of the past couple of days, the stress, the bloody *badminton*,
which he blamed above all for what had happened since – all of it
was Ben Helle's subconscious working through the fact that he was
a murderous git? Typical. And Ant had deserved better. To go out
with a bang, fine, that was one thing, and to die in his own bed – but
to have the one guy whom he'd always resented pulling the trigger?
It was a shame, it was a damn shame. Criminal. Well, obviously.

Wilson sunk the rest of his brandy. Torben? Of all people? What
had he thought to himself, the other night – that Tor was one of the
good guys? No, no, it didn't stack, there had to be, had to be some …
some what? His mind dried, the next line was missing. All the parts
had got mixed up. He reached for the decanter.

This, thought Kirsty, was what came of letting these properties
get into private hands. Young people, getting carried away; too much
money and too much drink. Really, it was surprising this sort of thing
didn't happen more often. Poor Mr Dodd – who, for all his faults, had
always respected the place. She hoped he was at peace now – that
was sort of a silver lining, when you thought about it. He'd told her
what was in store as the disease developed. And she suppressed a
shudder. There but for the grace of God …

Danny, who had given up trying to follow all of this some time ago,
was carefully inspecting his lighter for scratches.

Sara felt Frances lay her head against her shoulder. She wrapped her arm around her girl, placed her cheek upon her curls. There was comfort in the scent of her; in knowing that they had come through this together. It calmed the screaming shock of it all; let the part of her mind that wasn't reeling take a step back, and begin to draw conclusions. She wasn't sure what she thought about what Torben had done. On the one hand, Anthony Dodd was no great loss to the world, and his card was already marked. On the other, to play God like that … It hadn't even been about the will, not really – but did that make it better, or worse? Don't think about the will, she told herself. It's undignified; inappropriate. *Fifty thousand, though. And the same again for Frances.* Don't think about it.

Frances felt Sara twitch, and straightened back up. Sara was her harbour; her present, her future. But right now, it wasn't enough. Torben's revelation had torn a rent in her world; torn at its foundations. Was this the boy she had almost loved? To whom she had given so much? Anthony, she had thought, was the bad man in that story, the taint on those three otherwise glorious undergraduate years. Had she really got it so wrong? Her eyes blazed into Torben, as if she could find there, in the morning light, the broken thing inside him that she had not seen before.

Spent, Torben came to. Their faces reflected back something of his own pain, mixed with whatever rose most clearly to the surface in each – fear, disgust, incomprehension, pity … pity worst of all. Ruth had turned to contemplate the fire. It glowed lower now, the room almost all shadows.

Frances was regarding him as if a complete stranger had just walked into the room. 'I … I don't know you,' she said. The words fell from her lips as if unbidden, stones dropped from an inattentive hand, earth upon a grave.

Torben felt the tears behind his eyes. *I don't know you*. He had been saying the same thing to himself since the afternoon. Fear for Leyla had drowned it out, but now the voice was back. Who was he, to pretend he could still be that charming, harmless boy of a decade ago? Who was he, this man capable of such coldness? Was this what living alone had made him? Or, maybe worse, was this the old Torben of those murky teenage years, the one he thought he'd left behind for good? Had he been there all along, the guiding hand, had that been the problem with Anthony from the start?

It had been bad enough a decade ago, among others, a stranger – even then, it wasn't long before he'd started to judge Anthony. Then it had seemed a reasonable reaction. But all these years in London, a bachelor, in the business of exercising taste, aiming for a detached critical attitude on a daily basis – he had finally taken it too far. Let the coldest part of himself rule the rest. And even after the – the event – what had he done, but seek to judge his friends? *For helvede*, Torben Helle. Too late, now, for a shot at redemption. But oh, if he could have that time again! If he could learn only to understand, and always to accept …

He thought of the room Anthony had assigned him. Bare, dark, dank, its walls thick as a prison's. Anthony had sensed who he was, in this at least. He would go back there, go up to his prison, and shut the door. Remove the embarrassment of his presence from these ordinary people, who had not forfeited their right to company, to a place by the fire. He would shut the door upon them all, and then—

And then there was a clink, an intake of breath from Ruth, and Leyla was knocking back a full glass of brandy. 'Hook … hook, line and sinker,' she said.

23

MONDAY, EIGHT-THIRTY P.M.

'Argh, that's nasty stuff,' Leyla added. 'Torben ... you've fallen for it. Hook, line and sinker. You were – *we* were wrong, right from the start. Taken in by the one ... person ... you instantly excluded from the enquiry ...'

She shivered convulsively. Making a supreme effort of will, she stilled the shudders. 'Oh, just – just look at my phone,' she said.

He looked. What else could he do? The photo it showed was as random as her words. Ruth, younger, at some formal dinner. A nice picture, you really *got* her from it, but ... ?

'Torben,' she said, and he couldn't tell if her slowness came from the hypothermia, or her extreme frustration with his own simplicity, 'this is the picture my phone displays when Ruth calls me. I mentioned it back – oh, it seems years ago – to the others in the kitchen, but you weren't there. Now, look. Look at the hands.'

He looked. First, he saw Ruth's beaming face. Then her hand gripping a knife. And was that – yes, *Anthony's* arm at the left edge of the screen, his awful shirt, his digital watch, a hunk of what might be steak impaled on the tines of his fork ...

Anthony's left hand, holding the fork. His left wrist, wearing a watch.

'Is … is that flipped? You know, mirrored—' But even as he said it, he knew it was not. Ruth's face was correct, her hands, and besides, there was the corner of a printed menu just in shot, you could read the lettering.

'Anthony Dodd,' said Leyla, 'was right-handed.'

Leyla was visibly gaining strength; she seemed to grow before them. 'Torben, you convinced us all that Anthony was left-handed, because you remembered him—?'

'—ringing his spoon on the wine glass. Raising that glass in a toast. All with his left hand, Leyla, I can see it clearly.'

'But just before that, he'd made a pun. Remember? Try to remember!'

Had he? Yes, yes … something about dexter and sinister, from the Latin, dexter meaning right, sinister meaning left … 'Dextrose and sinister!' said Torben.

'Exactly. And when you didn't notice the first time, he said it again, just for you.'

'Yes. Yes, and it was precisely *because* I was thinking about that, that I noticed him using his left hand straight afterwards! But—'

'And, Kirsty, you told Ruth something at the end of that dinner, didn't you? You told her that you thought Anthony was getting better?'

'Yes, I, I suppose I did … see, he took his meals in private, like, because he said he was embarrassed about his eating now he'd gotten so poorly. And, I thought, with the whole me serving him thing as well … and at first you couldn't blame him, he made that much of a mess. Food all over, took forever, no appetite. But he must've been improving, because recently his plates were practically clean.'

'Improving,' said Leyla. 'Exactly. He *was* improving, but not in his health. He was secretly teaching himself to eat as if he were left-handed. Over time, he got less messy. You know, I don't even think most left-handed people *do* eat with their cutlery reversed – but he went the whole hog, just to make sure you'd notice.'

'Leyla, where is all this going? What do you mean, I've fallen for it?'

'Oh, Torben, isn't it obvious? Anthony set you up. All along, he's been framing you for his murder.'

'But ... but he *is* dead!' said Tom.

'Yes,' said Leyla. 'We know. He committed suicide, didn't he? You read his note, he told us so. Only, the whole thing smelt so fishy that we immediately ruled out the very thing he was admitting. Oh, Tor ...' and she grimaced, as another tremor passed through her. 'You've spent so much energy feeling guilty that you've lost sight of the one key fact in this whole situation ... which is that Anthony Dodd ... was an absolute shit.

'In fact,' she carried on, her voice now taking in the whole room, 'what with being an irredeemable bastard, Anthony didn't just invite us all to a party in order to have us here while he killed himself – which, in fairness, he confessed to outright. No; on top of that, he killed himself in such a way that, not only would Torben *in particular* think it wasn't suicide, but that Torben would end up falsely accusing *himself* of murder.'

'Obviously,' Wilson explained to no one in particular, 'everyone has now gone entirely mad.'

'Shut up, Wilson,' said Ruth. It was, in a way, the most surprising thing that had happened so far. Wilson shut up. 'Go on, Leyla,' said Ruth. 'Only,' she added, reverting to type, 'try not to over-exert yourself.'

'First I need to clear up one more thing,' said Leyla. 'Kirsty, when Anthony told you to put that record on after dinner, did he say anything else?'

'Yes – yes! He told me to mount his special pistols over the mantelpiece. He'd always had them out loose in the case before then, he liked to handle them … said he wanted something to really impress his guests.' She shrugged. 'Bit showy, I thought.'

'Hah!' said Leyla. This brought on a fit of coughs, and she spoke more carefully once they had passed. 'I *thought* we would have noticed them if they'd been there earlier. We're such snobs, me and Torben especially, we were critiquing everything – clearly it wasn't part of his plan to have us notice them when we were sober. He needed to set up a proper show and tell, so that we'd remember things in the right place, at the right time. He'd built the perfect stage set here, in secret, and all Saturday he was just dropping the crumbs in a neat little line.'

'Leyla—'

'Don't tell me that's a mixed fucking metaphor, Torben Helle, because that's precisely the kind of asinine observation Anthony was relying upon to make this work. What we're dealing with here is one sick, twisted genius – I mean the sick literally, and the genius is grudging – who, ever since his terminal diagnosis, had been plotting how to make his own end the coldest kind of revenge imaginable. You've been gaslit, Torben, from beyond the grave.'

'Compromised!' said Ruth. 'We thought the whole crime scene was compromised, because the killer had every chance to plant or remove evidence *afterwards*. But instead you … you mean Anthony planted all the evidence in advance?'

'It was, as they say, his party,' said Leyla. 'The note, the pen – he could have written them ages ago, maybe even at the same time as the invitations, because what's easier to forge than your own handwriting? A couple of deliberate mistakes and you're there. He placed the tell-tale pad and pen in Torben's room before any of us arrived, and had the note ready in place wiped of all prints – along with his own pen, on his own bedside. Of course, he needed to give you a clear run at investigating yourself. I assume he disconnected those phone lines in advance. And I saw he'd cancelled this knock-off tree-surgeon who was due on Friday afternoon – I'm guessing Plan A was to rig things so a tree would be primed ready to fall and block the gates once we were all safely here; he could've made some excuse about needing to nip down to the lodge and then finished the job off in minutes with us none the wiser – seeing this weather forecast must've made things a lot easier for him …

'Anyway, the props were set, so next he just needed to create the mood. Easy enough with that creepy atmosphere, which of course he himself created, to get us talking about murder, and he knew what Sara was studying – it'll be on her university profile, after all. He made sure to draw your attention, Tor, to the fact that he was left-handed – which allowed him later to shoot himself naturally, right-handed, just as you said anyone taking the decision to end their own life would want to. OK, so he had to strain his wrist a little bit to do it straight on – unpleasant, if not exactly difficult – but the satisfaction of that piece of one-upmanship must have been worth a little momentary discomfort.

'Next, the whole business with the will, so carefully stage-managed – he might have guessed that would piss you off, but mostly I imagine it was to provide an obvious motive – and then of course the strong hint about the pistols. Call it a very literal homage to Chekhov – Anthony may have been cunning, but he was never subtle. And then all that remained was to get you, Torben, completely pissed, whilst making sure you were reminded at a convenient moment about your track record of remarkable but instantly forgotten feats whilst under the influence. Job done, he could proceed to kill himself with the correct hand in the comfort of his own bed, thus getting one over on both his disease and his oldest enemy at a single stroke. Technically, I don't think he even *lied*, except by omission. After all, he *did* leave a genuine suicide note.'

'That's it!' said Ruth. 'Omission! I knew something had been nagging me. When we searched his room, oh, it seems like so long ago … there was something we *didn't* find, that I'd been looking for without knowing it. I've just realised what it was. A rosary.'

'A rosary?'

'Or a Bible, even – I had all this out with Torben. Anthony used to be a Catholic, so you'd expect *some* sign of that if he were still practising. It was his Catholicism that first convinced me he wouldn't commit suicide.'

Torben's body was still catching up, his stomach in turmoil, his hands shaking. But his mind was racing ahead, latching on to Leyla's words like a raft in a torrent. 'And above his bed,' he found himself saying, 'there's this funny patch of wall where something used to hang … oh, *for helvede*, a crucifix, of course!'

'Whatever faith he once had, he must have lost it,' said Ruth.

'Well, that's one thing I don't blame him for,' said Leyla, 'given his diagnosis.'

'But hang on,' said Ruth, whose mind was also limbering up. 'What did I hear, then? That door, opening and closing. If Torben didn't … I mean, it seems too much of a coincidence to think that Torben went sleepwalking to the loo or something at the exact time Anthony … you know.'

Leyla hesitated. 'I – I sort of assumed Anthony had done that

306

himself. Opened Torben's door knowing that he'd be out cold. Lurked in the corridor for a few minutes, shut the door again, stole back and did the deed. After all, he knew you were a light sleeper, Ruth, and he made sure to put you in *that* room, so clearly he wanted you as an ear-witness in order to implicate Torben. But now that I say it, it seems so risky …'

'Oh, shit!' said Wilson. 'Tom, was that when—?'

'Yes,' said Tom. 'It must have been.'

They looked at him; at his forehead glistening with sweat in the flickering candlelight. 'I was *going* to tell you all, of course I was, if it came to it, but …'

He dried up. No one seemed quite able to formulate the right question. Torben, now thoroughly at sea, was just concentrating on trying to breathe. He looked down at his hands, willing them to stillness.

After a moment, Tom took something from his suit jacket.

'Here you go, Ben,' he said. 'It's your watch.' He turned to Wilson. 'Happy now?'

Wilson shook his head. 'And the rest,' he said.

Tom sighed. 'Leyla,' he said, 'when we get out of this … I'll post you your necklace. The one you lost at the Gaudy, two years ago.'

'—?'

'He stole them,' said Wilson, simply. 'C'mon, Tom.'

Tom fished in his pockets, and brought forth a filigree ring, set with a small cluster of garnets. 'Sorry, Fran,' he said, handing it over.

'That was my grandmother's,' said Frances, very quietly.

Wilson coughed. 'He also stole Sara's gloves from the cloakroom. Oh, and an iPod of Torben's, but since that was more than ten years ago I wouldn't bother asking for it back. Same goes for your old laptop, Frances. Probably other stuff too.'

'Wilson found me,' said Tom, looking at his shoes. 'After that …
after the bloody badminton. Everyone was busy, and I was feeling …
feeling excited. Ashamed. I went to the cloakroom and started just,
I don't know, looking for things.' He raised his head. 'I haven't done
this in years! Somehow, all of us being together again, it took me back
to that place. It was like that at the Gaudy too. I had a real, a real
problem when I was younger. Remember when all those things went
missing in second year? I was out of control. Since school. I started
doing it during Games lessons, in the changing rooms – the badminton must've helped trigger it. Told you it was a fucking stupid sport.'

Wilson put an arm round him. 'He's promised me he's going to
get help.'

'I can put you in touch with someone,' said Ruth.

'In Daventry?'

'Well …'

'Look,' said Leyla, who was in no mood for sympathy; she had loved
that necklace, 'what exactly are you saying? That you stole Torben's
watch on Saturday night? At – when was it? – at two seventeen?'

'It must have been about then, yeah.'

'And you were just going to keep this silent? Let Torben think he
was a murderer rather than own up?'

'No, of course not, only … look, this isn't easy for me.'

'Evidently,' said Leyla.

'It was Ant,' Tom said. 'He took me off, last thing on Saturday
night – like I said, to apologise for not consulting me when he drew
up the will. I was pretty bloody keen to talk to him about that will, I
can tell you, it was just what …'

He paused. Swallowed. 'Well, since this is confession time, I might
as well admit it: I wanted an advance on the fifty thousand. A down
payment, if you like. He'd done it plenty of times in the old days,

before he cut all his ties and vanished up here and I'd, well, I'd sort of come to rely on the occasional—'

'Handout?' said Leyla.

'Favour,' Tom substituted. 'Anyway, when the tap turned off just before our wedding – which Ant had practically *promised* to finance – I found myself pretty deep in the shit, and with the baby on the way and no maternity pay to count on … Ant just said, yeah yeah, we could talk about it tomorrow, meaning Sunday, but that he wasn't going to make any changes to the will now, it had been too much trouble and there was some pretty sensitive stuff in there.

'That made me think of what he'd said to Kirsty, about the house and being his sister – yes, yes, I know *now*, but … anyway, it made me suspicious. So I asked why Kirsty had taken it away with her and he said, well, he didn't like leaving anything in this house as nowhere was secure from thieves, no locks on most of the doors, which is when I first started thinking about how easy it would be to— anyway, that's when I got tempted. Then we laughed a bit about how pissed Torben had got, and Ant said how funny it was – remembering that time we bunked up together in Wales – that however out of it Torben was, he always had these little routines before going to bed. How he'd noticed Ben always put his iPod in a certain place; how he took his watch off and laid it neatly on the table, even if he still had his shoes on … made quite a point of it, now I think about it. You mean he was – I was being played too?'

Leyla nodded. 'He didn't miss a trick, did he? You two were pretty thick together as undergrads. Did you ever tell him about the stealing?'

'The kleptomania. Yeah, well, one time he actually caught me. He was testing an early prototype of his STONi chip, and I actually managed to swipe the wallet he was testing it on, which ended up being fucking embarrassing when it went off.' Tom rubbed his eyes. 'The – the bastard! He thought he could use me like that, that he could drop a hint and I'd run off the same damn night, all so a door would open and close when he wanted it to?'

'Well, he was right,' observed Leyla.

'It's worse than that,' said Ruth. 'I almost think it's the worst part of the whole business. He didn't just count on you giving in to your kleptomania. He counted on you not admitting to it afterwards.'

There was a silence. Torben took it in at last: so, it had been his watch, not the pistol, that he had laid upon the desk that night. He had the impression of something slowly lifting – draining away – like sand beneath his feet as the wave withdrew. It was not entirely a comfortable sensation.

'Well, Tom's owned up now, hasn't he?' said Wilson, into the silence. 'Well done, mate.'

'Yes, it's all very touching,' said Leyla. 'But what a c— ... what a complete piece of work Anthony was. So controlling. Why be approximate with the timings when you can do things precisely? I can just picture him sitting up in bed, gun in hand, waiting for the noise of Tom creeping past. The click of the door, a few seconds' wait, and – *bang*. Sorry, *pffft*. A minute later, Tom shuts the door, watch in hand, and creeps back to bed. Anthony's little figures moving round like – yes, like clockwork, or like a piece of coding I suppose – to a programme he set in motion. And we've been doing it ever since. Tom, Kirsty – all of us playing our parts in convincing Torben to take the blame for Anthony's suicide.'

'You mean,' said Frances, 'this whole – *everything* – this was all just some kind of dick-swinging duel from beyond the grave? All this to get one up on Torben, because they've always been too repressed to sort this out when Ant was alive?'

'Yes, Frances,' said Ruth, 'I'm sure you're right; the most twisted part of Anthony's plan was definitely its undercurrent of toxic masculinity.'

'No, but, it *was* though, when you think about it – an' the whole superman detective thing, if Torben hadn't been seduced by that then we might've had a nice weekend …'

'I think Frances is right, Ruth,' said Leyla. 'This wasn't a crime – it was a demonstration. When I pointed out that Anthony actually left a legitimate suicide note, I wasn't just thinking about the irony – I was making a legal distinction. *Anthony* hasn't framed Torben for his murder. *Torben* has framed himself, that's the whole point. I don't think he wanted Tor convicted; frankly, I'm not sure he was even hoping it would get *this* far. There's no actual evidence, just a series of suggestive coincidences that we've interpreted. No; Anthony's revenge was never meant to be about a criminal sentence, it was about torturing Torben. About one-upmanship. I think he saw him-self as a posthumous puppet-master, pulling Tor's strings – all our strings – from beyond the grave. And he baited it so well. He just *knew* Torben wouldn't be able to resist showing off. And we played right into his hands.' She drew breath. 'He wasn't trying to consign Torben to eternal damnation. Just proving that he could put him through hell for a bit.'

For the first time in what seemed like hours, Torben stirred. He was coming back to himself, returning to a body reprieved, to hands no longer a murderer's. It hardly felt like victory.

'Why did he hate me so much?' he said. His voice was small, like that of a child.

Leyla put out a hand to him – then let it fall back. 'At last,' she said, 'you've asked the right question. All that time we all spent on how *we* felt towards Anthony, our grudges, our incentives, when we should have been asking, how did Anthony feel about us?

'It began to fall into place for me this afternoon,' she went on, 'when you, Tor, you said the answer was all there in our pasts. I remembered the blackouts, how we'd discussed them on Saturday night, and I guessed what you were thinking. And then I did some more remembering too. And it all began to fit. Maybe I, I should have said something right then, but I was distracted by what I thought I'd seen outside, and then Ruth also began talking about footprints—'

At this, Ruth shifted in her seat. She looked thoroughly ashamed of herself.

'—which seized us all, to be fair,' said Leyla. 'And for the rest of you, that lent extra credence to the outsider theory. But to me, it meant something completely different. I was worried the figure was Kirsty; when you said it was a man, that no longer fitted. But it *did* remind me, persuade me even, that I'd seen a man lurking where they shouldn't be once before ... But that comes later on. Anyway, this afternoon, when it all took off, I was starting to think along completely different lines. And I thought, evidence! I need more evidence. What I had was so inconclusive ...'

Leyla tailed off. Paused for breath. Then she turned to Frances. 'Frances,' she said, 'what I have to say – it takes us back. And, having gone there once ... I mean, you've made your feelings on this very clear, and I'm not sure I have the right to discuss it, but I need to revisit a ... a related aspect of the past, in order to explain why Anthony had so much hate in him.'

Frances stared at her for a long moment. 'Oh,' she said at last. 'You mean something to do with me and Torben? Everybody knows about that now, don't they?' She toyed with a loose curl of hair. 'You can – well, you can see I like to keep things private, for preference. But when I've just been outed and three people have been accused

312

of murder ... is it three? ... sure, you can talk about an old bit of bonking if it helps.'

Sara blushed.

Torben thought, *an old bit of bonking?*

'Thanks,' said Leyla. 'But – while I'm glad you can think of it like that – I don't think Anthony could. In fact, it was probably the final ... well, straw, nail, whatever cliché you think he's most likely to have employed. But in the long litany of offences against the name of Torben Helle – spoiling his quizzes, boasting about badminton triumphs, doing better in exams, publicly shaming his pronunciation, wearing outrageous clothes, mastering the theories that he spent forever struggling with – I think that getting the girl who was his great unrequited passion rather ... took the biscuit? "Took the biscuit" – now there's a strange one.'

'Wait wait wait – Anthony *knew* about that?'

'What do you mean, the girl he loved? He practically molested her – oh, sorry, Frances—'

Leyla raised a hand for silence. It was, perhaps, the very feebleness of the gesture that did the trick. 'I think, for Anthony, those stalker-ish propensities meant something rather nobler. And he's definitely carried the flame – Christ, we even found a locket of her hair upstairs, after all this time! Yes, it may seem rather sordid to *us*' – and as she spoke, Torben had a memory of Leyla holding up *Lovely Lasses* and *Rampant Redheads* – 'but I really think that, to Anthony, Frances was The One.'

'Just my luck,' Frances muttered.

'So,' Leyla pressed on. 'Most of us, I think, were aware that Frances and Torben had a thing going on in second year, despite their best efforts to keep it a secret. It started – I believe – at the beginning of term, after the first welcome-back Bop. Is that right, Frances?'

'Aye, but … you weren't even there, Leyla. That' – and now she blushed – 'that was sort of the point.'

'No,' said Leyla, her face impassive. 'I was pulling an all-nighter, working on some bloody essay about tort law. Too much caffeine, too little time. Around midnight I was distracted by the noise of all the people coming back to their rooms – I lived over in Meadows, remember? – and I looked up from the page for the first time in what seemed like forever. It was a stuffy night, my window was wide open, and – not to put too fine a point on it – it sounded like someone was recreating a Babylonian orgy outside. Imagine my disappointment' – she did not say chagrin, fury, shock – 'when, poking my head out to see, it turned out to be just Torben and Frances, rutting. Frances, you probably all remember, had one of the balconies, and she and Torben … well, you can imagine.'

'Uh-huh,' said Danny. Everyone stared at him. 'Er, sorry,' he said. Kirsty covered her face with a hand.

'Quite,' said Leyla. 'Naturally I slammed down the window and went back to work, but for some reason – hah, I've no idea why – I was finding it hard to concentrate. Kept glancing up, looking out at the avenue of trees down to the river. There was this weird moon, and all this light spilling out from the building, and as my desk was right up at the window and I had just the one lamp on, I could sort of see out. And I had this – well, what I thought was a hallucination – that there was a man, standing among the trees where no man could logically be, looking back at the balconies. In fact, from the way this figure was facing, it looked like he was staring up at Frances' balcony, and I thought – well actually, up until yesterday I've always thought – it was just my subconscious, projecting … a sort of stand-in for my own unintended act of voyeurism. It was bloody hard not to think about what was going on out there, frankly.'

Torben and Frances were both inspecting their shoes.

'But then yesterday,' Leyla went on, in a rush, 'the same thing happened – I imagined seeing a man, lurking outside – only, then Frances said she'd seen him too – and it all made sense. The final confirmation of my theory. I really *had* seen a man in the Meadow – and it was Anthony. Anthony, just standing there. Completely still. Watching it all happen.'

'But,' said Frances, 'you can't get *into* the Meadow at night, they lock all the gates, that's why we took the risk ... oh! That sneaky bathroom window on the ground floor; if you climb on the bin ... oh, fuck.'

Leyla nodded. 'I forgot too. But it was a *university* – of *course* people get into places you're not supposed to get into. I'm afraid he must've tailed you back from the Bop, and when he saw the pair of you heading up to your room ...'

Torben allowed himself a moment amidst it all – just one moment – to picture the scene. He and Frances above, naked, enwrapped. And down below, in the darkness, among the trees – the man watching, eyes burning into them. So still.

'Torben!' said Ruth. 'But, but you told me last night – you *met* him! Coming back in through the Meadows gate, looking like death. You said you thought he'd been for an early stroll, but – but he'd been out there all night?'

'Oh *for helvede*, and he immediately picked a fight with me ... wait, wait, he *sniffed*, and made this face, like I smelled offensive, and I thought it was just *me* he was smelling. But I must have reeked of Frances' perfume too— that is *not* a euphemism, by the way, you all remember how liberal she used to be with the CK One.'

Ruth groaned. 'He must have felt you were literally rubbing his nose in it.'

'But,' said Torben, 'but … oh, *for fanden*, even if he did have a … oh, let's call it *feelings* for her, it was – how did you put it, Frances? A bit of bonking?'

'Exactly,' said Ruth, 'that's *exactly* the point, Tor, don't you see? The fact you can say that is precisely what must have got to him. That you actually *got* the girl of his dreams, and could be so casual about it. For you and Frances, it was just this, this …'

'Highland fling?' supplied Leyla.

'Oi!' said Frances.

'Anyway,' said Ruth. 'It's what you've never really appreciated, Torben. His whole issue with you. With everything he made you stand for. That resentment against the system, against the people to whom it all comes naturally, like it's a birthright – the people who can make conversation and get the references, who can get away with expressing themselves through their clothes, their opinions … I get where he was coming from, I really do. How difficult it can be for those of us who spent our entire childhoods working *so* hard, sacrificing everything, to finally get to the place that was meant to be our paradise, our reward – only to find out, for one reason or another, that we still felt like we were on the wrong side of the gates. That was what Anthony was putting on you. And you've never stopped being that person for him. When he made his fortune, you scarcely even noticed – just the other day, you were conspicuously ignorant of what his app actually does. He was so disappointed when I told him you weren't coming to the Gaudy, which I took to be a good sign – but probably, he was just desperate to make a big statement, and you weren't even going to be there. All this time you're sailing on in this rarefied air of scholarship, and when he tries to show off in an area you actually care about, culture, Wilson blocks him from backing his play … well, if he then turns out to have been in love with Frances into the bargain—!'

'Plus,' said Leyla, 'that's some powerful imagery to fuel his anger. Up on that balcony you were almost literally in an ivory tower … All these years, it must have festered. And when he got his terminal diagnosis, he was on a timer. He settled his affairs, sold the business. Romance was definitively off the cards. I think all he had left, all that still *mattered*, was this one final chance to get one over on the one person who epitomised everything he resented. To hoist this big bag of overblown air by his own petard.'

'But,' said Torben, 'but that's *not* me! I was the outsider, not him, I – *for helvede*, I was still learning how to pronounce things!'

'But that's never bothered you,' Ruth said. 'Straight away, you asked me to correct you when you went wrong. Do you realise how much that says about you? How few people would have the confidence to let themselves be publicly corrected? You saw what that did to Anthony: it practically killed him. In a way, it actually did. I'm not – not blaming you exactly for the way you provoked him and went on provoking him just by, just by being you, but … look. Remember the way you went on to Tom about art the other night? Yes, I heard that, you were speaking rather loudly. Tom, who let us remember went to a minor public school himself, came over to me afterwards. Do you know what he said?'

Tom leant over. He looked like he was enjoying this bit, at last. 'I said, "Who the fuck's Giorgione?" It was like being pissed on from your ivory tower.'

Wilson laughed.

Torben put a hand to his brow. He felt, suddenly, extremely hot. This new version of himself – so much less awful than the last – but still. It was as if he had been dissected and shown to himself on a plate, raw, obscene. 'No one – no one ever said anything,' was all he could manage.

317

This time, Leyla did put a hand on his arm. 'Dear Torben,' she murmured, 'I'm sorry. I never put it all properly together, not until— god, was it really only a few hours ago? Maybe I should have said, but without the evidence, the photograph ... and I was so afraid, you know, that it might ... might lead you to do something you'd always regret. And then it almost did anyway.'

Torben shook his head. 'But for you, Leyla,' he said.

'Oh, Tor ...' Now it was done, her strength seemed exhausted. 'I thought – you know, I really thought you were going to do it too. Suicide. That you'd taken the other gun. That's why I went, why I had to find that photo right away – there would be no other way of convincing you.'

'Kill – kill myself? *For fanden*, where did you get—?'

'Yes! Yes, you said suicide was how you would want to go, you told Ruth you believed in it ...'

He looked at Ruth. 'Well, you did,' she said.

'And then,' said Leyla, fighting tears now, 'once you said you had the answer, I saw what you'd written, when we'd left you alone in the drawing room – your notes were just lying there, like you didn't even care anymore ... You'd been working it out; you said suicide could be a logical solution to an insoluble situation, a rational response – I thought you were condemning yourself – I had to save you—'

'Oh,' said Torben. It was all he could find to say. His book review. He could see that, out of context ... And all along, he'd thought it was he who needed to save Leyla. Was there anything he hadn't got utterly, entirely wrong?

'Hang on!' said, of all people, Danny. 'If you didn't kill Mr Dodd, why's your glove got blood on it?'

Torben hung on to the question like a man drowning. It might keep him above water. 'Oh,' he said again. 'I know. You see, I was trying to help an old woman onto a train ...'

24

SOME OTHER MONDAY, EIGHT P.M.

They had arranged to meet in a discreetly excellent Moroccan restaurant in Exmouth Market – the sort of place Torben had always
wanted to go to, but could never justify to his bank balance. Clean,
uncomplicated furniture, a couple of industrial pillars, packed
tables. And now he felt too nervous to eat. He hadn't seen Leyla
since … well, since everything.

She glanced at the menu. 'Yum. No offence, but are you sure you
can afford to eat here?'

'Well, yes, actually,' he said. 'In fact, it's my treat.'

She raised an eyebrow.

'Leyla, did you get anything unexpected in the post this week?
Anything in a STONi Ltd envelope?'

'Well, yes, but I haven't dared open it. I'm still half afraid his lawyers are going to start a defamation case or push an NDA onto all of
us. You mean it's—?'

'A cheque, yes. For fifty thousand pounds. I rather thought it was
one last trick from beyond the grave but, to hell with it, it could only
bounce – so I paid it in.'

'And?'

'The money cleared, no problem. Evidently Anthony's desire to make his plan watertight extended to making out a genuine will. It had to look convincing.'

'You know, that was the first thing that seemed suspicious to me?' she said. 'I lost hold of it in everything that followed, but it was something Frances said right at the start – "just enough". That it was just enough to kill for.'

'*I* should have realised,' said Torben, 'when I found all those detective novels in the drawing room. I took them for a sign of Anthony's humanity – an ordinary pleasure – when they were probably his research materials. I've been reading them ever since we got back to London. *Clouds of Witness* gave *me* the idea of checking the blank notepad; it gave *him* the idea of a suicide mistaken for murder. *Roger Ackroyd* – such a meticulous setup in advance to deceive all the guests. *Murder in the Mews, Gone Girl* – resources to help him with staging a death so as to frame someone for murder. Only he had to improve on them; he took an accidental slip over a right-handed gunshot and made it a deliberate part of his own plan. Piecing together the perfect trap from the work of people more imaginative than himself. A bit like writing a weekly essay. I was his tutorial partner, remember? His essays always were really well referenced, I'll say that for him ...'

'Mm. Another man taking credit for the ingenuity of women. Well, thanks for spoiling a bunch of books I was probably never going to read.' Leyla didn't seem especially interested in Torben's digression. 'Typical showing off, really. Especially when you add in flashing all that cash. Still, I bet the bastard spent ages deciding on the smallest amount that would sound plausible as a motive. I hope you're keeping the money?'

'*Er du sindssyg?* It's the least he owes us.'

'Hear hear. The only trouble will be persuading Ruth not to give her cut to charity ...'

He shrugged. 'If it makes her happy. Realising she's had two such controlling men in her life has been hard. I think that's why she's finally getting divorced – she can't do anything about the tragedy of Anthony, but she *can* save her own life before Jon ruins it for good. I think the whole thing's disillusioned her more than any of us. That anyone could carry such hatred within them – no, more than that, the fact that she hadn't seen it in him earlier, and done something ...'

Torben's mind strayed as Leyla ordered what sounded like the entire menu. That man he'd thought he'd known, Anthony Dodd, sitting up there in his monumental hermitage. Dour as the sky, hard as the hill, implacably constructing his instrument of revenge as illness ate within him.

Well, he supposed, everyone needed a hobby.

'You know,' Leyla said, once the waiter had gone, 'that's not how I look at it. Right from the start, even when you said it was murder, you also said you couldn't believe that any of us had killed him. Well, we hadn't! If he was hoping to turn us against each other, he failed. Even Tom bloody Goring's getting help for his kleptomania. Frances and Sara are officially an item and now, presumably, have a hundred grand to build their life with, which is as good a foundation for a relationship as I can think of. Ruth and Wilson have a regular date for badminton – something Jon would *not* have been happy about – and she's finally seen sense on that score too. When you think about it, we were all, at some point, suspicious of each other – but we've come out of it better friends than ever.'

'It's as if,' said Torben, 'Anthony took it upon himself to be a true scapegoat. He loaded all the sins of a houseful of people upon his back, and made himself a sacrifice so that we might be absolved.'

'God,' said Leyla, 'how he'd hate to think of it like that!'

The first plates of food arrived, bursts of bright colour that were almost fauvist in their exuberance. 'Shall we just share, each take half of everything?' said Leyla.

He nodded, wincing a little at her choice of words. With half his mind on Anthony's will, the phrase had too much of the marriage vow about it, at a moment when he had rarely felt further from her. He noticed she was wearing her old necklace again, the one that Tom had stolen.

'Ruth says the only thing we can safely conclude is that the middle classes have a major drink problem,' said Leyla, 'and that none of this would have happened without "a destructive level of consumption, made normative by our hypocritical approach to different forms of alcohol".' She popped a little ball of morcilla and apple into her mouth. Torben watched her lips as she chewed. 'I see you're on the – what even is that?' she said, gesturing at Torben's glass.

'Kombucha,' he said. 'It's a sort of fermented tea.'

She made a face. 'I'll stick to the Albariño.'

The conversation drifted. At its centre, unspoken, gravid, was the rest of that February weekend. The unbearable weight of the debt he owed her, the shame of it, the gratitude. The aftershock of great feelings, that had shaken them both as a dog shakes a rat. How close they had both come to irreparable loss – of themselves, of each other …

By the meal's end, she had talked him into a small glass of Pedro Ximénez. 'Moderation,' she said, 'is a far healthier life goal than abstinence.'

The sherry was sticky, rich, and reminded him of Christmas pudding. The lights were low, like amber, and the restaurant was emptying. She had a dab of labneh, flecked with pistachio, just above her mouth. Should he say anything? 'Leyla—'

But she was glancing at her watch. 'Look, I've got a case in the morning,' she said. 'Are you sure about getting this? Great!' And she rose from the table. Brisk, businesslike, she wiped her face with a napkin.

'*God nat*, Leyla.'

She nodded. 'Good night, Tor.'

Halfway to the door, she turned.

'Tor – when you're ready … the next one's on me.'

ACKNOWLEDGEMENTS

As a work of literature, it's really up to you to decide whether this book technically constitutes a criminal act. But if you think it does, then I advise you to avail yourself of a large country house, stuff the drawing-room full of sofas, and assemble the following parties for the denouement.

The inciting incident came back in 2018, when my dear friend Caroline Crampton launched her magnificent podcast *Shedunnit*. Without its fortnightly forays into the history of Golden Age detective fiction, I'd never have felt tempted to try my hand at the thing myself, nor really known where to begin. So she must shoulder a large chunk of the blame.

I was aided and abetted by my early readers, without whose encouragement, discernment, generosity, erudition and downright pedantry I would never have gone so thoroughly to the bad. Besides the felonious Crampton, aforementioned, I wish to indict Katherine Hambridge, Katy Hamilton, Elaine and Graham Head, Emily Kate Price, and – most egregiously of all – my own flesh and blood: my parents and my sister Freyja, who should really have nipped this in the bud at the start, but achieved precisely the opposite with a pernicious blend of love, support and really really getting it.

In further mitigation, I'm prepared to testify against my accomplices. I'm looking at you, Hayley Shepherd, the best copy-editor the black market can supply, while a swift raid on the shadowy head-quarters of Profile Books should suffice to bring to justice Emily Frisella (the ruthless runner of the operation), Charlotte Greenwood (the precocious fixer), Robert Greer (the gang's public face), and Samantha Johnson (the outrageously talented cover (up) artist). Alas, they'll just have missed Therese Keating, whose nous and enthusiasm throughout did so much to bring the dastardly scheme to fruition. (I hear she's heading up a rival outfit now: beware, for she is danger-ous.) But they might just nab the big cheese herself, Miranda Jewess, that Machiavellian schemer-in-chief who continues to merit her rep-utation as the Moriarty of the editorial underworld. I hear she's even amassing a collection of daggers...

Spare a thought, too, for the victims, lying in a heap in the corner. From that Frankensteinian pile, those in the know will be able to discern the hacked up corpses of a number of my best-loved friends, now mangled out of all recognition. Rest assured, absolutely no one in this book is actually based on a real person except, just possibly, silly old Torben himself, but I've gone on quite the spree of charac-ter-trait culling, for which sacrifice I thank them all. Some of them will recognise aspects of themselves, others won't, and others again will guess awry – but without their brilliance, their foibles, and their wholly unearned friendship, this book would be lacking at least two of its dimensions. I shan't name them, of course – oh, except for David Button, he's in there loads, mostly the really stupid bits.

There are but two partners-in-crime left to grass up. Emma Whipday does a fine job of looking all innocent, playing the part of my best friend, wife, one true love etc, etc. But beneath that mask she's a ferociously effective critic, her talents honed by multiple lit-erary atrocities of her own, and I want her on record as an accessory before, during and after the fact. Finally: my inveterate accomplice and agent, Joanna Swainson, who did all the dirty work on this job, as usual. Never was anyone more guilty of assiduous, relentless, inspirational criminality. And look, she's not even ashamed of it! And nor am I. Mark my words: we will kill again!

ABOUT THE AUTHOR

Oskar Jensen is an author and academic. He researches songs at Newcastle University, and has written scholarly tomes on Napoleon, ballad-singing, and most recently the London streets, with 2022's *Vagabonds*. He is a BBC New Generation Thinker, appearing frequently on Radios 3 and 4, as well as showing up in the *New Statesman*, on *Who Do You Think You Are?*, and as historical advisor for 2018's *Vanity Fair* and a forthcoming major motion picture. *Helle & Death* is his first novel for adults. Find him on X @OskarCoxJensen.